FIVE
Glass Slippers

ROOGLEWOOD PRESS

Raleigh, NC

Published by Rooglewood Press
www.RooglewoodPress.com

Printed in the United States of America

ISBN-13: 978-0-9894478-4-3

Book design by A.E. de Silva
Cover Illustration by nizhava1956

Table of Contents

FORWARD

F EW FAIRY TALES are as beloved as *Cinderella*. Something about her rags-to-riches adventure touches our hearts, encourages our spirits, and inspires our dreams. Hers is a simple story, but perhaps its very simplicity engenders the heroine's undeniable appeal. We as readers want to see her triumph again and again, in all the various dramatic retellings of her tale.

For *Cinderella* is about so much more than glass slippers. These are only symbols, tools used to achieve the heroine's goal, and easily exchanged for other tools of equal symbolic importance. Luke Skywalker's lightsaber—Katniss Everdeen's hunting bow—James J. Braddock's boxing gloves. The slippers are interchangeable; the story is universal. I doubt very much that readers will ever grow tired of reading Cinderella's tale in all its various manifestations.

With this idea in mind, I decided to host the *Five Glass Slippers* creative writing contest. There are so many wonderful fairy tales to choose from for a contest of this nature, but none with greater attraction and flexibility than *Cinderella*. Contestants were challenged to create new versions of the familiar tale, including many of the themes we know and love—the prince's ball, the evil stepmother and stepsisters, the pumpkin coach, the fairy godmother, and, of course, the glass slippers—while also shaking up the details to create brand new stories.

The results were astounding. Submissions came flowing in from across the world. Writers of all ages and experience levels crafted original versions of the fairy tale. There were mysteries, horror stories, romances, and comedies. There were historicals, fantasies, and modern-day retellings. There were tales of magic, tales of terror, tales of heartrending sadness. There were thoughtful allegories and high-flying adventures. There were steampunk and science fiction—just about every genre was represented in the selection of submissions Rooglewood Press received.

And the most amazing thing of all: No two stories were alike.

Oh yes, they were all *Cinderella*. But the brilliance of the original fairy tale was made all the more evident in that each writer could create something so unique with her or his retelling.

Narrowing these entries down to five winners was a task beyond anything I had anticipated. But the five stories you now hold in your hand are truly the perfect assortment.

What Eyes Can See is the romance of this collection. A gentle tale told in an old-fashioned voice perfectly suited to the subject matter. Elisabeth Brown's delicate writing style abounds in good humor. She writes characters you cannot help but like, even when they all work at cross-purposes to each other. By the time I finished reading this story for the first time, I had no doubt in my mind that it would be not only a winner, but also the perfect story with which to open this collection. Something tender, something sweet . . . and yet such a surprising twist on the original that readers are bound to enjoy it.

By contrast, *Broken Glass* is not at all a gentle story. It is a side-splitting comedy that caught my attention from the very first sentence. The characters are larger-than-life and so hilariously bent on their own various plots that I could not wait to turn pages and find out what would happen to each of them. Emma Clifton has a sense of humor that tickles my fancy and is sure to inspire her readers to many a smile. Or snort. Or snicker.

But it was the heroine of the middle story, *The Windy Side of Care*, who stole my heart and secured her place as my favorite incarnation of the titular Cinderella. Alisandra Carlisle is not a victim to her difficult circumstances. Indeed, she is a woman on a mission, and neither wicked stepmother, nor appalling stepsisters, not even the kingdom itself will sway her from her goal! Alis herself could not have sprung to such vivid life, however, without the equal vivacity of her creator. Rachel Heffington's quick wit and snappy narrative are a pure delight.

The very last story I read for this contest was *A Cinder's Tale*. By that time, I thought I must have read every variation possible on the original story . . . and I was completely wrong. Stephanie Ricker introduced me to a world so distinctive and yet so believable that I could not get enough of it. Science fiction can be a tricky genre for retelling a fairy tale, but this talented author wrote with such a strong sense of authenticity, I was totally caught up in the events transpiring in the space station above planet Aschen. It's the cast of endearing characters working together to thwart disaster, however, who really make this story. Readers will get the sense that there is more to this world just waiting to be explored.

Every reader loves a spooky little chill now and then; that is exactly what Clara Diane Thompson delivers in *The Moon Master's Ball*. Within a few paragraphs, I was spellbound. This young author has penned a mysterious story of eerie magic, a story which departs the farthest from the original source material . . . and yet Clara manages to satisfyingly tie in all the most important Cinderella elements. The secrets behind the Moon Master and his ball are sure to intrigue readers, offering plenty of gasps and thrills along the way.

Each of these five stories is so different from the others, yet their consistent *Cinderella* themes tie them together beautifully. I could not be better pleased with either these writers or this collection. Cinderella herself will go on to star in many more fantastic retellings of her tale. But I fully expect these particular incarnations—Arella, Evelyn, Alisandra, Elsa, and Tilly—to secure places as favorites in the hearts of Cinderella enthusiasts everywhere.

So, without further ado, I present to you the winning stories of the *Five Glass Slippers* contest.

Anne Elisabeth Stengl

What Eyes Can See

Can See

Elisabeth Brown

For Grandma Brubacher

PLEASE DON'T make me go," Arella begged, her large eyes pleading.

Her stepmother sighed. "It's a matter of etiquette. One simply cannot refuse an invitation to the prince's royal ball."

"But I'm insignificant, Stepmother. No one will even notice I'm missing!" Arella persisted hopefully. "You and the other girls will certainly be good enough representations of our family."

"At important functions such as this, child, everyone who attends or does not attend is noted. I assure you, your absence would be taken as a personal affront to the entire royal family. And they would not look kindly on the slight." The stern lines in Duchess Germaine's face softened. "Besides, Arella, you are far from insignificant. You are one of the most beautiful girls in the kingdom and will surely be noticed by the prince."

Arella's face filled with worry. "I don't want him to notice me," she said quietly.

Drusilla, Arella's older stepsister, gave her a sympathetic smile. But Anastasia, the youngest, rolled her eyes. "Goodness, Arella, why not? What more could you possibly ask?"

Drusilla watched the stepsisters exchange tense glances. The two were as different as light and shadow: Anastasia vivacious, sparkling— Arella quiet, retiring. Anastasia would never understand why Arella hated these functions, and Arella would never understand why Anastasia loved them. Drusilla, her personality falling somewhere between these polar opposites, had always acted as the buffer, doing her best to understand both of her little sisters and keep the peace.

"I just . . . don't want to meet him. That's all," Arella finally answered, her face revealing her discomfort. "Maybe you could tell them I'm ill? Or travelling to visit relations?"

"You should know better than to lie," said the duchess. Her brow furrowed in concern, and she placed a gentle hand on Arella's forehead. "Are you truly ill, child?"

"No, I'm feeling well, Stepmother," Arella admitted. "I just don't like balls."

"You are an aristocrat, and as such you are not always allowed to act according to your likes or dislikes. You are expected to attend, and attend you will. I cannot permit you to behave in a selfish and rude manner, Arella. Such would not be a credit to your father."

"Yes, Stepmother," Arella murmured, her downcast eyes filling with tears. Drusilla, always observant, saw that telltale glimmer and wondered. Did the mention of Arella's father cause this sudden sorrow? Or was the poor girl simply upset about not getting her own way? There was no way to know for certain. Even Drusilla struggled to interpret Arella's reticent moods.

The duchess gazed upon her stepdaughter with a mixture of compassion and exasperation. "There, there, child! It can't be as bad as that. After all, it will be the grandest occasion in many years. The royal family will spare no expense. Foreign nobles and dignitaries from across the world will be in attendance."

Arella didn't seem in the least cheered by this prospect.

"We shall all have new dresses! Lovelier dresses than we have ever had."

Arella's forlorn face remained unimpressed.

"And we shall take a silver coach, with our finest horses."

No response.

"And footmen!"

Still nothing. What did the child want? The duchess shook her head. "Very well. If it is this distressing to you, I shall allow you to leave at midnight—but no sooner. And then only if you promise me to do your best to be pleasant to the prince and the nobles. Agreed?"

"Yes, Stepmother," Arella whispered.

At least Stepmother had approved the notion of Arella's making her own dress. This was some consolation. Arella sat on the floor of the dusty attic among boxes and trunks, remembering her conversation with the duchess that morning.

"You don't want to go to the dressmaker's with us?" Duchess Germaine had asked in surprise.

"I'd rather wear one of my mother's dresses," Arella had implored. "I'll make it over so it won't look too old-fashioned."

The duchess had bowed her head. All these years, and she still didn't understand this girl. "You can wear your mother's gowns anytime. This is a special occasion. Don't you want something new, something that will look like all the other girls?"

"No," Arella had replied.

Duchess Germaine, tired of fighting, had conceded. It had been hard enough to convince the girl to go to the ball in the first place. Arella was so beautiful that it wouldn't matter if she wasn't dressed in the latest fashion, and perhaps if she wore one of her mother's gowns she would feel more comfortable. "Very well. Would you like to accompany us to help your sisters pick out their gowns?"

"If I'm going to make my own, I should probably start working on it."

"Very well," the Duchess had said again, sighing a little in resignation. "Drusilla, Anastasia, and I are leaving now, dear. We shall return by suppertime."

Now Arella was rummaging in the attic, accompanied only by one of her lively kittens. She loved the smell of her mother's things: lavender from the sachets tucked among the clothing, leather from the ornate trunks, a nearly imperceptible sweetness . . . Was it her mother's old perfume? She pulled out dress after dress, inhaling deeply with each one. Too much lace. Too bright. Too antiquated . . .

Ah! This one would do.

The rose-colored gown she held was simple, elegant enough to blend in with the fine apparel worn at a royal ball, yet not flashy enough to attract undue attention. Scrutinizing it carefully, Arella decided her mother had probably worn it as a breakfast gown. Such had been the fashion back then.

Arella smiled. "You probably didn't guess your daughter would wear it to the crown prince's royal ball," she whispered. She rubbed the smooth fabric absentmindedly. Was this one of her mother's favorites? Had her father liked to see her mother wearing it? Arella closed her eyes, trying to conjure an image of her mother in this dress, trying to find a memory.

None came. The only face she could see was the one from the portrait hanging in her bedroom.

Arella carefully repacked the long gowns in the old dusty trunk then picked up the selected gown and descended the attic stairs. "A little sash and some lace at the bottom should do to make this appropriate for the ball," Arella decided. She made her way to the sewing room and set to work. If she had to go, she may as well wear something she liked.

"What do you think?" Drusilla asked her mother and sister, holding the smooth silk up to her body. She hoped the pale green would lend some of its color to her murky eyes and soften the brightness of her red hair. Surveying herself in the mirror, she ruefully admitted that they were as murky and red, respectively, as ever.

"I like it," Anastasia answered. "It brings out the green in your eyes."

Drusilla glanced at her doubtfully. "Really? I didn't think it helped much."

"Try the darker green," her mother suggested. "I think it would suit your complexion better." The duchess handed her eldest daughter a different length of silk.

She nodded approvingly as Drusilla held up the new piece. "Very becoming. I think you should choose this one."

Anastasia and the dressmaker echoed the duchess's commendation. Drusilla wrinkled her nose at the reflection; nothing seemed to be particularly becoming. But if her mother and sister liked it . . . "All right then." Drusilla shrugged. "Dark green it is."

"Very well, my lady," said the dressmaker, taking the silk and placing it with the lavender Anastasia had already selected. "And how would you want them made?"

"Ball gowns for the prince's ball," Duchess Germaine responded. "Make them according to the latest fashions—full skirt, bustle, plenty of lace. After all, this is the event of the year. Perhaps of the decade!" She smiled brightly at her girls. New dresses never ceased to be exciting.

Except to Arella.

The Duchess's smile faded somewhat as she thought of her stepdaughter. Of course, it was understandable that the girl would like to wear her mother's things. Though Duchess Germaine had tried to take a mother's place in the girl's heart, Arella always maintained a quiet shell, especially after the duke passed away—scarcely a year after he and Germaine were married, when Arella was still so young.

Drusilla noticed when her mother's smile slipped and knew she was worrying about Arella again. That girl! She could have come to the dressmaker's with them today and found a bright blue to match her clear eyes. She could have at least come and helped them to select their silks.

Instead, she was by herself in a dusty attic and would probably pick the simplest dress she could find. It didn't matter too much—she was a beautiful girl, and a plain dress would not conceal that fact from the prince. Still, it would be nice if she could try to be involved with her family for a change.

Drusilla smiled at her mother, hoping to ease her worry. "And what about you, Mother? Shan't you have a new dress for the ball? It is the event of the decade, after all."

Duchess Germaine returned her daughter's smile. "One of last year's dresses will do nicely for me. *I* am not being evaluated for the prince's bride!"

Neither am I, thought Drusilla behind her smile. *Nor anyone else's bride, for that matter.* "But think, Mother," she replied brightly, "of all the nobility who will be there! You don't want to be the only one in last season's dress, do you?"

Anastasia added her voice. "Oh, do get a new dress with us, Mother. It would be such fun! And here's a silk that would look perfect with your complexion." She held up a pale peach fabric.

The Duchess laughed. "Goodness, child, I am much too old to wear that shade! But I think—yes, I shall have a new dress." She indicated a sophisticated silver. "If you please, Mrs. Montgomery. And while we're here, I shall order one for Arella—this blue matches her eyes so well. Perhaps she has changed her mind and would like a new dress after all. We'll surprise her."

Drusilla tapped gently on the half-open door then poked her head through. "Arella?" she called.

"Come in," replied her stepsister's gentle voice. Arella looked up from where she sat on a low stool surrounded by dull pink silk. One fluffy gray kitten napped on a chair near her while another pawed a spool of thread on the floor. "Did you need something?"

"No," Drusilla answered. She picked up the sleeping kitten and sat down. The little furry bundle curled up in her lap and fell immediately back to sleep. "I just came to see how you were getting along."

"Oh," Arella responded, focusing on her work. "Quite well, thank you. Did you have a nice outing?"

"It was very nice. Bustles are still in style, but sleeves have changed considerably. Apparently long sleeves are horrid now." Drusilla smiled at her stepsister. "Not that it makes any difference to you."

"Not much," admitted Arella. "I've never liked bustles. But I never liked those long sleeves, either. They got in the way."

"Did you need any help? A thread-snipper? Errand-runner? Someone to amuse you?" Drusilla asked cheerfully, stroking the drowsy kitten.

Arella smiled but shook her head. "No, thank you. I have everything I need here, and there really isn't much to do."

Drusilla watched her stepsister's nimble fingers move deftly though the layers of fabric. "Is that one of your mother's dresses?" she inquired, more to make conversation than anything else.

"Yes," Arella replied. "I think it's lovely."

"It is," agreed Drusilla, admiring what she could see of the gown draped over Arella's lap. The first Duchess of Abendroth must have been a woman of no mean taste; each of her dresses was costly and impeccably designed. This one, though simply cut, was no different. "What are you doing to it?"

"I'm just adding a little ruffle to the bottom. And I'll make a sash."

"No bustle?" Drusilla teased.

"No bustle," Arella answered. Considering a moment, she added doubtfully, "Do you think Stepmother will approve?"

Approve? Or understand? Drusilla thought. She paused before replying. "I think she wants you to feel comfortable." Their eyes met—Arella's blue, lovely, innocent; Drusilla's hazel, kindly, wise.

Arella nodded. "Do you think it will stand out if I don't?"

"You, my dear sister, stand out wherever you go and however you dress. So wear what you want."

Arella sighed. "I wish it were a masquerade," she said. "Costumes are much more interesting."

"You forget the purpose of this ball," Drusilla replied with a small laugh. "I believe the prince is trying to find a beautiful girl to make his wife. Masks would scarcely help him in that endeavor."

Arella made a face. "It's silly that I have to go then. I wouldn't marry him even if he wanted me to."

"You haven't met him," Drusilla said, arching a brow. "Perhaps he will sweep you off your feet with charm."

"He won't."

"If you say so."

A silence lingered in the room for some moments. Realizing there was nothing more to be had from her quiet stepsister, Drusilla rose. "I suppose I'll give Sleepy his chair back, then." She replaced the kitten on the chair, planted a quick kiss on Arella's head, and left the room.

Arella watched Drusilla go. And she thought, *No prince will sweep me off my feet. No one can.*

Seated in his mother's sitting room, Prince Frederick listened half-heartedly to the queen reading the list of eligible females who would be attending his royal ball. He had finished his education and was about to celebrate his twentieth birthday. Therefore, according to precedent, he must marry. And his bride would be found among the noble young ladies dancing in the castle two weeks from now.

"Princess Miranda—a good match, but not exceptional. Her father's kingdom is too small to be a useful ally. Alice, daughter of the Duke of Stelstek—sickly constitution. Amala de Perperand's family isn't old money. Oh, the daughter of the Emperor of Verdemons! She would be an excellent choice."

The prince listened to the seemingly endless list of names and descriptions, but none struck his fancy. The ridiculous thought crossed his mind that this process was like buying a horse. Except, unlike a horse, the woman he chose would stay with him for the rest of his life. The woman he chose would have the power to make him happy or miserable. The power to make his reign—his entire kingdom, even—strong or weak.

He sighed.

Queen Thalia looked up from her lists and raised her delicate eyebrows. "I am not wearying you, son?" Her voice, cultured and melodious, held the faintest hint of reprimand.

"Of course not, Mother," Frederick quickly reassured her. "I was just wondering what my life will be like if I pick the wrong one." He drummed his fingers nervously on his leg.

"Don't pick the wrong one, then," his mother replied calmly.

Frederick half smiled but without amusement. "Out of so many? How will I know?"

"My son, when you marry, you take not only a bride but also a queen. Make sure she is worthy to be queen." Queen Thalia returned her gaze to her lists, ready to pick up where she had been interrupted. "Lady Anna von Dalber, reputed to be very pretty. Elissa Galott, daughter of the Earl of Middlefield . . ."

Frederick found this advice scarcely helpful, but his mother was not a woman one questioned twice. Apparently she believed this information ought to be enough for him.

A woman worthy of being queen. He tightened his jaw. Challenge it may be, but Frederick had never been known to back down from a challenge. He would find her.

THE NIGHT of the ball rapidly approached—not rapidly enough for Anastasia, too rapidly for Arella. When the day itself arrived, Arella felt her stomach knotting itself tighter and tighter as the hours ticked by. If only there were some way she could excuse herself, some way to sneak out to the stables or the garden and vanish! But she knew that was impossible.

Early in the afternoon the hairdresser set about primping the four women. Anastasia's excitement could not be contained. This was her first ball—and what a first ball! The duchess smiled at her exuberant chatter. "I'm afraid no other ball will ever compare to this, child," she said with chuckle. "Every experience you have from now on will seem dull."

Anastasia was certain this couldn't be true. Different, perhaps, but never dull. And even if it were true, so be it! Any amount of future dullness would be worth the wonder of tonight. Would the prince dance with every girl there?

"Heavens, no!" her mother assured her, much to Anastasia's disappointment. "He doesn't have enough time to pay attention to everyone. You will be introduced to him, however, and there will be plenty of other young nobles to pay attention to you."

Quick to sorrow but quicker still to delight, Anastasia surveyed herself in the mirror, her dark eyes sparkling. Whether or not the prince danced with her, tonight would be the best night of her life.

Arella was silent, though this was hardly unusual for her. As the hairdresser expertly piled her hair into a mass of golden curls, she fought back the panic rising in her heart. She knew, as Drusilla had told her, that she would dance with the prince tonight. She could not deny her own beauty. But how did one act when dancing with a prince? Or with any noble, for that matter? Though she had officially entered society last year, she had avoided attending as many balls as possible. Crowds made her feel awkward and shy. She lacked the polish her stepsisters had acquired.

If only Anastasia had been the beautiful one, she thought with distress. *She knows how to behave around princes.* Arella set her jaw. *Please, don't let me be a disgrace to my family!*

Drusilla reached over and silently squeezed her sister's hand. Arella took a deep breath. At least Drusilla would be with her throughout the night.

"Arella," the duchess called merrily, "How did your dress turn out?"

"Very well, Stepmother. I have it in my dressing room," the girl replied.

"And you like it?" Duchess Germaine asked.

"Yes, Stepmother." After a moment she added, "It's pink."

"Very good, child. And you're sure you don't regret not getting a new one?"

"Yes, Stepmother."

"Wonderful. Run along then and get changed." Duchess Germaine had hoped Arella would show some sign of disappointment; she had so looked forward to surprising her with a new gown! However, Arella seemed happy with her choice, so the duchess wouldn't interfere.

"No," Arella moaned, standing aghast in the doorway.

She had stopped short upon opening her door, shocked at the scene before her. Earlier she had painstakingly laid out her dress, smoothing away any wrinkles with a loving hand, smelling once more the scent of her mother. Then she had shut the door and left.

She had forgotten that her kittens were in the room. Apparently they loved the scent of her mother, too.

"Sleepy!" she cried. "Frisky! How could you?"

One of the kittens scampered under a table to hide while the other lazily stretched, his claws catching on the smooth silk of her mother's gown, which lay crumpled on the floor. Arella ran to the dress and picked it up. The kittens had gnawed the bow at the waist and run their claws down the skirt. Arella squeezed her eyes closed, wishing the scene away like a bad dream. But when she looked again, she saw the same thing. The dress was certainly not wearable—sash in disarray, one sleeve half off. "What do I do now?"

From the room next door Drusilla heard her cries of chagrin and came over. "Arella? Is everything all right?"

"No." Arella turned to her, holding up the soiled gown. "I didn't know cats ate dresses."

"Oh, Arella!" Drusilla exclaimed, entering the room. "Your mother's gown! Is there anything we can do to fix it?"

"No," sighed Arella. "There isn't enough time."

Drusilla hesitated a moment, uncertain what to do. Then she took the dress from her sister and grabbed her hand. "I know. It won't be your mother's dress, but it will have to do." She led Arella down the hallway to the duchess's room. Knocking, she called out, "Mother?"

"Come in," the duchess responded. Drusilla and Arella entered, bringing the torn gown in with them.

"Arella's dress," Drusilla explained simply. "The kittens got it."

"Oh dear!" Duchess Germaine cried. "How dreadful!"

"What shall I do?" Arella asked, her eyes brimming with anxiety.

The duchess inspected the damaged gown. "Well, you certainly cannot wear this, can you?" She smiled, lifting a mysterious eyebrow. "But I may have something that will work." From her wardrobe she produced the blue gown she had ordered. "I wondered if this would come in handy."

Arella accepted the dress, managing a small smile of gratitude. "Thank you, Stepmother." The style was completely unlike the simpler frock she had wanted to wear, but it didn't seem she had much choice now. She turned to head back to her dressing room.

"One more thing, child," the duchess called. "Here." She handed Arella a shoebox. "The glass slippers I wore a long time ago when King Hendrick had his royal ball. By right, Drusilla should wear them—"

"—but my feet are too big!" Drusilla smiled encouragingly at her stepsister. "You don't mind wearing them for me, do you?"

"No," Arella returned. "I'm just sorry you can't wear them."

Drusilla waved an indifferent hand. "It's no matter. But enough chitchat—we have a ball to dress for!" She put an arm around her stepsister's shoulders and guided her from the room.

Her eyes prickling with tears she couldn't quite suppress, Arella clutched the shoebox tightly in both hands. Nevertheless, despite the ruining of her mother's dress and the dread she felt about the impending ball, she met Drusilla's warm smile and managed a small smile of her own in return.

Arella's heart beat faster and faster as they alighted from the carriage and swept their way up the palace stairs. The knot in her stomach tightened, and she fought to keep her face calm. Yards of skirt rustled about her, and the dainty heels of her glass slippers made a delicate tapping as she walked. She looked like a princess—which she certainly neither was nor wished to be.

They hesitated at the entrance to the ballroom. In due time the herald would announce them and they would go forward to meet the prince. Arella tried to control her heartbeat while they waited, watching the prince greet the numerous nobles. *Stepmother promised I could leave at midnight. That's not too long to bear.*

3

PRINCE FREDERICK repressed a yawn as a line moved along. "Alice Laroche of Stelstek," he heard the herald pronounce. Frederick bowed courteously over the hand of a young girl with a white face and lank hair.

"I'm delighted to meet you," he declared. It wasn't a lie, exactly, just like wishing someone a good day wasn't a lie even though one often didn't really care how good the other's day was. She tittered up at him, batting pale eyelashes. He forced himself to suppress a grimace. Did all these girls actually believe that tactic to be attractive? Alice moved on, throwing a flirtatious glance—or at least what she hoped was one—over her shoulder as she left.

No. Definitely not Alice.

"Duchess Germaine Abendroth, Miss Drusilla Bessette, Miss Arella Abendroth, and Miss Anastasia Bessette," the herald droned. The duchess moved forward, her daughters following.

And Frederick fought to keep himself from gaping as the loveliest girl he had ever seen approached.

She met his gaze and started in nervous surprise. *Is it even fair that one girl should possess so much beauty?* he wondered.

The four women curtsied deeply as they drew near, and he returned an even deeper bow. "Duchess, Miss Bessette, Miss Abendroth, Miss Anastasia—I am so very pleased you could come." *Especially you,* his eyes said to Arella.

She glanced at him before looking down modestly.

No simpering. That's new, he thought. "I trust I may have the pleasure of dancing with—each of you before the night is over?" It would hardly be courteous to single out only one. Especially when there was an older sister—or stepsister, apparently—involved.

Anastasia's eyes flew wide open in delight. *I'm to dance with the prince!* she thought jubilantly.

Drusilla felt only shock. *I can thank Arella's beauty for this invitation,* she realized. Glancing at Arella, she saw her stepsister's face flooded with blushes. They looked becoming on her. The prince was obviously smitten already. Drusilla smiled to herself but felt worried. Could the prince charm Arella?

Murmuring their "I would be honored"s, the family moved on. The duchess smiled proudly. All three of her daughters had elicited an invitation to dance with the prince himself. An accomplishment indeed!

"I have to dance with him!" Arella whispered frantically to Drusilla behind her fan, out of earshot of the prince. He continued to bow to young ladies and their parents but sent frequent glances in Arella's direction.

"Just what every other girl wishes to do," Drusilla whispered back. Now was not the time to let Arella indulge in solitude. Like it or not, she would have to make herself agreeable.

"Why can't he dance with every other girl, then?" Arella whimpered.

"Because you are the prettiest."

"I hate being the prettiest!"

It was the most vehement speech Drusilla had ever heard her stepsister utter. "I'm afraid that isn't for you to choose. Dance with him, agree with what he says, smile a little, and then it will be over. Surely you can manage that?"

Arella bit her lip.

"It will be just like dancing with any other young man," Drusilla continued. "Don't be nervous. Everything will turn out well."

Arella cast a dissatisfied glance at Drusilla. "I hate dancing with all of them, too!"

Their conversation was interrupted when a friend of the duchess joined their party to visit.

Drusilla sighed. *Please, Arella, just behave.*

The evening dragged on forever, Frederick thought. At least the part of the evening until he could dance with Arella.

First he had suffered through all those formal introductions, and now he must dance through a list of noble ladies at his mother's behest. The daughter of the Emperor of Verdemons, for example; it would hardly do to ignore her.

Just dance with her and a few more, and then I'll be able to speak to the beautiful Arella. Frederick sneaked another glance her way. She stood beside her sister, the picture of elegance and grace. As far as he had been able to tell, she hadn't looked his way once.

But a little shyness isn't necessarily a bad thing, he reflected as Amala de Perperand boldly fluttered past him, eyelashes batting for all they were worth. *In fact, I think I like that in a woman.*

"Excuse me." Drusilla heard a deep voice behind her shoulder. "I believe you honored me with the promise of a dance?"

She turned to see the prince waiting, hand outstretched. She dropped a graceful curtsey. "The honor is mine, Your Highness." She allowed him to lead her to the center of the room.

It was indeed an honor for her; this was the beginning of her fourth season in society, and she had never boasted any serious beaux. In the opinion of most young men, her fortune was not enough to offset her awkward height, plain face, and flaming hair. Thanks to her stepsister's charm, however, she was now dancing with the crown prince.

I believe this is one of those stories spinster aunts tell their nieces ad nauseam, she mused. *"Did you hear about the time I danced with the prince?"* Drusilla felt sorry for her future nieces.

The prince was charming in every way. His dancing was impeccable, and his smile made her heart beat faster, even though she knew it was on Arella's account. She could see why all the other girls in the room tittered foolishly at him.

Frederick forced himself to focus on Drusilla instead of letting his eyes wander to her lovely stepsister. "I trust you and your family are in good health this evening?" he began courteously.

"Very good health, Your Highness, I thank you. I trust the same for you." Drusilla didn't know if what she had just said was technically true; Arella seemed rather unwell, actually. But Drusilla was never one to be remiss regarding etiquette.

Frederick nodded an acknowledgment to her good wishes. He was tired of conversations such as this—polite tidbits that interested neither party. At least this girl didn't simper. And she danced well—very well, in fact. *No great beauty, but quite acceptable for a stepsister-in-law.*

Tired or not of such conversation, such conversation must be had. They spoke courteously throughout the rest of the dance. With the closing chord, he made an elegant bow, matched by her equally elegant curtsey. "I thank you for the dance," he said. "It was a pleasure."

"The pleasure was all mine, Your Highness." If she had lied a bit earlier regarding the health of her family, at least this statement was entirely true.

Another man claimed her. Though not sought after as a wife, Drusilla was a good dancer and had sufficient partners.

Frederick smiled. Now he could finally speak to Arella.

AS SOON as the music began, Arella found herself in high demand as a dancing partner. She hated it. But what could she do? She quietly submitted to dance with all the young men who lavished attention on her, but did not deign to grace them with smiles.

Across the full room she saw the prince approaching Drusilla. *That means I'm next,* she thought, her hands growing clammy inside her gloves. She had more difficulty than usual following her partner. Her mind was sick with worry over the next dance, the one when the prince would claim her. Her partner, a stout man with a freckled face, didn't notice her abstraction. It was enough for him to be close to her.

The dance passed silently. The ending chord sounded.

The prince threaded his way to her.

Frederick bowed low to the woman he had been thinking about all evening. "Miss Abendroth," he said, his eyes shining, "I believe you promised me the great honor of a dance?"

"Yes, Your Highness." Her words were barely audible, but Frederick didn't notice. He took Arella in his arms and whirled away to the strains of the new song.

Arella could feel her heart pounding in her chest. Her hand in the prince's was cold. Prince Frederick gazed at her admiringly. She, however, looked down, unable to meet his eyes.

"It is an honor to claim you as my partner," Frederick said.

She hesitated. What was the polite reply to this? "Uh . . . it's my pleasure." A bald lie, if one counted lies at times like this. But she couldn't very well say, "I'd rather not dance with you, if it's all the same," so the lie would have to do.

Frederick could scarcely lift his gaze from her lovely face. The curve of her cheek, the light on her hair . . . She was irresistible, so he did not resist. "You look very nice tonight," he said with a hint of bashfulness. "But I suppose you look very nice all the time,"

A deep blush spread its way across Arella's downcast face. *I wish you could see me when I've been helping Alfie muck out the stables,* she thought defiantly. *Tell me then how nice I look!*

They were silent a moment, but silence did not bother Frederick. He felt he could happily admire his timid partner for hours without her ever speaking a word. "Did you know you deprive society of its most beautiful jewel when you are absent?" he asked her softly.

No. Don't start the foolish compliments! "Uh, thank you, Your Highness." She grimaced and wished Drusilla were there to hide behind. She surely would know what to say to a prince!

He seemed not to notice her awkwardness, her reserve, her hesitant dancing. He knew only that this girl was remarkably beautiful.

And he was going to marry her.

"You—you have many beaux, of course?" He tried to sound nonchalant.

She bit her lip. "Not many, Your Highness." She did her best to freeze away any would-be suitors. But how did one freeze away a prince's romantic advances? Had any other girl ever wanted to do that before?

"I would happily fight them all for the chance of a smile from you," Frederick said.

"That is . . . kind of you, Your Highness." Arella gulped. How long would this song last? The music whirled on, heedless of her discomfort.

"Not just kindness," Frederick replied, his gaze full of meaning.

Why me? Arella thought desperately. She cast about in her mind for a change of subject.

"I saw you dancing with my stepsister Drusilla," she blurted. "She is a wonderful dancer, is she not?"

"She dances exquisitely," Frederick agreed. "But she has not your charm."

"And you are promised to dance with Anastasia?"

"Yes. But when I have done"—he looked at her with pleading in his dark eyes—"will you favor me with another dance?"

No, she said inwardly. "Of course, Your Highness," she said out loud.

Frederick's smile lit up his entire face. What had he done to deserve such joy?

Arella glanced at the large, ornate clock at the end of the room. Ten o'clock. Two more hours.

As the evening progressed, Drusilla watched Arella with concern. Once he had gotten through his obligatory dances, the prince had paid attention to no one but Arella. Her poor stepsister looked miserable, though she was hiding it fairly well from the general assembly. They were too busy gawking at her beauty to notice any discomfort anyhow.

Drusilla sighed with compassion. *Poor girl.*

Arella felt panic beginning to well up in her heart. Prince Frederick insisted on paying her attention. Marked attention. No shyness dissuaded him; no awkwardness discouraged him. What could she do? Whirling across the crowded floor in his arms, she forced herself to keep down her rising desperation.

The clock struck midnight. Arella stopped suddenly in the midst of the dance. "I—I must go," she told the prince, pulling to escape from his arms.

"Go?" Frederick echoed with bewilderment. "Where? Why? The night is yet young!"

But Arella had borne as much as she could stand. "You must let me go," she begged. "I cannot stay any longer." Slipping from his perplexed grasp, she turned and hastened through the crowded room.

"Miss Abendroth! Arella!" the prince cried, following close after her. "Don't go!"

She moved faster in her frantic efforts to get away, weaving through the dancing couples, ignoring the prince and his undignified pleas. Breaking through the last of the dancers, she glanced over her shoulder.

The prince was still pursuing.

Arella ran through the doorway, through the entrance hall. Yanking open the heavy front door with effort, she sped down the outside stairs, nearly tumbling in her haste. Bother these glass slippers! She kicked them off then thought better of it. They were her stepmother's heirlooms, after all. She found one . . . Where did the other go?

Too late now; the prince was at the top of the stairs. The other shoe would have to stay here. She ran through the darkness, down the long avenue, vanishing into the midnight. Anywhere to get away from the unwelcome favor of the prince.

Frederick hurried down the steps, stopping at the bottom. "Miss Abendroth?" he called, stupefied. Why had she run away from him? He gazed into the darkness, searching for her.

She was gone.

"Arella," he whispered, clenching the fist that had so lately held her dainty hand. Turning, he started back up the stairway, pausing midway. Her slipper lay forlorn, kicked aside. He picked it up, cradling the delicate piece in his hand. It was dainty, beautiful—just like its owner.

His eyes darkened with determination. Frederick had always liked a good challenge, and winning the heart of this charming girl seemed like a challenge of the best variety. But not just now. He couldn't very well leave his own royal ball to comb the palace gardens.

"But I will see you again, Arella," he vowed. "And next time, I won't let you run away from me."

DRUSILLA WATCHED in horror as her sister broke away from the prince and fled out the doorway. What was the girl doing?

"Arella!" she cried, making her way to the far side of the room where she saw her sister disappearing through the entrance. Weaving through the plethora of voluminous, twirling skirts, Drusilla finally arrived at the doorway. Neither Arella nor the prince was in the large entrance hall. Had her sister run into the midnight darkness outside?

Drusilla, skirts clutched in her hands, hurried to the open door. She met the prince at the top of the stairs. He held one of Arella's slippers. "Where did she go?" she cried breathlessly.

Frederick looked at her, his face a calm mask. "I don't know. She ran down the avenue."

"You didn't follow her?" Drusilla stared at him, aghast. What kind of prince was he?

Frederick looked slightly surprised. "Even I can see that she isn't exactly asking for my attention."

Drusilla clenched her jaw. He had let her little sister run into the night alone? Her good breeding kept the upper hand, however, so she did not tell him what she thought of him at the moment. Instead, she forced her voice into a prim, respectful tone. "I must look for her. I fear she is not well."

"There is no need for you to go out. I will send a footman."

"She needs me," Drusilla replied shortly. "If I have your leave?" She paused.

"Of course," the prince nodded. Somehow he felt rebuked as Drusilla bobbed a brief curtsey and hastened down into the gloom of the palace grounds. She had been polite—yet at the same time, she had almost imperceptibly chided him for his lack of action. But what was he to do? Leave his own royal ball to find a girl who inexplicably ran from him? It wasn't as if she were in any danger, save dampness. The gardens surrounding the palace were immense; she surely wouldn't leave them.

He sighed. None of the etiquette books he studied addressed this situation. Maybe he could write one: *How to Behave When the Girl You Adore Runs Away from You at Your Own Royal Ball.* Perhaps it would assist future generations of princes faced with this same conundrum. Frederick smiled wryly.

He beckoned to one of the footmen standing at the door of the ballroom. "Miss Drusilla Bessette is trying to find her sister, who is strolling in the gardens somewhere. Take a lantern and assist her."

The footman bowed and left to do as he was bidden.

The ballroom filled with whispered gossip. Many people had witnessed the sudden flight of the prince's favorite dance partner and the immediate pursuit of the prince and of her stepsister, and those who hadn't seen jealously wished they had. Behind fans, ladies murmured.

"Did you see the way she ran out? She was deathly pale!"

"See her! I *felt* her! She trod on the hem of my new dress and tore it."

"Maybe Prince Frederick will dance with me now."

"I think she took ill suddenly."

"Maybe she's an imposter and the prince discovered it."

"Perhaps there was a beauty spell on her and it faded at midnight!"

This royal ball would not be soon forgotten.

Drusilla ran down the long avenue, calling her sister's name. She was almost to the gate when she finally saw Arella sitting on the side of the road, sobbing. "Arella!" Drusilla knelt beside her stepsister, putting her arms around her. "Are you all right?" she asked.

Arella cried harder, hiding her face in Drusilla's shoulder. "I'm sorry, Drusilla," she moaned between sobs. "I couldn't stand it any longer. I had to get away."

"Shhh now," Drusilla comforted her. She put a hand to Arella's forehead. "You're warm! Do you feel ill?" She gazed anxiously into the girl's teary face.

"Yes," Arella replied, hiccupping. "I feel—terrible."

"Come now," Drusilla said, rising to her feet. "We'll go back to get the carriage and return home. You'll feel better tomorrow." She put out her hand to help her younger sister to her feet.

"I can't go back there!" Arella wailed. "I've disgraced Father—and Stepmother—and everybody." Her sobs, which had slowed under Drusilla's comfort, returned with greater vehemence.

"We can worry about that later," Drusilla answered calmly. "For now, you just need to go home. No one can fault you for being sick."

Arella continued crying but allowed Drusilla to help her stand. Her large eyes met her sister's penitently. "I'm sorry, Drusilla," she repeated. "I just . . . panicked."

"It's all right, Arella," Drusilla soothed. "Don't think about it. Just come back with me."

They walked up the drive, Drusilla steadying Arella's shaking frame. She felt feverish. Drusilla wondered if she had actually made herself ill. Rounding the bend in the avenue, they came back within sight of the castle.

A footman met them. "Miss Drusilla Bessette?" he asked, raising his lantern.

"Yes?" Drusilla replied.

"His Highness the prince sent me to bring you a light."

Drusilla stared at him dryly. She had run all the way down the lane and walked back in the midnight darkness—and *now* a footman offered her a lantern. "Thank you, but it is no longer needed," she answered. "Would you call our horses and carriage, please? The crest is Abendroth."

"Yes, m'lady."

The footman strode away to the carriage house while Drusilla led her sister to the outside palace stairs. "Why don't you sit here while I find someone to tell Mother we're leaving? We can send the carriage back here when we get home, and she and Anastasia may stay and enjoy the rest of the ball."

Arella sat on the lowest step. She still held one glass slipper in her hand. "I think I left the other one here somewhere," she whispered.

Drusilla glanced at her stepsister's bare feet. The girl had walked all the way down the avenue and back in her stockings! She must be in pain, poor foolish thing. "It doesn't matter, dear," Drusilla said, her voice compassionate. "Wait here for the carriage."

Leaving her sister sitting quietly with her hands folded, Drusilla mounted the steps. Someone had shut the front door. She hesitated a moment. Did one rap on the door at a time like this? Or simply open it and proceed in? She tried the handle; it turned. With a little shove, the door swung inward. She brushed off her dress—it was definitely not made for midnight runs—and walked sedately through the hall.

Summoning all the composure she possessed, she addressed the single footman standing at the ballroom doorway. "Will you please send a message to my mother, Duchess Germaine Abendroth? Tell her that Miss Bessette and Miss Abendroth have returned home and will send the carriage back to the castle."

With a "Yes, m'lady," the footman bowed and entered the ballroom. It was amazing the composure they kept, Drusilla mused as she returned to Arella. The servants certainly couldn't be used to scenes like this—ladies running away from princes, and other ladies barging in the front castle door—but to look at this fellow, one would think it all quite routine.

The carriage was pulling up to the entrance as she descended the steps. Drusilla uttered a sigh of relief. This night had not gone exactly according to plan, but it was almost over now.

RUSILLA SHIFTED uncomfortably in her chair. She sat in the library, trying to read, but the words would not make sense in her head. Was it because of the late night she had kept? Worry over Arella?

Or perhaps . . . could it be the memory of the smile of a certain handsome prince?

Whatever it was, it was getting in her way. She sighed and shut the book.

The day had not gone well so far. None of the members of the household had stirred until nearly noon. Even then, the duchess ordered breakfast in bed and did not appear. Arella was even more silent than usual, which was not surprising. She had, after all, behaved rather scandalously, Drusilla remembered with a grimace.

Anastasia was tired but still would have liked to chatter, rehashing every event of last night, if the atmosphere of the house had not been so tense. As it was, she felt rather depressed; after she had looked forward to it so much, her first ball was over already. And neither of her sisters even wanted to talk about it!

Early in the afternoon the duchess called Arella into her sitting room. Drusilla hoped her mother wouldn't be too hard on the girl.

She wandered aimlessly to the window. *What I need is to stop thinking about the whole thing,* she thought to herself. *It's over, so worrying isn't going to do anyone any good.*

But she could make nothing else occupy her thoughts. Perhaps she should go try to cheer Anastasia—the poor girl obviously felt repressed by everyone else's misery. *Not that I particularly want to discuss last night,* she thought, a wry smile twisting the corner of her mouth. *But it may make her feel better.*

The butler opened the door and announced formally: "His Royal Highness, the Crown Prince Frederick, my lady."

Drusilla blinked in surprise at the royal figure standing in the doorway. *Not exactly what I was expecting!*

With a pleased smile, she moved across the room. "Your Highness," she curtsied, "What a pleasure to have you here."

Frederick bowed to her. He held a package in his right hand. "The pleasure is all mine," he replied.

Ever gracious, Drusilla gestured with one hand. "You will have a seat?"

"Gladly, thank you." The prince sat on the edge of a large armchair.

Drusilla settled herself across from him. "Might I enquire to what we owe the honor of this visit?"

Frederick made a motion with the package he clasped. "I was hoping for a few words with Miss Abendroth, if she has the time."

"Of course." Drusilla looked to the butler still standing at the door. "Harrison, I believe my sister is with my mother in her sitting room."

"Yes, m'lady." The butler bowed and left the room.

Drusilla turned back to the prince. "I pray you forgive my sister and me for the manner of our hasty departure last night," she said smoothly. "I am afraid Arella was taken unwell."

"I hope she is feeling better today?" Frederick asked, his brow wrinkled with sudden concern.

"I believe so, Your Highness. A good rest will do wonders."

He looked relieved. "She is a lovely girl," he remarked. Rather irrelevant to the conversation, but quite true nonetheless.

"Very," Drusilla agreed. She saw that Arella's abrupt departure last night had done nothing to quench the prince's fervent admiration. There seemed nothing more to say. The prince fell into abstraction—meditating on Arella's beauty, Drusilla guessed. Poor Arella. First a scolding from Mother and then a visit from a young admirer of whom she was deathly afraid.

"Your ball last night was exquisite," Drusilla said. "I imagine it will be talked of for months."

Frederick started a bit. He had been thinking of Arella's eyes. So blue, so innocent, so sweet . . . What had Miss Bessette just said? "Oh. Thank you. Mother insisted on sparing no expense. I trust you had an enjoyable time?"

"It was quite enjoyable, yes." Drusilla nodded. "The musicians were wonderful; I should have been happy to simply listen to them. I didn't recognize the first waltz they played. It was beautiful."

"A new composition by Westley Doone," Frederick replied. "You are familiar with his other works?"

"Oh, yes. His 'Dreaming of Thee' has always been a favorite of mine."

Their small talk continued amiably in this vein for some moments, but was interrupted by the solemn butler once again. "Miss Abendroth."

Arella entered, pale-faced and frightened.

Frederick immediately stood and walked over to her, eyes glowing. He bowed over her hand. "Thank you for giving me the honor of a word."

Arella nodded reluctantly. "I must beg forgiveness for the way I left last night, Your Highness." Her voice was faint. "I'm afraid it was unpardonable." *I hope it was unpardonable.*

"Not unpardonable at all!" He smiled at her, still holding her hand. "Your sister informed me that you were taken ill. I hope you are quite recovered?"

Arella paused before she replied, casting a dubious glance at Drusilla, who had risen and was standing demurely in the background. "I still feel a little faint—that is, um, I feel much better, I think. Your highness." She made the slightest motion to withdraw her hand. Frederick flushed and promptly dropped it. They stood awkwardly for a moment. Arella looked at Drusilla, her eyes pleading for help. Drusilla nodded to a chair.

"Would you care to sit, Your Highness?" Arella remembered. She sat herself, looking stiff and uncomfortable. Frederick perched on the edge of his chair, gazing eagerly at the lovely girl. Drusilla, loath to leave her sister, quietly took her own seat, just close enough to interject a comment if needed.

"I found something last night," Frederick began.

"Oh?" Arella replied.

He unwrapped the package he had brought to reveal a glass slipper. Leaning forward, he continued. "It will only fit the lady who stole my heart."

Arella gulped. She glanced again at Drusilla, who shrugged.

"Will you try it on?" the prince finished, gazing hopefully at Arella.

"Oh. I—" she began, but stopped. What could she say? "Of course, Your Highness," she finished without enthusiasm.

He knelt to remove her shoe and try the glass slipper in its place. Arella bit her lip. Perhaps her foot had grown overnight?

No such luck.

Prince Frederick smiled up at her. "It fits you, my lady. Perfectly."

"Um. Yes. I'm afraid I dropped it." Arella grimaced even as she spoke. She certainly didn't want to reciprocate his romantic drivel, but neither did she want to sound too rude. She had already disgraced her family once. She stole a glance at him to see if he was affronted.

He wasn't. Unfortunately.

He rose, holding out his hand to her. "My dear Miss Arella," he began, his voice full of tenderness.

Drusilla coughed then murmured, "Please, excuse me." Frederick looked at her in surprise. When had she come in? Oh yes. She had been here all along, hadn't she?

Arella sighed in relief. He turned back to her, hesitating a moment before speaking again. "My dear Miss Arella," he reiterated, "may I have the honor of calling on you again tomorrow?"

Arella couldn't very well tell him she didn't want to see him again. So she muttered, "Yes, Your Highness."

"And perhaps we could speak . . . alone," he added.

"Um, if you wish to, Your Highness." Her face was pale and bleak.

He bowed again. "I will take my leave then." His dark eyes fixed on hers intensely. "And I shall look forward to it," he whispered, pressing her fingers one more time.

Then he was gone.

The moment the door closed behind the departing prince, Arella gave a little groan. "Drusilla, what do I do?"

Drusilla rose calmly. "What do you mean?"

"He's going to propose! I know it!"

"So?"

"I can't marry him, Drusilla! I won't!" She looked frantic, defiant.

"Then don't," Drusilla replied.

"How do I tell him that?"

"I believe the customary practice would be to say 'No.'"

"I can't just refuse the prince!" Arella cried.

"Why not?" Drusilla asked. "That would seem to be the reason for a proposal, after all: to give the girl the chance to accept or decline."

"It would be so much easier if he just wouldn't ask at all," Arella moaned.

"Or if you would accept." Drusilla looked at her sister steadily. "It wouldn't be a bad life, you know. You would have a husband who adored you, I think that's clear. And you would have every material asset you could ever desire."

Arella shook her head. "No." Her voice was firm.

"Why not?"

"I can't. I mean, I don't—it wouldn't—he's not—I just can't."

Drusilla gazed curiously at Arella's downcast face. "Is there someone else?"

Arella's eyes flashed up to meet her sister's, her cheeks flushing bright red. "No!"

"You can tell me, you know."

"I—I have nothing to tell," Arella murmured, then fled the room.

Nevertheless, Drusilla wondered. She sat most of the rest of the day in the quiet library, wondering.

HE PRINCE came back the next day and asked Arella to marry
him. She awkwardly but firmly declined.

Frederick sat in his study, fingers tapping a morose rhythm
on his desk. The memory of Arella's quavering voice went round and round
in his head. *"I thank you for the—the honor of your proposal, Your
Highness. But I—I must—I must decline."*

Squeezing his eyes shut, Frederick dropped his face into despairing
hands. He remembered the advice his mother had given before the ball.
Choose someone who is worthy of being queen. Who was worthy of being
queen if not this vision? No other woman could compare to her.

But she had refused his proposal!

Frederick sighed. It was a sigh that communicated to the world, "I am
done with everything; my true love has rejected me"—the kind of sigh
Romeo surely uttered before he took his own life.

Why on earth had she rejected him? He was far from lacking in money, fame, or position. His manners were excellent, he knew, and he was reasonably attractive. Frederick wasn't a conceited young man (no more so than the average prince), but he couldn't think of a reason Arella would turn down his suit.

Unless, perhaps, there was someone else. But when, dazed by her blunt refusal, he had asked if this were the case, she had denied it.

Well, if there was no one else, there was hope for him yet. She was shy; maybe she just needed to get used to the idea? After all, she had met him only three days ago. What a spineless, sniveling worm he would be to give up so soon! He would try again to show her his love, and this time he would win her.

Two weeks! Two weeks it had been since she declined the prince's offer, and still he came calling!

Arella suffered through these visits quietly, unsmiling, and answered him only in monosyllables. Frederick didn't seem to mind; he found the duchess and Drusilla to be good conversationalists, and it was enough for now to admire the lovely Arella. Sooner or later, he reckoned, she would warm up to him. He was determined to win her, and her silence only enhanced his determination.

Arella pursed her lips in a thin, unhappy line. She would never marry him. Why was he too stupid to understand? She sighed, absentmindedly rubbing the head of the kitten sleeping in her lap.

Someone tapped on her door. "Come in," Arella called, easing her face into its normal, more placid appearance.

Drusilla entered the sitting room. "Ah!" she said. "I was hoping you'd be here."

"Can I help you with something?" Arella inquired politely.

"Do you have a few moments to chat?"

"Of course." Arella motioned her stepsister to a chair.

Drusilla settled herself and smiled warmly at her sister. "I wanted to find out how you've been."

"Me? I am fine," Arella replied.

"You seem unhappy. Something to do with the prince, I think."

Arella tightened her jaw. "I won't marry him."

"Why not?"

"I don't want to."

"May I ask again why not?"

Arella looked at her lap. How she wanted to explain herself, to unburden her heart to Drusilla!

"It's because . . ." She bit her lip. How could she describe it? "I . . . just don't want to," she finished dully. How she hated herself, hated the way she couldn't open up her heart! She wanted to cry.

Drusilla paused a moment. Then, choosing her way cautiously, afraid of disturbing her stepsister still more, she suggested in her gentlest voice, "Have you tried wanting to?"

Arella looked up, and her eyes were desperate. "Drusilla," she began, "it's more than just trying to want to marry him. I could never be happy if we wed. And he wouldn't be happy with me, eventually. *You* know that I would make a terrible queen. Can't you understand?" It was a long speech for her, and she stopped, hoping Drusilla would comprehend all she was trying to say but couldn't.

Drusilla nodded. "I think I know how you feel, dearest." She smiled again and reached out to take her stepsister's hand, giving it a gentle squeeze. "And I want you to know, I'm on your side. If you honestly don't want to marry him, I support you in that decision whole-heartedly."

"Thank you," Arella whispered. Maybe she should tell her. She opened her mouth. "Drusilla . . ."

"Yes?" For a moment, Drusilla hoped against hope that some crack might appear in the wall around Arella's heart. Hoped that her stepsister would trust her, just this once, with whatever it was that so burdened her heart.

Arella hesitated. "Nothing." She couldn't. Not now. Maybe not ever. She uttered another sigh. "I'm just tired, I suppose."

"Maybe you should rest a while," Drusilla suggested as she rose to go. She placed her hand on the younger girl's forehead. "You don't feel warm."

Arella rose with her, dumping the kitten unceremoniously on the floor. He mewed a protest, but she ignored it. "I think perhaps I'll visit the stables. A ride might do me good."

"Would you like company?" Drusilla offered.

"I think not today," Arella replied after a moment. "I'd . . . like to be by myself for a while."

"As you wish," Drusilla responded. She made her way back to the door. "Just remember that I'm here if you ever need to talk."

Arella attempted a small smile while her stepsister left the room, but tears filled her eyes as soon as the door shut. She turned to don her riding habit. *The stables will help,* she thought. *They always do.*

Drusilla was nothing if not a lady. Anxious to make up for what she lacked in appearance, she had devoted herself to her studies in all fields of etiquette and accomplishments. She had never excelled at any particular art, but she had acquired an impressive amount of grace and tact.

Now, however, she had done something which was perhaps a little scandalous.

She frowned doubtfully as she rode along. She imagined her mother would not approve. She hadn't actually told her mother where she was going. She had simply said it was a nice day—which it was for late December—and she thought she would go for a ride.

She hadn't told her mother she was going to the palace.

Drusilla gulped as she approached the massive gates. She wondered if she'd made a terrible mistake. Too late now; the gatekeeper had let her in and she was trotting up the avenue. She concentrated on looking at ease, confident, respectful. If she was going to do this, she had better do it with skill.

As she approached the entrance of the castle, a groom appeared from somewhere, helped her dismount, and took her horse. She ascended the stairway and knocked on the door. A butler opened it, looking at her in faint surprise.

"I'm here for an audience with Prince Frederick," she said calmly, showing him the letter of invitation from the prince. The butler didn't need to know that Drusilla had written requesting the audience. That was the scandalous part.

"Of course, my lady," the butler bowed, showing her into the hall. "Will you please wait here while I notify His Highness?"

Drusilla nodded graciously as she sat down to wait. "Certainly."

The butler was back in moments, telling her the prince would see her in his study. She followed him up the grand marble staircase, down an elegant hall, through an imposing door. Prince Frederick stood behind his desk. "Miss Bessette," he bowed. "What a pleasure." He motioned for the butler to be dismissed. "Will you have a seat?"

"Thank you, Your Highness." Drusilla sat, as composed as if she were sitting in her parlor at home, embroidering a cushion.

Frederick studied her, curious to learn what could bring Arella's stepsister here. "I trust your family is all well," he remarked. After all, one must complete all the formal niceties of conversation before proceeding.

"Quite, Your Highness. And yours?"

"Yes, thank you. You had something you wished to speak to me about?"

"I do. I come on behalf of my sister Arella."

Frederick flushed a little. "She sends a message?"

Drusilla shook her head. "I'm afraid not. She is very shy, you know."

"Yes," he replied ruefully. "I know."

"And unhappy," Drusilla added.

The prince looked surprised. He waited for her to continue.

"Your Highness," she said, maintaining a respectful tone throughout her prepared speech, "my sister has no wish to marry you. I truly believe that it would be better for both of you if you were to end your courtship of her and find another woman to be your wife."

Frederick blinked. "You . . . you are telling me to forget Arella?" He stared at her, unable to believe his ears.

Drusilla inclined her head in agreement. "It would be best."

He continued to stare for a long moment, baffled. She did not flinch. At last he managed, "May I ask why this would be best? Do I not offer Arella everything—money, title, security, love?"

"I fear that my sister places little value on money and title, Your Highness."

"Surely she cannot place little value on true love!"

Drusilla chose her words carefully. "She may not want to accept your love if she cannot offer you hers in return."

"So you are saying I can never win her heart." Frederick sat back in his chair, his eyes flashing.

"Her heart recoils from society. She is a quiet soul. To marry you would be to thrust herself into politics and fashion, to be forever spoken of and scrutinized."

"Is it not worth it for love? She does not know how tenderly I cherish her image in my heart!" Frederick did not notice the curious look that flashed for a moment in Drusilla's eyes. He continued, "Her face is the one I see when I wake every morning. It haunts me all the day. To glimpse one smile from her would thrust me into paradise! She cannot scorn a love like this."

"I do not say she would scorn it," Drusilla replied humbly. "But I fear she cannot reciprocate it."

Frederick clenched his jaw. He looked like a man ready to leap into battle. Then suddenly his face relaxed and his voice calmed. "I believe I can win her heart, Miss Bessette," he said, his voice polite but firm.

Drusilla considered her words before speaking. After all, one does not like to offend a prince. Then she said, "I do not believe you can."

He forced a smile. "I suppose it's a bet, then." He leaned back in his chair. "Your prediction versus mine. I suspect the odds lie with me."

Drusilla's composure wavered. "It is nothing like a bet, Your Highness," she said, her eyes flaring with sudden passion. "It is Arella's happiness. I tell you that her heart is not easily won. I have been her sister for eight years—and I am *still* trying to gain her love and trust."

She rose, overcome by the sudden desire to weep. "You are free to pursue her as you wish, but I did not feel it was right to let you continue without cautioning you that your doing so will surely end only in unhappiness for you both." She curtsied. "I thank Your Highness for granting me an audience, and I wish you good day."

With that, Drusilla turned and left the room, shutting the door in her wake.

Frederick sat alone in his study, speechless, emotions boiling. What kind of woman waltzes into a castle and tells the crown prince he is unlovable? He stood up and paced the room.

"I love Arella. I will not give up so easily!" he said to himself, his face set like stone. "This woman can think what she likes, but a love such as mine cannot be suppressed. I will woo her and I *will* win her!"

Drusilla rode quickly away from the castle, no less emotional than the prince. She couldn't go home yet. She couldn't face any of her family, not in this mood.

What was this mood? She scarcely knew. She couldn't erase the image of Arella looking frightened and small and lonely. She couldn't stop hearing the inflexible tones of the prince declaring his eternal love for her beautiful sister. She couldn't get rid of the feeling that if only—

But no. She spurred her horse through the city to the fields beyond. There she let him gallop, trying to outride the thoughts crowding her mind.

A few hours later, somewhat calmed, Drusilla cantered back up to her home. She had missed supper, she was sure, and evening darkness was rolling into the city. Dismounting, she handed her horse to a groom. "Thank you, Alfie," she said wearily. The stable hand nodded, ever respectful, and led the horse into the stables.

Drusilla entered the house, attempting to think of an explanation for her long absence. She heard conversation in the parlor and made her way down the hall to it, stopping short as she came to the threshold. The family was gathered there, along with a visitor.

Frederick sat close to the silent Arella, speaking to her in tender tones. He glanced up as Drusilla entered, and their gazes met for a meaningful instant.

"There you are, child! I was nearly ready to send Alfie out to search for you," the duchess scolded gently.

"Forgive me, Mother. I felt in need of a long ride today."

"In this cold?" Anastasia asked. "I would have frozen."

"It isn't cold so much as brisk," Drusilla replied with a too-bright smile. "But you will excuse me now, Mother? I believe I will go beg leftovers from cook."

She left. Arella hopelessly watched her go even as Frederick redoubled his efforts to woo her.

8

SOAPY WATER slopped from the large bucket as Arella plunged her rag in. She wrung it out violently and began scrubbing the staircase. Sometimes her feelings could only be relieved by physical labor.

Prince Frederick did not seem to care that she disliked him. In fact, the quieter she was, the harder he would try to win a word, a smile, a glance. She had done her best to discourage him, to no avail.

"He can call on me until he's old and gray," Arella muttered. "I won't have him!" She rinsed out her rag again, twisting nearly every drop out of it.

The problem was that she didn't know how much longer she could withstand this. A month now he had been courting her, and he showed no signs of wearying. She, however, was weary to the bone.

"I can't marry him!" she said defiantly.

But could she continue ignoring him? She hated displeasing the people she cared for, and they were obviously displeased. Her stepmother showed strong disappointment at Arella's lack of courtesy. Anastasia was openly baffled as to why Arella would not accept such a charming prince.

Only Drusilla had any sympathy at all, and she was a little distant on the subject recently.

Even the old servants didn't seem to understand. Society was talking, too; Arella knew the gossipmongers called her spoiled and proud ("Too hoity-toity for the prince himself, she is!") and ungrateful and selfish ("After all her stepmother's done for her!").

Arella winced. "But I don't want to be the princess."

She scrubbed at the old steps harder, turning over scheme after scheme in her mind. *What if I could go away for a while?* But where could she go? *If I just tell him I will never have him?* She had tried that once already. *If I suddenly show interest—perhaps he'll tire of me?* But that was too risky. He would probably think she was serious, and she would end up having to marry him.

No, there was no way around it; there seemed to be no solution, no way to get rid of the prince's attentions. If things went on like this, she would have to give in eventually.

Arella finally made up her mind. She knew what she must do.

The sun shone brightly through a crack in the draperies. Drusilla yawned and rolled to her back. Stretching her arms, she smiled. It had been a lovely dream—though, of course, it was no more than a dream. She slid off her bed and walked to the window, pushing the curtains back to welcome the warm sunshine. The morning held promise of a cheerful day to come.

Passing through her dressing room half an hour later, she noticed out of the corner of her eye a letter on the side table. *How silly of me,* she thought, shaking her head. *I thought I had replied to Sheila's letter already.*

She strolled over and picked it up. Her brow puckered. This wasn't Sheila's letter; it was a clean, sealed note, blank save for the *Drusilla* written in Arella's neat hand. Worry in her eyes, she quickly broke the seal and unfolded the paper.

"What? No!" Hand pressed to her mouth in shock, Drusilla ran from the room. "Mother!"

Duchess Germaine was sitting up in bed, taking her breakfast, when Drusilla burst into the room. She shoved a letter into her mother's hands. "Arella!" she gasped.

The duchess glanced at Drusilla, puzzled. She scanned the page, eyes widening in disbelief.

"Arella? *Eloped*?" She stared at the page as though her gaze could burn away the words. "With the stable hand?"

"I knew she was unhappy but . . . but I never thought she would do something like this. And with Alfie! I didn't even know they spoke to each other!" A sob caught in Drusilla's throat. "Mother, what do we do?"

The duchess sat stunned. "Do? What can we do?" She turned to the letter again, perusing it more carefully this time. "It's nine o'clock; if they left at midnight, they will have reached Fallhall by now. Legally there is nothing to prevent their marrying in any county seat." She looked back at Drusilla, her eyes wide and hopeless.

Drusilla blinked back tears. Arella! Her little sister! Married dishonorably to a stable hand! Why? Why had she done it? She took a deep, shuddering breath and sank to the edge of her mother's bed. "She is lost to us, then," she whispered.

The duchess closed her eyes. *Forgive me, Alain. I thought I did my best raising your daughter . . . but I have failed you.*

The two women sat silently for a moment, each lost in her own thoughts and regrets.

If only I had tried harder to find out what was bothering her so much, Drusilla thought miserably.

Perhaps if I hadn't pressured her the way I did, the duchess brooded.

She was trying to tell me something. I should have known this was more than just not wanting to marry the prince. Drusilla bit her lip in frustration.

I should have seen that she could never love the prince. I should have let her live quietly the way she wanted. The duchess's heart ached.

And now . . . she is gone.

Germaine was first to rouse. "They couldn't have planned this on their own, surely. One of the staff must know something about it. I will talk to the head groom first." She paused. "Anastasia needs to know." She rang the bell for her maid. "Send Anastasia to me."

Drusilla suddenly gaped in horror. "Mother!"

"What is it?"

Drusilla slowly turned her panic-filled eyes to her mother. "The prince. He was going to visit for dinner this evening."

The duchess groaned. "We can't very well keep that engagement, can we?"

"But we cannot send a message saying, 'Arella ran away. Come some other time'!" Drusilla's paced the room, and both she and her mother lapsed into the silence of furious thinking. This silence remained unbroken until Anastasia tripped merrily into the room.

"You called, Mother?" Her voice, light as always, grated in the dark atmosphere of the chamber. She stopped, her brow wrinkling at sight of the distraught faces turned toward her.

The duchess motioned for her to sit. "I have a note from Arella for you to read."

Anastasia stared. What was that strange tone in her mother's voice? Why did Drusilla look as though she had been crying? Anastasia gulped, suddenly afraid. The duchess handed her the paper.

Anastasia's mouth dropped nearly to her knees as she took in the brief note.

"She ran away with the stable boy? But that's—Mother, that's almost *romantic!* Arella was never *romantic.*"

Duchess Germaine shot her youngest daughter a stern glance. "There is nothing romantic about running away and disgracing your family," she replied. "Neither is there anything particularly romantic about living in poverty. And there is certainly nothing romantic about offending the crown prince."

Anastasia opened her mouth, ready to protest. But a hasty motion of Drusilla's hand cut her off. She submitted with a meek "Yes, Mother."

"We still need to decide how to inform the prince," Drusilla pointed out.

"We will send him a note saying that unfortunate circumstances prevent our being able to receive him for dinner tonight as we had hoped," the duchess replied resolutely. "That is all he needs to know for now. I'm sure the entire matter will be out in the open before long." She got up. "Drusilla, ring for my maid. I will dress and interview the groom. We are too late to prevent their marriage, but we may still find them and do what we can for them."

"Yes, Mother." Drusilla's heart sank as she rang the bell. Despite her mother's brave words, she knew there was very little to be done now.

THE SUN shone cheerfully as the wagon rattled down the quiet dusty lane, away from the oppressive capitol and town house, away from the prince with his annoying attentions, toward space and freedom and a life with Alfie. He held the reins in one hand and Arella's hand in the other.

Arella gave him a nervous smile. "Are we doing the right thing, Alfie?" Her worried eyes searched his for reassurance.

"Yes," he answered. He rubbed her fingers lightly. "Are you having second thoughts?"

"More like twenty-second," she replied, leaning her head on his shoulder. "Are you disappointed in me?"

He kissed the top of her head. "Never."

"I don't want to be a disgrace to my family," she whispered.

"A disgrace is a man who assumes he can have whatever he wants just because he was born royalty. A disgrace is a man who sees you only for your beauty—which is remarkable, by the way." He grinned as she wrinkled her nose at him, but quickly became serious again. "A disgrace is a family that expects you to forfeit happiness for money and position. You would disgrace your family if you were like that, Arella. We are not a disgrace."

Arella loved how secure she felt with his arm around her, nestling into his side, hearing his confident voice. "I love you, Alfie." She turned to look up at him. "Very much."

Alfie was the happiest man in the world.

The wagon kept rattling down the lane.

Frederick re-read the elegant note from the duchess. He wondered what had happened in the Abendroth household. Was Arella safe and well? And how unfortunate this was! He was almost certain Arella had smiled at him last night. Well, perhaps not *at him*, technically. But she had smiled in his presence, and that was an improvement.

Frederick's mouth twisted in a wry grin. Was he actually excited because a girl had *almost* smiled at him? Perhaps Arella's strange sister was correct . . . perhaps this was a hopeless cause.

The young page broke his reverie. "Is there an answer, Your Highness?"

"I suppose," the prince replied, considering a moment before he began writing. He carefully penned a few lines expressing his regret at the change in plans and his fervent hope that he would have the honor of seeing the family soon.

And by "family," he meant Arella.

Because even if she would only almost-smile at him, she was a woman unlike any other, and she was worth working for.

"Nothing?"

"Nothing." The duchess rested her forehead on her hand wearily. "No one knows anything—where they went, when they left. Apparently they didn't consult with anyone. They didn't even take one of our carriages, just Arella's horse."

"They couldn't ride out of the city double horseback," Drusilla objected.

The duchess raised her eyebrows. "They certainly aren't here."

Drusilla closed her eyes, willing herself to think of something that would help them find her sister. Why did they not take a carriage? Where would they have gone—and how were they getting there? "Did they fear recognition?" she mused. "Is that why they didn't take a carriage?"

"They could have taken the little carriage without the crest," the duchess replied.

No, that wasn't it. Something tugged at the back of Drusilla's mind, an idea she couldn't quite put her finger on. She frowned, concentrating.

"Arella left a note so we would know she was safe. They didn't take a carriage." A thought hit her. She looked at the duchess. "Mother, Arella didn't take a carriage because she didn't want to be accused of stealing anything—or she didn't want Alfie to be accused of anything. She ran away, but she's trying to be . . . I don't know. Respectable, I suppose."

The duchess pursed her lips and slowly nodded. "Yes. I suppose that makes sense. The note she left was quite respectful."

Drusilla half smiled. "That's so like Arella—rebelling without actually breaking the rules." Then she sighed. "But that still doesn't help us discover where they went."

"Sullivan informed me that this stable boy's full name is Alfred Stone.

His family is from Finch-under-Clay, and he's been working for our household for five years. He came with excellent recommendations from the vicar in his hometown, so Sullivan gave him a job in the stables. Apparently he's been a good worker; no one has had any complaints against him until now."

"I'm sure Sullivan feels terrible."

The duchess nodded. "He blames himself. Though he could have had no idea that this would happen."

"Do you think they're heading to—what was it?—Finch-under-Clay?" Drusilla asked.

"I've already sent a man that way, hoping to overtake them. I also sent someone to Vilihania—though that would be a little too obvious. And Pressley, of course, as the closest place they could be married. But they could have gone anywhere."

"If they are overtaken, what then?"

The duchess rubbed her brow again. "If one of the men finds them, he is to bring them back. Then we can . . . have a discussion."

Drusilla chose her words carefully. "What can we discuss?"

The duchess shook her head. "I don't know."

The dusty lane rolled on and on, and the wagon—passengers sitting close together—rattled on with it. Finally the wagon rattled into a respectable town full of whitewashed houses and cobbled streets. Alfie pulled up the horse outside an imposing courthouse and grinned at the lovely girl sitting by his side.

"Here we are," he said, swinging himself to the ground and extending his hand to help Arella. He grinned up at her, eyes shining. "I love you, Arella," he said softly as she stepped out of the wagon. He pulled her close.

"Marry me?"

"No word yet?"

"Still nothing."

The hours had been agonizingly slow. Each one that passed carried Arella farther away, farther to—where? Drusilla's mind was tired from the endless swirling of worries that had filled her thoughts since morning. Would they be found? Were they already married? How would they live?

And what would Prince Frederick do when he found out?

For he would find out. And soon. Rumors were already beginning to accumulate like mists rising from the marshes in the evening. Some servant girl had told her beau; some old cook had gossiped with her neighbors; some younger stable boy had told his parents—it didn't matter who began the rumors. But they had begun, and they would not be stopped.

How would the prince respond?

Frederick dismounted from his horse and patted its black flank. "Good ride, Midnight," he said as he handed the gelding's reins to a groom. It *had* been a good ride, he considered, walking briskly to the castle. Missing dinner with Arella last night had preoccupied his thoughts. He'd needed this ride to clear his mind. He glanced at the sky. It must be nearing the dinner hour. He would call on the Abendroth household afterward.

Frederick strode into the castle and made his way to his mother's sitting room. He stopped short and grimaced outside the door because he knew the voice now ringing through the hallway. Lady Lloyd, a distant cousin of his father's, could be conversing in the deepest inner chamber of the entire building, and her voice would still resound through the halls. Anything he needed to say could wait until the old gossipmonger left. He turned to leave.

But he paused before he'd gone two steps, his ears perking at the sound of a familiar name.

"Yes, Miss Abendroth and a cook! Or maybe it was a footman. It doesn't matter. I have it on the best authority!"

The queen's voice now, fainter. Frederick strained to hear. "And whose authority would that be?"

"One of the maids told one of Sir Humphrey's footmen, I think, and he told Nurse Linnet who was caring for his wife, and she told Countess Laroche, that sniveling invalid,"— Frederick smirked; it was well-known that the two old women had been determined rivals for nearly forty years— "and *she* can't keep a secret, so she blabbed it at her luncheon today, and Lady Allistra told *me*."

"So it's an unfounded rumor, Lady Lloyd?" The queen's quiet voice held disapproval.

Behind the door, Lady Lloyd sniffed disdainfully. "Rumors are never *unfounded*, Your Majesty. They may not be completely accurate, but there is always a *foundation*."

"Until there is proof that Miss Abendroth has indeed eloped, I would prefer you not to speculate on the matter," Frederick's mother said firmly.

Eloped? Arella? What utter nonsense! Arella wouldn't—

Frederick's stomach dropped as he recalled the abrupt way Duchess Germaine had cancelled their dinner invitation last night. He turned on his heel and ran back to the stables. "A horse, now!"

A KNOCK at the door interrupted Drusilla's fruitless attempt at sewing. "Come in," she called. Could it be news of Arella?

A maid curtseyed. "Company in the parlor, ma'am. It's the prince again."

"Oh no," Drusilla moaned before she could catch herself. She restored her composure and looked calmly at the maid. "Is Mother still out?"

"Yes ma'am."

"I shall be right down."

"Thank you, ma'am." The maid bobbed again and left.

Drusilla closed her eyes and tried to keep herself calm. Of all people she didn't want to see at the moment, Prince Frederick was highest on the list. With Mother gone to seek her brother's help finding Arella, Drusilla and Anastasia would have to face the prince by themselves. And Anastasia wasn't readily available, so that left . . . Drusilla.

She took a deep breath and descended to the parlor.

"Prince Frederick." Drusilla gave a formal curtsey.

"Miss Bessette," Frederick replied, hastily rising from the chair he had been sitting in. Drusilla noticed that his hands were clenched and his face, though calm, was strained. "I . . . came to inquire after your sister. Miss Arella. She is . . . well?" His anxious eyes searched hers.

Drusilla felt pity for him. *Obviously he's heard rumors. No use trying to keep it hidden.*

"Arella," she began slowly, "is . . . not here at the present."

Frederick's face paled. "Is it true?" he asked in a low voice. "Has she run away?"

The poor man. It's almost as hard for him as it is for us. Drusilla nodded. "She left sometime before yesterday morning."

"With . . . with a servant?"

"One of the stable hands, Your Highness."

Frederick slumped back into the chair and hid his face in his hands. Drusilla watched helplessly. He looked up after a minute. "Have you heard from her?"

"Not yet. My mother sent out men, but Arella's location has yet to be discovered. My mother is with my uncle, asking him for advice and help."

"Of course," Frederick replied. His face had gone completely blank. They were both silent.

"I'm sorry," Drusilla said quietly. "I know you were attached to her."

Frederick looked at her with hollow, pain-filled eyes. "I loved her. But . . . she never loved me." His voice broke. After a moment he continued with a bitter smile. "You knew that she didn't, that she never would. I believe you tried to warn me this would happen." He stood and strode to the window. "I suppose this means you won our little bet."

"I never dreamed Arella would do something like this. I'm sorry."

"Don't be," he replied, turning to face her again. "It's not your fault. None of it's your fault. It's all mine. I should have respected her wishes and left her alone instead of driving her to . . . this."

"It's no more your fault than it is mine, Your Highness," Drusilla replied. "Arella made her own choices."

Frederick sank into a chair again. "And she chose to run away with a servant."

Drusilla opened her mouth but changed her mind. What was there to say? Instead, she simply sat. They passed several moments in silence.

Finally Frederick looked up. "I suppose I'm not needed here."

"We're just waiting for some word," Drusilla said. "But . . . you may stay and wait with us if it comforts you."

He looked at her hesitantly. "You won't mind if I stay a while? I won't be in the way? I know I'm not doing anything . . . but I feel closer to her here."

"I understand. Please make yourself at home. If there's anything I can do or get for you, simply say the word."

"No, no, don't bother yourself. Please. I would just like to wait with you."

Drusilla nodded. "As you wish, Your Highness."

The duchess returned late in the afternoon and found Drusilla and Frederick still sitting in the parlor, Drusilla with her sewing again, Frederick absentmindedly stroking the kitten that had climbed into his lap. All three startled when she entered the room, and the kitten leaped from Frederick's lap and slipped under his chair, where it set to washing its face.

"Any news, Mother?" Drusilla asked anxiously.

Germaine paused, noticing the prince. Then she indicated a letter in her hand. "Arella sends a note."

Drusilla jumped up, hand outstretched. "May I read it?"

The duchess handed it to her wordlessly. Drusilla fumbled to unfold it and scanned the lines. Frederick stood by while she read.

Finishing the note, Drusilla took a deep breath. "So. That's that?"

The duchess nodded slowly. "It appears so."

Drusilla read the paper again, more slowly. Frederick cleared his throat. She turned to him in surprise. "Oh yes. Your Highness." Drusilla looked at her mother. The duchess, not knowing how much he knew, hesitated.

"Arella writes? She is . . . married?" he inquired.

"Yes, Your Highness," the duchess answered. "She was married yesterday."

"Would you care to read it?" Drusilla offered the note to the prince.

He took it but hesitated. "You don't mind if I see it?"

"You are feeling as hurt as we are," Drusilla replied. The duchess nodded. Frederick unfolded the paper.

Dear Stepmother, Drusilla, and Anastasia, it read, *I married Alfie this morning. We are going to live near his family in Finch-under-Clay, and we are very happy together.*

I hope and pray most earnestly that you will not hold this against me. I know that my marriage did not start conventionally, and I know that you will perhaps face some criticism. I can say only that I hope you can forgive me for the hurt I caused, and I hope you will allow me to continue corresponding. If you would rather not, I understand.

Much love,

Arella Stone

"Well," Frederick said as he finished reading the brief letter, his face a mask. "I suppose that settles that. Is there anything we can do for them?"

"I think not," the duchess replied. "I shall write back—naturally we don't want to ostracize her—but I think they must be on their own now, at least for a while."

"To be sure," the prince assented. He glanced down at the paper in his hand again and let his eye rest on the signature. *Arella Stone.* So plain, so strange, so final! It could have been *Princess Arella d'Arceneau.* But it wasn't.

Frederick took a breath and forced himself to remain composed. He refolded Arella's letter and handed it to the duchess. "I believe I must be going," he remarked as calmly as he could. His manner fooled neither woman.

"Of course, Your Highness," the duchess assented. "And please allow me to apologize for the way you have been treated in this sad situation."

"No, please, don't apologize," he replied, swallowing hard. "I hope Miss Arella—er, Mrs. Stone—will have a happy and prosperous life with her . . . with her new husband. Thank you for allowing me to stay so long. Good day."

Drusilla's heart ached for the forlorn prince as he left the room. *If only he hadn't been so stubborn in pursuing Arella! If only Arella hadn't been so shy.*

Drusilla shook her head. Such meditations were worthless now. All she could do was pray that Frederick would be able to find someone who reciprocated his love.

11

"DID YOU see the way he looked at me when I told him I was already engaged for the waltz?" Anastasia asked, her face wreathed with delighted smiles. "I think he likes me!"

Drusilla smiled at her excited sister. "Making him just one more on an increasingly long list," she replied. "The question is, do *you* like *him*?"

Anastasia blushed. "Well, maybe a little. He's such a gentleman, and so nice, and so handsome! And he isn't just a gentleman in company, either. Why, just the other day Eloise told me that—"

These interesting confessions were interrupted by a maid bearing a note. "For you, ma'am." She curtseyed to Drusilla.

"Thank you, Mary." Picking up the note, Drusilla's brow puckered. *That looks like the royal seal . . . but why would anyone from the palace write to me?* She quickly broke the wax seal and scanned the contents of the letter.

"I've been summoned to the palace," she said, blinking in surprise.

Anastasia's jaw dropped. "Whatever for? When? By the queen?"

"I don't know why, whenever it is convenient for me, and by . . . Prince Frederick."

"The *prince*?" Anastasia's jaw miraculously found a way to open wider. "What on earth could he want?"

"I have no idea," Drusilla said. "But I believe this summons is scarcely one I can put off." She rose to go, thinking aloud. "I'll tell Mother . . . I suppose I'll need to change. One goes to the palace by carriage at a time like this, I believe."

She stopped and turned at the door, smiling mischievously at her sister. "But, when I get back, I still expect a full report of everything Eloise told you about the gentlemanliness of this young man!"

Duchess Germaine looked up from the letter she was writing. "Yes?"

Drusilla entered the sitting room and handed her mother the letter from the castle. "Prince Frederick would like me to call on him at my earliest convenience."

Duchess Germaine looked surprised. "The prince? At the palace?" She looked at her eldest daughter in confusion. "Do you know why?"

"I have no idea!" Drusilla replied. "We haven't seen him since the day Arella sent that letter, and that's three weeks ago. What could he want?"

The duchess read and re-read the note. "I suppose the only way to find out is to go as he requests." She surveyed her daughter critically. "Put on your blue visiting dress, but leave your hair like it is. I shall order the carriage."

"Yes, Mother," Drusilla submitted. But inside, her mind was awhirl. *What on earth could he want?*

Prince Frederick stood courteously as the butler showed Drusilla into his study. "Miss Bessette! Thank you for coming," he said, bowing over her hand. "Please, take a seat."

They exchanged formal small talk as Frederick resumed his chair and studied the woman sitting across from him. She didn't look uncomfortable, even though he knew that his note must have come as a surprise. But Drusilla always had an ease of manner, no matter the situation.

"I suppose you are wondering why I asked you to come here today," Frederick said.

"I'll admit I am a little curious, Your Highness." Drusilla smiled. "It isn't every day one is summoned to wait upon the crown prince."

Frederick grinned. "And it's a good thing, too. One would find it rather boring."

"Indeed?" Drusilla laughed. "All those years of education, and you are a boring conversationalist? Your mother must be disappointed."

Frederick shook his head woefully. "Can't live up to everybody's expectations, you know." Then, turning serious, he added, "But that is actually why I wanted to speak to you."

If Drusilla was confused, she didn't show it. She merely waited for the prince to go on.

He cleared his throat. "You know that I held a ball some time ago in order to find a suitable bride."

Drusilla nodded.

"At which task I failed." Frederick drummed his fingers on his desk and smiled wryly. "My royal mother gave me a firm upbraiding yesterday for my still-unattached state and instructed me to remedy the situation as soon as possible. However," he glanced at Drusilla, "I have no idea what to do. Which is where you come in."

"I?"

"Yes. You may remember a similar conference we held some weeks ago regarding your sister."

Drusilla remembered that interview quite well.

"In light of recent circumstances," Frederick continued, "I have come to realize that you demonstrated a goodly amount of wisdom that day. And I need some wisdom now. You see . . ." he paused, considering. "Mother isn't the sort of person to give advice. Not *personal* advice, anyway. And Father told me to just pick someone, which wasn't exactly helpful. So I thought, given your good sense, perhaps you could advise me as to what course I should take now that, uh, my original plan fell through."

Prince Frederick is asking me for marriage advice. Drusilla took a deep, calming breath. He looked at her expectantly, waiting. She struggled to put her thoughts in order, hoping her voice sounded somewhat normal when she responded.

"I thank you, Your Highness, for this compliment. However, I must confess that I am not exactly sure what you would like me to say."

"Just . . . tell me what you think I should do. Whom to choose," he said, a note of pleading in his voice. "I don't know how to go about this bride-selecting business."

He's completely serious, she realized. *He needs help. Oh dear.* But she maintained her composure with masterful care and said simply, "I believe that you already know what you need to do."

"I need to find someone to marry," he replied. "How do I do that? I didn't do well the first time I tried."

Drusilla waited a moment before answering. "Your Highness," she began, making certain her tone was respectful, "why did you choose my stepsister?"

"I fell in love with her."

"What made you fall in love with her?"

"Arella was perfect. Beautiful. Unlike any girl I'd ever seen."

"And?"

He looked at her in surprise. "And what?"

"What else?"

"What else? I don't know. I didn't need to know anything else. I think I loved her as soon as I saw her."

Drusilla was quiet.

"This reminiscing will hardly help, I think," Frederick objected in frustration. *I need to find someone new. Not think about Arella. Arella! Mrs. Stone, now . . .*

"Your Highness," Drusilla continued, ignoring the prince's last comment, "you had no reason to marry my stepsister besides the fact that she was uncommonly beautiful?"

"Of course that's not why I wanted to marry her! I already said I loved her. Surely you saw that!"

"But you only loved her for her beauty."

Frederick stopped, aghast. Had this woman really just dared to accuse him of loving Arella for so base a reason? Had she really just insinuated he was that shallow?

And worse, was his heart agreeing with her condemnation?

Drusilla's heart thudded uncomfortably. Perhaps that had been a little too harsh. Still, he had asked her opinion, hadn't he?

Stupid girl. Her mind raced. *One doesn't just tell the prince what one actually thinks!* Too late now. Drusilla forced herself to meet the prince's gaze steadily.

The silence lingered awkwardly. Frederick cleared his throat. "Miss Bessette," he said stiffly, "I fail to see how this conversation pertains to the question I asked you."

"You described your first choice as a failure. Perhaps, in order to make a better second choice, you need to discover why your first didn't succeed."

Her humble tone did little to ease the pain Frederick felt upon hearing her words. *This is not exactly the kind of advice I expected,* he thought in frustration.

But maybe it's the kind you need, another part of him prompted

"So," he ventured to say. "What do you think I need to do now?"

Drusilla smiled. "I think you need to be honest with yourself." Frederick stared at her moodily. She continued. "Just as you are more than a title, so must your queen be."

He waited for something else. "That's all you can offer me?" he asked.

"I'm afraid so." Drusilla rose to go.

He eyed her for a moment and then nodded. Rising and bowing graciously, he said, "Very well. And I do thank you, Miss Bessette, for doing me the honor of speaking with me today."

"I'm only sorry I could not be more helpful, Your Highness."

The prince watched her go with a sigh. *Well, that didn't go exactly as planned.* But what had he planned, anyhow? For some reason, asking Drusilla's advice had seemed like a very good idea earlier. Frederick supposed he'd thought she could tell him which girl on his long list would be the best.

I guess I'm on my own. He stared down at the paper in front of him. Written in his mother's stately hand, it was the list she had prepared for him before his ball.

You never really loved Arella.

The voice rang in his head with painful clarity. That was what she had said, wasn't it? The insolent woman had accused him of—

—*the truth.*

Frederick pushed his chair away from his desk and paced across the room. How could anyone say his love was untrue? Had he not persevered in the face of rejection? Had he not patiently labored to win his beloved's hand?

And why did you do those things? The voice continued. *Why take so much time on that girl?*

Frederick stood at the window and crossed his arms. He didn't want to know the answer. But he couldn't stop his thoughts, which answered the question with dreadful honesty: *I pursued her because I couldn't face the thought of failure.* He hung his head as another part of him interjected, *But I failed anyhow.*

The study felt stuffy, oppressive. Frederick considered going for a ride on Midnight to outrun these painful thoughts. He stared out the window longingly but remained inside. *I need to understand this. I need*—Blast it, that woman had been right!—*to be honest with myself.*

Sighing, he seated himself at his desk. He bowed his head. *I chose Arella because she was beautiful, and I never actually took time to know who she really was. I was too proud to admit that I could be the wrong man for her.*

The realization stung. It stung horribly.

I was so concerned with living up to everyone's expectations that I never gave a thought to what Arella would want. Only to what would be best for me.

"I'm sorry, Arella," he whispered. But it was a little late to apologize now. He could only hope that the life she had chosen would make her happy. Meanwhile, he was responsible to choose someone else to be queen.

Restless, Frederick stood and began pacing the room again. "I failed you, Arella," he said out loud. "And Mother," he added, remembering the stern conference they had had yesterday. "And society"—thinking of the scandal he had caused when Arella ran away to escape his unwanted attentions. "Come to think of it, I've failed the nation. One job: Find a woman to be the future queen. And I, the classically trained Prince Charming, couldn't manage it." He clenched his jaw.

And what could guarantee that the next woman he proposed to would be any more interested in him, the shallow prince, than Arella had been? Needless to say, he knew any number of young ladies who would be happy to reside in the castle and be called "Princess." But he seriously doubted he could stand being tied to any of them for life.

There must be one woman in the kingdom who has sense!

"I suppose I need to follow Miss Bessette's advice and look deeper than titles and appearances." With a sigh he added, "Which means I need to get to know them." He strode back to his desk and sat down. Taking up his mother's list, he decided to pay some calls.

Drusilla shook her head as her carriage took her home. Of all the strange conversations ever to take place, that one had to be the strangest.

Prince Frederick had summoned her to the castle to ask her whom he should marry.

She had accused him of never truly loving Arella.

Drusilla winced. *Goodness, Drusilla,* she condemned herself. *What a thing to say to the prince! You could have counseled him to choose . . . say . . . Miss Clea. She would make a charming princess. Or you could have put in a good word for cousin Fabienne. But no. You had to go and tell him that his love was shallow and untrue!*

It didn't matter. Even if she hadn't offended him dreadfully, she was sure the prince would take no further interest in her. She sighed.

You blamed the prince for loving Arella for her beauty . . . but your own head was turned by Prince Frederick's charm. How is that any different?

Drusilla felt herself flushing, though the voice was only in her head. "It isn't just his charm," she defended herself to the empty carriage. "Though certainly he has that in abundance." A self-conscious smile briefly passed over her face. "Prince Frederick is more than charming," she continued, then considered a moment. "He's a good man, a trustworthy man. He's trying so hard to be everything he needs to be, and he's worried, I think, that he won't be."

She folded her arms. "I know he could never think of me—I don't ask him to." She thought ruefully of her flaming hair and plain face and the way she had probably just offended Prince Frederick for the duration of his reign. "But I can't blame myself for . . . for liking . . . and respecting him. And for hoping he finds a woman who will love him properly."

If the empty carriage observed the break in Drusilla's voice as she finished her defense, or if it noticed her struggle to regain her composure before reaching home, it never told. Drusilla's secret was safe inside it.

ADY LLOYD'S annual ball was the most important social event of most seasons. This year she had been trumped by the prince himself, yet her ball still boasted a great deal of grandeur.

Duchess Germaine watched her girls happily. The certain someone Anastasia blushed over was, indeed, paying her marked attention, and Anastasia was giving him no reason to believe it was unwelcome. If only the young men who danced with Drusilla would notice her after the ball was over!

On the other side of the room, Drusilla fanned herself while her partner went to find refreshments. It had been an enjoyable ball thus far. Although the family was still branded by Arella's scandal, they were liked well enough that few people treated them any differently.

Anastasia is looking well, Drusilla mused. *We could have a wedding on our hands before this time next year—*

Her ruminations were cut short by a familiar voice.

"Are you claimed for the next dance, Miss Bessette?"

Drusilla turned in surprise to see Prince Frederick. "Yes, actually," she admitted.

"Oh." Was that disappointment on his face? "But the set after that, are you free?"

"I am." How could it be that he wasn't still offended?

"May I have the honor?"

"The honor would be mine, Your Highness."

Frederick smiled as Drusilla's partner returned. "I will look forward to it."

Drusilla was afraid her current partner would have to suffer through a rather distracted dance.

"You were right, of course," Frederick admitted, a little bashfully. He and Drusilla were whirling around the floor, not unlike the first time they met. This time, however, the conversation was not made up of stilted polite nothings while his attention was focused elsewhere.

Drusilla wrinkled her brow in confusion. "I was right, Your Highness?"

He hesitated. "About your sister. Miss Abendroth—Mrs. Stone. How I treated her. You were right."

Drusilla blushed, her pale skin flaming as bright as her hair. "I should not have said what I said," she replied. "It was quite rude."

"It was completely accurate," he countered, "and I thank you for it. I've been trying to follow your advice."

Drusilla tried to remember what she had advised him to do. "I'm glad I was able to be of service to you, Your Highness."

"Please, no more 'Your Highness'-ing," Frederick begged. "As I mentioned, I've been trying to do like you said—look beyond titles and appearances—but I've found quite a few young ladies who seem to be concerned only with the outward, and the continual simpering and 'Your Highness'-ing is getting a little old."

Drusilla smiled. "Surely you've found some young ladies who are more than that, Your . . . um, Prince Frederick."

He grinned. "Not many. In fact, one day this week I was so sick of the simpering that I actually decided to call on your family so I could hear some sensible conversation. But you were out."

"I'm afraid we have quite the busy social life," Drusilla replied.

The prince twirled her so that her skirt swished, then drew her close once more. "Judging by the difficulty I had obtaining a dance with you, I believe it," he said.

"Waiting one dance isn't so difficult, is it?"

"One that you know of," he answered with a wry smile. "Besides, I'm not used to waiting for dances."

She considered this a moment. "No, I suppose you wouldn't be, would you?"

Frederick shook his head. "Royalty is spoiled enough, and being the only child rather increases the problem."

Drusilla laughed. "You poor thing," she said unsympathetically.

"It's a serious problem!" he protested. "For example: When Arella refused me the first time, I had no idea how to react. I've always gotten what I wanted."

"Well, Arella would confuse most men," Drusilla replied. If her gaze suddenly dropped from his face to focus on the embroidery of his collar, she doubted anyone would notice in the middle of a dance.

"Have you heard from her again?"

His voice sounded natural. Drusilla wondered if he felt as calm as he sounded. "Yes, we've been corresponding. Her husband is working for a blacksmith, and they have a cottage to live in. She sounds very happy. Happier than I've ever known her to be."

"I'm glad for her," Frederick said.

Drusilla met his gaze for a moment, saw that he was sincere, and nodded. "Thank you," she replied.

Frederick didn't ask what she was thanking him for. They both seemed to understand.

The conversation moved to other subjects, lighter ones. Frederick and Drusilla chatted easily. She forced herself to enjoy their dance instead of thinking about the fact that he soon would be choosing another lady to be his bride.

VER THE past month, Frederick had studied his list of suitable marriage partners, made his own list of qualities necessary in a future queen, visited the young ladies who struck him as likely prospects, narrowed his list, and visited some of them again. He had whittled his list down to four women, and the merits of these seemed about equal. They were all high class enough to suit society and possessed, in addition, personalities more substantial than those of average young ladies. Frederick had conversed with them to make sure they had at least some sense, and observed them to ensure they had kindness.

Beyond that, he didn't really have time to know them better; Mother had been particular that he fulfill his princely duty soon. He must simply pick one and hope she turned out to be gentle and lovable.

And have a sense of humor, Frederick added. He surveyed his now-short list dubiously. The names all looked about the same to him. He wasn't excited about marrying any of them. But one of them it must be. He closed his eyes and jabbed the paper.

Miss Maud Alize Clea.

He frowned. She had been nice enough, but he didn't exactly want to marry her. Not at all, as a matter of fact. He jabbed again.

Miss Elissa Galot.

He frowned again. There was nothing really wrong with her, either. But just the same . . .

Frederick sighed. His problem was that he expected too much. Noble birth, good looks, sensible mind, gracious manner. And on top of all this, he thought it necessary to have feelings for the girl? He must stop being so particular. One more jab couldn't hurt, though.

Miss Gwendolyn Beckett.

She was no better than the first two. Neither was his last option. He tapped his pencil nervously against the desk. "Feelings come and go, Frederick," he lectured himself. "You'll surely fall in love eventually."

But it wasn't simply a lack of emotions, he realized. Were any of these women worthy of being queen? Were they women who would make strong leaders, strong supporters?

"Honestly, Frederick. You won't find someone who's perfect—and goodness knows, you aren't perfect. You're looking for an above-average measure of wisdom, grace, kindness, tact, and humor; and you won't find that—outside of Drusilla, of course," he added as an afterthought.

Drusilla.

The idea hit him with the force of a thunderbolt.

Arella surveyed the messy kitchen despondently. It had not taken her long at all to realize that occasionally "helping" prepare food in a large, rich household was a far cry from preparing daily meals on a limited budget. Alfie was sweet about it, but she knew that she had a long way to go before she could be called a good cook, or even a mediocre one. She wondered if he ever regretted not choosing a more competent wife.

She sighed and set to scrubbing burnt goo from the pans. She hadn't realized before how much she took for granted. She wouldn't trade this life with Alfie for anything, but it certainly was different from the life she had known.

And it was different from the life she had expected. If she had thought running away from the city would leave behind all prying eyes and unwanted attention, she was wrong. The prying eyes here were lowlier than those of the society she used to know, but the gossip mill ran just as smoothly here as it had in the city. Arella was new, unused to this way of life, and the principal player in a rather shocking scandal. At times she felt as uncomfortable in the center of this village as she had in the center of the castle ballroom.

No, cottage life wasn't as romantic as she had imagined it would be.

Alfie stopped in the doorway to admire his pretty wife. She was working furiously to scrub something off a large pot, her forehead furrowed with concentration. With a frown? Alfie wondered if she was unhappy. After all, this life was a far cry from what she had known, though he was doing his best to make a good home for her.

Arella saw him out of the corner of her eye and turned, a smile lighting her face. It was replaced immediately with an embarrassed look. "Alfie! Supper's . . . almost ready. I don't think it will be much good."

He smiled. "It will be wonderful," he replied, walking over to kiss her. She hoped it would be edible, at least, for his sake. "I brought you something," he continued, pulling a letter from his pocket.

She took it, her eyes shining with delight. "From Drusilla!"

"Do you miss them very much?" he asked, a hint of anxiety in his voice.

"Very much," Arella answered with a sigh. "They were so kind to me, though I doubt I deserved it."

Alfie thought this ridiculous. Arella deserved every kindness! He hesitated a moment. "Do you . . . ever wish you hadn't left?" He looked around their small home. "I know I can't give you what you're used to."

"No, Alfie, never," she replied. "I mean, that is . . . you give me *you.*"

Alfie felt his heart flip at the sweetness of her smile. He put his hands on her waist and pulled her closer. "Don't you think I should get something in exchange for the letter then?"

Arella blushed and wrapped her arms around his neck.

Yes, she was very happy in the life she'd chosen.

MARRY DRUSILLA. Why hadn't he thought of it before?

"Because it's crazy!" Frederick argued with himself, shocked at his own idea. "Your brother-in-law would be this—this—Alfred Stone! Your sister-in-law would be *Arella*!"

It wouldn't work. It couldn't.

"She's only the daughter of a baron, and she isn't pretty at all." He felt the walls staring at him. "Well, she's not," he protested.

But, on the other hand . . .

She was wise; she had proven that. And he trusted her. She was gracious, easy to talk to, easy to like. Every time he had called on Arella, Drusilla was pleasant, keeping the conversation flowing and peaceful. Her manners were excellent—those born royal could not have better. And she could laugh and make him laugh in turn.

What more could he ask? And furthermore, the thought of spending the rest of his life with her didn't fill him with dread. Actually—he smiled to himself in disbelief—he rather liked the idea.

"*Find a woman worthy of being queen,*" his mother had instructed. It was as if she'd been telling him to marry Drusilla.

He shook his head. "That's impossible," he said to himself. "You forget, prince, that it takes two to make a match, and Drusilla is probably too good for you." Hadn't she seen his fault when he had been blind to it? Hadn't she known him for the shallow, thoughtless man he was? Why would she want him?

And yet, even when she condemned him for his shallowness, she had called him more than a title. Was it possible that such a woman could accept him, could even love him eventually?

"It's crazy," he smiled to himself. "But, if I can get her to agree . . . it's perfect."

"Where are you off to, Drusilla?" Anastasia asked, looking up from the latest in a series of love letters.

"Mrs. Wright sent word that the little Willow children have been taken ill," Drusilla explained, buttoning her coat. "I thought they might like these." Next to her sat a basket. Anastasia observed the contents: warm food, a ragdoll, several picture books.

Anastasia smiled at her older sister. "You're so kind," she said. "It isn't contagious, though, is it?"

Drusilla laughed at her sister's anxious look. "I'm sure it isn't," she replied. "Mrs. Wright would have warned me if it were." She turned before walking away. "Did you want to come?"

Anastasia replied with a trace of guilt. "Not today. It's cold. Besides, you never know if someone important might come."

Drusilla laughed. "If someone important comes, tell him or her hello for me."

The awkward thing was deciding how to go about it. Frederick had finally determined to pay a call and declare himself to Drusilla. Then . . . he would see what happened.

He felt a knot growing in the pit of his stomach as he rode closer to their house, which was nonsensical. He didn't love her. He had just thought of marrying her this morning. Yet he still felt nervous.

There could be no harm done except to his pride, and that had already suffered a blow; it could surely handle another. He took a deep breath and dismounted at the door of the town house.

The afternoon light was fading as Drusilla got home, a little tired but happy. So she faced a life of spinsterhood. What of it? She could be useful and spread joy.

Anastasia, grinning mysteriously, met her as soon as she entered the house. "Someone important came," she said.

"Oh?" Drusilla raised an eyebrow as she unbuttoned her coat. "The butcher, I suppose?"

Anastasia's grin grew wider. "Prince Frederick himself."

Her news carried the intended surprise. Drusilla looked up, startled. "What did he want?"

"*Does* he want," Anastasia corrected. "He's been locked in a private conference with Mother since right after you left. *And* you're to join them at your earliest convenience."

Drusilla wrinkled her brow. *If he's here for more courtship advice, I re-*

fuse, she thought stubbornly. Then, with a sigh, *Though I suppose he's my future sovereign, so I'll aid him in any way I can.*

"Well?" Anastasia prompted.

Drusilla looked at her, startled.

"Don't you think you should change out of that wet coat?"

"Oh yes. Of course." Drusilla looked down at her outfit.

"After all," Anastasia reminded her, "you'll want to look your best for your audience with the prince!"

Frederick rose when Drusilla finally entered the room.

"Your Highness," she said, bobbing a curtsy. "I hope I didn't keep you waiting."

"Not at all," he replied. "I've been having a very pleasant visit with your mother."

Duchess Germaine beamed at them and bowed her way out of the room. Drusilla tried to mask her curiosity. "You will sit down?" she asked, indicating a nearby chair with a gracious wave of her hand.

Frederick sat, but his hands fiddled in his lap. He cleared his throat. "Miss Drusilla," he began. "I . . . came today to discuss something with you."

Drusilla waited.

"Actually, you may remember my asking advice from you a few weeks ago," he continued. "You know, about whom I should marry."

"Yes, Your Highness." *Not again . . . .*

"I've been thinking a lot about it." He shifted in his chair. "And I've been trying to look deeper than just outward things this time." He met her gaze, but Drusilla couldn't tell what he was thinking. "Whomever I marry will have to be queen someday, so I want to marry a special woman—if she'll have me," he added quickly. "Someone who is kind and wise and gentle and good. Someone I trust." He paused and looked at her again.

"Yes, Your Highness?" Drusilla prompted.

Frederick took a deep breath. "Someone, in short, like . . . you."

Drusilla felt her breath catch in her throat. Could her ears have deceived her? But no, there sat the prince before her, gazing at her with a mixture of earnestness and fear. She turned quite pink, refusing to meet his eyes now.

"I know that it comes as a surprise," Frederick hurried on, rather red himself, "and I know that you could probably choose from many better men than I"—Drusilla would have laughed had she not been so surprised—"but, well, I thought about marrying someone else and I just didn't want to. I would like to marry you."

Drusilla stared at her own hands, her eyes very round.

Frederick stopped, uncertain whether or not to go on. Drusilla glanced up at him briefly. Encouraged, he continued. "You don't have to give me an answer now if you don't want to, and I'll understand if you cannot accept my offer," he assured her, "but, Drusilla, I would be honored if you would consent to be my wife. I don't know a lot about love, you know that. But . . . I'd like to learn. With you."

Drusilla couldn't quite suppress the pull at the corners of her mouth. Prince Frederick finished his speech, out of breath, hoping against hope, hardly daring to look at her but determined not to look away. Why wouldn't she meet his eyes? Was she laughing at him?

Blushing, Drusilla finally looked up and smiled at him.

He startled. *How did I ever think her plain?*

ABOUT THE AUTHOR

ELISABETH BROWN has always loved words. The third of seven children, she enjoyed being homeschooled through her senior year of high school, and is now studying piano performance at Appalachian Bible College. When she's ignoring the fact that she should probably be practicing more or doing Greek homework, you'll find her sewing, baking, reading, singing along to basically any musical ever created, hiking through the woods, or laughing at incredibly silly puns.

What Eyes Can See is Elisabeth's first published story, but she also rambles at www.MetaphoricalCello.wordpress.com.

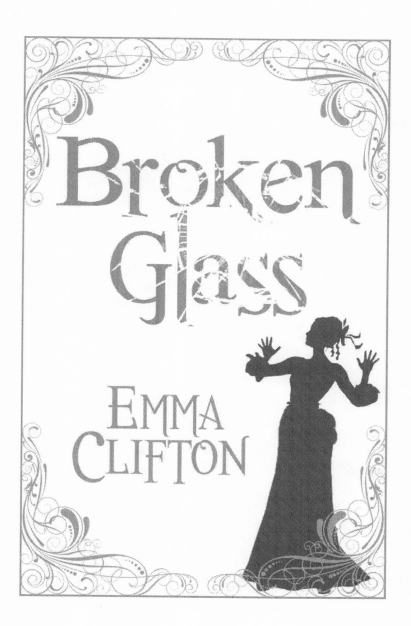

Broken Glass

EMMA CLIFTON

To my wonderful mom:

I am so grateful for all the time, energy,

and love you give me every single day.

You've taught me so much and have always

been there for me when I needed you.

Thank you so much!

Chapter 1

I T'S NOT me, I promise!" Lady Rosalind Copper glared fiercely at the palace attendants before her. Then her glare shifted to her foot, which wore a glass slipper bearing a delicate, swirling *R*. "Yes, this is my shoe, but I wasn't wearing it last night!"

"All the evidence points to you, miss," one attendant responded hastily, giving her a sympathetic smile. But when Rosalind's eyes narrowed, he shrank into his silk livery and backed away.

"It wasn't me." Too outraged to care about proper grammar, she crossed her arms. "I went to the ball with Henry last night. I didn't wear these shoes! I don't know *how* they ended up at the palace. Tell them, Henry. It wasn't me!"

The young gentleman standing beside her wasn't acting like his normal, cheerful self. Even his curly brown hair seemed to droop. "My father's orders are pretty much law," he mumbled, and shrugged lamely. "Sorry, Roz."

Rosalind flung her hands into the air. "So what if your father is a king! You're a prince! Doesn't that amount to something?"

"Not really." Henry's gaze remained fixed on the floor, intently studying the toes of his boots. "I'm his third son, you know."

"You are all *hopeless!*" Rosalind shrieked. "Doesn't my word count for *something?* Isn't there *anything* you can do?"

"Goosie," her father said in a soothing voice, patting her on the back, "I'm sure the king will understand. Just go with them to the palace, explain what happened, and it will all turn out well. Am I right, Helena?" Lord Copper turned to his wife, who nodded and offered a dainty smile.

But Rosalind, a high-minded young woman of eighteen, only scowled at her father. "Don't try coddling me. I *know* the king won't listen."

"Miss?" the guard began cautiously.

"What?"

"We . . . um . . . are allowed to use force, if necessary."

The other attendant snorted. "To think we'd ever have to force a girl to marry the crown prince. All the other girls in Arcadia are lining up to try this shoe on!"

"You're going to *drag* me out of here?" Rosalind's bright green eyes widened; she latched onto her father. "You wouldn't dare."

"Rosalind. Rosalind." Her father gently patted her hand before prying it off his arm. "Just go quietly, and things will turn out better."

"Now you're taking their side!"

Henry mustered up his last bit of confidence. "Roz, come on."

With as much reluctance as possible and with more glares all around, Rosalind followed Henry out of the house. Her house—the house she was being forced to leave! To marry a prince she didn't want.

I already have a prince. She sniffed to herself. *What has the kingdom come to? It would almost be better to be a cinder-girl.*

This was an exaggeration, of course. A cinder-girl had the lowest job in the factories of Arcadia: cleaning the ashes from the furnaces and keeping the fires burning. It was practically slave labor; protests over the conditions in which cinder-girls worked happened all the time. As a member of higher society and the daughter of a factory owner, Rosalind tried not to have an opinion on the subject, but that nasty little thing called her conscience wouldn't let it go. She participated in monthly clothing and food donations to cinder-girl charities; wasn't that enough?

All these thoughts and more swirled around in the boiling stew of Rosalind's mind as she marched down the front steps of her home. Neighbors crowded on the sidewalk, eager to catch a glimpse of their future queen. Rosalind knew they were all wondering why on earth she looked so cross.

If only they knew, Rosalind thought, her mind whirling with thunderous anger. *Our king is a tyrant, that's what.*

Rosalind shoved past the attendants who tried to help her into the steam carriage. A very meek Henry clambered in across from her. She acknowledged him with a sniff and crossed her arms. Moments later the steam carriage sputtered to life and began bumbling down the road.

As Rosalind expected, several minutes passed before Henry spoke.

"It's all right with me if you danced with my older brother," he offered in a quiet voice.

Rosalind shot him a glare prickling with daggers. "Are you calling me a liar?"

"No . . . not exactly. But you can be honest with me." He gave her the cute little smile that had stolen her heart only a few months ago.

But she wasn't in a susceptible sort of mood now.

A dramatic sigh burst from her carefully painted lips. "So you *are* calling me a liar. Even you, Henry; even you. Why does everybody doubt me?" She flopped back in her seat and stared balefully out the window. Their carriage pulled away from the lower city, leaving behind the conglomeration of metal smokestacks and shingled roofs.

"But how did your shoe end up on someone else's foot?"

Rosalind moaned and rubbed her face. "I don't know."

The twisting topiaries in the palace garden sailed past. Gardeners paused their trimming to catch a glimpse of their future queen. But their future queen did not care to catch a glimpse of them.

"Should we tell my father about us?" Henry suddenly asked.

Rosalind's eyes narrowed. "What do you mean? Have you never mentioned that you are courting me?"

Henry took his turn at studying the scenery outside. His answer came slowly, after he had carefully mulled it about in his head. "He never asked. He never asks anything about me." He laughed, yet Rosalind thought she heard a hint of bitterness in his voice.

No, she must have imagined it. Henry wasn't capable of bitterness. He was too weak. The thought almost made her smile, but she repressed it with the self-control of a well-born lady. Instead she continued to glare. "He's your father," she persisted.

"He's the king," Henry corrected. "And the king worries about the future king."

"Marius." Rosalind sniffed. "Whom I'm being forced to marry. What has this kingdom come to?"

"Now, now, I'm sure Father will understand," Henry started, but her shrill voiced sliced through.

"Oh, really? And that's so likely. What are you going to do? Stand up for yourself? You could've done that back at my house. Aren't attendants supposed to listen to the king's sons? You don't even have the guts to stand up to your own attendants; you'd never be able to stand up to your father."

"I . . ." Henry floundered. "I just don't like to cause trouble."

Rosalind groaned. "This is your future we're talking about! My future! Our future! Don't you love me?"

"Of course I do," Henry hastened to assure her. "But I can't go against my father's wishes."

She gave him another wilting glare. "You have no imagination sometimes."

Henry opened his mouth to reply, but the steam carriage interrupted him by jerking to a halt. Moments later, a pair of scurrying attendants opened the door and bowed to them. Rosalind swept past them without so much as an acknowledging glance, but Henry muttered a quick "Thanks."

Fists clenching her silk skirts, Rosalind marched along the halls of the palace and through the yawning double doors of the throne room. The guards and courtiers parted before her, opening a walkway to the throne.

Rosalind got her first good look at King Cygnus. She'd glimpsed him at the ball, of course, but not up close. She wasn't impressed. To be sure, he wasn't the pleasantly plump little man her childhood imagination had always pictured; he wasn't stuffed in a comical silk suit overflowing with lacy ruffles. No, in reality he was disappointingly normal. His close-cropped graying hair, hard face, and dark eyes made her hate him even more.

The king's stony face twisted into an expression that took Rosalind several moments to decipher. Then she realized—he was smiling. "Ah, well done, Henry! You've found her."

Rosalind thrust her chin into the air. "No, he hasn't. I'm *not* the girl you're looking for."

The king's eyebrow slid up. "Really? Then who are you?"

"Lady Rosalind Copper," she pronounced with a stiff curtsey. "And Henry is courting me."

"Is he?" King Cygnus's uninterested gaze shifted to his youngest son.

"He never mentioned it."

The courtiers began to chatter, ladies tittering to each other from behind their lacy fans. Rosalind scowled around at the lot of them, taking in the size and scale of the throne room as she did so—two rows of vast marble columns soared up to the vaulted, gold-tiled ceiling. This very spaciousness might have daunted another, but to Rosalind it simply meant she'd have to talk louder to be heard. This had never been a problem for her.

The king rubbed his chin thoughtfully as he studied Henry's chosen love. "You do realize that Henry is only the *third* son, yes?"

"Yes, but—"

"Then I don't understand," the king continued just as though she weren't speaking. "Why don't you want to marry Prince Marius? Every other girl does. He is the crown prince, after all. If you need reminding."

Rosalind exploded with a shriek worthy of a tea-kettle. "I'm courting Henry! I love Henry! What is so hard to understand about that concept?"

Waves of whispering rippled over the courtiers and guards. What was this girl thinking? Snubbing the crown prince, yelling at the king—Who did she think she was? But Rosalind's mind was a rock amidst the sea of others' opinions, impervious to the crashing waves of gossip. They broke and ebbed on her determination.

One voice, however, spoke louder than the rest. "The shoe belonged to her; it fit perfectly," one of the attendants from the steam carriage called timidly.

"Indeed?" The king's face turned back to Rosalind with an unreadable expression she liked less and less.

"I'm not the right girl," Rosalind insisted. "Ask your son Marius. He'll agree with me."

For a moment she thought the king was displeased with this statement. After all, she was practically giving him a command. But did she care? Not a jot. It was actually kind of fun.

"Father?"

A new voice drifted to Rosalind's ears like a cold draft. She almost shivered. A young man slid out of the shadows behind the king's throne. He glided across the floor as if his boots were made of oil instead of black leather. His smile was equally greasy. Black hair, with the slightest suggestion of waves, fell artfully around his face. A few rebellious strands dared to cover his left eye. The other eye glittered brightly at Rosalind. She glared back at him. The man paused beside King Cygnus's throne.

"Shall I fetch Marius?" he asked and, though he spoke in almost a whisper, his voice carried across the hall.

Cygnus didn't spare his second son so much as a look. "Yes, Darcy. Your assistance is most welcome."

Darcy's thin lips stretched into a smile. "It is my pleasure."

The doors of the throne room barely creaked as Darcy slipped out. A minute or two passed before the quiet chatter resumed.

"Courting Henry?" the king mused, a small smirk curling his lips. "Who would've thought? Tell me, how long has this arrangement been going on?"

"Since last winter," Rosalind replied, raising her head proudly. "And it's not going to end."

"Indeed? We'll see about that."

Any further conversation was cut short by the loud banging of the double doors.

"What now, Father?" a sharp voice rang across the room, matched by the clack of a pair of boots on the marble floor. Rosalind turned to glimpse her supposed future husband. She'd heard much of the crown prince but had never seen him up close. He was the sort of person God had blessed with good looks and not much else. Honey-gold hair, blue eyes, a well-shaped face; yes, he was attractive. But he wore an expression of utter contempt.

He took one look at Rosalind. "That's not her," he growled.

"I told you!" Rosalind cried. She whirled around to smile triumphantly at the king. "May I go now, Your Majesty?"

The king laughed. "Of course not, my dear! You'll do."

"What?" Marius and Rosalind yelled at the same time. Henry might have mumbled something as well, but nobody heard; frankly, nobody cared.

"But Father!" Marius protested.

"What?"

"You promised."

"Promised what?"

Marius crossed his arms. "To get me the girl I danced with!"

"And you promised to marry the girl I found."

"But Father! This isn't the right girl!"

"Your Majesty!" Rosalind snapped. "See here—I don't like him. He doesn't like me. Why on earth would you force us to marry?"

Darcy gave them both a dark look that Rosalind interpreted to be a smile. "You'll make an *amusing* couple," he said.

But King Cygnus waved a dismissive hand. "What don't you like about my son? He is crown prince, after all."

The entire court stared at her in disgust for snubbing Marius, for he was the court favorite. But to Rosalind, the courtiers were no better than paintings or nice vases. They were excess ornaments in an already over-trimmed room. "I don't *dis*like him. I just like Henry better," she answered, staring the king squarely in the face.

"Henry?" Marius repeated. He snickered. "I have a hard time believing that. You must be very desperate."

The first hint of annoyance crossed the king's face; he turned to his eldest son. "And what is your issue with her, Marius? Lady Rosalind is a well-born lady and the daughter of one of the most successful factory owners in the city."

Marius examined his nails impassively before sparing a glance at Rosalind. "She doesn't sparkle quite like the girl I see myself marrying." He studied her face for a moment, his eyes narrowing. "Fairly decent looks, I'll give her that. But she's not thrilling. Not amazing. Not the girl I danced with last night."

"Oh, and you can discover your future soul mate by dancing with a random stranger?" Rosalind snorted. "Likely."

He cocked his head and grinned. "I'd expect a comment like that from someone like you. Someone desperate enough to settle for Henry."

"Yes, yes, I'm sure you'll get along splendidly. So it's decided," the king declared, beaming down upon the courtiers as if he were the sun granting its blessed light to the earth. Two pairs of angry eyes stared at him.

"You . . . you can't possibly mean—" Marius stuttered.

"I have to marry him?" Rosalind spluttered.

"Oh well," Henry mumbled. But nobody heard him.

The storm at last blew over the throne room, leaving behind an unsettled lull. The future queen now sulked in her chambers while the future king moped over a boring novel. But the king and his middle son remained in the empty hall.

"Darcy," King Cygnus said, breaking the silence, "I need you to do something for me."

Every day is the same, Darcy growled inwardly. *Do this. Do that.*

But another voice in his head replied. *The more you help him, the more he'll see that you are more worthy than Marius.*

He'll never notice. He doesn't care.

Darcy smiled anyway. "What is it, Father?"

"Marius will try to find the other girl. The one he really danced with. He had that look about him, as if he were about to disobey me. And that Rosalind . . . she'll try to get away too." The king looked to his son and frowned. "Make sure nothing gets out of hand. Watch them closely and report back to me."

"Of course, Father. You can trust me."

The king's frown softened somewhat. He patted Darcy's arm. "You're always here for me, aren't you? It's just a shame you weren't born first."

Behind his smile, Darcy ground his teeth. *I've been telling myself that for the last twenty years.*

Chapter 2

THE FATEFUL moment arrived in under twenty-four hours: Rosalind found herself alone in the same room with Marius. To be more precise, Marius found her. That is, he barged in on her precious reading time. The library had seemed a safe haven—surely someone as snobbish and childish as Marius would have no desire to read and thus would never disturb her there.

"What are you doing here?" Rosalind snapped, closing her book. She sat up from her reclining position in the window seat, leaving warm impressions in its stiff cushions. Like many other rooms in the palace, the library was intended mainly for show; in this case, to display the king's vast collection of rare, boring books and expensive, uncomfortable furniture.

Marius shrugged, sauntered to an armchair, turned it to face her, and settled his lithe form onto the embroidered upholstery. "It's my castle. I can go where I please."

"Actually," Rosalind said with a disdainful sniff, "it's your father's *palace*. The words 'castle' and 'palace' are not synonymous."

Marius clapped. "Bravo. I wouldn't have believed you capable of using a word like 'synonymous' correctly."

Anger swelled in her breast and threatened to bubble over. But Marius would have found her wrath gratifying, so Rosalind simply gave him a cool smile. "Then you are even denser than I supposed. Henry, on the other hand . . ." She let her voice trail off and returned to reading.

"Was that supposed to insult me? Because I think you're extremely dense for courting Henry."

Rosalind bit her lip to keep from scowling. Turning a page and keeping her eyes on the book, she said in a distant tone, "If you're here to distract me, you'll find I'm not so easily swayed."

"Yes, that would be a fun reason to be here," Marius agreed with a solemn nod. "But no, I just came to be a general nuisance." When she glanced up, he gave her a smile that managed to be attractive even while dripping sarcasm. She glowered, and his smile widened. The books and wood-paneled walls around her began to lose their charm; she inwardly groaned at the necessity of finding a new place to hide from Marius.

"I'm still curious how you and Henry got together." Marius lounged across his chair like a cat upon a warm windowsill.

"Why?" Rosalind gave him a sharp look, and her book snapped shut. "He's capable of falling in love."

"With you?" Marius laughed softly. "I doubt anyone closely acquainted with you could fall for you. And anyway, Henry would never have the guts to ask you."

Her cheeks burning, Rosalind turned to the window and folded her arms. "He just needs a little push now and then."

Marius suddenly sat upright, and that horrid grin spread across his face once more. "I can see who's driving the steam carriage in this relationship. So he didn't ask you?"

"Well . . ." Rosalind's reply trailed off as the memory floated through her mind. It had happened last winter, in the palace gardens. She remembered the tickle of snowflakes flitting onto her face and the cold that seeped into her bones from the marble bench beneath her. Henry was smiling that cute little smile of his, and Rosalind was just realizing how nice his curly hair looked with snow in it, when . . .

"I like our walks," Henry said with a musical lilt in his soft voice.

"So do I." Something felt strange inside her. Was she nervous? Stuff and nonsense! The fearless Rosalind was impervious to nerves. Her mind must be playing tricks on her.

"Neither of my brothers ever takes time for me," Henry continued. "But you do. You're so . . . engaging. Interested. You actually listen."

The thought struck her—she liked him. No, this feeling surpassed mere liking. Was it love? The idea was a sip of hot tea on that cold day; it radiated heat, spreading even to the frozen tips of her toes. Rosalind felt a blush and a smile erupt on her face at the same time. "You're an interesting person! I can't imagine why your brothers would ignore you."

Henry rolled his eyes. "Marius is too busy fixing his hair, and Darcy is, well . . . too busy glaring at Marius and thinking up clever retorts and asides to shoot at us lesser mortals."

"Poor, friendless Henry," Rosalind agreed, suppressing a smile. That weird fluttery feeling hadn't ceased; it was beginning to disrupt her usually organized senses.

Henry's eyes widened, an adorable little curl falling into his face. "But we're friends, aren't we?" He smiled playfully.

"Of course, silly boy." Rosalind giggled. "But you know . . ." She let her voice trail off, hoping he'd pick up the hint.

"Know what?" He tipped his head down and stared up at her with wide eyes.

Good heavens, I am falling in love, she thought.

"We could be more than friends," she finished in a near-whisper. But her voice still held all the firmness of fearless, determined Rosalind.

Henry blinked. "I'd like that," he said.

"So would I." She could feel the warm clouds of his breath brush against her cheeks. "Is that a 'yes'?"

Henry leaned forward and kissed her cheek; just a second later he pulled away, leaving a spot of warmth on her face. Her skin tingled and a smile glowed in her eyes.

"We should tell my parents," she stated, her practical side coming alive again.

His eyebrows drew together. "What, that I kissed you?" He wore the expression of a wet puppy; it was too sweet for words.

"No," she sighed, smiling. "Tell them we're courting."

"Oh." His grin wiped away the wet-puppy look. "Good idea."

"Hello, Rosalind?" Marius called. "Have I lost you down memory lane?"

Rosalind blinked back into the present and stared vacantly at Marius's smug face. Her mind was too tangled in the shrouds of memory to think of a clever retort. "What did you say?"

His harsh laugh was a splash of cold water in her face. "You asked him to court you?"

She felt her cheeks redden. "Not really."

He smirked nevertheless. "Were you that desperate for a man? You must be a lonely soul indeed to settle for Henry."

Rosalind rose with majestic hauteur, stalked over to his chair, and stared down at him. "Henry is a wonderful young man. Far better than you'll ever be."

"Oh, I'm so hurt," he sighed, putting a hand to his heart and gazing up at her mournfully. She could've slapped him.

"Well, you certainly don't seem successful in love," Rosalind quipped. "All you've done is fallen for a beautiful stranger and ended up with me."

"Horrible, I know," he agreed with a solemn nod. How she wished to pick up a heavy book and smash it into that perfect nose of his! How very gratifying it would be to see him writhe in pain.

Some hint of her thoughts must have leaked onto her face, for Marius actually looked concerned. "Planning a murder?" he asked. "Let me guess the victim: me. That's not very ladylike, you know."

Rosalind tried to speak, but all that came out was a frustrated "*Oh!*" She stomped out of the room. He had gone too far, toggled her switch once too often.

Perhaps she wasn't capable of murdering him, but she was perfectly capable of wishing all manner of unfortunate accidents on him.

Chapter 3

THE NEXT day found Henry and Marius engaged in a game of chess, slouched over the battered wooden board that Henry had dominated since early childhood.

"I can't marry her," Marius groaned, flicking his pawn off the chessboard. "Just win already, Henry. I know you're holding back."

Henry smiled faintly down at the chessboard. "We'll call it quits."

"It must be terrible for you," Marius continued. "How are you not exploding with jealousy? Father is making me marry your sweetheart. Not that she's very sweet, mind you."

"Life happens," Henry said with a shrug. He picked up his queen and rolled it around in his hand. "Things change. I try not to let it get to me."

Marius snorted. "Obviously I didn't inherit that ability."

"It's not something you're born with," Henry replied. "You have to work at it."

"She's vile, you know. I don't know why you like her." Marius rubbed his temples. "How do you put up with her?"

Henry shrugged again. "I don't think she's all that bad."

Letting his hands drop to his lap, Marius looked up at his brother. "But do you love her?"

"Why . . . yes."

Marius snorted. "And you sound *so* confident when you say that." He began to set the captured chess pieces back on the board.

Henry's mind was already a murky mud puddle of emotions; he didn't appreciate Marius's sloshing around in it. "So, what did she actually look like?"

"You're changing the subject." Marius balanced a queen on the tip of his index finger.

"I'm trying to help you."

"Hmm." Marius tossed the queen in the air and caught it backhanded. "Ha! Did you see that?"

"Can you just answer my question?"

"What are we talking about again?"

Henry groaned, earning him an approving look. "I must've roused the beast," his brother mused. "I didn't think you were capable of being annoyed."

"I was asking about the girl you actually danced with at the ball."

"She was fair-haired, for one thing," Marius began. He leaned back in his chair and clasped his hands behind his head. A dreamy smile spread across his face. "And she had these pretty brown eyes." His expression darkened for a moment. "Nothing like the little green-eyed cat I'm currently engaged to."

"Go on," Henry urged.

"She was a tiny thing, almost looked malnourished. She wasn't nobility, I'm certain of it. Tottering around in her glass slippers, tripping over her skirts—she wasn't used to fine clothes. I liked her all the more for that. It was refreshing. But you see, Henry, even if we had found her instead of your darling Roz, Father wouldn't have approved. She's a member of the lower class."

"And you didn't get her name," Henry concluded.

Marius sighed and rolled his eyes. "No, I didn't; we covered this earlier. That's why we had to use the glass slipper to find her, right?"

"Why didn't you ask her name?"

"I don't know!" Marius threw his hands into the air. "I just don't think of those sorts of things."

"I asked Rosalind's name when I met her," Henry mumbled. "It wasn't that hard to think of."

"Well, isn't that grand? You win the prize! And I lose. Is that what you want?" Marius scowled.

Henry shrank back into his chair. "No. I'm trying to help you."

"I appreciate the offer, but I doubt you can do much." Marius picked a book off the table next to him. "I'm going to read now, so could you leave?"

"Why? Why do you think I can't do much?"

Marius didn't look up from his book. "Because you don't have the guts. You didn't have the guts in front of Father. It's just your nature."

Ophelia had broken her promise. Oh well. Most people did.

Evelyn the cinder-girl paused in her work for a moment, squatting on the squalid factory floor, and smiled ruefully. How silly she had been to get her hopes up. Marry a prince? Likely! No, the nice lady had been exactly that—nice. But misguided. A dance, a silk gown, and a pair of glass slippers couldn't solve Evelyn's problems. She would be a cinder-girl at a factory just as long as there were factories and cinder-girls.

The memory of her stepmother's words still burned in her mind: *You don't deserve anything better.* And her stepmother was right.

Catching a flicker of motion from the corner of her eye, she turned and watched a thin, scraggly rat scurry into a crack in the wall. *I'm a rat,* she thought. *I'll never be anything better—*

"You there! Evelyn!"

Evelyn jumped at the sound of her name, an ill omen for a cinder-girl. The floor inspector only used a name if someone was in deep trouble. She trembled at the thought of her punishment. Scrubbing the latrines? Emptying the rat traps?

"What, s—sir?" she stammered, spinning around and stumbling to her feet. The floor master looked like any upper gear in the grand machine of the factory: polished, cold, and hard as metal. It was all a front, Evelyn knew. She'd seen these men when their families came to visit. Their faces would light up at sight of their children, and a little spot in Evelyn's heart would warm. They were human too.

But the young man standing beside the floor master was not a part of the factory. Though he wore the clothes of an upper-class citizen, he looked rather uncomfortable in them. His brown hair, dark eyes, and kind smile all added up to a very attractive gentleman.

"This man would like to speak to you in private." The floor master glared at her through his monocle. "Don't give him a hard time, understand?"

Her head bobbed up and down until he looked sufficiently satisfied. "Good. I'll leave you to it."

A moment later, Evelyn was alone with the strange young man. His face reddened and he scuffed the floor with his foot. "Sorry. I hope I'm not getting you in trouble," he mumbled, and grinned. It was probably the most adorable grin Evelyn had ever seen—not that she saw very many adorable young men or had time to pay attention to such things. Cinder-girls didn't marry. They weren't worth marrying.

"What do you need?" she asked, feeling a bit breathless. Her cheeks flushed too.

"Well, your name; but I'll give you mine first. I'm Henry." He grinned again and bowed politely.

"Evelyn." Since he was treating her like a lady, she politely offered her hand like one—and flinched when he lifted it to his lips and kissed it.

His eyes widened in a puppyish expression. "Sorry. I didn't mean to startle you. That's just, you know, the sort of etiquette—"

"No, forgive me," she replied hastily, reclaiming her hand. "I wouldn't know."

"It's nice to meet you, Miss Evelyn. Before you say anything, I don't care that you're a cinder-girl." He paused, working up the nerve to continue. "And my brother doesn't care either."

"What?" Evelyn's heart skipped a beat. She wrung her soot-smudged apron in her hands.

"You see, my brother's the prince. Prince Marius." He grabbed her shoulders to prevent her from curtseying. "Don't. Please don't. There's no need. Look, I need to know if you danced with my brother at the ball a couple nights ago. You were there, weren't you?"

How could he know? Could this really be happening? She vaguely felt herself nod.

Henry let out a huge sigh. "Good." He let go of her and ran his hands through his thick curls. "You wouldn't believe how awkward the last few hours have been, interviewing all the wrong golden-haired cinder-girls." He grinned again. "So you're the girl who left a glass slipper behind?"

Evelyn nodded vigorously.

His grin diminished a bit. "May I ask how you got them?"

Her heart stopped for a moment. Ophelia had told her to keep it a secret! "I . . . I found them," she stammered.

"Did you steal them?" Henry's voice softened. "You won't be in trouble, but I need to know. You see, the girl who really owns those shoes got chosen instead. And she doesn't want to marry Prince Marius."

"So that's why they didn't come," Evelyn murmured, more to herself than anyone else. Then, seeing the question in Henry's eyes, she hastily said, "I didn't take them. A friend gave them to me."

"Did your friend steal them?"

Evelyn's eyes drifted to the floor. "I . . . I don't know."

"What is your friend's name?'

Evelyn's tongue stuck to the roof of her mouth. "I can't tell you. I made a promise."

Henry exhaled loudly. "I appreciate that you want to keep your word, but you must know that this could be the only thing standing between you and your happy ending."

Evelyn felt her cheeks burn as a strange mix of shame and guilt swirled in her head. "But I promised," she whispered. "I'm sorry. I can't help you."

She almost jumped when he reached out and took her face in his hands. Gently but firmly he raised it until their eyes met. His voice was sweet but urgent when he spoke. "I'm here to help you; and I won't stop trying."

Then he let go and stepped away. "Look around you, Evelyn. Do you want to stay like this? Do you want to be a cinder-girl?"

Letting her gaze wander around the factory, Evelyn took in the familiar sights. The stinking, smoking furnaces, the grind of the machines and the screech of the conveyer belts—all controlled by workers who had become more machine than human themselves. She felt a spark of discontent in her stomach, but a stronger feeling rapidly crushed it.

"No," she whispered. "But I deserve to be one."

Chapter 4

I BELIEVE we may have gotten off on the wrong foot."

Rosalind didn't look up from her sketching to acknowledge Marius's presence. He'd taken his sweet time to finally speak; for the last few minutes Rosalind had felt him looming over her chair like lightning ready to strike.

A crackling fire and several strategically placed candelabra lit the king's private drawing room. It was King Cygnus's after-dinner tradition to coop all his family up in this posh little room. To Rosalind, having all the royal family together was an overdressed grenade ready to explode. The queen could never join them, however. Apparently she was too ill and kept to her room most of the time.

Rosalind was the only one drawing in the drawing room. Everyone else had their noses in books. Of course, Rosalind did enjoy reading. But Marius disliked drawing, particularly the scratching sound of pencil against paper, so Rosalind enjoyed drawing even more.

King Cygnus dozed in his chair, and a dark shadow curled up in the window seat. That dark shadow happened to have a name, which happened to be Darcy; but nobody really notices dark shadows, even named ones. They have a habit of lurking about. People learn to ignore them after a while.

Across the room from the king, Rosalind scratched harder at her paper. "Hmm. And I suppose I'm responsible for the bad start of our relationship?"

"I never said that."

"You implied it."

"You're putting words in my mouth."

With one fluid movement, Rosalind raised her head and delicately tossed the hair out of her eyes. "What are you getting at?" she demanded. "I'm trying to draw, and you are standing in my light. So either start talking or get out of the way."

"I'll block your light as long as I like." Marius crossed his arms. "It's technically my light, by the way."

The pencil snapped between Rosalind's fingers. "We've been over this," she hissed. "It's your father's palace. Your father's light. Can you stop avoiding my question?"

"You were the one changing the subject."

Half of the pencil sailed from her fingers and smacked him squarely between the eyes. "Ow!" he cried, rubbing his forehead. "What was that for?"

"Figure it out, genius," she grumbled. "By the way, that was *your* pencil."

His fingers curled into fists. "How I'd love to smack you . . ."

"You're scared of hitting me." She smiled sweetly up at him. "Aren't you?"

Marius let out a groan and clutched his head. "This is exactly what I wanted to talk to you about," he seethed through clenched teeth. "We'll kill each other before our honeymoon is over."

"I think you're being a little too optimistic," Rosalind replied. "What would you like me to do with the other half of your pencil? Stick it up your nose?"

"Stick it up your own nose, I don't care," he grumbled. "Or throw it at Darcy. He probably deserves it."

From behind his book in his dark corner, Darcy glared at them and mumbled something clever. But they didn't hear him, of course.

"What I'm trying to get at—"

"And doing a poor job of expressing yourself," Rosalind cut in.

"Because you keep interrupting me!"

"I'm making clever asides," she sniffed. "There's a difference."

"Well, be like Darcy and mumble your clever asides. As I was saying, I want to help you. And myself."

"What? How? By spontaneously combusting so that I can marry Henry? Most considerate of you!" She continued to smile sweetly at him. "Or do you have other suggestions?"

"That's what I'm saying," Marius lowered his voice. "If we work together, we may be able to get out of this somehow. Does that sound all right? I'll tolerate you if you tolerate me."

Rosalind thought for moment and then extended a hand. "It's a bargain," she said.

Darcy watched them shake hands. He glared. But shadows go unnoticed.

Dull embers glowed in the fireplace, casting more shadow than light across the king's private sitting room. Sitting up, King Cygnus yawned and rubbed his aching neck, realizing that everyone else had disappeared, possibly hours ago.

"They're conspiring," Darcy said quietly, melting out of the darkness behind his father's chair.

The king jumped. "Good gracious; you've got to stop lurking about like that," he sighed, rubbing his forehead. "Who are conspiring?"

"Rosalind and Marius. To undo the engagement."

"Just keep an eye on them, won't you?"

Darcy leaned against the fireplace mantel, draping one arm across the wood. "There's something else."

"What?"

"Henry found the real girl."

Cygnus's eyes narrowed. "And who is she?"

"A cinder-girl."

A dark expression passed over the king's face; it might've been the shadow cast by his son, but it would be hard to tell with all the shadows skulking around them.

"Then you must watch them with even more care. I will not have a cinder-girl for a queen."

Chapter 5

IN THE library, a notebook and a tray of tea things rested on a table between the two battle-camps. This no-man's-land was the meager sign of a precarious truce.

"So, what are your marvelous ideas?" Rosalind swirled her spoon in her teacup, the soft tink of metal against china echoing around the room. "Have you even got any?"

"I thought I'd leave the planning to you," Marius said with a wink. "Isn't your father a brilliant businessman?"

Rosalind's spoon clanged louder. "And isn't your father the king?"

Marius growled and slumped in his chair, chin in his hand. "You win," he muttered into his palm. "But that means you have to come up with the first idea."

"Isn't there a fairy godmother in the city? We could ask her for help."

"No. She'll cause far more trouble than she's worth. Fairies are always muddling things around. Turning you into frogs, stealing your shoes, getting you lost in the forest with a household of dwarves. And anyway, I doubt any fairy godmother would help the royal family of Arcadia since . . . the fountain."

"The fountain?" Rosalind took a sip of her tea and gave him a questioning look. "Do elaborate."

"Don't you remember? I'm not so many years older than you, but I remember it distinctly." Marius sat up a little straighter, eager to pontificate. "Arcadia had a treaty with the city Lucernis, which is, you could say, the capital of magic. The city sits on the last spring of magical water. Whoever drinks the water—"

"Gains magical powers; yes, I know that," Rosalind cut in.

Marius glared at her. "Other cities, such as Arcadia, paid tribute to Lucernis to have connecting wells dug in their town centers. That way they could have a share in the magic. Arcadia's fountain resided in the palace courtyard under heavy guard."

"So where'd the fountain go?" Rosalind asked. "Last time I looked, there was no fountain in the courtyard."

"About twelve years ago, Lucernis started demanding higher tribute. But they didn't stop there. Their city leaders, some of them the most powerful fairy godmothers, wanted a say in our government, and in the governments of other cities benefitting from magic. They wanted heirs to the throne, such as me, to be schooled by them. Indoctrinated, my father explained to me."

"They were trying to take over," Rosalind concluded.

Marius shrugged. "That's what Father suspected. But their official reason was 'to stop the misuse of magic and ensure that rulers do not abuse their power.' Father didn't like the sound of that." Marius leaned forward in his chair. "So he destroyed the fountain. He blew it up. Arcadia severed all ties with Lucernis and has been on the brink of war many times." He gave her a superior look. "I can't believe you don't know about any of this."

"I seem to remember hearing something about Lucernis and magic," Rosalind said. "But I was only six then and didn't pay much attention to politics."

"What did you pay attention to, dolls and tea parties?"

She glared. "Actually I preferred tin soldiers and wooden swords." Then she sighed and set down her teacup. "You're right, I suppose; that puts the fairy godmother out of the question. Do you have any other ideas?"

"Well, I was thinking . . ." He glanced around the empty library and leaned closer. "We could fake your death."

"*What?*"

"Shhh," Marius hissed, startling forward in his chair and hastily putting out a hand to cover her mouth. "Not so loud. We don't want the whole of father's court to know, do we?"

Even after he removed his hand, she scowled at him. "So how do you want to kill me?"

"I was thinking you'd get lost in the woods. We'd inform Henry, of course. You two could run off to the next kingdom."

"And what would stop your father from finding us?"

"I'd totter home, bloody and bruised, telling him that we were attacked by an evil fairy. The foul creature dragged you back to his lair—"

"Stop. Please." Rosalind set her teacup on the tray and fixed Marius with an incredulous stare. "That's much too dramatic. No, I think the steam carriage should blow up while we're taking a ride in the country."

"With you in it?"

"No, you biscuit-face! I'd get out first!"

Marius held up his hands. "Sorry. Just wanted to clarify."

"Do you really think I'm that stupid?"

"I probably shouldn't answer that question."

"No, you shouldn't. Unless I can tell you how stupid you are."

They could have continued in this vein for some time. But just then a new voice spoke, startling both Rosalind and the prince so completely that they jumped.

"So how are you going to get the steam carriage to blow up?" Darcy leaned one shoulder against the doorjamb, hands in pockets and mouth twisted into an amused expression.

"Darcy," Marius growled. "What are you doing?"

"I can hear you arguing from my room." He sauntered into the library, still smirking.

Rosalind picked up her teacup and lifted it to her lips. "And now you can leave," she said, and took a sip of tepid tea.

Darcy raised one brow. "But I want to help."

Both Marius and Rosalind stared.

"Look." Darcy lowered himself into a chair. "There's going to be no peace in Arcadia as long as you two are engaged. So I want to help. I know where to get explosives and how to arrange everything so that our attendants see only what they need to see. Details are my specialty, not yours, Marius."

Marius shrugged and looked to Rosalind. "Unless you can make the steam carriage explode by touching it, Rosalind, I think this is our next-best option."

Rosalind narrowed her eyes at Darcy, uncertain how much she trusted the elegant smile he turned her way. But then, what other choice did she have? "Fine," she said, setting her teacup down in its saucer with a decisive clang. "But we need to inform Henry."

Henry was forthwith summoned to the library. But he received the scheme they related to him without the expected cheer. At least, so Rosalind thought.

Indeed, he sat stiffly on the overstuffed armchair, strangely quiet and unenthused throughout the explanation. His silence was simultaneously insulting and confusing to Rosalind. The tea in the cup she'd poured for him had long since grown cold. *He always drinks the tea I give him,* she thought. Just one more thing that seemed off about Henry.

If Marius noticed any change, he didn't show it. He lounged in his usual chair, which he had dragged over beside the settee on which Rosalind perched.

"What do you not like about the plan?" she snapped.

Henry shrugged. "Everything? Anyway, I'm busy for the next few days."

"Busy with what? Do you have something more important to do?" Marius laughed. "This is your future hanging in the balance."

"There's probably a better way." Henry shrugged, offering a lame smile with no spirit whatsoever behind it.

"Like what? Talking to your father again?" Rosalind gave him a condescending look.

"We could try that."

Rosalind folded her arms. "And we could try kissing a frog." She gave her head a small shake, and her voice became sweetly persuasive. "You will cooperate, won't you?"

Henry hesitated before rising from his armchair. "I'll see what my schedule can manage."

Rosalind's perfect little mouth hung open as he strolled from the room.

"Your spell over him is beginning to wear off," Marius whispered.

Chapter 6

HERE TO see the floor master again?"

Henry smiled nervously at the receptionist and shoved his hands into his pockets. "Um, yes."

She squinted behind her spectacles. "And the girl?"

"That won't be necessary."

"Good." With one swift motion, the receptionist swiveled around to the wall and flipped a complicated series of switches before speaking into a receiver. "Mr. Jones? A gentleman is here to see you. Yes, the same one." A few wisps of her mousy hair escaped her tight bun as she turned back to him. "He'll be here soon."

"Thank you."

She continued to stare at him, picking up a pen and tapping it against the desk. The gray dullness of concrete walls around him began to oppress. "You disturb the schedule," she said suddenly.

"I beg your pardon?"

"You don't make appointments. You barge in and upset the rhythm of the factory; Mr. Jones isn't pleased." Her eyes narrowed into dark slits. "What does one cinder-girl matter to you?"

Henry was saved from answering this question when the door to the office flew open. "You again," Mr. Jones huffed. His hand shot out automatically to shake Henry's, but there was no warmth in the gesture. "How can I help you?"

"I need more information about the girl I talked to last time: her family, her background, anything." Henry squared his shoulders and lifted his chin. "It's rather urgent."

"Is that so? Well, Agnes," Mr. Jones said with a glance at the woman behind the desk. "Give him anything you have."

"Thank you," Henry said with a warm smile. "You don't know how much this means to me."

"No, I don't," Mr. Jones agreed blandly. "But it apparently matters to your brother; he came to the factory asking about you."

Henry's mind whirled as he accepted the papers from Agnes. "Which brother?"

"Said his name was Darcy," Agnes cut in. "Have a nice day."

Thus Henry found himself ushered out of the office with a handful of answers and a mind full of new questions.

Once again, Rosalind sat in the library. It had become a refuge to her, though not quite as secluded as she had first anticipated. Indeed, she was as likely to meet Marius here as not, for he had a way of barging in rather often.

He barged in now, interrupting her perusal of a suspenseful gothic romance. Even as she was about to read the mysterious, tortured hero's declaration of undying passion to the piquant young heroine, Rosalind found herself obliged instead to look up into Marius's decidedly unmysterious and non-tortured face. "Yes?" she demanded.

"It's time you met Mother," said Marius. It was about as far from a declaration of undying passion as a man could get.

Rosalind felt anything but piquant. "I rather forgot you had a mother." She sighed, closing her book. "Do I really have to meet her?"

"Yes," said Marius. "She's sick and kind of dying, so it would be the thoughtful thing to do."

Rosalind gave the gothic romance a regretful look, wondering if she'd ever learn the haunting secrets of the hero's past. But she set it aside and rose. "Now?"

"Why else would I waste my precious time bothering you?"

She waved him dismissively towards the door. "Lead on."

The queen resided in just the sort of place one would expect: high in a tower, surrounded by pillows and posh finery. Everything bubbled over with lace and light pink. Rosalind spotted upwards of five cats lounging on various windowsills and chairs. Finally, at the last door in the hallway, Marius paused with his hand on the latch and gave Rosalind a solemn glance she couldn't quite interpret.

"Marius!" a voice cooed as they entered. The queen was drowning in a sea of blankets and pillows, smiling like a child at a candy-cart. She was small, with papery white skin that could flake away at any moment. It was a wonder she wasn't a pile of dust. She had Marius's eyes; or rather, Marius had hers. Her hair floated about her head in a wispy gold cloud that echoed the glorious waves adorning Marius's head.

Her haunting eyes rested on Rosalind. "Who is this?" she cried delightedly. "Come closer, darling."

Rosalind and Marius approached at the beckoning of her spindly fingers; as soon as Rosalind reached her bedside, the queen snatched up her hand. For such a frail woman, she had a strong grip.

"This is my fiancée, Mother," Marius announced. "Her name is Rosalind."

"Rosalind," the queen repeated. Her face glowed. "What a pretty queen you'll make. How soon is the wedding?"

Marius shrugged. "Soon, I think. As soon as you like."

"This is all so wonderful but—" The queen paused and glanced between her son and Rosalind. "Do you love her?"

Rosalind wished she could yank her hand away and run.

"We're going to be married," Marius replied slowly. "Aren't you happy? Isn't that what you want?"

"But you don't love her."

"That doesn't matter. What matters is—"

"Your father is making you do this, isn't he? Because I want to see you married before I die." The queen's eyes glittered with tears.

"I admit I don't know Rosalind very well. But over time, that can change." Marius added a reassuring smile. "Really, Mother, I will be happy."

"You won't. Not like this . . ." Her eyes and voice drifted away from them. "I'm tired."

Rosalind finally found words to say. "Then we'll let you rest, Your Majesty." With a gentle tug, she freed her hand from the queen's grasp and led Marius from the room. He dropped onto a windowsill as soon as the door closed.

"My life is miserable," he groaned. "I can never please them."

"Maybe you shouldn't do things for them," Rosalind said, patting his shoulder awkwardly. "Do something for yourself."

He looked up at her. "Like our plan?"

She smiled. "Yes."

Chapter 7

FROM THE exterior, the Sevrays' house was a mirror image of Rosalind's and all the others on the street. Soft memories ached dully in Henry's heart as he knocked on the door. It was almost the same color as the Coppers'. How quickly the sweetness of that fragile romance had faded! Yet the pain was faint, far fainter than Henry would've expected.

He shook his head to clear his thoughts, and his fist rapped harder against the wood. A moment passed. Then two. Rosalind had always sent a servant to answer the door much more speedily than this if, having spotted Henry from the window, she didn't hasten to answer it herself. Maybe he shouldn't have come. Maybe this was none of his business. Did he really want his brother to marry a cinder-girl, anyway?

His indecision grew firm roots tying him to the doorstep. He had almost conquered it and was about to leave—

The door opened.

The maid standing across the threshold stared dully at him. "Lady Sevray was not expecting visitors."

You're the king's son, Henry reminded himself. *Use that power.* Gathering all his courage, he drew himself up to his full height and showed the girl his signet ring.

"I am Prince Henry. I wish to speak to your mistress on a matter of business."

The servant's filmy grey eyes widened. "Oh yes, um, of course." She scurried back, motioning him to follow. "I'll take you to her right away."

Henry trailed after her with firm steps, though she stumbled up the curving staircase. A bucket and sponge lay neglected halfway up the marble monstrosity. No expense had been spared in any corner of the house, from the avant-garde gold-laced carpet to the garish butterfly-print wallpaper. The maid stopped at a pair of double doors, mumbled something to Henry, and slipped into the room.

A cold voice snapped beyond the doors. "The prince, here to see me? Which one? Never mind. Show him in and then finish the mopping!"

Stammering a thousand "Yes ma'am's," the girl opened the door for Henry. He gave her a sympathetic smile before entering.

The room and its occupant wore the same mask of finery as the rest of the house. Lady Sevray rose from her chair, fully armored with the necessities of beauty. Pins and spray and fine little glittery baubles helmeted her hair; layers of powder and a good dose of blush protected her face. All these were as nothing when compared to the starched conglomeration of fabrics, lace, and pearls fitted so snugly to her slim figure. Yet these precautions proved useless against the assault of age, for Henry saw through her mask. She was old.

Nevertheless, like any gentleman he kissed her extended hand and accepted her offer of tea.

"Your Highness," she said while pouring his tea. Her voice reminded Henry of the low hum of factory machinery. "How may I help you?"

"I'm making inquiries about a certain young lady I believe you know." Henry paused, noticing a shift in that carefully powdered face. "In fact, I believe you are her stepmother."

Lady Sevray stiffened but continued to smile. "Are you referring to Evelyn?"

"Yes." Now came the hard part. Henry fidgeted with his signet ring, wishing it could magically fill him with confidence. He was a prince, after all. These things shouldn't be impossible.

"Have a biscuit?" She extended the plate with a polite smile.

He declined with equal politeness. Even the thought of food nearly made him choke. "I do not wish to be blunt, madam, but I can think of no other way to say this. You live quite comfortably in your house, and yet your stepdaughter works as a cinder-girl in a factory. Why?" His own words filled him with enough courage to look her in the eye.

Her eyes narrowed. "That was her decision."

He set down his teacup. "To sell herself away? And why didn't you stop her?"

"She felt it would compensate for her guilt." Lady Sevray glanced indifferently out the window. "And I am not the hard-hearted sort of woman who would forbid a girl from satisfying her own conscience."

"And why was she guilty?"

"Your Highness," she said with a kind smile, "so many questions! Might I ask why?"

The smile was the final straw, the final layer of her masks and makeup. "Whatever you may say, Lady Sevray, I believe your stepdaughter has been wronged. I looked into her eyes and saw—"

"You spoke to her?" A laugh erupted from her painted lips. "She puts on quite the act, doesn't she? Making herself seem like such the repentant little daughter."

Henry simply folded his arms and stared at her. "Will you please answer my question? I think we both want this to end as soon as possible."

"Oh yes. Of course." Lady Sevray seemed to shrink a little in her chair. "It was her father, actually. He dearly wanted her to accept my daughters and me when we married. But the girl couldn't stand me. She threw such tantrums and locked herself in her rooms." She sighed. "It destroyed him. To lose his first wife and then his relationship with his daughter . . . He worried day and night, overworked himself. He had a condition, you know. Some sickness of the lungs or another delicate part of human anatomy. He died."

"But how does this relate?"

"My dear prince, have you missed my point entirely? She caused him to sicken and worry himself to death. The selfish child! And when he died, she came weeping to me, asking how she could fix it. I told her she was a disgrace to her father and his house. She asked me where she should go. I told her I didn't care. I'd give her what she needed, as she was my step-daughter. But then she got the notion into her head to become a cinder-girl. So you see it was entirely her decision."

Henry drew in a deep breath to keep his emotions from spilling out. "Thank you for your time and for the tea, Lady Sevray." He rose from the chair and motioned her to stay. "I'll see myself out."

Chapter 8

"A RIDE through the country?" The king stared at his son over the morning newspaper. "But it's such a wilderness! People get lost and never return! The next substantial city isn't for a hundred miles. Whatever possessed you with such an idea?"

Rosalind, seated beside her intended at the breakfast table, slipped her arm through his. "Oh, but I know I'll be safe with Marius. And he's so anxious to show me around the wilder parts of his future kingdom! To prove to me that he's the strong prince everyone says he is." She squeezed his arm and showered him with smiles, then glanced shiftily around and leaned forward, her necklace nearly trailing in the butter dish. "Even though I already know he is," she whispered loudly to the king and giggled.

Still grinning, Marius drew her toward him. "You're overdoing it," he murmured in her ear.

Rosalind cast him another fawning glance, leaned against his shoulder, and whispered back, "Just play along, dimwit."

Henry watched them, picking forlornly at his food. Rosalind stifled the prick of her conscience at his melancholy expression, telling herself it was all for the greater good. And pretending to be giddily in love was rather fun. *I should do this more often,* she thought.

The king finally spoke again. "You shouldn't go alone. It wouldn't be proper. Perhaps Darcy would be willing to tag along?" He gave his middle son an encouraging smile.

"Yes. I'd be delighted." Darcy smiled back. Rosalind couldn't tell if he was choking on his egg. But he gave her a subtle wink. It was all going according to plan, of course. Darcy had been very helpful—far more helpful than moping Henry.

Henry kept glancing from Marius to Rosalind, his eyes widening. *No, no, no!* Rosalind let go of Marius's arm and clasped her hands together in her lap. She wanted to scream. *I don't love Marius! I'm doing this to help us.*

But part of her wasn't so sure about that anymore . . .

A look from Marius seemed to settle the conversation. He would talk to Henry and make certain he was aware of all the most updated details of their plan. Good. The orderly part of Rosalind's mind settled back down again, allowing her to finish her toast and tea in peace.

The machinery of the factory slowly ground to a halt. Evelyn's feet joined the scuffling train of cinder-girls. She watched the cold little coins fall into the other girls' hands.

"Are you sure—"

She didn't even look at the floor master. "Only on Fridays. You know the routine."

He stood aside for her to pass. "Suit yourself. If you want to starve."

Every day he asked the same thing. And every day she gave the same answer. There was a time when she had taken a week's wages; but that was before she encountered her stepmother while Sunday thrift-shopping with the other cinder-girls.

"You seem rather well-off," her stepmother had said coldly. "Have you forgotten so soon why you chose to work at the factory?"

And with that, the guilt Evelyn tried so hard to fight off had come crashing down upon her all over again. Her decision to give up her wages relieved some of the pain; the money she earned was better spent feeding the orphans of factory workers, anyway. But the floor master had insisted she take one day of wages at least. A dead cinder-girl would do the factory no good, he'd said.

A cold, gloomy mist had settled over the street. Evelyn clutched her bare arms, her body accustomed to the blazing heat of the factory. She kept her eyes on the pavement, avoiding the disapproving stares of other citizens. She turned into the alley that led to cinder-girl housing; it was a short cut to the back entrance. But instead of making the last dash to the door, she collided with something—or someone.

"I thought I'd find you here."

She backed away, staring wide-eyed up at the young man. Sadly, it wasn't Henry.

"I know who you are," he continued in his soft voice. "And where you were a couple of nights ago."

Evelyn allowed herself to hope for a moment. "Did Henry send you?"

The man laughed and his dark eyes glittered. "Ah, Henry. I knew he'd talked to you. Always the kind-hearted soul."

Evelyn shrank away from him and hugged herself tighter. "What do you want with me?"

"Just some information, never fear." The stranger gave her what was probably meant to be a reassuring smile. But his mouth seemed incapable of forming a friendly expression. "Where did you get the glass slippers?"

Her heart sank. "I can't tell you that."

He stepped closer. "I think you can." He paused, examining the alley around them. "Your life is miserable, Evelyn. Anyone can see that. But I can make it worse." He gave her that awful smile again.

"I don't care about myself."

"What about Henry? I can ruin his happiness with a snap of my fingers. So tell me, where did you get the slippers?"

Evelyn's shoulders sagged. Another promise she'd have to break. Another failure. But she couldn't ruin Henry's life.

The house had been difficult to find, but no secret was too well hidden for Darcy. Very little magic remained in the kingdom of Arcadia. Genies, fairies, and sprites had been relegated to children's tales. Few took the time to care about magic anymore; few believed it existed. But Darcy knew where to look.

The decrepit building crouched in a dark alley, wedged into a row of equally ramshackle structures. The street was empty except for a few rats and a couple of lowlifes loitering in the shadows. But their presence didn't bother Darcy. If anything, they made him feel more at ease.

He raised his fist and knocked hard, but the door creaked open with the slightest touch, revealing a short hallway and curling staircase.

"Hello?" he called, stepping inside.

"Come upstairs," a voice replied.

The voice was female, as he expected; it was young and had a cloying lilt, rather like the smell of perfume mixed with the sound of bells. He climbed the stairs, a dim light slowly stealing away the gloom the farther up he went. At the top, he pushed aside the curtain in the doorway.

Candles, faded silk, and the faint smell of vanilla filled the room before him.

A young woman sat in an old, tattered chair. She stood up and smiled. "Hello there! How may I help you?"

"Many ways," Darcy replied. She appeared to be the flighty, vain sort of girl that would hang around Marius in court. Her loose golden curls bounced as she walked, and her blue eyes were framed with dark lashes.

"Then I suppose you'll stay for tea." A teacup appeared in her hand. "Would you care for some?"

Darcy shook his head. With a shrug, the young lady flicked her wrist; Darcy wasn't sure what was supposed to happen, but the cup fell to the ground and smashed to pieces.

"Bother," she grumbled. "That's the fifth broken teacup this month." She waved her hand again and the shards of china disappeared. "Please, sir, do be seated."

With an amused smile on his face, Darcy waited for her to sit then settled himself into the chair across from hers.

"I see you have . . . abilities," he began carefully, as knitting needles and yarn materialized in her hands.

Her cheeks dimpled when she smiled back. "You could say that."

Darcy watched her fingers fumbling with the needles and yarn. "That scarf won't be for you, will it?"

She paused in her work. "No."

"You can't use your abilities for yourself, can you, Ophelia?"

The needles slipped from her hands, clattering to the floor. She huffed, frustrated, but turned the huff into another brilliant smile. This she flashed at Darcy. "It's not customary for my type to serve ourselves. How did you get my name?"

"From Evelyn Sevray. You helped her, didn't you?"

Ophelia's smile faded into a slight, uncertain frown. "What do you want from me?"

"Your help. I'm pretty sure you can do that."

"Possibly," she replied, twirling a bit of yarn around her thumb. "What do you need?"

"It's complicated." Darcy laced his fingers together. "I need you to hide someone here."

"Hide someone?" Ophelia raised an eyebrow. "That sounds terribly exciting. Why?"

"The reason doesn't concern you," Darcy said, stiffening. "You're supposed to help people, aren't you?"

She pulled the yarn so tight that it snapped. Her eyes were guarded. "And you seem to know a lot of about me. But I can decide not to help you—I can force you from this building if you threaten me."

He sighed and gave her a smile, all threats melting into charm. "Forgive my manners. I'm used to dealing with very difficult people. But you seem like a kind-hearted soul. What do you say? Can you help me?"

A moment passed before she answered. Then she snapped her fingers, and the fallen knitting needles floated up from the floor back into her hands. "Tell me what you need, and I'll do what I can."

Chapter 9

THE DAY of their appointed ride dawned sooner than Rosalind expected. For the last week Marius's words had kept nagging in the back of her mind. *"Your spell is wearing off."* But she persistently pushed that thought aside.

Darcy had done all the hard work with the steam carriage and the explosives. Rosalind would have three minutes to get out of the carriage before it blew. Marius, of course, would make some excuse to get out earlier. The lever was simple enough to turn to get the device started. Thanks to Darcy, none of the accompanying servants were aware of their plans and all were stupid enough to be fooled.

But King Cygnus still looked unconvinced as he saw them off. "Have a nice ride," he called, his tone implying that he very much doubted this was possible.

Marius helped Rosalind into the carriage. Darcy sat up front with the driver, an unprepossessing fellow who appeared inadequate to the task of driving. The other servants rode on the back with the picnic hamper. The carriage coughed and snorted to a start, and soon they were puttering through the city.

Although Rosalind occupied the same side of the carriage as Marius, she managed to maintain a good three-inch distance between them; she would have sat on the opposite side, but Darcy's exploding contraption lay concealed under the seat. Rosalind turned away from the device when her stomach began twisting into nervous knots. Instead, she pressed her forehead against the window and watched the people flooding the streets and waving at the royal steam carriage. They approached the outer walls of the city.

"Where exactly are we going?" Rosalind asked, waving absently out the window.

"Into the forest, out the north gate," Marius replied. "I showed you on the map last night, remember?"

"Oh, yes," she answered, not very convincingly. The previous night, Marius, Rosalind, and Henry had met to go over their plans. Rosalind's disconcerting feeling about Henry had only grown stronger. He seemed increasingly apathetic about their plot.

"Is the forest dangerous?" Rosalind asked.

Marius draped his arm across the back of the seat. "Why? Are you scared?"

"No! I just want to be prepared. Will Henry have any weapons on him?"

"What do you expect? He's Henry, protector of small, fluffy, harmless creatures. He wouldn't hurt a dragon if it were about to roast him alive."

"That's comforting," Rosalind grumbled. "Does he know where he's supposed to meet us?"

Marius rolled his eyes. "Yes, Rosalind! I told him last night *multiple* times."

"I'm not sure he was listening. He seemed distracted."

Much to Rosalind's surprise, Marius reached over and caught hold of her fingers, giving them an encouraging squeeze. "This'll work. Trust me."

Rosalind stared at his hand and then, eyebrow lifted, raised her penetrating gaze to Marius's face. He looked embarrassed, dropped hold of her fingers, removed his arm from behind her, and turned to the window, suddenly interested in the passing landscape.

After this they were quiet for most of the journey, watching the trees go by. Occasionally Marius tried to crack a joke. Most of these were weak, but against all odds he actually did have a sense of humor.

"You smiled," he said suddenly.

"What?"

"At my last joke. I thought you didn't like me." He grinned at her.

She growled, "Oh, be still, will you?" but barely repressed a laugh. Still, her stomach fluttered with nervousness. *Pull it together, Roz*, she thought. *Your plans always work. Nothing can go wrong.*

However, she knew very well that many things could go wrong, and it took all her willpower not to imagine herself trapped in the carriage, about to be blown to tiny bits.

They stopped for a picnic after a tension-fraught hour of driving. Their chauffeur drove the steam carriage to the edge of a meadow, then backed it up to a thick forest of trees. As soon as the engine switched off, a chorus of birdsong surrounded them. A few lazy butterflies meandered between the little yellow flowers dotting the meadow. A light breeze played with the grass, sending ripples across the green sea. But most of the location's beauty was lost on Rosalind as she imagined carriage debris exploding across the field; it wasn't hard to picture her body among the debris.

Darcy opened the door. "I'll get the device ready," he said, his voice oily with conspiratorial cunning.

The servants spread out a blanket and a few silk cushions; another set down the large wicker basket almost overflowing with small, buttery pastries and fruit. The sight of food sickened Rosalind as she sat down facing Marius. Sprawling across the cushions, he beckoned for one of the servants to hand him food.

"How can you eat?" Rosalind asked, scowling as the servant practically dropped grapes into Marius's mouth.

He reached up and caught the next grape mid-fall. "Why not?" he winked at her. "No reason to let a good picnic go to waste."

Rosalind crossed her arms. "Considering the circumstances, you could at least have the dignity to feed yourself."

"Someone's in a lovely mood today." Marius laughed, then lowered his voice so only she could hear. "Good heavens, we're not actually murdering anyone . . . though if we did, it would be you, of course."

Rosalind fingered the edge of the blanket and glanced at the servant. His expression remained blissfully ignorant as he watched a butterfly land on his tray of drinks. Rosalind leaned over to speak into Marius's ear. "Are you hoping I actually die?" she asked. "Would you care?"

Marius sat upright and stared at her. "I would! Naturally, I would. Do you think I'm that heartless?" Then he looked closer, his eyes narrowing in concern. "You really are nervous!"

Rising fear had withered her pride into dust. Rosalind nodded, and her voice sounded quivery as she asked, "What if something goes wrong? What if—"

"No," Marius said firmly, taking her hands in his and giving them a warm squeeze. "Nothing will go wrong. I just can't let that happen. That is . . ." Eyes suddenly wide, he let go and straightened. "Henry would turn into a mud puddle of despair if you died. And then who would beat me in chess? No one at all."

Rosalind smiled in spite of herself. "Such a disaster cannot be allowed. Someone needs to keep you humble."

"Me? Humble?" Marius raised his eyebrows in mock surprise, lay back on the cushions, and linked his hands behind his head. "Humility courses through my veins. If you looked up 'humble' in the dictionary, you'll find my name as the definition."

Unable to sit still, he scrambled to his knees and tossed her a grape. "Here, catch. Eat something to keep up your strength. It'll take you a while . . . you know." He jerked his head in the direction she and Henry would be making their escape.

Seeing the servant give Marius an odd look, Rosalind grimaced then surreptitiously pointed at the fellow. A look of comprehension replaced Marius's puzzled frown. "Ah, you there—Bartholomew, right?" Marius waved vaguely toward the meadow. "Go and . . . uh . . . catch some butterflies to take back for the queen. Yes. Butterflies."

Clearly doubting the prince's sanity, the servant wandered off. Moments later they saw him pounce and miss an elusive swallowtail. Marius snickered.

Butterflies seemed to inhabit Rosalind's stomach, which still wouldn't bear the thought of food; she let the grape roll out of her hand and into the hamper. "I keep forgetting this is the last time I'll see you," she said, reaching over to run her fingers across the grass tips and flower petals.

Marius tilted his head. "Will you miss me?"

Rosalind glared at him. "Certainly not."

Leaning gracefully on one hand, he sipped his glass of sparkling water and inclined his head toward her. "Are you going to wish me well?"

"With what?"

"You know, finding my true love, ruling the kingdom, figuring out how to lie about your disappearance." He gave her a winning smile. "Just a few suggestions to get you started."

"You'll do fine without my well-wishing." Rosalind suddenly felt cross. "But maybe when you're king you can try not to run the kingdom's coffers dry."

"Oh, I don't know," Marius replied with a mischievous quirk of his brow. "That's a tall order. A king needs to stay in fashion."

Rosalind rolled her eyes. "Arrogance like yours will always be unfashionable."

He simply shrugged. "I might say the same to you."

Just as Rosalind opened her mouth to retort, Darcy approached. "Are you ready?" he asked. "Everything is prepared."

All the cleverness drained from Rosalind's mind as her fears and flutters returned. But she managed to keep her composure. "I'm ready."

Marius extended a hand and helped her up. "Let's part friends," he said. "Please?"

Rosalind shook his hand firmly then let go. "You'll be my brother-in-law soon enough, anyway."

At this, Marius gave her a strange look. "Has Henry proposed yet?"

Rosalind stiffened. "No. But I'm sure he will."

"I see." He pursed his lips and raised his eyebrows.

She opened her mouth to object, but when he reclaimed her hand and linked their fingers the arguments vanished. Hand-in-hand they traversed the space between their picnic blanket and the steam-carriage. On cue, Darcy ordered the servants to pack up the leftovers and do various other tasks that would keep their attention away from the carriage.

A noise like pounding drums suddenly filled the meadow. Rosalind and Marius whirled around to face a rider on horseback. As the horse slowed to a trot then a jog, Rosalind recognized the hatless rider's head of bouncing curls. It was Henry.

He checked his horse a few feet away and stared down at them, his face full of a determination so foreign to him that it frightened Rosalind.

"Henry! What are you doing here?" Marius asked with a hollow laugh, as if he were uneasy too. Rosalind hardly noticed when Darcy approached and stood by silently.

"You don't need to do this," Henry announced, dismounting. One of the servants took his blowing horse and walked it away. "I have another idea." Though his words came out in ragged gasps, he held eye contact with Marius.

"Talking to father won't help," Marius snapped. He took a step closer to Henry. "You'll ruin our plan. What are you so scared of?"

"This isn't right," Henry replied. "This will cause more heartache to everyone. Have you thought of what this will do to your parents, Roz?"

"Don't bring my parents into this," Rosalind growled. "Don't you love me? Don't you want to marry me?"

A deadly silence dangled between them like a garish piece of washing hung out to dry. It hung there for several long moments. Marius's grasp on her hand tightened.

"I don't know anymore," Henry finally whispered.

Rosalind sucked in a sharp breath. "You're not . . . you're not yourself," she said, regaining her composure. She wrenched her hand away from Marius and marched to the steam carriage. "Darcy, open the carriage door."

"With pleasure," he said.

"I found your girl, Marius!" Henry shouted, his eyes burning with something strange—was it anger? "If you would stop trying to order me around, I could help you! I'm forming another plan. Listen to me for once in your spoiled life!"

Ignoring the argument taking place between the two brothers, Rosalind leaned into the carriage and surveyed the device. "So I just pull down on the lever?" she asked Darcy.

He nodded and smiled. The device was an ugly jumble of wires and whatnots. Its mangled appearance was enough to make her feel sick. With a glance out the window, she noticed Marius and Henry were still at it. The lever was cold and slim in her shaking fingers. She pushed down. It began to tick.

"You can close the door now, Darcy," she said.

"Of course." He leaned into closer. "Best wishes."

Rosalind felt a sudden prick in her arm, and watched as he withdrew a small needle.

"What are you doing?" she cried. Darcy made no reply, only shut the door and smiled. She heard the click. He'd locked her in.

Frantically she pounded on the window but found her strength slowly fading away. Then she remembered—she had to get out the other door. She was almost relieved . . . until she discovered the other door to be locked as well.

Waves of dizziness washed over her. *Not now, Roz!* she thought angrily. *Keep your head!*

But her head did not want to be kept. It slowly dropped on the cushioned seat, and as her vision clouded over, she saw the watch ticking down the last seconds. She would die faking her death. All she could think about was how much Marius would laugh at her funeral.

Chapter 10

YOU DON'T care about Rosalind, do you?" Marius growled, marching up to Henry. The two were only inches apart; Marius could almost feel Henry's breath on his face. His fingers curled into fists.

"I do care. But pretending to—"

"Don't you dare spoil it!"

"I will spoil it," Henry snapped. "Unless you stop this nonsense right now."

Marius tensed, ready to strike Henry if he tried anything. But the sound of the steam carriage door closing made their heads turn. The plan was in the final stage; there was no stopping it now.

This was Marius's cue. "I'll go round up the servants," he said, giving Henry a look of false cheer.

"Don't you dare walk away!" Henry shouted, running through the tall grass after his brother.

"Come along, Henry," Marius called back over his shoulder. "The servants might need your help choosing butterflies to bring back for mother."

Behind him, Darcy drew even with Henry. "I suggest you clear out," Darcy whispered to Henry. "Don't cause any more trouble—"

Then Marius felt a sudden jerk; the ground shook, and a loud bang followed. He whirled around to face the fiery orange explosion just as Henry tackled him to the ground. Small bits of metal shot into the sky. Several servants began to shriek and run towards the three princes; another had his hands full with the terrified horse.

As soon as he could, Marius pushed Henry off and staggered to his feet.

"This is your cue, Henry," he said. "Time to take Rosalind and go."

But Henry simply stared at the steam-carriage debris. "Not anymore," he choked.

Marius followed his gaze and staggered back. A crumpled body was visible beneath the melted steam carriage's roof.

"What have you done?" Henry whispered.

"Rosalind is dead? You mean to tell me that the carriage just . . . *exploded?*" Cygnus folded his arms and leaned back in his chair.

"It was an unfortunate accident," Darcy said slowly. Marius and Henry stood on either side of him, their vacant stares fixed on the floor. "The machine itself was defective, I presume."

"A defective steam carriage in the palace's carriage house?" The king stood up suddenly. "I can't believe it."

"You must believe it, Father," Marius snapped. "Because we saw it happen. Because now she's—" He choked on his words, his face contorting. Henry gave his brother a sympathetic look. "She's dead," Marius finished in a near-whisper. "She's dead just when I was beginning to realize how much I liked her. And I'll never get to tell her so."

With that, Marius turned and strode from the room, slamming the door behind him.

"I should go with him," Henry said quietly. His face pale, his shoulders bowed, he hastened after his older brother.

Now the room was empty of all except the king, Darcy, and silence. The king slumped into his chair, his head in his hands. "Something is strange about this whole affair," he muttered.

Darcy picked up a vase from a nearby table, examining the delicate painting across its white surface. "Like I said, it was an unfortunate accident. It couldn't have been anything more, unless . . ." Darcy let his voice trail off.

The king sat up a little straighter in his chair, lifting his head and fixing Darcy with a keen eye. "Unless what?"

"I don't mean to cast suspicion or blame in the wake of such a tragedy. Forget I said anything." Darcy set the vase down and turned, smiling apologetically at his father.

"No, no, nothing you say will leave this room. You may speak freely to your father," the king urged. "I'm always willing to listen."

Pushing an errant lock of hair from his eyes, Darcy let out a short sigh. "It just . . . it would seem so out of character for him! Yet I had such a nagging suspicion. I was afraid he'd try something stupid." Darcy hung his head, waiting for the king's response. He would want to hear more. He always did.

"Who, Darcy?"

Darcy slowly looked up. "Marius," he whispered miserably. "In the wreckage of the explosion, our attendants found remnants of wires and a watch." He waited, watching his father put the pieces together.

"Which means someone rigged the carriage to blow," the king finished. "Marius was trying to get rid of her."

"I should've thought of that. Oh, I should've stopped them from going on the ride!" Darcy moaned. "I should've known."

"You can't blame yourself all the time," the king replied. "I thank you for your courage in telling me."

Darcy gave his father a short bow and turned to leave. "Just . . . if it does turn out to be the worst . . . if Marius did this, don't be too hard on him."

The king's face darkened. "He will get what he deserves, like any other murderer. No man is above the law; not even the king's son."

Chapter 11

EVER SINCE she could remember, Rosalind had wondered what Heaven would be like. Glorious, golden, filled with light . . .

Wherever she was now, it was not Heaven. Heaven was not musty, dark, damp, and cold. And she was pretty sure you couldn't feel drugged and achy in Heaven.

She groaned and sat up. Something metallic clinked as she moved, and her arms felt heavy. A few seconds later, a floating light appeared before her. Then she realized it wasn't floating—something or someone held it.

"Hello," called a voice. It was a strangely timid and sweet voice. And there was a person: a tall, fair girl dressed in a faded silk dress that might once have been pink. The light also revealed the metallic something— chains linking Rosalind to the wall.

"Am I dead? If so, this is a terrible disappointment," Rosalind said, slumping against the wall.

The girl might have smiled, but the shadows her lamp cast made her face look ghoulishly contorted. "No."

"Why am I here? What happened?"

The girl stepped closer, but her foot appeared to catch on something. The light slipped from her hand and clattered to the ground. It sputtered for a moment; then the room was back in darkness.

"Bother," the girl grumbled, and light reappeared a moment later as a candlestick standing on the floor. "I hope you like ham and cheese," she said, setting a tray down beside the candle. It held two dainty sandwiches and a cup of water. "Though if you prefer, I made some lovely little cucumber sandwiches yesterday."

Rosalind put her head in her hands. "Why I am locked in a dungeon and getting fed tea sandwiches?"

"Of course!" the girl cried. "Your tea. I forgot the tea. Black or herbal? And how much sugar and cream do you like?"

"I don't care about tea! I want to get out of this *stupid dungeon!* Since you're clearly incompetent, let me at least speak to your master, superior, or whoever's in charge of this deranged establishment."

The girl shifted her feet a little. "Then that's a 'no' on the tea? Are you sure? It's a bit cold down here."

Rosalind sucked in a deep breath. "No tea. No sandwiches."

The girl considered a moment. "I'll leave the food in case you get hungry," she said. Then she smiled, her cheeks dimpling. "Would you like a blanket?"

"I would like answers."

"Oh." The girl shrank back a little. "I'm not supposed to tell you much, and I'm not really sure how long you're supposed to be here. My name's Ophelia, by the way. You're Rosalind, correct?"

"No, I'm Daphne," Rosalind snapped. "Of course I'm Rosalind! You've locked me in your dungeon and you don't even know my name? Lovely."

Ophelia stiffened. "This isn't a dungeon; it's a cellar, and a very nice cellar at that."

"Oh, and chaining people to the wall in cellars is totally normal."

"You don't understand: I'm doing this for a friend. Well, actually . . ." She paused and giggled. "I *think* he's my friend. I don't really meet a lot of gentlemen. But he seemed nice."

"What's his name?"

"Sorry, I can't tell you. But give a shout if you need anything! I'll be upstairs."

Then she vanished.

Rosalind let out another moan and rubbed her temples. Was she going insane?

"You wanted to speak to us?" Henry said.

Henry and Marius stood in their father's council room. Darcy leaned against the wall behind Cygnus's chair. He might have been smiling, but his face was veiled with shadows. It was strange for their father to call his sons to the council, and even stranger to have the council members present. Every single one sat in the room.

Cygnus noticed the direction of Henry's gaze. "I wanted all members of state to hear what I have to say. To hear what has happened."

"To Rosalind," Marius whispered hoarsely.

"Yes. And why it happened." The king beckoned Darcy. "Tell the servant to read the proclamation."

Darcy stepped forward and handed the scroll to an attendant. Any sign of a smile had vanished, but his dark eyes glittered as the attendant unrolled and began to read.

"By royal decree of His Majesty King Cygnus, approved by the members of the State of Arcadia, Prince Marius is hereby charged with the murder of Lady Rosalind Copper. His sentence will be decided by an official court to be held a week hence. Any person having aided the prince in this foul crime will be punished alongside him." The attendant cleared his throat and stepped back into the shadows.

"That can't be!" Henry cried. "That just can't be! Marius didn't murder her, Father. It was an accident!"

"All evidence is to the contrary," the king replied coolly. "Do you have anything to say, Marius?"

But Marius was a statue. He didn't blink; he didn't move. He simply stared at the floor.

"Come on, Marius, defend yourself! You didn't do it!" Henry gave his brother a quick jab in the ribs. "Don't just stand there like an idiot!"

"He is clearly guilty," King Cygnus declared. "Look at him, Henry. He won't deny it."

"He won't deny it because he's in shock! His fiancée just died!"

Darcy stepped out again. "You mean the fiancée he so desperately *didn't* want to marry? Why would he care if she died? He had an excellent motive."

"Marius is not a murderer," Henry insisted.

"Henry." Cygnus fixed his son with a stern stare. "You may leave."

Henry returned his father's stare, but not for long. He couldn't fight him; he wasn't strong enough.

"Henry."

Henry didn't look up from the chessboard. "I really don't want to speak to you, Darcy."

Darcy sighed and slowly sank into the chair beside him. "And I don't want the events from earlier today to be a wedge between us."

Henry knocked half of the chessmen off the board. "You were there. You helped us! You *know* he didn't murder Rosalind!"

"Of course I know that," Darcy said softly. "Because Rosalind isn't dead."

Henry stared.

Darcy reached down a languid hand to retrieve a fallen pawn. He toyed with it, twirling it in his long fingers as he continued. "She's . . . somewhere safe. The worst that will happen to him is banishment. The throne will come to me. We both know Marius is not fit to rule! He's vain and stupid and petty. You and Rosalind could go off and live your lives peacefully. Isn't that what you want?"

"There was a body," Henry said numbly.

Darcy smiled. "It was an illusion; a friend of mine helped me with that bit. The explosion released a toxin that toyed with your minds, making you think there was a corpse there."

"But . . . it's all wrong." Henry stared at Darcy, aghast at what he was hearing. "Marius is innocent."

Darcy's face darkened. He closed the unlucky pawn in his fist, knuckles whitening. "I'm not asking for your blessing, Henry. Just stay out of my way."

"Or what?"

Darcy stood up and stretched. "I have ideas; I guarantee you won't like any of them." He smiled and tossed the pawn to land at Henry's feet. It rolled in a circle and was still. "Oh, and don't even think of visiting that little cinder-girl again. She'll be out of the way soon enough. But honestly, Henry, I'm not concerned that you'll be a threat. You don't have the guts." He ruffled his brother's hair and strode out of the room.

Henry watched him go, his mind a broiling sea of decisions and consequences.

He could be happy. He could be with Rosalind. All he had to do was stay quiet.

But a little voice in the back of his head nagged him.

You could be more. You could be brave.

Henry slowly stood. He had a factory to visit.

Chapter 12

THE SUN was setting as Henry approached the factory. His ragged breath formed little white clouds in the cold air. Shadows filled the alleys behind the factory, relieved only by gloomy little lanterns. *Surely there'll be a door back here*, Henry thought. Then he saw it: a delivery boy opening a back door. A steam cart had pulled up. Henry hurried forward, hoping to sneak in.

"You there!"

Henry's head turned in the direction of the speaker. He was a rough-looking man, probably a factory floor master. "Are you one of the incompetent haulers I always have to deal with?"

Henry blinked. Then he nodded.

"Get yourself over here and move these boxes!"

Henry picked up the nearest box and almost fell to the ground, thus proving his status as incompetent hauler forever. But he managed to regain his balance. A few snickers rang in his ears, probably from the other haulers. But Henry didn't care. He kept his head down and followed the men inside.

It had been hard to find commoners' clothes, but with a little digging around he had managed to "borrow" a delivery boy's outfit. He'd left some money behind and hoped he hadn't caused the boy too much inconvenience.

The groan of gears and the oppressive heat of the factory made Henry shudder. How could any human being work in such a place? The smells of oil and human sweat hung in the air, along with other acrid odors that were not meant to be in one's nostrils. Hoarse shouts rang from various parts of the factory, and always the dull, rhythmic clinking and clanking of the machines. Henry dropped the box as soon as he inconspicuously could.

He crept through the factory, his eyes sweeping over the endless rows of machinery. Where was she? There were too many furnaces in the room, looming black pillars with fiery jaws. It was nearly impossible to differentiate the silhouettes crouching at their mouths, feeding the flaming beasts with shovels of coal.

His pace quickened. He had to find her first. Whatever Darcy had in mind—no. He couldn't let it happen. If Marius would not stand up for himself, Evelyn certainly wouldn't.

Then he saw her. At first she was just another shape, just another slave to the belly of the factory. But her small figure and bright hair were unmistakable. He strode straight into the cinder-girls' midst, receiving many surprised and frightened looks.

"Evelyn," he whispered, placing a hand on her shoulder. "You have to come with me. Now."

It took her a moment to recognize him. Suddenly her eyes widened. "Henry! I mean Your Highn—"

"Don't," he hissed. "Just come."

"I can't," she replied, shrinking back. "I signed the document. I am bound to this place."

Henry grimaced and readjusted his cap, nervously glancing around. His stomach twisted. The floor master approached. "Trust me," he said.

Then he took her hand and ran. They wove between the rows and rows of machinery. He felt the stares of many and heard the shouts of even more.

"Oi! You there!" the floor master called. "Stop!"

Henry shoved his way past the stunned delivery boys and out the door. But he knew they were not yet safe. He heard a gunshot, and his stomach did another twist. Where should they go? He hadn't thought that far ahead. He couldn't run to the palace like this. Who knew how deep Darcy's influence ran? The constable's whistle rang in his ears.

"In the name of the law, I command you to stop!" the constable yelled.

Evelyn jerked him from his thoughts by pulling him down an alley. He followed her wordlessly, glancing over his shoulder. Their pursuers were close; he could hear their shouts and thundering footsteps. The road slanted downwards and took several sharp turns. The buildings became progressively more dilapidated on either side of them. The city walls grew larger and larger on the horizon. Then a sound met Henry's ears: running water.

"The canal," he said to Evelyn. "You're taking us to the canal!"

She gave him a short glance over her shoulder, the faintest hint of a smile on her face. In older days when Arcadia had been more suspicious of her neighboring cities, a moat had surrounded the city. Now that the kingdoms fought a war of commerce instead of swords and muskets, King Cygnus had converted the moat into a canal, one of many in an intricate web that entangled the neighboring commercial cities.

They passed through the slums by twilight. Faded, threadbare laundry hung limply on sagging lines above their heads. Noise filled the street, but none of the happy sort: toddlers and babies screaming, parents shouting, and young men exchanging brusque words, dark threats in their eyes. But Henry and Evelyn simply shoved past these folk, leaving startled stares and mutterings in their wake.

The sound of water and the smell of boats at dock intensified. Evelyn pulled Henry around another sharp curve. As night fell, hardly any light pierced these small dark roads. Suddenly they were crouching and then crawling down a dark tunnel.

"There's a metal grate at the end," Evelyn informed him as they sloshed through the tunnel. "This drain is flooded during the day, but it works for a nice escape route at night."

"My first impression of you is turning out to be entirely wrong," Henry said with a grin.

"I had a life once, before my work at the factory."

They reached the metal grate. At first it would not open, but when they pushed, the rusted hinges gave with a shrill whine.

"And now you can live again," Henry said, helping her up on the other side. The city was at their backs. The street lamps slowly flickered to life as the last light on the horizon melted away.

"Can you do some explaining now?" Evelyn rubbed her arms from the cold. "I—well, we've broken the law."

"Marius is in trouble," Henry said. "And so are you."

Evelyn knew of an abandoned bargeman's shack along the canal. Concealed amid a tangled web of ivy and overgrown shrubberies, the dilapidated hovel was barely visible from even a few feet away. Henry managed to scrape enough vines away to break the door free. A small rusted coal oven sat in the middle of the dirt floor, and a few dust-coated boxes lay in the corners.

Evelyn dug matches out of one box. "I used to sneak out here after my father remarried," she explained. "I had a small stash of things I'd smuggled here." She motioned to the open box. "There might be some coal in there and some canned bacon."

"Looks like some animal got to it first," Henry replied, holding up a battered and chewed tin. "Oh well. But there is coal."

The oven glowed to life after some persistent coaxing. The two crouched on the floor before it, rubbing their hands and arms.

"So what happened to Marius?" Evelyn asked quietly.

"He and his fiancée had a plan. They tried to fake her death . . ." Henry's voice trailed off, remembering the foolhardy craziness of the scheme he'd allowed himself to be dragged into. Then he shook himself and continued. "They rigged their steam carriage to explode, but Rosalind just disappeared. We saw a body in the rubble, but it was only an illusion."

"What then?"

"I believe you've met my other brother, Darcy," Henry continued.

Evelyn's eyes dropped to the floor. "Yes," she whispered.

"I think Darcy framed Marius. He was eager to help with their plan. Strangely eager." Henry looked at Evelyn, his eyes narrowing. "Is something the matter?"

"I told Darcy some information. He threatened you." Evelyn wouldn't look up.

"He threatened me?"

Evelyn nodded. "He wanted to know who had helped me. I broke my promise and—"

Henry took her hands in his. Her fingers were thin and cold, and he found he longed to press warmth into them, to comfort her any way that he could. "Evelyn," he whispered. "You don't have to be sorry. I understand. And I'm touched that you would go so far as to break a promise for my sake. I know that must have been difficult for you." He smiled. "You have a good heart."

She pulled away from him and shrank into the shadows. "Then you don't really know me," she mumbled. "You don't know what I did to my father."

A sympathetic look replaced Henry's smile. "Actually, I do. I visited your stepmother."

Evelyn's slight form slumped. "She told you—"

"That you caused your father's death?" Henry finished. He prodded the coals in the heater with the rusted poker. "Is that really why you chose to be a cinder-girl?"

"Yes . . . and my stepmother helped to persuade me." Evelyn scooted a little closer to the heater again. "But in the end it was my decision."

"I don't believe that's entirely true." Henry set down the poker and stared at Evelyn. "I think you allowed yourself to be bullied into it. From what I saw of your stepmother, I could see she's the extravagant sort of person who probably married up the social ladder. She married your father for money, Evelyn. You had good reasons to dislike her."

"But that doesn't excuse my behavior," she cried. "I drove my father to sickness and eventually death. I killed him." Tears trailed down her pale, sooty face, leaving streaks when she brushed them off. "I don't know how to let it go."

Henry moved closer to her and took her hand in his. He reached into his coat pocket, drew out a handkerchief, and gently wiped her tears away. "Start by making me a promise: After this is over, you won't go back to that factory. Your father would not want you to punish yourself like this for

the rest of your life. He would want you forgive yourself. Will you promise?"

She offered him a faint smile despite her tears.

"Will you promise, Evelyn?" Henry persisted.

"I promise," she whispered.

The two sat in silence for a little while. Then Evelyn took the handkerchief from Henry's hands and blew her nose. "Her name was Ophelia,"
she said. "The woman who helped me—her name was Ophelia."

"How did she get Rosalind's slippers?"

Evelyn shrugged. "I don't know. She said she was a fairy godmother,
delegated by her superiors to serve in this city. Somehow she knew I
needed help, knew how much I wanted to go to the ball. So she gave me
clothes to wear and the glass slippers. She transported me inside the
palace."

"Why did you run away from the dance?"

"I was dancing with your brother . . . trying to, anyway, and making
something of a hash of it. But he wouldn't stop smiling, and I felt so light,
so free. Then I saw her. My stepmother." A shadow fell across Evelyn's face.
"I should've known she'd come. And she saw me. She recognized me,
maybe. Now I'll never know, because I ran."

"Where did the clothes and the slippers go?"

She smiled faintly. "Well, I lost one slipper on my way out of the
palace. By the time I reached the factory, I was wearing my normal work
dress."

"So you told Darcy about Ophelia," Henry confirmed.

"Yes."

"Do you know where she lives?"

"I have ideas."

Henry stood up and stretched. "Then we should set out at once."

Chapter 13

DARCY SHOULD'VE been happy.

He sat at his desk by the window, with a pen in hand and a document waiting to be signed: a witness statement condoning Marius's banishment. A few drops of ink, and all his problems would be gone.

Or would they? The cinder-girl had escaped from the factory. No, someone had helped her. Henry must have helped her.

But Henry was weak. Henry couldn't do something like that.

But what if he did?

"I will stop him. I will stop them all," Darcy whispered, clutching the pen. With a swift flick of his hand, he signed the paper. There. Marius was out of the way.

Being the second son was like coming in second place. Marius was first, so he got all the glory. Henry was third. He was the baby, coddled by their mother until her health declined. But Darcy had the worst of both worlds. He was both older and littler. Neither young enough to be loved, nor old enough to be heir. Of course his parents said they loved him. But he didn't care.

He didn't need them. He didn't need any of them. No one could be trusted. Well, no one except Ophelia. She was a fairy godmother; therefore, her sole purpose in life was to serve others. A foolish occupation for her, but useful to him.

Darcy smiled at the thought of Ophelia and set down his pen. How kind she'd been to him, how willing to help! If only all the world were like her and would simply step aside for him to take charge.

He rose, paced to the window, and looked out upon the city. He scowled. Arcadia had become a machine. In the days of old, the days Darcy's nursemaid had told him stories about, magic had lived in the city too. Progress and special ability had lived side by side, those with magic always having the last word.

But some people hadn't liked that. They didn't like being weak and powerless.

You are weak and powerless, a little voice reminded Darcy. *You rely on another to provide you with your magic.*

Darcy shoved the voice aside, replacing it with a memory he clung to, his memory of the fountain's destruction.

The royal family stood in the courtyard of the palace, smiling and waving to the gathering crowd. But nine-year-old Darcy didn't smile. He only stared blankly ahead.

"Citizens of Arcadia," King Cygnus called out. "You are witnesses to the greatest day in Arcadian history. Today we are ridding ourselves of evil! Wiping a source of temptation and destruction from the city! Look before you. What do you see?"

Darcy looked in the direction his father pointed. The fountain.

"As you all know, the magical waters contained in this fountain are property of the royal bloodline of Arcadia. It is my family's sacred duty to protect this fountain and delegate the water only to those who are worthy. But this fountain has become a source of division in my kingdom! The palace is not safe. Looters, greedy for more magic, dare to break into the royal house."

Whispers ran among the crowds. Darcy bit his lip. What was his father doing?

"So, to rid the kingdom of this problem once and for all, I hereby order this fountain to be destroyed! No more will the worth of Arcadians be determined by how much magic is in your blood, but by hard work, good character, and successful enterprise!"

The crowd burst into applause. Darcy heard them cheer. He heard them clap.

He scowled.

"Pierre, if you please," the king said to a thin man standing behind him. The man promptly rolled out a cart with a cloth-covered object on it. With a dramatic sweep, Pierre removed the cloth. The ugliest conglomeration of metal sat on the cart, an eyesore beside the beautiful white marble fountain. Pierre picked up the machine and dropped it into the waters. He pulled something out of his pocket; a little copper box with a crank on it.

"The mechanism is ready, Your Majesty," Pierre announced in a nasally voice.

The king smiled and turned back to the crowd. "Citizens," he cried, spreading his arms, "behold what Arcadia can accomplish, not by foreign magic, but by her own strength!"

Apparently this was the cue for Pierre. He hastily turned the crank a few times and stepped back.

The mechanism shuddered and whirred to life. To Darcy's horror, cracks began to form in the fountain's base. The water quickly dried up and then—

BAM!

Chunks of marble flew into the air. The crowd screamed and covered their heads. But before the chunks ever neared the earth, they exploded into tiny sprinkles of silver. The rest of the fountain's base began to crumble, the dust of the marble methodically sucked up by tubes sticking out of the mechanism.

"This is the beginning of new age," Cygnus announced. "An age of progress!"

The memory stung every time. Darcy knew the real reason for the fountain's destruction: Lucernis, the city in control of the fountain's source, had been pressing for more tribute. Cygnus wanted an independent Arcadia. That meant an Arcadia without magic.

"But it's not all gone," Darcy whispered, a crooked smile spreading across his face. He opened a little drawer in his desk and removed the false bottom. A small glass vial winked up him in the lamplight. The last bit of magical water. He'd been saving it for just the right moment.

Darcy picked up the vial and looked out the window. The time was right.

Chapter 14

MARIUS STARED vacantly at the plate in front of him. A crust of bread. He deserved less. His mind flashed back to that awful image: Rosalind's crumpled corpse underneath the steam carriage. He dropped his head into his hands and wept, the clink of chains echoing with every shudder of his body.

I should be happy now. She's gone. That's what I wanted. Well, what I thought I wanted.

"Having a good cry?"

Marius slowly raised his head and scowled at his brother. Darcy leaned against the prison cell bars, grinning like the devil he was. "You," Marius hissed. "You miserable traitor. Can't even stand by your own brother, can you?"

Darcy shrugged. "Not when he's the only thing between me and the throne. Don't take it too personally. We all know you would've made a horrible king."

"Have you come to gloat?"

Darcy ran his thin fingers down one of the cell bars. "Actually, I came to reassure you. Rosalind's not dead."

Marius's heart skipped a beat. "What? Is she all right? Where is she?"

"Don't worry; I'm keeping your Rosalind safe and well." Darcy smiled in his insinuating way. "I might just pop in and see how she's doing later. She's probably confused, scared, and alone. Eager for comfort."

Marius flew to the bars. He shot his hand through and caught his brother by the shirt, dragging him hard against the iron so that he could snarl into his wicked face. "What have you done to her?"

"I think I'll keep you hanging," Darcy whispered, giving him a wink. Then with surprising strength he twisted himself from Marius's grasp and adjusted the lines of his shirt. "Sorry, but I have business to attend to. Business with Father. Sufficiently miserable now? Good. You can go on blubbering, if you like."

And Darcy vanished.

The door of the ramshackle townhouse was locked. The lock appeared weak, but no matter how hard Henry and Evelyn shoved it, it wouldn't budge.

"She's probably enchanted it," Henry said, panting and stepping back. He gave the door one last kick. "Open up, Ophelia! We need your help."

"Wait," Evelyn said, crouching before the lock. "Even if this lock is enchanted, it's still made by the factory I work for." She fished around in her apron pocket and pulled out a slender metal rod.

"You can pick locks?" Henry said.

"I can do many things," she replied, giving him a quick smile. With a few twists and clicks of the metal rod, the lock gave way and swung open.

Henry stepped inside first, blinking in the dim light.

"She's probably upstairs," Evelyn whispered behind him. "Come on."

The staircase let out a cacophony of groans as they ascended. Henry pushed aside the curtain at the top. A cozy but musty-smelling room awaited them. So did the fairy godmother.

"Hello." She sat in a dusty old chair in the corner of the room, reading a book. She didn't look up. "I wondered if you'd return, Evelyn."

"Do you know a man named Darcy?" Henry demanded.

"What does it matter? Is it a crime?" The book closed itself with a loud snap and floated onto the table beside her. Ophelia looked up. Although she smiled, Henry saw fire in her eyes. The pistol in his coat pocket felt heavier.

"What did he ask you to do?" Henry inquired quietly, slipping his hand into the pocket.

"That's none of your concern. And I know what's in your pocket."

"Can it hurt you?"

"Yes." Ophelia rose from her chair. "But I can hurt you too."

Henry's hand returned from his pocket empty. "I believe you know where a young woman named Rosalind is."

Ophelia smiled and moved to the rusted stove in the back of the room. "Would you two care for some tea? I also have sandwiches."

"You're avoiding the question," Henry replied. "And no, thank you, I don't want tea."

Pausing, Ophelia laughed. "You're much politer than Rosalind. She yelled at me when I offered her tea." She turned to face them, kettle in hand. "What about you, Evelyn? Tea?"

Evelyn folded her arms. "Have you hurt her?"

The smile disappeared. "Of course not!"

"Then where is Rosalind?" Henry said, stepping forward. "Whatever

Darcy's threatened to do, you don't have to fear him. We'll stop him."

Ophelia turned away again. "He didn't threaten me," she said quietly. "He asked."

"Then why are you doing this?" Evelyn suddenly exploded. She marched up to Ophelia and snatched the kettle from her hands, banging it down on the stove. "Prince Marius is being charged with murder, and you're going to stand by and watch? I thought you were supposed to help people!"

"I am helping someone," Ophelia replied softly, picking at the lacy cuff of her sleeve. "I'm helping Darcy."

Evelyn took her hand. "To do what? Take over the city with treachery?"

"Good heavens," Henry muttered. "You're sweet on him, aren't you?"

Ophelia froze. "Yes. Is there a problem with that?"

"You would stand by and let Darcy banish an innocent man because *you have feelings for him!*"

Ophelia blinked rapidly; tears shone in her eyes. "But . . . I think he likes me too. No one's ever liked me before!" She stopped for a moment to wipe the tears away. "That's why I became a fairy godmother. My friends all found someone to love them. They all married. But I didn't find anyone." Ophelia let out a sob. "I am a burden to my father. Mum died ages ago and his job doesn't get him much. He can barely support himself. I thought, maybe, with magic . . . someone would . . . maybe . . ."

"Love you?" Evelyn whispered. She took Ophelia's hand.

"I know I sound terribly selfish," Ophelia sniffled, "for a fairy godmother. But I only want to be loved."

"You helped me out of kindness," Evelyn said softly. "I'll never forget what you did for me."

Ophelia let out a laugh. "But I broke the glass slippers," she said, her voice somewhere between a sob and a giggle. "That's how this all started. I dropped them—I always was clumsy. I didn't have time to create more. That sort of magic takes time. So I summoned a pair."

"Summoned?" Henry raised an eyebrow.

"I didn't know they'd be Rosalind's. It was a random summoning. And I didn't notice the *R* on them. Don't you see? I always make bad choices. Becoming a fairy godmother, summoning the slippers, helping Darcy." She sighed. "I'm a disaster. Can you believe it? This whole tragedy is because of broken glass."

"People can change," Evelyn replied. She cast Henry a knowing look then returned her gaze to Ophelia, squeezing her hand. "You can change."

"Or you could let Rosalind go, and we'll leave you in your misery," Henry cut in. "Really, I don't mean to be rude, but this is the throne at stake. Putting a crown on Darcy's head would destroy the kingdom *and* him."

Ophelia, her eyes still watery, looked from Henry to Evelyn. Then she bowed her head and said very softly, "All right. I'll let Rosalind go."

"You're doing the right thing," Evelyn said, smiling encouragingly.

"I hope so." Ophelia's shoulders sagged. "I'll be right back with her."

Ophelia disappeared into the other room, leaving Evelyn and Henry alone.

"I didn't know you had it in you," Henry said quietly.

Evelyn turned to him. "What do you mean?"

"To yell at Ophelia like that. It was impressive." He gave her a smile.

"You are an inspiration yourself, Henry . . . Your Highness. The way you broke into the factory to save me!" The smile Evelyn turned upon him was brighter than he would have believed possible on a somber cinder-girl's face. It was a warm, lovely smile. "I honestly didn't think you were capable of that."

"Really?" Henry tilted his head.

"You were very nice the first day you came, but you seemed weak. Downtrodden. I see men like that all the time at the factory. They have the potential to be strong, but they allow themselves to be pushed aside."

Henry shoved his hands into his pockets. He wasn't sure he liked hearing this evaluation of himself coming from Evelyn. "And I seemed like that?"

"Yes. But today you changed."

He glanced up hopefully. "Was it a good sort of change?"

Evelyn opened her mouth to answer when another voice interrupted her.

"Really, you are insufferable. One minute you're locking me in your cellar and the next—" Rosalind appeared in the doorway and stopped. "Henry," she said rather flatly. "What are you doing here? Who's that?"

He looked at Evelyn and grinned. "A friend."

Rosalind crossed her arms, turning her head to one side and narrowing her eyes. "Where's Marius? I thought he'd come."

"He would've, I'm sure, but he's detained in the dungeons."

"What?" Rosalind's face paled. "What do you mean?"

"Father thinks he murdered you," Henry replied.

"But didn't you *stop* him?" Rosalind cried, flinging up her hands. For a moment Henry half-expected her to fly at him in a rage. "You knew he didn't kill me!"

"I tried!" Henry shouted back. "I tried at everything! I tried to please Father. I tried to please you. I tried to love you."

Rosalind froze, her eyes wide and her mouth hanging open in a little red o. Slowly, the hard lines of her face melted into something that may have been vulnerability. Seeing this, Henry forced himself to adjust his tone, speaking a little more kindly than before. "But these last few days, I've realized something: I don't love you, Rosalind. Not like you want me to. You are a beautiful young woman and you deserve a good man. But that man is not me."

"Well then," Rosalind said slowly. Then she laughed, and her cheeks flushed bright pink. "That works out rather nicely. You see, I actually fell in love with Marius. I tried not to. But . . ."

"He's hard to resist," Henry finished. He wondered momentarily if he should be jealous. Or even just a little vexed. But he found to his satisfaction that he wasn't. Not even a bit. "Yeah, I've heard that before." He smiled wryly. "I was hoping you wouldn't be crushed."

"Excuse me," Ophelia called. "You should see this."

Three heads turned in her direction; Ophelia stood in front of the mirror, wringing her hands. Only the mirror wasn't a mirror. It was a window into the palace. And Darcy was in full view.

Chapter 15

DARCY COULD feel the power coursing through his veins. It burned painfully, but it was a pain he relished. He was strong.

He let out a laugh, waving his hand in the direction of a vase. It flew from its stand in the hallway and smashed on the ground. Though he strode through the widest hallway in the palace, his surroundings seemed too close, too small to contain such power as his.

The doors to the throne room flew open with only the slightest flick of his fingers. The throne was vacant. King Cygnus and a few of his advisors stood around a small table, conferring over a map. At a mere mental command from Darcy, the map burst into flames and shriveled up. The councilors and the king turned in his direction, their faces expressing astonishment.

"I was not informed about this meeting," Darcy stated. He sauntered over to the throne, running his hand along the armrest. "But I trust you won't let that happened again."

Cygnus blinked rapidly. "My son!" he cried. "What is the matter with you?"

"Magic," one of the councilors hissed, pointing at the char marks on the table. The table suddenly levitated and knocked the man in the head. His unconscious body dropped to the floor.

Darcy smiled and lowered himself into the throne. "You fear me, don't you?" His head tipped toward his father. "You especially."

"I do not fear my own son," Cygnus replied stoutly.

"But your thoughts betray you, O King, for I can hear them like the frightened cries of a child." Darcy's smile widened. "Isn't it marvelous? And to think you could've had power like mine. But you destroyed it."

The color melted from Cygnus's face. "You . . . you saved some of the fountain's water?"

"It's funny how it happened," Darcy laughed. "Marius dared me to steal some. I was young and wanted to prove my worth. But, after I had done the deed, I thought, 'Wouldn't it be better to save this for a more auspicious moment?'" Darcy's fingers clenched the armrests. "And what better time than now, when you're just about to banish your heir?"

"Darcy, I command you to come to your senses," Cygnus barked. "I destroyed the fountain so that this would never happen!"

Darcy tilted his head and stared at his father. "You feared me even then. Even when I was a boy. Splendid."

"I didn't fear you. I don't fear any of my family. But I did fear *for* you and for Henry—the seed of jealousy is easily planted in the younger sons of kings. It could've been you. It could've been Henry."

Darcy's laughter rang through the hall. "Henry? He doesn't have the courage. He doesn't even have the courage to stand by you now."

"What exactly are you trying to do?" King Cygnus asked, stepping back.

"I'm gaining what I deserve and giving Marius what he deserves."

"And you think you can just take this"—Cygnus gestured towards the throne—"with a little bit of magic in your veins?" The king barked a laugh that was perhaps not as confident as he would have liked.

Darcy's smile disappeared. He leaned forward in his new throne. "Don't underestimate me, Father. What do you think I've been studying so hard all these years? Why do I pore over books late into the night? Magic. You wouldn't believe how many books are about magic: how to use it, how to gain it, how to hurt people with it—"

"You'll suffer for this, Darcy," Cygnus said, raising a warning fist. "And the worst suffering will come, not from others, but from yourself. Through your actions you will reject all the love and friendship that has been offered to you. In the end you will die friendless, lonely, and unhappy. Power is not everything, Darcy. Think carefully."

"I have thought carefully for twelve years," Darcy hissed. "But apparently you never noticed. Have you ever been in your dungeons, Father? I think you should have a look."

Cygnus's eyes widened and he stretched out his arms to Darcy; but chains had already wound their way around his body. The next moment he disappeared.

"Councilors," Darcy announced, turning to the remaining men cowering on the floor. "Send out an edict that King Darcy will be crowned tomorrow. Oh, and don't forget to mention Marius's banishment. If you can't manage that, I'm sure I can find some brainless and adoring underlings to replace you." Darcy smiled. "You may grovel and kiss your new king's hand, if you like."

Darcy's triumphant face stared back at the group gathered around the mirror. Rosalind backed away.

"Where did my father go?" Henry cried, turning to Ophelia.

"Darcy must have magically transported him to the dungeon," she whispered, her hands clasped to her cheeks. "I didn't know he had magic." She lowered her hands for a moment and sighed. "You must admit, though, he looks rather classy on a throne . . . and burning the map was a clever bit of magic. Even I can't do something like that."

Rosalind groaned and plopped down into Ophelia's chair. "You've got to be joking," she moaned. "You're sweet on Darcy! How can you even *like* him?"

Ophelia blinked several times before responding softly, "I don't know."

But Henry marched towards the door. "I'm not going to stand here doing nothing," he announced. "I'll hopefully see you all at the palace." He drew the pistol out of his pocket and paused for a moment, weighing it in his hand. His mouth set in a grim line. "I never thought I'd use this on my own brother."

"Please," Evelyn said, grabbing his arm, "Don't go. You saw what he did to those council members—and he wasn't even trying! He's too powerful."

"She's right," Rosalind agreed, rubbing her face. "Don't waste your life, Henry."

"But we must do something," he persisted. "We can't step aside and let him take over the kingdom without a fight!" Henry looked to Ophelia. "I may not be able to do anything, but you can. You have magic."

Three hopeful pairs of eyes turned to her. Ophelia backed away.

"I can't!" she cried. "I just can't."

Rosalind's eyes narrowed. "But surely there's a way to stop him. Can't you just take away his magic?"

Ophelia bit her lip. "Yes, but you don't understand. If I take his magic, I lose everything too!"

"But we're talking about an entire city of people who are going to suffer from that deranged man's rule," Rosalind retorted.

"He's not deranged," Ophelia snapped. "He's just . . . jealous. And maybe a little obsessed."

Evelyn cocked her head. "What do you mean by saying you'll lose everything? You'd be helping Arcadia."

"Taking magic is illegal for fairy godmothers," Ophelia replied slowly. "It's stealing of the highest form. I'd be removed from the program."

"Removed?" Henry repeated.

"I'd lose my powers, my memories . . . my name . . ."

"Your name?" Rosalind's face screwed up in a confused look. "That's odd."

"When a girl becomes a fairy godmother, she chooses a new name; it's a symbol of letting go of her old life," Ophelia explained. "But don't you see? I'd lose everything! My father is poor; he makes carts for a living. Nobody buys carts now that there are steam carriages! But as long as I am a fairy godmother, he receives a little money to support himself. If I am removed . . ." Ophelia buried her face in her hands. "I just can't."

Henry let out a slow sigh. "I understand," he said quietly. "So we'll leave you in peace. Come on, Roz; don't argue."

"I can do something for you, though," Ophelia called as the three started to leave. "Save you some time. I can teleport you to the palace."

"Thank you," Evelyn said, giving her a wide smile. Rosalind only glowered.

As he felt himself begin to melt away, Henry shot one last look at Ophelia. "Please," he mouthed. "For Darcy's sake."

Ophelia looked away, tears glimmering in her eyes.

Chapter 16

DARCY'S EYES snapped open; he sat up in the throne. Three bedraggled figures stood before him, all giving him their best impressions of a murderous glare. Only Rosalind succeeded, but Henry was doing surprisingly well.

"Interesting," Darcy said. "Have you come for my coronation? You probably didn't hear the good news: It's tomorrow. How unfortunate that I'll have to get rid of you before then."

Rosalind marched up to the throne. "Let Marius go *right now*," she snarled. "Or else!"

Darcy laughed. "Or else what? You'll give me the evil eye? That seems to be the only thing you can do." He flicked his hand, and she flew back, crumpling onto the marble floor. Evelyn screamed.

"Who's next?" Darcy called, smiling cheerfully at Evelyn and Henry. Evelyn had caught hold of Henry's arm, and both stared up at Darcy, unable to mask their fear. "I'll look forward to getting rid of you, Miss

Evelyn. You've caused me more problems than I thought you capable of."

Henry stepped in front of her. "Please, Darcy," he started.

"You've come to beg?" Darcy put on an expression of mock sorrow. "How . . . what's the word? *Adorable*. Of course I hardly expected any better from you."

Henry's jaw set. "You're making a mistake. Think about what you're doing—"

"Father said the same thing," Darcy mused. "Keep this up, Henry, and I might let you stay alive. But only to be my dinnertime entertainment. You'd make a good dog. You beg just like one." His eyes widened in cruel delight. "How hard will you plead for your beloved cinder-girl, I wonder?"

He raised his arm, but Henry was faster. His hand whipped the gun from his pocket, and a loud bang followed. Darcy slid from the throne, clutching his arm. A cry escaped his lips, rendering him momentarily inarticulate. Then he gathered himself together, his teeth clenched in a facsimile of a smile. "You dared to shoot me?" he growled, staring at his now-bloody shirt sleeve.

"I will do it again," Henry hissed, cocking and pointing the pistol at Darcy once more.

Darcy raised his head and laughed, his face contorted in a strange mixture of agony and delight. The lights in the throne room flickered and flared from his power. "You do have some spark, Henry. And I thought you were incorruptible. Let's see how far you're willing to go." Darcy staggered to his feet, taking his hand off his blood-soaked shirt. "Come, little brother," he spat. "Let's play."

A *poof* interrupted them as a figure materialized in front of Henry.

"Um. Let's not," spoke a hesitant voice.

Darcy's cold eyes shifted to the glimmering, slender little form. "Ophelia," he growled. "What are you doing?"

She steadied herself, her hands out on either side. Then she looked at Darcy and lifted her trembling chin. "What do you think?"

Darcy laughed again and paced towards her. "Well, let's see: You're betraying my trust, acting very stupid, and protecting the most pathetic pair of people in this entire kingdom." He shook his head and sighed. "You, of all people. I thought I could trust you. Yet again, I am disappointed." He lifted his hand to blast her against the wall, but she grabbed it.

"What are you doing?" he hissed. His eyes narrowed.

"I think you know," Ophelia answered, raising her chin.

Darcy tried to wrench his hand from her grasp. "You wouldn't dare. You know what will happen."

"I see you've done your homework," she replied simply. And she closed her eyes. As the veins in Darcy's arm began to glow, he let out a scream of pain.

"Please!" he howled. "Stop! I have worked all my life for this. Take my power and I am nothing. I thought you cared for me!"

"I do care," Ophelia whispered. "That's why I'm doing this." Though he desperately thrashed and twisted his arm to break her grasp, her seemingly delicate fingers held on with astonishing strength.

Darcy began to crumple to the ground. Ophelia knelt in front of him, still holding his hand firmly. She looked to Evelyn and Henry and called, "Goodbye." Gazing down at Darcy, she smiled sadly. "At least I won't remember you."

A bright light flashed through the throne room; the palace shook. Henry and Evelyn staggered back, barely able to support each other.

When the light faded, Ophelia was gone.

Chapter 17

R OSALIND."

There was that voice again. That persistent, annoying voice. Rosalind's head throbbed enough without someone talking at her.

The voice sounded familiar, and Rosalind had a nagging suspicion that she should recognize it. Her eyelids cracked open for just a second. Obnoxious amounts of sunlight surrounded her. She let her eyes close again.

Someone shook her gently.

"Roz, please. You've been out cold for a day already!"

Rosalind sighed. "I don't want to wake up," she mumbled. "Go away."

"Don't order me around, young lady. You're in my palace," the voice replied. It was a deep voice and a little uncertain, but there was a familiar teasing undercurrent to it.

Rosalind's eyes flew open and she stared up at Marius. "You're safe!" she cried, a smile lighting up her face.

"Glad you care," Marius replied with his usual cocky grin. "I was beginning to wonder if Henry had forgotten about Father and me in the dungeon."

"What happened?" Rosalind asked. She looked around and found that she lay in her own bed, clad in a modest dressing gown. Embarrassed that Marius should see her at such a disadvantage, she tried to sit up and take charge of the situation. Her head strongly objected to this move, however. She groaned, closing her eyes.

"Whoa, stay calm," Marius said, gently taking her shoulder and pushing her back down. "It all turned out fine. Well, except for Darcy. And that fairy godmother. She vanished."

Rosalind settled back into her pillows. Then she raised an eyebrow at Marius. "Vanished?"

He shrugged. "According to Henry and Evelyn. Did you know they're engaged? Mother thinks it would be splendid if we have a double wedding."

Rosalind opened her mouth to make a quick, sarcastic reply. Then she saw the look on Marius's face and thought better of it. Suddenly feeling shy—an odd sensation for her—she studied her hands, twisting the edge of her quilt. "Do you actually *want* to marry me?"

Marius looked down at his own hands, twiddling them nervously. "If you will actually have me. Look, I understand if you're upset about Henry and Evelyn, but if you'll give me a chance—"

Dropping the quilt, Rosalind reached out and took his hand. "You're the crown prince, Marius. Why on earth would I prefer Henry?"

Lighting up, he clasped her hand tightly in both of his. "I'll get a ring later and make it official."

"So, what happened to Darcy?"

Marius's smile disappeared. "About him . . . I'm sorry for what happened to you. I should've known Darcy had a trick up his sleeve. Did he hurt you?"

"Aside from bashing my head on the floor, you mean? No, but I would love to break his nose for locking you up."

"Well, you can't, unless you want to travel a hundred miles south of here to a pokey little island in the middle of a stormy lake." Marius grinned. "Father set Darcy up in a nice little castle there. With many of his finest guards, of course."

"Sounds cozy. How long will he be there?"

"Oh, until he learns to behave. But, knowing Darcy, that may never happen. Father's pretty upset over the whole ordeal." Marius sighed. "And I was pretty upset when I found you unconscious on the floor in the throne room." He gave her hand a quick squeeze. "Do you know what Henry said? 'Oh, I forgot about her.'" A look of gleeful delight passed over Marius's face. "I didn't know Henry had it in him to be so un-thoughtful! I almost applauded him, but I was too busy making sure you were still alive."

"Henry has a lot of things in him that I never noticed," Rosalind said with a laugh. "I think he's grown . . . maybe Evelyn's had an effect on him."

"They both want to have an effect on the kingdom; Henry's lobbying to improve the situation for cinder-girls in the factories. They'll now be paid better wages and sign no binding lifetime contracts."

"And what does your father think of this?"

"Considering that Henry helped defeat Darcy, I think Father is willing to do pretty much anything for him. Sadly, I missed out on the opportunity to show my bravery and earn rewards." Marius sighed dramatically.

"And what brave act would you have done?" Rosalind asked with a smirk. "Given Darcy a fabulous look of disdain?"

"Surely that would've crushed his self-esteem, seeing how much more stylish I am," Marius replied with a toss of his handsome head. "No, it was kinder of me to spare him such pain. He is still my brother, you know."

Rosalind grinned back at him. "And you're not disappointed about Evelyn?"

Marius gave her hand a squeeze. "She is nice, but not my type. You were right about something, Roz. It does take more than one dance to find your soul-mate."

"What does it take?"

"In my case it took a scheming brother, a stubborn young lady, an exploding steam carriage, and a bit of broken glass." He leaned down and kissed her on the forehead. "Thanks for being stubborn, Roz."

"I would smack you if you weren't kissing me," she replied.

"Then I'll kiss you again. I'd prefer that you not bruise my beautiful face."

# Epilogue

EVERY DAY Darcy sat by the window, picking at his food and muttering. The servants hated him. He hated them. He was above them, but they were practically his guards while he rotted in his overdressed dungeon. A beautiful island in a lake, his father had said. Darcy scowled. Though the castle was impressive in size, most of the rooms wallowed in dust and disrepair. Darcy had servants to clean his apartments, but most days he would allow them in only to deliver his food. A few chairs in the room were missing legs from being hurled against the wall. The remnants of last night's china lay in a shattered heap in a corner. His bed could boast no better state: The snagged silk coverlets might have been the scene of a particularly violent goose fight, judging by the amount of down floating in the air.

Eventually Darcy would run out of furniture and chinaware to vent his anger upon. He clenched his teeth. A lifetime of this misery was going to drive him insane.

A timid rap on the door startled him from his thoughts. The servants usually didn't dare knock. They were in the habit of leaving his food on a tray outside the door and sneaking away to avoid his wrath.

"Go away," Darcy snarled, his nails digging into the arms of his chair. "I don't want anything my father has sent."

"It isn't anything from your father, Your Highness," a small voice replied. "It's . . . a visitor."

Darcy stood up quickly and turned to the door. "A visitor?" Other than the servants, he had seen no other human being in these last three weeks. For a moment something inside him yearned. Was it loneliness? Darcy clenched his teeth and shoved the feeling deep down. No. He didn't need companionship. He wasn't that weak.

"I don't want to see anyone," Darcy growled. "Send him away."

"I tried to tell her that, but she wouldn't leave," the servant replied nervously. "She . . . um, insisted on coming in."

When Darcy heard the door creak open, he prepared to give the servant a good tongue-lashing. But the strange figure in the doorway caught him off-guard.

An old woman tottered past the servant, entered the room, and gave Darcy an almost toothless smile. She surveyed her surroundings with one sweeping glance. The destruction only seemed to amuse her.

"Accept my humble gift, Prince," she wheezed. From beneath her dark cloak she withdrew something.

"A rose?" Darcy raised an eyebrow. "Why would I want a stupid flower?"

"All I ask is to stay the night, and then I'll be on my way." The woman stretched out her hand. The flower didn't even look fresh. The tips of the petals were shriveled and turning black. "Will you take it?"

Darcy laughed bitterly. "You can take your rose and your ugly face somewhere else, old crone. The home of a prince is no place for the likes of you." He turned his back on her and stalked to the window. "Leave me in peace."

The old woman's tone changed to disappointment mixed with disapproval. "Is that so, Darcy? Appearances are not always what they seem. The exterior is weak and temporary; true beauty can exist only on the inside."

"I said leave me, not lecture me." Darcy didn't spare her another glance.

"Oh, I shall, never fear. But mine will be the last face you see for a while . . ."

ABOUT THE AUTHOR

EMMA CLIFTON has been thinking up stories since before she knew how to type them out. Reading books such as the Chronicles of Narnia, *The Door Within* Trilogy, and *Redwall* inspired her to take her writing more seriously. Though her rigorous homeschool education keeps her busy, she also enjoys sewing, reading, and spending time with her family in beautiful Northern Virginia. *Broken Glass* is her debut novella.

You can find out more about Emma and her writing on her blog: www.PeppermintandProse.wordpress.com

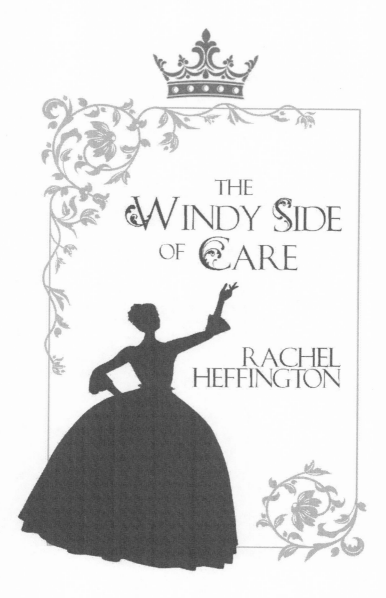

THE
WINDY SIDE
OF CARE

RACHEL
HEFFINGTON

To MKF, without whom there would be no Alis.

May London happen sooner than we dream,

may our dreams happen sooner than London.

Much laughter and more love from:

your own crazy girl.

CHAPTER 1

Don Pedro: "In faith, lady, you have a merry heart."
Beatrice: "Yea, my lord, I thank it, poor fool.
It keeps on the windy side of care."
Shakespeare's *Much Ado About Nothing*

I COZIED an apple in my hand and tried the weight of it against my palm, contemplating whether or not beaning a judge with half-rotten fruit would qualify as contempt of court. Quite probably.

"I swear before the Court of Ashby, the birth certificates were *switched!*" I shouted. "How else have *I*, Lady Alisandra Carlisle, obtained the features of our royalty? If Auguste Blenheim is Ashbian to the core, can you explain why he is short and dark as coal smuts when every royal has been fair and tall since the Ancient Days?"

I imagined that the band of rooks in the pine above me were actually court folk, blinking in unison at my reference to coal smuts. I lobbed my apple at the tree and listened to the taffeta-winged disturbance it created among the quarrelsome birds.

It would be the judge's turn to speak now, and I took the pins from my bun and shook my hair down to make it as much like a horsehair wig as possible. I could *feel* the role in this state. "It would seem, Lady Carlisle, that you are making claims of fraudulence against His Majesty, the King," My throaty voice rang out with all the conviction of an experienced barrister's on the stillness of our orchard.

The rooks fell silent, each leaning from his perch into the cloying, windfall-scented air. They listened to my one-woman trial and would probably have been against me had they possessed voices with which to speak.

"Your answer, Lady Carlisle?" I asked myself ominously.

It was important that I practice these situations, considering my aspiration to one day take the throne I knew should be mine. Would I answer the real court confidently? Could I?

Yes. Say yes.

I willed my tongue to form an affirmation, but it balked, stumbling before a jury of birds. How could I stand before the Court of Ashby and hope for better results?

Addlepate.

Furious for failing yet again in this daily exercise, I bundled my skirt like a basket, rolled a few chill apples into it, and headed toward the house.

"If Auguste Blenheim the Pig had not stolen my birthright, I should never have had to stand out here making myself stupid for an audience of rooks." I wasn't sure if I spoke to myself or to God. Did it matter, really? I pushed through the gap in the orchard fence, sliding easily through the narrow opening, and trotted across the stable yard. The old-faithful smell of breakfast tumbled out of the stone kitchen, and I followed its cinnamon beckoning.

Ellen-Best turned as I dropped my apples on the table. "Have you seen yourself in the mirror?" she scolded. "You're all over with straw bits."

"No." Today I was glad for the absence of a looking glass in the kitchens; I wished not to look at my royalty. Some days it was just too infuriating.

"TEA!" The imperative broke in on our conversation with a suddenness almost electrifying.

"COMING!" I shouted back. Serving girls in manor houses were not supposed to shout at anyone, much less at their betters. But the makers of Proper Etiquette had doubtless never lived in a house with this many passages, corridors, and miniscule staircases.

I had instituted my own etiquette early on.

Ellen cocked an eye at the main house. "She's chirpy." She pulled me to her side and gathered my thick hair back into a sleek knot.

I escaped and darted to the cupboard. "Has Stockton come up yet?" I clattered several teacups onto a tray and righted them in haste.

"Stockton? He's never been on time these eight years. Why, please God, would he change habit now?"

"I need him to deliver a letter for me. I've gained ground, Ellen."

"Have you?" Her tone was doubtful.

"I have. The first thing to do was try to find Father's certificate of death."

"Naturally."

I scooped tiny, curled tea leaves into the silver bobber and dropped it into the teapot. "There never was a certificate—birth or death—for a single Bickersnath Carlisle in the whole Kingdom of Ashby, according to the Records."

"They must be a healthy race, those Bickersnaths." Ellen stirred the porridge and raked a cone of sugar over-top.

Brows knitted, I pondered how best to respond to this non sequitur. "Either that or my real father has a less ludicrous name." I dropped my fingers on Ellen's shoulder and pulled her to face me. "Ellen. You have always told me that I am truly a daughter of Blenheim. A royal. How do you know?"

Ellen's eyes traveled down my slender frame and back to my face with a wry smile. She smoothed my uncouth eyebrows with one finger and winked. "You have too much Blenheim going on for anyone to deny."

I groaned. "That will not stand in court, Ellen."

She waved me off. "How do *you* know you're a royal? Were you born with gold flowing through your veins, teething on jewels?"

I made a precise pyramid of sugar lumps and shoved them next to the saucers on the tray. "They say my father—Bickersnath—died and left me to that awful woman he had married a few weeks before. They say my heart was broken."

Ellen and I both knew that wasn't the case. I never had a father. Well, biologically I must have had one, but I certainly had never looked him in the eye and given him the filial kiss. There was more than one thing wrong with the whole story anyway. Had no one thought it remotely suspicious? Unhappy man marries beautiful woman. Beautiful woman shapes up rather nasty. Man unhappier than ever; woman unhappy as well. Three short weeks . . . Oops, he's dead! Oh, poor dear child. Let's see what we can do with her. Free labor!

One would think there would have at least been an inquest. If it was true at all.

We knew it wasn't.

"Their story is pale cider," I said. "Were I really nothing, Laureldina wouldn't let me keep my title. They would not bother to tell me this story about Bickersnath Carlisle."

If Ellen and I were right, then King Henri and his queen were my parents. They had given me up because the people of Ashby had expected a princeling. And when the people of Ashby expect one thing and are given another they are prone to a nasty little thing called Anarchy. The House of Ashby would not last long under a gale of the common-folks' fury. The common-folk generally scour the countryside with fire *and* sword, and sometimes a plague or two for good measure: the People's Way.

There are many problems with a system of King's Justice, but Anarchy is not one of them; sometimes I rather thought a tyrannical ruler might behoove the people of Ashby. Anything would be better than their own dictatorial tendencies. But there it was: The way of Ashby was writ in blood, and not many would be fool enough even to try to convince them otherwise. My father, the king, had obviously not been a fool. Per his wisdom, I was a dethroned royal living an interesting existence as a kitchen drudge.

The only question then: Who was my substitute? I mean, who was Auguste really, and how was I going to make sure that I was recognized as heir and Auguste deported back to whence he came?

My current scheme was to firm up the facts I already knew and then work at becoming a "Lady of State" as they call the girls up castle way. If anyone was to denounce Auguste, I wanted it to be me and I wanted it to sting. One isn't given the chance to depose a royal on a daily basis. I'd rather get acquainted with the man that my triumph may be greater.

I snitched half a piece of bacon from Laureldina's tray. "Ellen-Best, tell me when Stockton does drag in; I've a letter for Lord Humphries and it mustn't wait till tomorrow. What a disappointment it would be to find someone else had poisoned Auguste's coffee and ruined *my* chances forever."

I carried the tea things upstairs, one tray on my head, one in each hand—a practiced art.

"TEA!" the shriek came again, but this time I was prepared for it. I backed into the door to push it open with my hip and rump then glided through the room, careful to deposit the trays in perfect silence.

I raised my gaze enough to meet Laureldina's chin, refusing to look any higher. "M'lady, would you like a syrup? Your voice sounds like a crows' caucus."

By her stiffening, I knew my stepmother had taken the hit. "No, thank you, Alis. You might, however, have the decency to pluck your eyebrows. They offend reason, child."

"They are a patriotic gesture," I said in honeyed tones. "A nod to Ashby, madam, in light of the prince's approaching birthday. *All* the Blenheims have incorrigible brows."

Laureldina sighed one of her insinuating sighs that could mean anything from, 'Oh dear, surely you aren't making this up?' to 'Oh heavens, of course you are.'

I decided to bide my time before saying anything else. I spread the tea things on Laureldina's side table and began the laborious and precise process of making her First Cup.

"Elbows *straight*," Laureldina chided, tapping my elbow with her fingers. "I don't know why I bother training you. I'm sure it is my native goodness and gentility that has kept you from the poorhouse thus far."

"I'm sure it must be." I wondered how far one could stretch the definition in good conscience. "Are the girls awake, madam?"

She tossed her hands. "God only knows, child. Go wake them before the tea is worthless. Do you want them to feel as if they're drinking from chamber pots?"

"Yes, madam. No madam."

In truth, I rather wished to reverse my answers.

I backed out of the room with the remaining trays, to all appearances submissive. Of course I recognized my propensity toward impudence as one not terribly helpful for a grown woman, but it is a harsh person who expects overmuch from a disinherited princess.

Biting my tongue both mentally and literally, I pushed through the latticed door dividing My Lady's chambers from those of her daughters. Vivienne and Clarisse reclined in their beds, quite angelic-looking. How ill-tempered women are blessed with all the beauty has forever been a mystery to me; how men can stand enough of the poison to marry them a greater mystery still.

I clashed the trays onto the dressing table then twitched the curtains open, flooding the room with sunlight.

"Oh, Alisandra!" Clarisse flung one bare, white arm over her eyes.

"You'll blind us all!" Vivienne sat up and parted her red curls. "Since you're stupid enough to wake us like that, come fix my hair." She slipped from her bed and sauntered to her dressing table, where she sat and proceeded to fix her own tea, yawning the while. "Has the mail come yet, Thing?"

I twisted her curls into ornate coils, spearing them into place with jeweled pins. "No, Vivienne."

"Marvelous." She took a letter from her bosom and handed it to me. "See that this is delivered to Lord Grosvenor." She took a bite of toast with a dreamy sigh and rested the point of her chin in her hand. "*J'adore mi amour.*"

"Don't even try to speak French, Vivienne." Clarisse rolled out of bed and pulled a yellow silk wrapper from the chair onto her Junoesque frame. "It's so inelegant."

"You told me last month that French was the height of fashion."

Clarisse pushed me out of the way and hugged Vivienne's neck. "Of course I did, darling, but that was before *you* started trailing Spanish through it."

Vivienne scoffed and pushed her sister away.

Clarisse trod on my bare feet and stumbled backward. "You horrid thing!" she cried. "Why aren't you wearing your slippers?'

"The cat made a mess in them," I said in my most tranquil tone. "You can't have wanted me to come upstairs wearing them in that state."

Clarisse pressed a hand to her midsection. "No . . . no, you are correct . . . But your *feet*, Alisandra!"

I bent my knees so the skirt hem might hide my grass-stained, roughened toes. "I am having a pair of crystal slippers made, you know," I said with a smirk. "Soon my beautiful feet will be showcased in the finest glass-work for the public's viewing pleasure."

Vivienne's green eyes widened and Clarisse glared at me. "You wretched creature. Mama!" she howled.

"What is she doing now?" Laureldina warbled from her gilded cage.

I smiled and curtsied to my sisters, fingering a second letter I'd pilfered from the pocket of Clarisse's gown. "I shall mail that letter, Vivienne, only I wondered: would you like to translate it into Italian first?" I peered at Lord Grosvenor's name and the pretty scrawl in Clarisse's handwriting below: "*La mia bella amante?* Oh my, Clarisse! That *is* bold. Calling Lord Grosvenor your 'beautiful, illicit lady-love' will certainly win his affections. It might affront his masculinity, but he'll be quite glad you think him beautiful; he's so sure on that point himself." I tapped Vivienne's arm with the letter and winked. "She's besting you, Vivienne. You had better call him 'the burning heat of your passion' if you hope to keep up."

Clarisse's eyes were livid. "Vile pig! Horrible sneak!"

I made my way to the hall door and turned on the threshold. "You don't think, girls, that Lord Grosvenor cares which of you he kisses so long as you're both possessed of good looks and reasonable fortunes?"

"Mother!"

But I was already halfway downstairs, laughing.

My laughter was destined for a short life. Laureldina's son, William, stood at the bottom of the staircase, grinning. I stopped short and made an effort to meet the eyes of this young man who, by virtue of being the half-brother of my stepsisters was no relation to *me* at all.

"Alis, Alis . . . always causing a row." He offered his hand to me, and though the gesture befuddled me, I knew enough of him not to refuse.

I gave him the tips of my fingers. "Has Barnaby been up with your coffee?"

"He has *not* been up. I was hoping you'd do it."

I stepped backward, took my hand from his, and raised my eyebrows. "Your kindness is too great, sir, it overwhelms me. That you would think to offer *me* a chance for *more* drudgery . . . benevolence itself."

"Not so fierce, Alis." William ran a hand over his smooth chin and shook his head, smiling at me from under a shock of bright gold hair. "You're the sort of thing they write about, y'know."

William's manner confused me. As usual, I was made to feel a fool as I stood there beneath his roving eyes. My tongue was the prized mechanism by which I ruled the house, putting this one in his place and raising another to a higher station. I knew not what to do with a man who begged for more of my backchat.

Wordless, I passed William and ducked down the hall to the kitchen, glad he did not try follow today as he sometimes did. Two months he'd been home, and I still hadn't found a solution to the dilemma of his infatuation.

Young Stockton was perched on a stool by the sink, three cookies stacked on one of his patched knees and a mug of goat's milk raised to his mouth. He made a face at me over its rim, swallowed with a gulp, and wiped his lips. "Well, Alis?"

I grinned at the throaty up-and-down cadence of his changing voice and snatched one of the cookies. "Well?"

"Have you got anything for me to take up Ashby-way?"

"I have. Two letters to Lord Grosvenor"—I laid them on the table with a wink—"and a letter from myself to Lord Humphries."

"Is old Humphries going to help you, then?" Stockton stowed the letters for the younger lord in his leather bag and stared at the sealed note I offered. A beam of sunlight from the window above the sink ran through his red hair and lit the freckles across his pale face.

I kissed the letter to Lord Humphries with a prayer and handed it to Stockton. "He has agreed to help in any way he can, and since I found that not a single Bickersnath Carlisle has ever lived or died in the kingdom . . ."

"Never one?" Stockton stuffed the last cookie in his mouth and slid off the stool. "You're just building your army, ain't you? First me and Ellen, now Humphries."

"I wrote to Lord Humphries a month ago, setting forth my ideas of a claim to the throne."

"And did the old mumbler gobble it?"

"He did." I tucked a loose strand of hair behind my ear and took a bucket of eggshells and vegetable peelings to the doorway, flinging them to the chickens around the stoop.

Stockton tossed the strap of his leather bag over his shoulder. "What did you write in this letter?"

I had worked on the letter late into the night and could have quoted its entirety for Stockton had we the time. "I told him that my alleged father, Bickersnath Carlisle, had never existed. I told him that I would be eager to examine any evidence in my favor that could, perhaps, point the way to my rights. I told him that I would need . . . help."

"Why would Humphries want to help *you*? You've got no claim to him."

"No." My heart plummeted with the risk I'd taken. "But William has claim by virtue of being Lord Humphries's nephew. And I'm afraid . . ."

Stockton lowered his brow. "What did you do stupid, Alis?"

"I asked William for his help."

"In claimin' your rights?"

"No!" I cast a nervous eye over the several entries to the kitchen, afraid William might be lurking in one of them. "I told William nothing except that I would like to correspond with Lord Humphries about certain points of the law I did not understand."

"And William wasn't suspicious?"

I held my breath and offered another prayer that, please God, he was not. "William thinks me amusing and was all too glad to recommend me to Lord Humphries as 'a fine little woman.'"

"Did he say that to your face?"

"If only."

Stockton flashed his impish, knowing smile. "Alis, you steamed the seal open and read William's letter before sending it, didn't you?"

I felt my face go hot. Stockton was too keen. "And was I supposed to let him write to his uncle accusing me of treason? 'Lord Bickersnath Carlisle' is an invention, but who invented him? For years I have been stowed away as an orphan, put *here* by someone who did not want me to keep the throne. If Laureldina and William suspect me of plotting anything, they won't expect me to fly into danger's face."

"Danger's face?" Stockton ground his boot in a bit of flour spilled on the floor. "I'm not following."

I tried to sort the mayhem of my brain. "Let's suppose I am who we think."

"Right."

"That means I was deposited here as a *baby*. Laureldina was considered trustworthy enough to keep me—heaven help the man who made *that* mistake! The story says she made a third unfortunate marriage in my widowed father. This would account for my presence, would it not?" I backed into the doorway, ticking the points on my fingertips.

"Aye . . ."

"Oh, Stockton, you aren't listening."

"I *am* listenin'! But you're going on so long and complicated, I can't keep up with you!"

Still standing in the doorway, I folded my arms and leaned my forehead against the low lintel, feeling the whole world teetering. "I was given up. For some reason Laureldina took me. She must be aware of who I am and, having concealed it this far, must mean to continue to conceal it forevermore. If she thought I knew anything, would she expect me to reach further into the family, contacting her uncle to aid me?"

"No . . ." Stockton drawled his reply as if still muddled and only trying to give the answer I desired.

I pushed away from the doorframe, fingers pressed against my temples to still the dizziness. "Well, I am safe. For now."

"Safe from what?"

William's sudden, lazy voice sent a jolt up my spine, and I wished for one moment that I was the kind of girl who fainted.

CHAPTER 2

THE EARLIEST tinge of autumn spread over field and wood, and the hounds would soon be rallying for a foxhunt. Pheasant and quail would hide in the hayricks, and every brook forget its summer stupor and chuckle in a self-satisfied manner as it danced over rocky streambeds. All nature was alive and beautiful and free.

Except the one man who was to rule it all.

"Prince Auguste, if you would only attend."

Auguste shoved off the stone windowsill with a moan. "I don't want to *attend*, Belkin." He ran a hand through his black, wild hair till it stood further on end. "I don't want to *hear* about the state of my nation or listen to one more suggestion of a suitable wife or do anything that is my duty. I'm a man, Belkin, not a pig-headed scarecrow."

"Such language, Your Highness!"

"Hang my language!" Auguste snapped. "And hang you, Belkin."

The secretary blinked from behind his glasses. "Do you mean that, Your Highness?"

Auguste crossed his arms and offered a wry smile. "I think I do." He made the mistake of looking out the window again onto the rich oil-painting of field and forest. "Oh, *blast* it. Do you know what I want to do? No, you would not guess; you're much too refined." With a quick step Auguste grabbed Belkin by the jacket and shoved him toward the window, pressing the man's nose against the pane. "I want to go out there and find myself a plump village lass and kiss her—hard. Y'understand? I want to dig my hands in a furrow and bring up a fistful of potatoes and . . . and cook them myself. I want to ride Feather-Fellow at a gallop and risk breaking my neck if I take a fancy for it, and I want to miss every cabinet-meeting from here till kingdom come!"

Belkin wriggled out of Auguste's grasp and adjusted his spectacles with a pale finger. "Now, Your Highness, let's not get ourselves into a foul humor."

Auguste raised one eyebrow and stifled a sigh, lapsing into the royal speech: "We are not in a foul humor, Belkin. We are in a corrupt-tempered mood. There is a difference, you know."

"Is there?"

"There blasted better be."

"Your Highness, if you would only attend—"

"*Belkin!*" Auguste put every crumb of his considerable frustration into that bellow, and the mouse-colored secretary trembled under the weight of it. Smiling a bit wickedly, Auguste patted the man's shoulder. "We only want you to know that nothing you can say or do will make a difference. You might save your breath, or we'll have to consider this prospect of having you hanged."

"Very well." Belkin made a desperate effort at a display of authority. "I shall have to inform your father of this unseemly outburst."

"Do," Auguste said, feeling pettish in the extreme. "Then he might have an 'unseemly outburst' himself, and we'll all be in perfect agreement."

"You are twenty-four years old, my prince. You ought to start behaving like a king." Belkin's face was even paler than usual, which was quite an accomplishment.

Auguste cast his himself into a red chair and crossed his legs. "Tut-tut, Belkin. That could be construed as an assassination plot. My *father* is the king."

"And you will be someday—if you aren't killed beforehand for being a bone-headed woodpecker."

Auguste clapped his hands, stood, and made a bow. "Bravo, Belkin. Standing up in the face of supreme royalty? I should have thought you'd have fainted before daring to do such a thing. I only wish you would—Oh, hang the fellow. He *has* fainted."

So saying, Auguste dragged Belkin to the doorway and called down the hall, "Someone! You there, soldier. Come get the man. He's fainted."

A clattering fool in pie-pan armor bent to administer smelling salts. Auguste pulled on a fistful of his hair again, wondering what he ought to do. He was feeling giddy himself, what with the closeness of the hall and Belkin stretched pale and senseless on the sweating stone floor.

He needed a ride on Feather-Fellow, that's what. Auguste saluted the soldier with two fingers, turned on his heel, and exited his chamber by a side staircase—one of many secreted in the castle walls like providential rat tunnels. He wanted to go riding and, if at all possible, never return.

CHAPTER 3

A FTER THAT unfortunate episode of William walking in on the conference between me and Stockton, I thought it best to refrain from letter-writing and had Stockton deliver a *verbal* message to Lord Humphries that all communication between us should be finished until he heard otherwise.

We were scheduled to travel as a family from Cock-on-Stylingham to Weircannon, the capitol of Ashby, at the end of the month. I would no doubt see Lord Humphries in person while we were in town for the Season, and he could attach a face to this bold schemer playing with the crown.

I was little troubled by the thought of my treason: Ashbians are never over-particular about their loyalties. As far as they're concerned, one monarch is as good as another provided taxes don't rise. In addition, I was doing them rather a favor by booting that swarthy imposter off his *regia solia.* Satisfied, I went about the yearly business of the Season's preparations in as good a humor as one could wish.

This lasted one week.

"I hope Lord Grosvenor breaks your hearts!"

I ran downstairs, fleeing my stepsisters' company, bundling the gowns they'd flung at me. William met me as usual at the foot of the stairs, but this time I was grateful when he eased the heap of dresses from my tired arms into his own.

He clutched the bundle to his chest and gave me his loose fool's grin. "Why're you smiling like that, Alis-mine?"

I shook my head and took the gowns from him. "You look like a tomcat gone to play in the laundry line. News might get around that you're a washerwoman, then where'd you be?"

"In no less of a ruddy hash than I am now."

I seemed to have stolen William's confidence. He ran his fingers over his cheek with a preoccupied hum then put a hand against my back and steered me toward the end of the hall, out toward the wash house.

"Alis, it's a horrid business," he said in a despondent and confidential tone. "Laureldina insists I'm married by the Prince's birthday; or I've at least chosen my wife."

He looked so stricken I began to feel sorry for him.

I steadied the pile of silks in one arm and squeezed his shoulder. "Don't be a goose; someone will have you." We were all accustomed to my stepmother's whims; if she wanted William married by October twenty-first, so be it. "You must make shift as you can, I suppose."

As we walked, a plan burbled in my flow of thought like the shallow bends in the streams that fed River Lin. I wanted to make my claim to the throne sometime before Prince Auguste's birthday, which would double as his ceremony of accession. An extra day in Weircannon would only pave my way smoother. A week would help enormously.

Hope buoyed the rest of my steps to the wash house. William stayed outside, one hand pressed against the low stone lintel, his face speckled with shadows from the alder tree.

I tossed the gowns over a rack and returned to him. "Listen, old fellow—"

"You've got that clever look in your eye. Tell me what the deuce I'm to do, pretty Alis."

Though the words presented flirtation, they lacked assurance. I gave William a smile and picked a few leaves off the alder, rubbing them between my fingers. "If you persuaded your mother to leave early, there would be an extra fortnight for courting the lasses," I said.

William tugged his eyebrow. "Alis, you're the only one I want, you know that. Can't y'do something?"

I tossed the leaves aside. "You can't have me, William, so there's no use pressing there."

He shoved off the wash house and kicked at the turf. "I wish I were the prince."

My heart flipped at the word *prince*. "Why the blazes?"

"'Cuz I'd not have trouble finding a wife. *You'd* marry me if I were prince, wouldn't you?" His brows drew together in a churlish look. "*You'd* take my hand."

My only desire as far as the prince was concerned was to give him a rousing kick in the *derrière*. I contemplated kicking William instead, but that would hardly put him in a temper to agree to going to town at the earlier date.

I thrust my chin in the air to make a point of how little I cared. "I should *not* take your hand. You know me, William! If you were the prince, I should take your throne. A crown fits better than a ring any day."

Realizing how close I'd come to confessing my plans, I knocked my stepbrother under the chin. "Don't fret, old bean. You're handsome enough and decently rich. Girls don't usually worry over the dose of brains."

It had been a mistake to come that close to him. William wrapped his arms around my waist and pulled me close, resting his chin on my head. "Alis, what's a man to do?"

Struggle was useless. I folded my wings like a stubborn bird and made my head as much like a stone as possible. "Do about what? Ask Laureldina for the extra two weeks. We'll go up to Weircannon. All will be well. Your sisters know lots of people. I'm sure they could find you a nice girl." My voice sounded rather squashed, my face pressed against William's chest as it was.

William released me and pushed me ahead of him toward the house. "I don't know. Girls don't like my sisters, y'know. Men-trouble and all that."

"Oh." *God bless them.* I had forgotten the girls' vicious reputation as beau-stealers. "Whatever you do, William, don't fret. Demand those two weeks and"—I might as well try my own strategy here—"if the deadline looms, I'll find you a scullery maid and dress her in silk, and you can present her at court. No one would know the difference." *I pray most fervently, Lord.*

William's lazy eyes shone inquisitive blue. "Bless you, Alis; you are a clever girl." He laughed to himself and threw an arm around my waist.

I swiftly moved out of reach, speaking lightly, "I try."

"Could you try to love me?"

I hurried toward the kitchen on the south side of the house. "Afraid not; standards and all that."

William took a couple of leaping steps ahead of me then turned, both eyebrows raised. "You have standards?"

"I've heard people do."

"Aye, but you're a *maid.*"

"The only thing that divides me from the rest of the world is my occupation. Clean me up, dress me in silk, and *I* could steal the prince's heart."

He drew close. "You've stolen mine."

I ducked into the safety of the kitchen, pushing a surprised Ellen in front of me as a guard. "How clumsy of me! Remember, I don't deal in hearts—diamonds, yes. Have you diamonds? Then please leave me alone and ask Laureldina for those two weeks."

William went into the main hallway off the kitchen, shaking his head. He turned and saluted me. "Alis, you're a marvel. I'll do it, by Ashby: I'll find myself a wife."

"That's the stuff. A wife." And the sooner the better if he didn't want a blackened eye.

CHAPTER 4

I DRAGGED the last of the girls' trunks into the house at Weircannon and thanked God Laureldina had agreed to William's pleas for more time. Not that I hadn't paid for my brainchild—sleep, of which my body requires little, had vacated my life for the last ten days—but here we were now, and no harrowed, slumberless nights could dampen my spirit.

The cabman took his fare, and I slammed the door on the city street, gold-specked as it was with lanterns here and there. Time enough for the beauties of the royal city later. Now, I must help Ellen get Laureldina's infernal tea and feed her obese cat a bowl of liver paste sent up by Lord Grosvenor.

The house in Portfellow Street was one of those residences one finds within cities where convenience buckles to the owners' sense of fashion. I took the six turns of the kitchen staircase.

"Charlotte Russe!" I yelled for the cat and took the last two steps as one. The kitchen was bare and at-odds, wearing that affronted expression of a room left empty for six months. Charlotte Russe waddled to my feet and batted the hem of my skirt as if to demand solace after being deposited unceremoniously in a basement kitchen by a dirty cabman who swore and smelled like sardines. Shoving her away, I dumped the liver paste onto a white china plate and clacked it on the flagstone floor. "Compliments of a trifling reprobate. I hope *you* enjoy it—your mistresses seem to find anything *a la Grosvenor* delicious."

"Has her royal highness stooped to talking to the cat?" Ellen squeezed out of the small pantry and reached out to me for a hug.

I wrapped her plump frame in my long arms, resting my head on her gray topknot. "I can't believe we're here." I laughed nervously and pulled away, hugging myself now. "I have just three weeks to discover why I was dumped and how I can make my claim for the throne. Lord Humphries will help me." *I pray.* "But Ellen, it might not work."

"I've known that since the start. Hadn't you thought of it?"

"I prefer to assume myself right till proven wrong." Finding my hands shaking, I busied them with prying open wooden crates and distributing the contents throughout the kitchen. "How will I ever pass for a princess?"

"You don't have to pass for one. You *are* a princess."

"Yes, and wouldn't that be a joke: show up at the royal birthday feast in these rags, making social blunders right and left."

Ellen took the precarious stack of crystal saltcellars from my trembling hands, and pulled my face downwards. "Alis, you haven't much to go on, but if you are meant to rule, then rule you will. Neither man nor throne in this world can stand against the plans of our blessed Lord."

"I know." I took the tea tray from one of the crates and slammed it too hard on the butcher-block table. "I wish I had a fairy godmother. Taking the throne would work like a charm."

"And you'd lose half the pleasure of it. You should listen to an old woman: A fairy wand has never done anything money can't."

"You'll recall I'm a pauper." I reminded her.

Ellen scoffed. "You're a king's daughter! You'll have plenty of money come your crowning time. Lord Humphries'll lend you whatever you need in the meanwhile, if you ask him for it. Simple logic."

I leaned against the table, hands pressed on the cool wood, and stared at Ellen. "You are a conniving devil!"

She shrugged her shoulders. "I'm a woman . . . which is much the same thing."

"It is a brilliant scheme, really now."

Another shrug, and her black eyes snapped with intelligence and humor. "Just give me the tea things and get yourself to writing letters. Lord Humphries will be needing to make haste if you're to be outfitted in time. And when are we going to meet this high-and-mighty coxcomb?"

"Laureldina is having him to dinner Wednesday."

Ellen dug both fists into her hips. "Joy and jubilation. I suppose she'll want a grand to-do?"

I sighed. "Three courses at *least*."

Ellen pointed a knife at me with a warning eye. "You'll be helping serve. You're not a princess yet, for all your aspirations."

CHAPTER 5

AUGUSTE TIPPED his glass to one side and watched petals of wine furl from the rim. He did not want to look up at his father, because acknowledging his presence would mean a reconvening of conversational doomsday: marriage. The one and only topic on which kingdom business currently bungled.

"Auguste, it's no use. We'll have it out now."

His father's brisk tones brought Auguste to a straighter position, and he fastened his eyes on the king's lean, intelligent face. "As you say."

King Henri rose and clasped his long, thin hands behind him, pacing the floor before the breakfast table. "I don't wish to be awkward, but seems to me you're playing the bally pouting child."

Auguste rubbed his eyes and pushed the wine goblet away, feeling the tax this whole business was taking on him. "Is it such a terrible thing to want a *normal* life?"

"The people haven't given you a normal life," his father said. "They've chosen us as kings."

"And I suppose it's their business?" Auguste spat.

His father ran his lean hand over his lips, interrupting the start of a smile. "It is their *right*. No, don't argue whether it's a wise *system*. Wise or not, it is ours to abide by. I'll warrant a nation's happiness depends less on the wisdom of its system than on the wisdom of its ruler."

Auguste growled low in his throat. "Then it's my duty to be a cunning leader and dispense with my dreams of a simple life in order to save our heads from a mob of displeased subjects?"

Henri's chin jutted as he laughed. "Duty and dreams are so often mistaken for each other."

"Is that supposed to make me feel tolerant of the kingship?" Auguste asked.

"You could try."

"Mmm." Auguste's wry smile came before he had a chance to smother it.

Henri pointed a finger at him. "Ahhh, you see my point, don't you? The crown is not just homage and glory. It's a trade itself. The carpenter has his hammer and nails, the sculptor his chisels, the merchant his ships . . ." His voice trailed off in a thoughtful pause. "And we our thrones," he resumed. "A funny business, but I was born to it."

"And me?" Auguste scraped his initials with his thumbnail into the wooden tabletop. "Why do I lack your passion?"

"You're a Blenheim," Henri said with a wink. "A stubborn fool."

With a sigh, Auguste hauled himself out of the chair and clapped his father on the shoulder. "I wish I had your courage." He laughed, a bitter enough sound. "I seem to have inherited will without valor. Quite frankly, the idea of being locked up in this castle with servants watching every move I make gives me the creeping ghosts."

Henri laughed. "It's for your own good. As is a *wife*."

"Excellent segue."

"Your Accession is in three weeks. Find a sweet girl and marry her. Give them a bit of pageant and a future queen." King Henri's mouth eased into a lopsided smile. "All will be well."

Auguste knew his father considered the topic closed. He watched King Henri leave the breakfast room and wished to high heaven that he could *want* the crown.

But when an inconclusive cough from the hallway heralded the approach of Belkin, Auguste's blood rebelled. He would not live his life under the public eye with every movement recorded in the royal chronicles for posterity. And he was currently far from interested in one of Belkin's motivational speeches on how overcoming one's fears was the way to manhood.

Stuffing one muffin in his mouth and a second in his pocket, Auguste slipped into a side passage and away. He'd just take a wander 'round the city and hope some assassin made a merciful move.

CHAPTER 6

I DID as Ellen told me, and my heart dared hope again. There was nothing left but to wait and trust that Lord Humphries was rich enough to gamble his money on my ability to take my throne. I'm sure he'd wagered it on more useless things in the past.

It was three o'clock on Tuesday when the doorbell rang. I knew destiny and treason were on the other end of the bell rope, but those aren't things you rush toward as if you were glad to see them; you're likely to end with your neck in a noose.

These thoughts playing herald to the summons, I removed my apron in dead calmness and hung it on the coat peg, then wrenched open the door. Bright, city sunlight glared into my eyes, and I had a hard time seeing the person on the steps.

"Message from Lord Humphries, miss," a voice said. Through the blaze

I could make out a red feather curled over a purple velvet hat and a fat face adorned with a bit of mustache.

"I'll take it," I said.

"It's for Lady Alisandra Carlisle, miss."

"I'll take it."

"For her hands only, miss."

By now my eyes had adjusted to the white light, and I glared at the fat man on the doorstep; he was so short as to require me to tilt my chin downward. "If you must know, *I* am Alisandra Carlisle. What have you for me?"

The jowls quivered like an unstable blancmange, and two beady eyes took the measure of me. At last the man put a plump hand into his pocket and brought it back out grasping a velvet sack and a letter.

I grabbed the sack, and my pulse quickened at its weight and the dull clink. These were not silver coins; Lord Humphries had lent me gold.

"Any reply?" the messenger asked.

"A moment, Sir Imperative." I broke the heavy amber-colored wax and unfolded a single sheet upon which were scrawled the following words:

Lady Carlisle: For the love of king and country, don't delay. Or, in your case, for the hatred *of king and* astonishment *of country, make haste. Women are expensive; hence, I have never kept one. There should be enough money here to supply you with a dress or two and a bit of lace. Jewelry too. Don't look shabby; I hate shabby women, as do all anarchists. I expect to see you Wednesday when I attend your stepmother at dinner. You will be present and you will have made your purchases. That is all.*

Until I See Fit to Excuse Myself,

   Lord Humphries

I folded the note with a quick glance at the messenger. "You may tell his lordship I thank him and am his humble servant always."

The man nodded, turned on his heel, and waddled away to a cart and pony waiting in the street. Emblazoned on the side were what I knew to be Lord Humphries's arms: a sleeping cobra harassed by a flock of blackbirds, one large bird leading the attack. The cobra, I supposed, was the King, and the head of the flock, Humphries of Sandisturn: a house notorious for leading Ashbians in their frequent bouts of anarchy.

Watching the pony cart wheel away in the dazzle of sunlight, it seemed to me I'd done right to choose this man as my ally, for he was bred for mischief-making. I needed a man of this temperament on my side.

I needed a flock if I was to crush the serpent.

Wednesday, the day appointed for Laureldina's dinner, dawned bright and fair with a hum of pigeon wings and cartwheels filling the streets.

I left the house by a back street and breathed deeply the scents of baking bread and steaming carriage horses, trodden hay, and the fermented-apple undertones of manure. All these scents were familiar to me from Cock-on-Stylingham, and it was a pleasant reminder that I was still in possession of a bit of my normal world.

I made short work of the maze of back streets and, before the tower clock showed eight-thirty, had gained the shopping district of Weircannon. Though I'd come uptown every year with Laureldina and her daughters, I had more often than not been relegated to housework and had seen very little of the city. Still, not prone to timidity, I was confident that I could accomplish my goal of setting up as a Society girl.

I paused a moment to fix the neckline of the blue gown I'd taken from the girls' wardrobe. It was too short in the waist, too large in the bust, but Ellen had pinned me here and there until I looked presentable.

With a smile and a deep breath I stepped into the first shop, setting off an officious bell. A pale, pinched-in woman emerged from her lair behind the counter. She smiled at first, but the expression froze over, and I could see her mind at work behind the icy glaze.

"I am here to be fitted for several gowns," I said, raising my voice so it was not so throaty and making an effort to conduct the words at a drawl. "La, but it's a beautiful morning. I had thought to do my shopping before anyone came abroad. The crush is *suffocating.*"

The woman presented a tape-measure and a vicious pincushion. "Indeed, Lady . . . ?"

"Carlisle." I thought against extending my hand and yawned. "Egad, but it is early, though."

The woman smiled. "Never too early to serve m'lady. I do not recall seeing you before. Are you a great traveler?"

Curiosity will kill you yet, old cat. "La, *all* over. My uncle, Lord Humphries, thinks it a prerequisite for accomplished women." In my mind I defined "all over" as the width and breadth of Cock-on-Stylingham, in which case I lied not.

"Your uncle is Lord Humphries?"

"Does it trouble you?"

She paused with a strange smile. "None, m'lady—though I have never heard him mention your name."

What had I done, claiming Lord Humphries as my uncle? I skirted the unspoken questions with a giddy laugh. "Does he frequent this shop?"

"He does. My husband is the tailor; I do the fancywork. We specialize in men's *and* women's clothing." Her eyes were sharp and inquisitive, and I all but saw the end of her nose twitch like a rat's.

"How very modern." I closed my eyes for a second and prayed Lord Humphries would not take it into his head to pop into his favorite tailor's for a morning fitting. We had yet to meet, my co-conspirator and I. How awkward.

I yawned again, hoping to disguise any betrayal of nerves. "If we could proceed with the measurements, I should be grateful. I have only just arrived on the continent and have many more errands."

The shopkeeper took my measurements, and I gave directions for three day dresses and one ball gown to be made up according to her taste. The total sum due the woman frightened me, but I found that "Uncle" Humphries's cash was more than adequate. Bless the old traitor; he'd dealt me a generous hand.

Assured that the gowns would be ready and delivered by the end of this week or the beginning of next, I continued on my way.

Each shopkeeper stared at me in the same glazed fashion, and I soon recalled that my greatest claim to the throne was how very much I looked like the royals. What a puzzle for Weircannon. Far from feeling at ease with this notoriety, I finished my errands in haste.

Hands occupied with my purchases, I shuffled the lid from the topmost box. Nestled inside was a pair of blue slippers and a receipt for the order of another pair to be formed in glass to my particular measurements. I had not forgotten how much Clarisse hated the sight of my feet. I wanted to see her eyes when I descended a staircase in those glorified rowboats.

Congratulating myself on my clever jest, I turned down a side street and from the corner of my vision saw Stockton barreling toward me on a pony cart.

"Alis, move!" he shouted. They were but ten yards away. Stockton jerked the reins to steer away from me and shouted to his pony, but it was too late for me to contemplate grace and dignity. I threw my purchases onto the sidewalk and leaped after them, not caring if I ended face-down on the flagstones so long as I escaped getting trampled by Stockton & Kin.

They flashed by in a blur of yellow wheels as I fell, but rather than rough stones cutting into my face, my landing place was . . . human.

I opened my eyes and found my cheek pillowed on the waistcoat of an unshaven, wild-haired young man.

"Forgive me." My voice had gone throaty again. Of all the stupid things to do, colliding with handsome gentlemen was the stupidest.

"No harm done. Are *you* well?"

I refused to look at the man as I pushed myself upright, focusing instead on Stockton, who had managed to stop his cart farther down the street and now ran toward me. "I am not hurt," I muttered gracelessly, brushing off my skirts, and flashed a timorous glance at my savior.

Stockton grabbed me by both shoulders. "Alis! Oh, Alis, you've got to be more careful. You're lucky you're not dead by now, or at least bleeding."

Humor flowed in as the shame flowed out. "No, my fall was cushioned by a gallant knight." I gestured toward the young man who had, by now, got to his feet.

He made a bow and smiled, though without looking me in the eye, and then set about picking up my boxes. Somehow this bashfulness on his part put me at ease. "At your service, dear lady," he said. "I hope always to be conveniently near when princesses collide with cart-horse dragons."

My heart skipped three beats at the word *princess*, but I realized he could not know who I really was. When he straightened from gathering my packages, I took a good look at his face. My heart thudded once more, and this time I felt sick before it beat again.

"Prince Auguste."

He jumped at the name as if scared of it and gave a shame-faced smile, still not meeting my eye. "I had hoped I might go unnoticed, not being in the palace and all."

This was not how I'd planned our meeting. I gathered my hair back into a bun. "I'm afraid you're a terrible hand at making yourself inconspicuous, standing on street corners just waiting for hapless girls to fall into your arms. What *do* they teach young men these days?"

Auguste's eyes snapped to my face, and immediately the blood rushed into his cheeks. "Jove," he breathed. "You . . . you . . ."

I bridled. "If you're going to stare at me like a pickled herring, have the good courtesy to tell me why."

He swallowed, and a muscle twitched in his cheek. "My apologies, but you . . ." He blushed redder and kicked the cobbles with the toe of his boot. "You look just like my father."

Stockton's face was the incarnate image of tragedy, eyes pleading, jaw slack as if to say, *The game's up.*

I tapped Auguste on the shoulder and smiled at a passing cab driver so we might not look like a trio in the throes of a political drama of national importance. "Perhaps we'd better continue this discourse elsewhere. And one comment if I may: You haven't an inkling how to speak to a woman."

CHAPTER 7

AUGUSTE STARED at the tall, thin girl who so resembled his father. He tried to suppress the urge to laugh. He had rather hoped not to meet anyone that morning, preferring to dwell on his depression without the bore of exerting himself socially. But he'd never thought to meet someone who looked for all the world like she'd stepped down from the Hall of Portraits just to jerk him into an alleyway.

"Are you enjoying it?" she asked, a taut edge to her voice.

"Enjoying what?"

Her eyes bored into him like gimlets, and he watched the lad beside her tense as if waiting for the girl to explode. "The *throne*," she spat.

Auguste stretched his arms and tipped his head from one side to the other to loosen the muscles in his neck. "The throne? Deuces, no."

"Oh."

She sounded disappointed, and Auguste looked at her with fresh curiosity. "Who are you?"

"That isn't the proper way to introduce yourself to a lady," she said.

He smirked. "No, but I don't suppose it's *proper* for a lady to throw a gentleman to the ground and land with her head pillowed on the fellow's chest."

The girl straightened, chin high, shoulders back, until she stood a good inch taller than he did. She was the picture of scornful indignation. "Next time I'll just let myself be flattened by an out-of-control vehicle, and you can mop up the mess afterward. I bleed quarts when injured."

A short laugh exploded from the depths of Auguste's belly, surprising even him. "Well played, my lady. Is there a point to this interview, or may I resume my mournful wanderings in peace?" She was uncanny, this girl with his father's eyes and that regal snap to her movements.

Some uncertainty seemed to occupy her mind for a moment, and while she wavered, Auguste considered all the strange qualities and questions of this meeting. One: It happened in broad daylight when such things never do occur. Two: It happened outside of the palace, certainly an oddity amid his typical social experiences. Three: The girl obviously had Blenheim blood and, if so, what sort of relation was she? And why had they never met before?

Four: What was he to do with her now?

By the shifting of her position and the pucker of her thick brows, Auguste knew that she had come to some decision. He clasped his hands behind his back, feet apart, and waited for her words.

"I am the Lady Alisandra Carlisle." Her eyes appraised him, and a flush rose in her cheeks. "I don't expect you've heard of me. It's a recent title."

"Then you're *married*." It came out as a statement rather than a question. Shocked by a keen sense of disappointment, Auguste could have bitten his tongue for speaking his thoughts so bluntly.

Lady Alis laughed. "Good heavens, no. I'm not the sort of thing people go around marrying." Her cheeks grew even redder, and Auguste thought he would be rather inclined to contradict her statement if all men felt as he did. There was something delightfully uncouth about her—something in her coltish stance and the way she moved her hands that sent a surge through his body. *Keep your wits, fool.*

Auguste ran his tongue over the inside of his cheek. "Lady Alisan—"

"Alis." She offered a chummy smile. "Everyone calls me Alis."

"Lady Alis, you must tell me about yourself. I know it's rude of me, but I do terribly want to know how we're related. You're so obviously kin."

"To you?" The question was loaded with hidden meaning, and Auguste wished he were clever enough to figure out what she meant by it.

"Look, I don't know who you are or what sort of charade you're playing, but there's not a person in Ashby who could put you and my father side by side and say you weren't blood relatives. Who are you, then? I've never heard of the House of Carlisle in relation to my family. What are your arms?"

Lady Alis shifted, her eyes revealing a momentary loss of poise. "It's . . . not really a *house.* More like . . . a gypsy wagon? We don't have a coat of arms."

More confused than ever, Auguste waited.

Lady Alis patted the shoulder of the lanky boy beside her and deposited her packages in his arms. "You'd better run along, Stockton. Ellen will be missing my help with the tea trays. Put these in the kitchen. I'll be along soon." She spoke in a low voice, but Auguste heard.

Stockton pushed back a shock of pumpkin-colored hair and looked at him. "Good luck t'you." He ran down the alley and climbed into the pony cart on the other side of the dust-dim street, rattling off a moment later.

Auguste now took a sweeping view of his companion, wondering. Tea trays and gypsy wagons? The girl was a riddle from one end to the other. It was evident she had not spent much time in Weircannon, else they would have met at the parties his mother held every Season.

Auguste rumpled his hair and followed Lady Alis, who had taken a stalking course farther down the alleyway. He wanted to say the clever things princes usually said when meeting fair cousins, but his mind was a cat's cradle of impertinent questions he didn't think she'd answer. Maybe if he began on the topic of mutual friends.

Dash it all! He'd never been fond of *any* of the people introduced to him at court and could think of no one about whom he could inquire. The only person he *really* liked was bombastic Lord Humphries and him only because years ago he used to take Auguste aside and make comical criticisms of the cabinet members while feeding him lozenges.

Auguste had always liked those lozenges.

"Do you know Lord Humphries?" he asked as they neared the termination of the alley.

Alis turned with a relieved smile and bounced on the ends of her toes. "*Yes.*" An emphatic statement. This was progress.

"Oh, jolly. Do you like him?" *Idiot. People aren't compelled to like their acquaintances.*

That worried pucker came back to her brows, but she laughed and flicked her hands. "He's my uncle. Good, dear Uncle Humphries."

Good, *dear* Uncle Humphries? She didn't sound like she knew him at all. Of course she could be one of those nieces who stayed conveniently out of the way most of her life, but a suspicion took up residence in Auguste's mind that perhaps this Lady Alis with her tea carts and gypsy wagons wasn't quite what she made herself out to be.

"Did he give you lozenges too?" Auguste masked a shrewd smile by feeling his jaw.

"Oh yes."

Liar. "What flavor?" He presented his most roguish smile and rolled his fingers. "I always forget."

Lady Alis bent her head. "Lemon, I think."

Auguste clapped his hands. "Peppermint. Why do you lie?"

"I'm not lying," she countered. "*My* lozenges *were* peppermint—I mean . . . lemon?" She ended in a pleading question.

"You are dealing with the royal prince, you realize."

"Don't I know it." The crackle mounted in her eyes, and she started off down another alley angling toward town.

Auguste kept just a step behind the girl like a herding dog. "Why are we doing this? Either you are a singular flirt wanting to get me down a back alley for some childish romantic reason or you know something I don't and refuse to tell me."

"You're clever," Lady Alis said, turning her head just far enough that Auguste could see her distinct profile. "Not as . . ."

He kept one step behind her, enjoying the sensation of protecting something, though in all honesty there was nothing from which to protect her. "Not as . . . ?" he prompted.

"Bad as I expected. Or as ugly."

"What sort of venom did they breed into you? Oh, I forgot. You're a *Blenheim.* Deny it if you will, but I know."

She gave him a curious, intelligent look. "As much as it pains me to notice, you're actually—"

"Decent?" he supplied.

Lady Alis nodded. They emerged back into the shopping district, and Auguste saw her stiffen. Her eyes focused someplace distant.

"What is it?"

Alis had gone pale and she drifted away. "I must go. Laureldina and the girls. I—it's just—Oh, *goodbye*, Your Highness. I'm sorry again for crashing into you!"

"And laying me out like a corpse."

"That too."

She had taken his hand in hers, and Auguste realized that it felt perfectly natural and pleasant to let her hold it. He twined his fingers through hers and squeezed. "Must you go just now?" He didn't want this strange and fascinating girl to leave. Not when they'd just started to get along.

She squeezed his hand. "I really must. Goodbye."

She dropped a curtsy, gave a salute, dashed down the alley, and was gone, leaving Auguste to wonder at all he'd been missing by staying in the castle all these years.

CHAPTER 8

LAURELDINA ONLY bludgeoned my head slightly when she came home from their shopping expedition and complained of my absence. Evidently she had not seen me with Prince Auguste when I glimpsed her from the end of the alley. I answered her questions with honesty: I was shopping for a new gown because she couldn't expect me to live in squalor my entire life if she ever hoped to be rid of me. I deserved my chance to find a husband as much as her daughters. Furthermore, I wanted to be present tonight when Lord Humphries came to have dinner with the family.

Laureldina laughed in her scornful way but otherwise made no protest.

I went upstairs a half hour before Lord Humphries's scheduled arrival and pulled my battered travel case from the foot of the bed. Inside was a cast-off dress from Clarisse, altered and mended ages ago to make an almost-presentable gown. It glowed insipid mauve in the light of the tallow candle. The color was atrocious, but I took the gown from the trunk and laid it out, straightening the old lace here and there where it had been crumpled.

Beneath the dress was a framed ink drawing of Prince Auguste's face, clipped from a newspaper ages ago. This I kept on my basin-stand at Cock-on-Stylingham, accustomed to lecturing it *ad infinitum* on my worst days. Now, as I turned it to the candlelight, I was able to see the points in which the face was far nobler than I'd ever before been willing to admit. The brow was heavy but loyal, and I had seen the stony mouth form a wry grin several times. And yes, though I had tried to erase it from my memory, I still felt his strong hand shaking mine, like a pleasant, troubling ghost.

I tossed the frame back inside and slammed the lid. I could not *like* the man when I'd sworn to depose him.

"You are going to take his throne, you recall," I muttered. But though Auguste's portrait was now face-downward in a dank chest, the essence of him danced in my head with maddening clarity; a rogue wearing *my* crown with a grin that made it impossible to hate him. A grin that attracted me.

And what did he mean by saying he was *not* enjoying the throne? Could it be that he would volunteer his crown without a brawl? Only a madman would do it.

"I don't care," I reminded myself and wriggled into the unappealing remodeled gown. "I shall take the throne whether or not I am in love with Auguste."

In love with him? I astonished myself. My reflection in the speckled mirror by the door showed my eyes round and concerned. I couldn't love him. I didn't believe in love at first sight. And even though knocking a man prostrate, arguing, and laughing was not an ordinary how-d'you-do, I refused to acknowledge the idea. I was Alisandra Carlisle, a girl with her wits about her. I couldn't fall in love with just anyone, and certainly not at first sight. I was not living in a fairytale.

I reached over my shoulders to button the dress, tied the sash in an anemic bow and stepped into my new slippers. I looked nearly presentable, and Lord Humphries would just have to grin and bear it if he was displeased with the "heir" on whom he'd pegged his money. I might explain that the dresses I ordered were not ready-made, and I had not worn this atrocity through fondness for it.

Nothing further to do. I left my room and joined Ellen downstairs.

"Are you wearing that thing to dinner?" She wrinkled her nose. Drips from the soup spoon ran onto the cobbled floor.

"Nothing better till the dresses come. And I do hope that snobby tailoress stabs herself with a needle for each of her insinuations. I hate people who insinuate."

Ellen only laughed and began ladling the soup into a tureen. "I heard Lord Humphries come in the door. He'll be upstairs now, and I only hope he's colorblind; looks like you've got ague."

"Thank you, Ellen-Best, for that confidence, but as there really is no remedy for fashion tragedies, I shall hope along with you. I wouldn't want Lord Humphries to think he'd financed a chronically ill upstart."

"You've only got to start talking. You're a nice-looking lass in general but not in that color. Let's hope your wit makes up for your complexion."

"If there is one comfort, it might be the fact that Clarisse looked even worse in it than I." I hefted the heavy tureen, careful not to slop, and hoped Stockton had remembered to set the table for the first course. "Off I go. Pray."

"I will." Ellen gave me a whiskery kiss and patted the place on my cheek with her old fingers. "You're a princess sure and certain. Go show the old bats."

With this benediction, I hurried up the stairs and squeezed past

Stockton in the hall without speaking. My nerves played hopscotch with my stomach. At the top of the stairs, I set the tureen down on a serving cart, checked to make certain I'd remembered a fresh ladle, then pushed the whole to the doorway of the dining room. I paused there a moment, grimacing as one of Laureldina's vapid remarks reached my ears.

Oh Lord, if it is pleasing in your sight, let nothing go wrong. I smoothed the front of my dress, gripped the handle of the serving cart with both hands, and pushed it into the dining room.

The clink of crystal and silver suspended as I read displeasure and annoyance on the girls' faces. William sat back and grinned, and Laureldina made the weakest show of a smile as if she severely regretted having given permission for me to be there.

The man at her right was Lord Humphries, presumably. I had expected someone a bit older. Someone who looked less like a sea captain and more like the grandfatherly sort who'd pat my head and ask me to play a round of whist. His hair was unpowdered, and he wore no wig. By the strong set of his jaw I knew I had chosen a good ally. He was the sort of man who courted revolution and juggled firebrands for the fun of watching the world gape.

His eyes, so pale as to almost look silver, met mine. "Is this the Lady Alisandra Carlisle?" With one hand he swirled his wineglass while the other drummed aimlessly on the cloth.

Laureldina put her hand to her stomach and gave a matchstick smile. "This is my stepdaughter." Her voice was breathless, brittle.

I stepped forward, pushing the serving cart and its bountiful soup tureen over beside the table. "And you are Lord Humphries?" I asked, even as I took up the ladle.

He stood and bowed. "At your disposal."

Laureldina toyed with her ebony necklace. "Oh, no one is ever at her disposal, uncle. La, you make it sound as if she were important. And in the presence of His Royal Highness . . ."

I froze and swiveled on one heel to face the all too familiar apparition: Auguste stood at the side table, wineglass in hand. Blood rushed into my face, and if I had lacked color before, I made up for it now.

"Your Highness!" I made the lowest curtsy I knew, ladle still in hand. "I am honored to make your acquaintance." If I hadn't been so weakened by shock I might have remembered to be proud of the way I played the astonished kitchen maid meeting a future king. But if my words were feigned, my shock was not, and I was grateful for the table hard by and the generosity of Auguste in raising me and kissing my hand as any benevolent ruler would.

Laureldina laughed. By the tremor in her tone I suspected the prince had not deigned to kiss her daughters' hands. "Alis, this isn't an *acquaintance*. The prince, I am sure, has much better things to do than know you." She said the words for my hearing alone, but Auguste was close enough to hear them all, I knew.

His eyes poured out a torrent of questions. I silenced him with a panicked shrug and prayed he would not mention our meeting.

"I had not met *this* daughter when you came uptown last year, Lady Ecksmore," Auguste said. "I am pleased to know her now." It might have been my imagination, but I fancied a trace of pointed amusement as he spoke, as if he wanted to irk her.

Laureldina closed her eyes, and her collar bone shifted under the heavy gems. "Alis has not been well the past few years," my stepmother lied with a compassionate smile at me, frightening in its frailty. "Arthritis in all her joints. The doctors did not think the activity of the Season would be good for her health."

Auguste shot me a look and clicked his tongue. "And yet she serves the soup? Oh no, Lady Alis, let *me*. It would be my delight to serve." He took the ladle from my hand and, before I could even think to make a protest, began to fill the bowls himself, pushing the cart as he went. Scoop, pour, step to the next place, repeat.

I bit my lip and made a helpless face at my stepmother who sat, red faced and ashamed, at the head of the table. Strange as it was to sympathize with this woman, I shared in her mortification that the Prince of Ashby was scooping our broth. Gladly would I have taken the spoon from him, but that would have deepened my disgrace. What kind of prince served soup to his subjects?

And then the irony struck me: What kind of prince? A good prince.

Oh, heavens.

"Please sit down and let me," I begged, bending close to his ear.

One corner of his mouth tipped, but he shook his head, shy and determined. "It is my pleasure to serve you."

Clarisse turned as pale as her mother was red, and Vivienne picked at the cloth with her fingernails. William looked merely interested, like a St. Bernard who finds the comely spaniel has been given the job of raking the kennel's sawdust. Lord Humphries sat back in perfect composure, spreading his big brown hands on the table and fingering the lip of his wineglass now and then in a thoughtful manner.

The whole company was silent except for Auguste, who tried to make small talk as he filled the bowls. I dropped in a spineless heap in my chair and winced as His Majesty filled my bowl last and moved the serving cart to the other side of the room. Then he returned and sat at the other end of the table. My nerves were reduced to their lowest state. I wished nothing more than to retreat to the kitchen and resume my former life as a nobody.

Lord Humphries said grace in a rumbling Northern accent that ill suited the petite phrases from the Book of Common Prayer, but somehow the bluff thunder of the words stroked my fur down.

When the soup course was finished, Stockton's polite cough at the doorway reminded me that Ellen would have finished roasting the quail. I excused myself with a curtsy to Lord Humphries and the prince and exited the room in a whish of mauve skirts.

"The prince came up for dinner." Stockton gripped my elbows, his face tragic, and steered me toward the stairwell. "I was going to tell you, but you were so quick down the hall I hadn't time."

I waved Stockton off and re-tied the feeble sash of my gown. I needed fresh air and a moment to think, and the wide hall provided both. I had not prepared myself for the day's second interview with my rival. Heavy footsteps thudded on the wooden floor behind me, and I stiffened, willing it *not* to be the man who had stolen my throne and composure.

"M'lady Alis, a moment please?"

Chills sprang up my backbone at the introduction of the voice, and for one hair's breadth of a moment I thought it was Auguste's. But a heavy hand descending on my collar announced the new companion as Lord Humphries. Stockton scuttled downstairs per the direction of my eyebrows.

"Alis, you devil." Lord Humphries kissed my hand and winked. "What a blunder, introducing yourself to the prince this morning before *we'd* even met. How much does the man know?"

I shook my head. "I couldn't say. We met in town, and I babbled on for a bit—can't even remember what about. We argued, I think."

"He mentioned as much when I invited him for dinner."

"He knew he was coming here? To my house?"

Lord Humphries took the decanter of cheap brandy from a silver tray on the hall table and poured a glass. He lifted it to his eye and stared at me through the amber liquid, then handed it to me. "Auguste did not know that I was coming here. I only mentioned having dinner with my niece, Laureldina Carlisle, and her children. You are a recent production, my dear. I made no mention of an Alisandra Carlisle. What a nice surprise it was for him, I'm sure, seeing the breathing copy of his own father in female form. What did you say to him? He's smitten."

I spluttered through the foul brandy, but the little that made its way down my throat fortified me. "*Smitten*?" I spat.

"Mmm, yes. You've cut the cloth a bit close if he's in love with you. Will you lose resolve for our campaign and let your beloved take his ignoble throne without ever trying your hand? And after all the work we've done. You know, Alis, I had confidence in you from the moment I saw you come in tonight, saluting his royal highness with a soup spoon. Plucky."

"He's not my beloved," I snapped.

Lord Humphries's eyebrow twitched, and he grinned as if he had a cramp. "But he will be. Auguste is a fine man, and I congratulate you."

The man enraged me. I crossed my arms and leveled at him. I was just as tall as he and quite as dignified. "I will beg you to hold your tongue."

"You aren't my queen yet. And since I am financing this precarious theatrical production, madam, you may think of me as your godfather. In which case," he added, taking the rest of my brandy for himself, "I can say anything I like."

The point was too correct to dispute. I considered him a moment then went down the stairs. "Follow me, aged godfather. You might catch cold from the draught."

He did as I said, and we hastened down the narrow staircase into the kitchen. Ellen stirred her pot and brushed away a bit of damp hair. Stockton looked up from chopping potatoes, wearing that increasingly frequent crease between his brows that came on when he noticed I'd fallen into hot water.

I laughed and gestured to my companion. "This is our general, Lord Humphries."

Ellen nodded, wordless. Much help she and Stockton were when I was trying to be humorous. "As you know, he gave me the funds to buy the things I'll need if I'm to pass for a royal." I addressed Lord Humphries then, saying, "I shopped this morning."

Lord Humphries nodded. "Hallelujah. You look like a drudge in that color."

"Thank you, godfather."

"Do you really have arthritis or was my niece lying?"

"Laureldina is the picture of honesty."

My sarcasm met with an answering glint in Lord Humphries's eyes, and he stretched both arms before clapping his massive hands together. "What a lark, booting Auguste off the throne just before his Accession."

I garnished Ellen's quail with a few pinches of parsley and hurried them onto a tray, sending Stockton upstairs to feed the guests. "Are you satisfied?"

Lord Humphries leaned against the butcher-block table and smirked. "With you? Of course. It's obvious you're Blenheim to the bone. Actually, I wondered when you would put the pieces together. Either you were stupid or Laureldina told her little lies with more cunning than I gave her credit for."

"What pieces? You mean about my father being a fake?"

"Aye." When my self-appointed godfather said the word, one eye drooped in a sardonic wink. "And the other things."

Much though I wished to appear omniscient, I was curious. "What things?"

"*Auguste's* parentage." Lord Humphries took a knife from the table and tossed it in the air, firelight from the range catching on its steel blade. He laid it aside with care and crossed his arms over his chest. "Wasn't this a pleasant little family dinner?"

He studied me, watching the effect of this little speech, and the words hung empty in the quail-scented warmth of the kitchen. Ellen made small scraping sounds with her spoon against the bowl of creamed carrots, and my gaze followed the repetitive motion. I felt like a clod. What was I supposed to get from that cryptic change of subject?

And then it pierced me: family dinner. Auguste. Laureldina!

My heart thudded to a careening halt, and I gasped for air and comprehension, wishing the floor would crack open and gobble me. "Do you mean to tell me that the prince is my . . . stepbrother? He's Laureldina's *son*?" I dropped onto one of the empty crates. "And I'm in *love* with him?"

"Ah, now you admit it." Lord Humphries chuckled and waved his hand at my harmless snarl. "Oh, now where's the real harm in that? Your places were swapped, as you suspected all along."

"Please explain."

Lord Humphries lounged away from the table and squatted at my side. Though my head drooped, I could see him very well from this angle. His composure needled me. "Alis, promise not to bite me."

"Bite you?"

"You're a vixen and you're peeved."

I snapped to attention at this remark and summoned my most imperial tone. "Gallant Knight of Hell's outer rim, wouldst thou deign to enlighten me?"

"Good girl." He patted my knee and stood, hands clasped behind his back. "Your father and mother are the king and queen."

"Are you *certain*?"

"Please don't interrupt. I'm quite sure: *I* managed the transaction."

"You—" But I stopped at his upraised finger.

"This evening is not the first time we've met. You were no more than a week old when I lugged you in a padded fish trap all the way from Weircannon to Cock-on-Stylingham. A puny thing with a lusty cry and sharp fists with which you insisted on banging me. I really *am* your godfather; King Henri made me so at your birth. Of course he was mildly drunk at the time and probably thought I was the Bishop, but one doesn't care so much about these things. You were three days old when they decided they'd rather have a prince."

"You put it all so coldly." The chill of it seeped through my bones and into my marrow. I'd been given up for the sake of public opinion.

Ellen rolled her eyes and dried her hands on a rag. "Don't be upsetting Alis."

"Forgive me, dear lady," Lord Humphries said with a sparking cast of his grey eyes in her direction, "but my *nature* is blunt, and I never tamper with it. Let me continue, and we'll have done in a second. The thing plays out like this: A prince was more pleasing to the people of Ashby, so when your father's cousin caught the eye of an unprincipled Lord of State—"

"Laureldina is the king's cousin?"

"Aye." The lid closed halfway over his eyes again. "This unprincipled lord got Laureldina with child and seemed to forget all his vows to wed her, though he was more than willing to bed her." Lord Humphries looked around as if for commendation on this witticism, but I was not in the mood to fabricate laughter. My godfather tucked his chin and strode up and down the kitchen. "This occurrence left the king with a tangle of political yarn: Would it do for his lovely cousin to waltz about bearing other men's children? No, of course not. What was there to do then but fabricate a marriage for Laureldina and offer to raise her child as the royal heir in exchange for her rearing of you? Thus the kingdom was saved from an expensive revolution, your stepmother's reputation was saved from demise, and you, my little harpy, were saved from being murdered by an angry mob."

"Oh my." My brain was a sailors' knot. "No one will believe this."

Lord Humphries dipped his finger in Ellen's creamed carrots and licked it with a considering expression. "Rather tasty. *They* don't have to, dear girl. *I'm* rich, Auguste doesn't want the throne, and I can produce the real birth certificate if King Henri makes a stir. The people won't mind a change. They're growing bored with the idea of Auguste. My nephew is clever enough to see that this is the only way to keep from the same revolution he feared."

I wove my fingers in and out of one another. "Sorry to be thick, but who's your nephew?"

"Thick as fog. The *king*, little princess. If Laureldina is my niece, and the king is her cousin, then that makes him my nephew. Haven't you studied genealogy?"

"Not extensively."

"'Not extensively,' she says with the composure of an angel. God save us." He whipped about and gained the stairway then stalked back and jabbed a finger under my chin, forcing me to meet his eyes if I didn't fancy a puncture wound.

"You are to study your real lineage till you know every twig and leaf on the family tree," he said. "Memorize the most influential of your enemies and the fastest of your allies. Live with me for the next few weeks—don't worry, I shan't let Laureldina interfere—and you are not to blab this to Auguste. He doesn't know." Lord Humphries removed his finger and passed his hand over his eyes. "It's a messy affair." His lips pulled back in wolfish grin. "But the messier the affair the better, I say. Pack your things, madam. You are the official ward of Lord Humphries of Sandisturn. I have two weeks to make you presentable."

Lord Humphries wriggled his fingers in my direction and disappeared up the stairs as suddenly as if he'd been a fairy godfather come to spirit me off.

I was still as stone. After a stretch of time during which I existed rather than *lived*, I gathered a shred of energy and stood. "It's happening," I muttered. "I'm going to take the throne."

"You shouldn't count your chickens before they've hatched," Ellen said with a fond smile.

"My, aren't you just the essence of edification?" I pinched the bridge of my nose and wondered if this was how it felt to be eaten from the inside out.

CHAPTER 9

AUGUSTE RETURNED to the palace in such a high humor, he felt he could almost tolerate Belkin if he'd stick his pale nose into the room.

He'd seen Alis—knew where she lived and how she was treated—and his royal blood burned to know what it must be like to have that wretched Laureldina Carlisle-woman for a stepmother. He approved wholeheartedly of Lord Humphries's scheme to keep Lady Alis at his own house for the duration of the Season. There Alis would be out of reach of her awful relatives, and Auguste could certainly find time to take her driving if she'd consent. And, aside from the fact that he was a royal, he thought his chances none too shabby; he thought he'd seen a certain encouraging spirit in the way she looked at him.

Auguste continued in this buoyant mood for the better part of the next week. In that time he threw himself so wholly into the issues of State that his father came to him over breakfast.

"My dear boy," he said, pumping Auguste's hand. "I'm proud of the way you've been handling your affairs of late."

Auguste looked up from one of Belkin's neatly scrawled list of minutes and smiled. "Thank you, Father."

King Henri took one of the decorative rapiers from the wall and fiddled with the basket. "May I ask . . . what occasioned this sudden change?" He drew the blade from its sheath and stabbed an imaginary opponent.

Auguste stiffened in defense. He didn't want everyone knowing about Alis. A tender, young love like this wasn't the sort of thing one talked of in the conversational tone used for other, less important things like the weather or which courtier had recently fallen prey to highway robbery. However, life at home would be easier if his parents would stop inviting foreign dignitaries to parade their daughters before him in hopes of striking a match.

He sighed. "As a matter of fact I . . . I have chosen a young lady."

"You have? Oh, Auguste!" His mother, the queen, swooped in from a side passage, and for once Auguste was rather angry with the brilliant man who had designed his personal method of escape. What right did his mother have to use it?

"Mother, yes, I have." He suffered her kisses and ran his hand through his hair to stand it on end once she'd finished.

The queen put her arm around King Henri's waist and turned to Auguste, beaming. "Well, tell us about her! Who is she?"

"Not at present, Mother. You don't know her, and the poor girl doesn't even know I have chosen her as the woman I want to spend my life with." That bit of the predicament nettled him. He was in love, he knew. But if she didn't know it—or, worse still, refused to reciprocate the feelings—what was a fellow to do? "I wouldn't want to embarrass her or make her feel pressed into a marriage."

King Henri nodded and looked so much like Alis with the expression that Auguste groaned and ruffled his hair again.

"What do you like about her, Auguste?" his father asked. "Love isn't just admiration, y'know. What's it about Lady Mystique that caught your heart?"

Auguste thumbed through a list of the tiny things he loved about Alis and shrugged. "She doesn't seem to want to make anyone fall in love with her. She doesn't worry about being lovable . . . and that makes her all the more so."

King Henri swung the rapier in his hand then returned it to its mounting on the wall. "Ah, one of your virtuous girls who'll never kiss you unless asked and'll hardly tell you the time of day, much less talk to you."

Auguste thought of his Alis against this picture and chuckled. "Nothing like. You'll meet her soon enough. I can't wait forever."

King Henri strode to the desk and stuffed all of Auguste's papers in the drawer then clapped him on the shoulder. "What are you doing looking at matters of state at a time like this? Go chase down your silly bride, and the sooner the wedding the better, I say."

"Be gentle and quick with her, Auguste," his mother added. "Girls don't like to do difficult things."

Auguste came to the queen and kissed her cheek, restored to good humor. "Such as?"

"Choosing whom to marry and staging murders and robbing banks. Oh, Auguste." Smiling fondly, she patted his chest. "Don't be a gander. The most difficult thing for a girl is to sit alone wondering if she's the only one who has feelings. Go tell her everything, and do be careful going out. I'd hate to see you killed just as you're starting to act like a normal prince."

Auguste saddled Feather-Fellow and pelted to Sandisturn, Lord Humphries's mansion on the edge of Weircannon. At the massive door he threw himself from the saddle and barged through to the interior of the house, knowing Humphries would care little how he announced himself.

"Humphries!" he bellowed when he gained the entrance of the great library where Humphries could always be found. Auguste wondered where Alis might be and if he'd get to take her driving or if she'd say something put-offish and make him cross. The jolting crack of a pistol disarmed him until Auguste saw the noise had been made by Lord Humphries snapping together the covers of a ponderous folio.

"Come in, Auguste, and don't drag your feet about it. We're busy brewing an especially nice batch of treason."

Auguste stepped into the room and found Humphries and his own beloved crowded over a dusty volume. Alis's finger traced the lines of a family chart much like the ones Auguste had been made to study with his tutor long ago. He smiled at the pucker between her dark brows.

Humphries sauntered over and clouted Auguste between his shoulder blades. "What business is so pressing that you break in upon my lair?"

Auguste beat a tattoo on the table with his riding crop and willed Humphries to understand so he wouldn't have to outright ask for an interview with Alis. He watched a spasm of humor pass over the man's face; then Humphries dragged the book of bloodlines from under Alis's nose.

"It appears His Highness would like to speak with you, my girl. I'll just be in my alcove." Humphries saluted and took passage up a tortuous little staircase toward a balcony to the right of where they stood.

Auguste thrashed at nothing with his riding crop then crossed his hands behind his back, rocking on his toes. Jove, this was harder than he'd expected!

"Ummm . . . Alis?"

CHAPTER 10

I LOVED that silly beggar.

There was no getting around the fact now that I was in his presence again and remembering his dogged service with the soup tureen after hearing Laureldina invent infirmities for me. I loved him. I had not overlooked my inconsistency, but I had found time to think and remember that Auguste was really innocent of each wrongdoing I'd piled at his door. Prejudices removed, I now stared down the throat of a bewildering case of lovesickness. My own love for a man I would prefer to view as my foe.

Auguste waited for me to answer his halting "Alis?" with something clever, but this fresh love for him could not trump my longer-ingrained love of mischief. I wanted this moment of absurd bashfulness on his part to last forever. Had Auguste any idea how adorable he looked while rocking back and forth on his toes like a schoolboy brought forward for exams?

"Are you here on business, Your Highness?" I began to trim a feather pen in order to hide my amusement.

"Business? Ah—no." He took his ridiculous riding crop from behind his back and fingered the braided leather. "I was wondering . . . Oh, *dash* it all, Alis. You know I can't speak to women."

"I've noticed." This time I graced him with laughter, and the surprise on his face was worth my cruelty.

"You're happy to see me," he whispered with a grin that showed two dimples I'd never seen before scoring either side of his mouth.

I put the back of my hand against my mouth to stifle another laugh; I always laughed at the wrong moments, but that was my nature. "Yes, Auguste, I am *happy* to see you."

He tossed the riding crop onto the table and came around to my side, taking my hand in his. "Please don't interrupt me, because once I've begun I can't stop or I'll never try it again. Lady Alisandra Carlisle, you have captivated me: heart, soul, stomach, and all the rest."

"Stomach?"

"Well, perhaps not that. I haven't tasted your cookery yet."

"Oh, you have." I tossed my head. "The soup was mine."

"Stomach too, then. I'm not much of a prince—ask Mother or Father or anyone—but I think I'm being perfectly honest when I say I make more than a decent man. I'll go away and never bother you again if you say you don't want me to love you, but it'll be deuced hard. What I mean to say is: Alis Carlisle, will you be my bride?"

I had never been so eager to agree to any proposition in my life. But, for me, honesty had to come before love, for love, in its purest essence, is honesty. Hang Lord Humphries's caution not to tell Auguste about our little plot. He'd just have to chump it.

I patted Auguste's arm and drew him toward the window at the back of the library. "My answer will come shortly, but before anything else you must know this one rather awkward thing about us: I have planned to take your throne from the day I was old enough to know who I was. Or was *not*, rather. I have come to Weircannon with the intent of claiming my rights, never thinking to find you anything like passable."

"Your rights?" Auguste's thunderous brows rumpled together like great black caterpillars. "D'you mean to tell me you have a legitimate claim to the throne?"

"I'm the king's daughter," I said with a nervous chuckle.

Auguste pushed away from me. "You're my sister!" His tone had in it the desperate groan of a speared boar.

I grabbed his arm and, being one inch the taller, managed to drag him near again. "It is *not* so, thank heaven. I'm you, and you're me. I mean, I am really your parents' daughter and you . . . well . . . you belong to . . ."

"That terrible Carlisle woman?" He looked positively battered, poor soul. "That Laureldina-piece?"

I wrapped my arms around his neck and smiled. "We were swapped at birth because the people wanted a prince. Don't fret, dear. Lord Humphries will be dreadfully cross with me after he put forward all the money and dragged out old favors from the more sprightly gentry, but . . . I don't *care* about the throne for myself anymore. Truly, darling! Besides, if I marry you, I'll still be queen. We can just skip over all the unpleasantness completely."

Auguste blinked like a dozy badger and turned his muddled gaze on me. "You're saying you'll marry me, Alis?"

"I will." I smoothed his pitted brow with my fingertip and smiled again.

He sighed. "Well then, I don't mind the rest so terribly much." With that he grew brighter and picked me up and spun me in a circle. "I feel as if I've been through a five-minute hell and found myself in heaven after all. Oh, Alis. You're such a pigeon!"

He kissed my lips once, twice, and I blushed, feeling that this moment was worth a number of conquered thrones. "You'd shock most girls."

"I know. But I don't want most girls. I want Alis, one Alis. And she's here in my arms right now. Oh, Pigeon, I am hopelessly happy." Auguste pressed a kiss to my forehead.

I did not pull away, but I felt that something ought to be said, since I had no practice in how to deportment oneself while being kissed. "Is there anything that could make you happier?"

Auguste's brows drew together once more. He set me down and mussed that eternally electrified hair of his. "Well, I don't much like this business about the throne. 'Specially if it's yours." He hugged me. "I want to live in a little stone cottage with goldenrod and blackberries round the door and a rooster to shout at every morning. Cats too, and a smart collie dog with a crooked smile. Oh, dear. I should be rather indebted if someone would kill me."

"Kill you?" I asked, aghast.

He smiled the finger-caught-in-the-pie smile I liked so well, which had a mollifying effect. "Well, not *actually*, darling. But I do so hate being a prince. Now I understand it all, of course, since in reality I belong at the farm, and you here. If I could be killed without having to die . . . that'd solve all my problems, wouldn't it?"

I pushed my palms against his chest, eyebrows raised. "You mean a staged murder?"

Auguste grabbed my hand and chafed it between his, brown eyes full of sweetness. "Well, rather."

A plan bubbled in my mind, and it scared me in its audacity and in the way it meant I'd never get my throne. "Auguste, I love you."

"I know y'do, Pigeon."

"And I'm clever."

"Yes? Are you? I should think you are. You look clever."

"And I've always loved to play chess," I continued. "Especially the winning part."

He chuckled. "Alis, darling, dearest, love, does this have any bearing on the conversation?" He kissed me again, but I pulled away and looked at him sternly.

"I love you so much, Auguste, that I'm not afraid of what it'll mean for us. I know we'll lose the throne, and if I'm found out I'll lose my life but . . . *I'll* kill you if you'd like."

He sighed wistfully but shook his head, and his eyes were determined. "It is too risky, even for my clever girl. I couldn't let you do that for me."

"Would you do it for me?"

"Yes . . . But, Alis, see here, it's the man's duty."

"And it is my choice. Love is risk, darling. And I'd rather risk my life for you than let you drear your own life away in misery. It's the pattern set a long time ago by a far, far wiser Mind than mine, you know."

"*Greater love hath no man than this, that he lay down his life for his friends,*" Auguste whispered the familiar canto over me, and a great peace settled on my heart.

I tipped his chin. "Let me?"

"If you insist."

"I do."

"I now pronounce you man and wife. I see you've already been kissing her." Lord Humphries's loud proclamation startled us so that Auguste's slow kiss landed in an awkward place halfway on my cheek.

I turned in his arms, face burning, to see Lord Humphries leaning out of his alcove. He applauded. "Alis, you're a devil incarnate."

"I'm a woman," I retorted, borrowing Ellen's words. "And that's pretty much the same thing."

"Do you think I'll actually let you both get away with this . . . alone?" Lord Humphries asked. "You're both ruddy fools and not very efficient murderers, either, plotting in front of company."

"We're doing perfectly well," I protested.

"Shut up, darling." Lord Humphries waved his book and leaned over the railing. "Leave the details to your godfather. A thing like this must be handled with finesse, and I'm rather an old hand at scandal."

CHAPTER 11

THE NIGHT of the Prince's birthday had arrived. The night on which I had long planned to steal his crown. In a way, I'd still be stealing the crown, as after tonight there would be no Prince Auguste. I would kidnap and "murder" my love, and we'd flee the country forever, taking up residence in some foreign chateau where Auguste could have the trappings of his idealistic life and I a prince if not a throne.

I laid out the gown I had ordered from the tailor and his wife and called for Lord Humphries's maid, Jane, to help me fasten the multitude of stiff petticoats and rustling tulle that comprised the under-layers of the concoction. After wrestling the under-things in place, I wriggled into the gown; Jane laced the stays and the ribbons that held the back of it together while I sucked in my waist.

I rustled to the dressing table and tried to sit in the little red chair before the mirror. After a futile attempt, I knew there would be no sitting for me in this costume and wondered if it would impair my escape. Jane gave me a long look and, before I could stop her, had taken the pins from my bun and let loose my mane.

"Jane, what are you doing?" I grabbed my hair in both hands, unused to seeing the waves of it crowding my face, though my reflection looked unusually pretty, I thought.

"You're not going to th'ball with a topknot, Lady Alis." And, with a few deft movements, Jane coiled my hair into an elegant, twisting mass on the back of my head. She tucked something into the coils and handed me a mirror. "There y'are. Clean up nicely, don't you?"

"Bless you, Jane." I kissed her cheek and squeezed her arm in my abundant gratitude.

"One would suspect she had never touched a dishpan in her life," Lord Humphries said in a voice thrilling with amusement.

My heart galloped and I turned to greet him. His arrival had kicked off the faint sense of girlish satisfaction attending preparation for my first party. "I've kept you waiting."

"You have." He held out his arm, which I took. "By Jove, woman. You're a raving beauty." But even this light-handed flattery could not still the roiling of my nerves.

"Is all well?"

"All is *ready*," he said with a grunt. "You know the prospects of success."

The ride to the palace was quiet and uneasy, punctuated only by gruff remarks and instructions from my uncle as to exactly what I was to do and how we were to get Auguste away from the party. We were to make our move at midnight, just before the proclamation of his Accession. If all went as planned, the gathered well-wishers would discover the pool of blood on the balcony at a quarter past twelve.

Our driver pulled up to the front staircase of the palace. Lord Humphries handed me out, and I adjusted the train of my gown before sweeping, pale and desperate, up the staircase like a tall, gilded statue mechanically moving between rows of armored soldiers. Had there been a chronicler of fairytales about, he would have pegged me at once for an enchanted princess looking for true love's kiss and worrying she'd melt when the clock struck twelve. I had no fear of melting—freezing in my tracks was the more relevant and very real terror.

Lord Humphries was close at my heels, and I paused at the top of the white stairs to look over the town of Weircannon, glowing amethyst and gold like the edge of dusk. Down in the valley beyond Town, the River Lin wound in shining, silver coils like a tranquil dragon, its edges feathered with night. Before us, carriages wound up the white-chalk road and deposited their expensive cargoes in pools of laughter and lamplight at our feet.

"It looks like fairyland," I whispered.

"And you're the fairy princess, I suppose." My uncle's words were rough and sarcastic, but in his eyes I caught a glimmer.

I slid my hand up his cheek and rubbed the weather-worn skin with my thumb. "And that makes *you* the fairy godfather. Thank you." I mouthed the last two words, and my fairy godfather—for surely he was if anyone could be—adjusted his gloves and took me in on his arm.

The Crier announced our names, and the hum of voices suspended for one heartbeat, silent and curious, then resumed like a bird hovering on the wing and darting off again. As we moved down the staircase and into the shreds of space between the silk-clad gentry, my breath started to come shorter and shallower. I tightened my grip on Lord Humphries's arm.

"You will not faint," he said through teeth clenched in a polite smile.

I waved at Laureldina and the girls as we passed, and the looks of hatred spitting from their faces would have been enough to scald me were I not numb to everything but the necessity of finishing this night in possession of my life. "You would kill me, wouldn't you, dearest uncle?"

"You'd die of shame and deprive me of that pleasure," said he.

Having reached the other end of the glittering splendor, Uncle Humphries backed me against the wall and spiked my nerves with a drop of spirits from a silver flask. He pressed another flask into my hands. This I stored in my bosom. Against the comparative flatness of my chest, no one would notice the slim bottle. This flask was to be our savior, for it contained blood from the butcher's with which to spatter the balcony and make Auguste's disappearance all the more convincing.

I wondered where Auguste had hidden himself then noticed the dais beneath a balcony at the left-hand side of the room. There each person came to pay respects to the king and queen and their heir. Auguste sat in his chair, a compact, dark blot on the white marble of his palace. The lad and his throne—what an ill-suited pair! No wonder he hated his life.

My uncle led me to the back of the queue, and we waited our turn to pay homage to our royals. I tapped one foot on the floor, and the *tink* of my crystal shoes filled the small pocket of emptiness around me with fairy bells.

Lord Humphries jerked my elbow. "Stop that. You're upsetting my psyche."

I forced myself to stand still and found it miserable. Finally, like a pair of elegant snails, we came to the throne. Lord Humphries bowed, and I sank into a deep curtsy on the lowest step of the dais. To think that I was now, for the first time, in the presence of my mother and father. A thought large enough to overwhelm me.

I felt a strong grasp and was raised by Auguste himself, cradled in his arm. The warm touch of his hand called forth a flicker of courage. I smiled at the king and queen—my parents—and could think of nothing to say that wouldn't be treasonous. I didn't think it good form to inquire here and now why they'd dumped me off the throne as a week-old baby. Even if my gender *had* upset them, it was a silly thing to do.

"Mother and Father," Auguste said, and his voice was a towline for my clipper ship of a brain, "This is my chosen one: Lady Alisandra Carlisle. You will please announce, along with your other statements, that we are to be married."

He and I stared at them, and I could tell by the start and flush on the queen's face that she knew me. King Henri turned the exact shade of red I knew I was turning myself. He took a futile half-step forward.

"Good evening, Mother and Father," I said, and though I was sorry for it afterward, I threw a handful of knife-points into my tone.

"Good evening, Lady Carlisle."

None of us breathed for the ten seconds of pulsing humiliation that followed. Then Lord Humphries tugged me away from the thrones and onto the dance floor.

I led a dull life for the next several hours. When cooped up at Cock-on-Stylingham I had been accustomed to daydreaming of gorgeous parties like this. Now that I attended one, I had to admit it was nothing like it ought to have been.

Where was my handsome prince? Perched miserably on a chilly throne. Where was the dashing dance partner? Likewise absent. Lord Humphries steered me through the dances like a tug pushing a lumber barge down the River Lin.

William cut in on Lord Humphries at half-past eleven. "Alis, you're gorgeous."

"You waste no time. Neither do I. I found a bride for you."

He blinked. "Did you?"

"Her name is Jane."

"Jane what?"

"Just Jane."

He spun me away from him and back in again with a chuckle. "I take it she's a drudge like you?"

"But of course."

"I seem to be fond of drudges."

I saw then how hard it was going to be for me to leave everything familiar. Even William, whom I had never expected to miss at all. I wondered if Auguste had considered how the news of his murder would affect his so-called parents. "You will find your bride in your uncle's employ," I said.

"Oh, *that* Jane."

"Indeed." As we danced I managed to view the gold-figured clock built into the ceiling above. A quarter till twelve. Fifteen minutes more and I would spread the blood on the white stones of the outer balcony; a half hour, and the murder would be announced. I needed to be on and off the balcony by twelve, and still the orchestra rattled out the music so that I must keep dancing.

Another five minutes ticked by and I saw that I would have to slip the knot. I slumped in William's arms.

"You all right, Alis?"

"Feeling faint."

"I'll take you for a—"

"No, thank you! Fresh air is adequate. No need." I pushed away his hands and ran from the center of the dance floor, my crystal heels clicking like pattens.

No one paid heed to the lanky, reckless creature flitting through the crowd and out the door. I found Auguste's carefully described steps hidden in a cove of ivy. These steps were little more than narrow stone ledges wedged between a false wall and the side of the castle. As I climbed, the church bells of Weircannon chimed midnight.

"Alis, what are you doing?"

William's voice jolted me with a symphony of shivers. I whipped around and saw him at the foot of the stairs. A witness. We couldn't afford a witness.

"Please don't interfere." My tone was too calm and clear.

"Are you . . . killing yourself?"

"And if I am?"

"I won't let you."

"Leave me alone."

"*Are* you?" William put one foot on the first stair as if about to remove me from the wall by force.

I took from my hair the knife Jane had concealed in the thick coils. "Of course I am not killing myself—for once in my life I am happy. Go away, William, and there shan't be trouble."

He looked at me with an intensity that spoke volumes. I knew he guessed this was my happily-ever-after.

A nightingale sounded from afar, and William grinned a rather wolfish grin. "God grant you a decent burial."

He was gone in a moment. I leaned against the prickling ivy until I was confident enough of my balance to continue. Breathing was a shaky business. I gained the balcony and swung myself over the rail, blessing God for the muscles, gained in menial labor, that allowed me to throw my weight while arrayed in sumptuous chains of satin.

I paused one infinitesimal moment to force a normal breath then slipped my hand into my bodice and removed the flask. The lid came off, and I poured the cloying, dark blood onto the white stones in a pool, careful to keep my hem from the crimson stain of it. I took also the knife Jane had concealed in my hair and tossed it into the pool like a penny in a wishing well.

A few drops of blood pilled on my skirt and ran in sticky rivulets down the folds. I bit my lip, but there was naught left to do but drop Auguste's signet ring alongside. This I did just as a step came on the stair, and my heart fell dead until I recognized the first few bars of the tune we had determined Auguste should whistle when ready. He passed through the gauzy curtain dividing the interior from the balcony and showed himself for one moment with a two-fingered salute. Then he disappeared again, as planned, down one of the passages hidden like rat's tunnels in the walls of the palace.

I counted to ninety and heard below me the fanfare of trumpets heralding the time for announcements. We would not be there when sought.

I gathered my skirt into my arms and slipped back over the railing, praying I would encounter no one else. William might or might not come looking for me. If he did, my life was forfeit.

I ran down the hidden staircase and meant to continue across the courtyard to the stables on the other side, where Stockton had readied Auguste's horse. A sentry passed the opening of the hidden staircase at that moment. I pulled short in panic, wrenching my ankle. I bit my tongue and tasted blood then spat it and crept out of my hiding spot, darting over the white stones as if Hell's hounds pursued me. It would be a miracle if I lived to see dawn.

CHAPTER 12

AUGUSTE HELD the reins on either side of Alis's slim form and fed them to his mount, willing him to despise the ground and fly farther with each stride. Faster, faster, farther, farther!

All he hated was behind; all his future, ahead; all his love, in this moment.

Then Alis stiffened. "Oh no!"

"Alis?"

"Oh God, be merciful."

Auguste pulled off in a copse of trees at the side of the road and forced Alis to face him. Feather-Fellow labored to breathe beneath their combined weight. "What is it?"

Alis pulled back her skirt, revealing one foot bare, one shod in the singular crystal slipper she had thought such a pleasant joke.

A spasm of annoyance and fear passed between them.

"I told you I'm clever," Alis said with a forced laugh and darkened eyes. "I murder a man and escape with the body but leave behind my own shoe."

Before he knew what he was doing, before he'd thought to be gentle, Auguste grabbed Alis's ankle and wrenched the slipper from her foot.

She cried out and grabbed her leg. "You brute!"

"I promise that hurts much less than a hangman's noose." Several emotions rioted in Auguste's blood and throbbed in his temples. What a choice he was for the throne; he couldn't even fake his death without bungling it. He hefted the slipper in his hand then drew back his arm and hurled it into the brush.

"That was my slipper," Alis protested with a steaming glare.

He glared back. "And your death sentence, my lady."

She drew herself tall and slipped from the saddle onto the ground, bobbling a bit on her hurt ankle. The passion withdrew, leaving Auguste feeling winded, regretful. Had he hurt her so much?

"If you're going to ruin my things, at least do it properly." She hobbled into the bushes and returned with the slipper in hand and her brows arched in black authority. "Like so."

Without flinching, Alis slammed the slipper onto one of the rocks sunk in the mossy roadside. It shattered with bell-like song into a pile of crystalline shards. She sprinkled handfuls of leaves over the glass to hide them then turned to him with her fists buried against her hips in the folds of satin.

Auguste's stomach flipped. "Do you think this will help?" he asked. Mechanical words in his mouth; he knew it was useless. "How would they know it was you? Won't they think we were both kidnapped? Oh, don't look at me like that. I'm sorry, Alis."

Relenting all at once, Alis came to him and pressed her forehead to his thigh, which was as high as she could reach when he was still mounted. His awkward, lovely bride.

"William followed me," she said. "And you know there was only one woman's foot in Ashby that would fit those spectacular gravy boats, which were, I will remind you, crafted to my specific measurements. I'll be missing, you'll be missing, and William will know the truth. Besides, your parents know I have returned and want the throne."

Auguste wondered if it was any use cursing. "They'll be one jump behind us then. God's my witness, I wish we'd let napping dogs lie." He jumped from Feather-Fellow's back, hoisted Alis up, and handed the reins to her. "You go on. I'll meet them, and you'll be safe till it all blows over."

"I won't leave you to face the mobs yourself. They'll kill you just as easily as me once they know you're an imposter."

Alis looked as determined as his father—*her* father—ever had. Auguste tugged his eyebrow and wondered if either of them would survive this night.

"Checkmate it is, then."

She clasped his wrist as he climbed into the saddle again, then passed him the reins. Turning Feather-Fellow about, they started back toward the smatter of golden lights on the purple horizon, toward the wreckage of their slapdash scheme.

Six distinct figures barreled down the white road in pursuit of the one who had killed their prince. Capes flying, cries ringing, swords drawn, they encircled a foaming horse and its rider. *Riders.* The captain of the guard stared for a moment, then swore softly. Here was the prince, looking quite whole, and before him a tall woman with the face of their king.

Something, the captain thought gravely, had gone monstrous awry.

CHAPTER 13

LADY CARLISLE, have you anything to say in your defense?"

The judge's glare was hot on my head. I cleared my throat and stood in the defense box. Any words guttered before they came as I realized that I was living the game I'd played so many times in the orchard at Cock-on-Stylingham. Everything—William and the shoemaker in the witness stand, the lords and ladies at court, Auguste on the front row—everything was just as I had dreamed.

Only for once my audience was human, not a band of rooks.

The familiar script caught in my throat, though I knew it verbatim: *I swear before the Court of Ashby: The birth certificates were switched.*

If I said this, Lord Humphries would back my tale. He would be able to produce evidence that I was the lawful heir to the throne of Ashby. But to do this, I would have to expose my mother and father as fraudulent rulers, makers of the very chaos they acted to avert. Surely this was just action on my part, and no one could blame me for making the claim. Surely I had a right to overturn the carefully kept secret in order to save my life. I knew the penalty for treason.

A faint stir at the back of the courtroom caught my eye. My stepmother and her daughters entered the room and took places on the bench. The girls made faces and giggled at the sight of me, handcuffed and mud spattered. But it was Laureldina's face that struck me. The cold beauty had left her features, and I saw nothing but a frightened, damaged woman who knew I held her reputation in my hands and expected no mercy from me.

"Lady Carlisle, your defense, please, or we shall proceed to the hanging."

My attention snapped back to the judge and jury. Time, motion, breath, *life* paused while I weighed my next words.

Then I smiled. "I have no defense, my lord."

My father, the king, started up in shock from the front row, and I cracked a half-smile. Laureldina sank, pale and relieved, into her seat.

"None, my lady?" the judge asked.

"None."

"You staged the murder, kidnapped the prince, and have no defense?"

I yawned and shook back my hair. "What makes you think it was I?"

"Your skirts are speckled in blood, madam, and one of your slippers, you will realize, was recovered at the scene."

The judge motioned for a page to come forward. He bore on a red velvet pillow the offending object.

"Lord William Stylingham said he followed you outside last night when you claimed illness and that you seemed shaken. The shoemaker assures me that it was *you* fitted for those slippers in his shop."

"Where is the other slipper?" I asked.

The judge bridled. "You would know."

"Would I?"

Hackles of stubbornness arched along my back. I would not tell the jury I had kidnapped their precious Prince Auguste because he so much despised the throne he'd do anything, even feign his own death, to be free of it. I would tell them nothing.

"You may try the slipper," I cried out. "If it fits, you may hang me. Of what value am I?"

The judge motioned for the page to come forward and the people of the court held their collective breath.

Auguste sprang out of his chair and in a few steps cleared the space between us. "Your Honor, *I* will fit the shoe on Lady Carlisle."

The judge smoothed his eyebrow, chuckling. "A man who fights his own battles, hmmm? Very well."

Auguste took the shoe from the page. It looked strangely small in his rough hands. "Alis," he murmured, "please come forward."

I left the witness box and came to him on the floor of the courtroom, gathering the soiled shreds of my ballgown in my arms so all might see the business with ease. I did not know what Auguste planned to do, but something told me my trial would not end at the gallows.

I sat in a chair provided for me. Auguste knelt, and I raised my foot. He had only to tip the shoe and it would slip over my foot as if enchanted; the glass slipper could fit no other. Our eyes met for a sliver of a second, but he tossed all his love into that look. My heart slowed peacefully.

Auguste halted and stood again, the mate to my shattered shoe cozied in his hand like the apples I had thrown at the rooks long ago. I had half a wish he might sling it at the judge's head, but that would seal my fate.

My legs cramped and I stretched them before me; how ironic, being once again barefoot and throneless.

"Your honor, who was kidnapped?" Auguste asked.

The judge blinked, appearing a bit disappointed the slipper had not yet been tried. "Why, you, my liege."

"Was I? I find myself hale and hearty this morning. Rather hungry now that it comes down to it, but present in this courtroom. And who was murdered?"

"You . . . my liege?"

Auguste moved toward the judge. "Hit me, please."

"What?"

The courtroom leaned forward. Had Auguste lost his wits?

He flicked his big hands. "If I've been murdered, I am a ghost. I should like to know if I am. Hit me." Auguste presented his face and the judge recoiled.

"Your Majesty, I cannot—"

"Then you will take it on my authority that I am unharmed?"

"I . . ." the judge swallowed. "I will. I must."

My prince stepped back and tossed the slipper up and down in his hand. "My good people of Ashby, do you see me before your eyes? I am not kidnapped. Do you see me in the flesh? I have not been murdered. The case against Lady Alisandra Carlisle, then, is delicate." He tossed the slipper higher, spun, and caught it on his index finger low to the ground.

The crowd gasped.

"Delicate," Auguste said, tossing the shoe backward over his head and catching it behind his back with the other hand, "as the evidence." He grabbed the slipper and waved it over his head as a cat might wave its tail. "If the slipper fits Lady Carlisle, what does that signify? That she has feet? My, my, what is the world coming to, that women should have feet? Even large ones!"

"But, Your Majesty," the judge protested.

"You will say it is custom-made, and far be it from me to disappoint the trust of the people of Ashby in our justice system. I will try the slipper on her foot. If it fits, you may do with her what you will. I will be ruler of Ashby one day: I realize the people's way is the king's way."

I froze. He had defended me bravely, but the shoe would fit and there was nothing for it. Auguste backed toward me, brandishing the shoe. Just as he turned to kneel, his foot caught on my outstretched leg, tripping him. His arm flung out, and the slipper flew from his hand. An explosive crystal sound deafened me for a moment. When I was brave enough to turn and look, I saw the slipper—what remained of it—wrecked beneath a marble effigy of some long dead Ashbian royal.

My body shuddered. They would think I had done it on purpose; they would think I had tripped Auguste to destroy the evidence. I would be hanged without delay. I cast an agonized look at Auguste.

But his eyes were *laughing*. Only then did I realize he had tripped on purpose, knowing full well my legs were stretched out behind him.

My love winked and pushed himself to his feet. He turned to the stunned courtroom. "That was unfortunate."

Someone—Lord Humphries, I presume—dared to laugh, but the others stared at their prince, wary. They had been cheated of a scandal. There would be no hanging. A beehive hum sprang up as the people of Ashby began to whisper among themselves.

"My lords and ladies of the court, listen to your future king." Auguste's voice rang out strong and bold, stilling the hum of the courtroom with its authority. "If but one of you speaks, I shall lose my temper. Now then: every party must have a pageant. Tell me, is this not the custom?"

The people of Ashby exchanged glances, and my eyes found Lord Humphries in the corner, twitching as if to stifle laughter.

Auguste winked at me. "And as for kidnapping, a far worse crime is a woman's thievery of a heart, which, I grant you, she has committed. You demanded a bride, a future queen. You asked for a splendid occasion and a grand speech. This is the grandest oration you'll receive, for no fairy attended my birth to give me a gilded tongue. Furthermore, last night I gave you your pageant with all its trappings of blood, daggers, and forgotten slippers, which many of you understandably took for reality."

The hum rose louder. My heart soared.

Auguste raised me and brought me to his side. "And now, O people of Ashby, look well. For here I give to you the Lady Alisandra Carlisle, my bride, your queen. She has committed no crime . . ." and in a lower tone, meant only for me: "for indeed, she has saved the throne."

After this, I remember a thrum then a kiss, warm and passionate. I remember applause and exclamations, and Auguste turning what should have been another kiss into an outburst of laughter next to my ear. I remember my real parents rushing forward and making whispered reparation, and Laureldina fading in and out of my sight like a specter that could haunt me no more.

I was incandescently happy in our wholeness. Then came a surreal, ironic, quiet thought that made me bury my head on Auguste's shoulder: Heavens, what a mother-in-law!

Someone dropped a paper crown on my head, interrupting this terror, and I looked up to see Lord Humphries. "How now, little Alis?" He nodded at Auguste. "All well with your fairy prince?"

I ran my fingers through Auguste's wild hair, kissed his rough brown hand, and winked at my godfather. "Lord help you, sir, look at him! Prince, yes. Fairy? Never."

Lord Humphries beckoned me aside to where Auguste had slain the glass slipper. My godfather stood behind me as if to ward off anyone who would approach.

"I'm going to write out your story for posterity," he whispered, his breath tickling my ear. "*The Cinderwench: from rags to riches by way of her tongue.* And you can't stop me. The world needs a bit of amusement in its old age."

"Never, dear Uncle," I cried, turning to him. "You'll have it all wrong. I know you will. You'll probably say we lived happily ever after and thwart any possibility of further adventure."

His eyes narrowed with scathing amusement. "You're sincerely worried." He stepped to the side and ground bits of the glass slipper under his heel, absently. "To your own attempt then, Madam Literary."

And I knew in that moment that I really meant to write the tale down; if only, I thought, to live again on the windy side of care.

ABOUT THE AUTHOR

RACHEL HEFFINGTON is a Christian, a novelist, and a people-lover. Outside of the realm of words, Rachel enjoys the Arts, traveling, mucking about in the kitchen, listening for accents, and making people laugh. She dwells in rural Virginia with her boisterous family and her black cat, Cricket.

In February 2014, Rachel released her debut novel, *Fly Away Home*, and is excited to collaborate on *Five Glass Slippers* with her fellow authoresses. She hopes to release her second full-length novel and first mystery (*Anon, Sir, Anon*) in autumn 2014. For more on Rachel, her current projects, and writing in general, visit her on her blog: www.InkpenAuthoress.blogspot.com

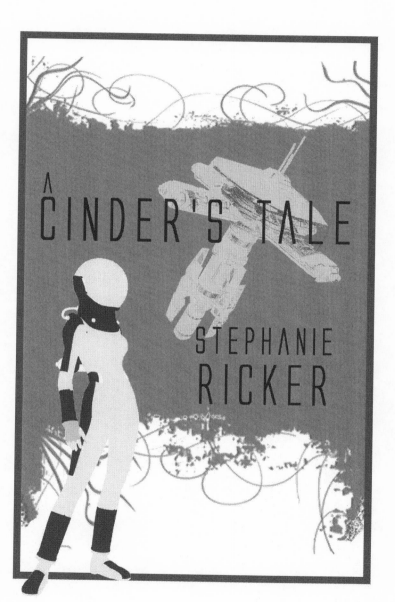

A
CINDER'S TALE

STEPHANIE
RICKER

To Christian, with many thanks

for making days in the cubicle farm enjoyable.

CHAPTER 1

N ITS GLORY DAYS, Aschen had been a gas giant. Circling too near its sun, it was a roaster—a hot Jupiter—locked in tight orbit around a red giant star. Gradually, over many years, hydrodynamic escape had stripped the planet of its atmosphere, leaving only the metal-rich core behind.

Elsa skimmed her miner's coach low across Aschen's molten surface, her eyes flicking from the heat-resistant controls in front of her to the carefully darkened viewscreen protecting her from the sun's intensity. The planet's fast rotation and proximity to its star meant that each miner spent a hefty portion of each shift on Aschen's blistering-hot dayside.

A deep, gruff voice came through the comm line inside her helmet. "Watch yourself, Elsa. Reading a lot of activity in the pumpkin patch to your left."

"Copy that, Bruno," she told the older miner. "I'm watching."

Through her viewscreen, Elsa eyed the patch of bubbling lava warily. Pumpkin patches, so named because the superheated lava puffed out in large bubbles, were notorious for blowing up without a moment's notice.

Any sane person would want to get as far away from them as possible.

Of course, any sane person wouldn't sign up for a job as a cinder in the first place. The pay was good, but the life expectancy left something to be desired.

The work was necessary, if perilous. Aschen had made its debut on the galactic scene as soon as long-range mining scouts determined that the planet's volatile outer atmospheric layers had boiled away sufficiently to allow the deployment of mining teams. The big mining companies sniffed at roasters like hungry dogs, waiting for their moment to harvest the planetary dregs.

And few worlds were so ripe for the harvest as Aschen.

The substance that put hitherto-ignored Aschen on the map was cendrillon. Strong enough to withstand the tidal forces of planets and light enough to manipulate even in standard gravity, the material could be found only in the forged remains of a chthonian planet, a gas giant compressed and drained of its atmosphere. From such planets, named after the denizens of the Greek underworld, came the cendrillon to build better space stations, starships, and weapons. The galaxy could hardly spin without the stuff.

Pity it lurked in the hottest, most inhospitable corners of the worlds, Elsa thought. She maneuvered her coach closer to the pumpkin patch, avoiding the hottest spots, her eyes glancing from the heat sensors to the spectroscope on her console and back again. The patches harbored large concentrations of cendrillon. The temptation of a big ore haul lured many cinders to brave the dangers of explosive magma.

Her machine picked its way daintily over the lava flow, and Elsa edged the coach right up to the perimeter of the patch. Her spectroscope chimed obligingly. A lovely concentration of cendrillon lay just beneath her. Elsa deployed the collectors, watching as the arms descended from the body of the coach, plunged elbow-deep into the lava, and scooped up the heavier cendrillon beneath.

Dripping liquid fire, the collector scoops emerged again, dragging their burden into the body of the coach. Elsa's gloved fingers hovered over the thruster controls as she kept her gaze on the heat sensors. She couldn't stay in this position much longer. The first of the heat alarms sounded quietly just as the scoop arms completed their retraction. Time to go.

She slapped the thruster controls, and her coach leapt into the air. The pumpkin patch exploded in a fiery splash, the superheated magma splatter just missing the underside of Elsa's coach.

Elsa let her breath out in a whoosh, enjoying the adrenalin rush and checking her displays for damage to her vehicle. The reports were all clear. She grinned and activated her comm line. "I can feel your disapproval from here," she told Bruno, "but I was timing it carefully."

He grunted. "You know how I worry," he said dryly. "But you also know what you're doing. Get a good haul, did you?"

"That I did," she said, unable to keep a smug note from her voice. From her higher vantage point, she saw Bruno's coach arc away from the planet's turbulent surface. "Calling it a day?" she asked in surprise.

"Yep. Bells are in only ten minutes."

Elsa glanced at the chronometer. Bruno was right; the shift was nearly over. She saw several other coaches making their way across the planet surface like a small swarm of grasshoppers above the swirling magma. She followed suit in her own vehicle, feeling the slight drag of the full load she carried. High winds, whisking heat from the dayside of the planet to the nightside, buffeted the coach, and she had to work to maintain her course. The end-of-shift bells rang on her comm line as the heavily laden coaches around her flung themselves at the sky towards the gleaming space station.

Tremaine Station, the current darling of the Tremaine Mining Company, was ringed with docking ports for ships of all sizes, but the coaches had a different destination. The station's mining hub, set at a distance from the main station to accommodate the loading of the gargantuan ore barges that transported the cendrillon to distant star systems, was designed to unload and house the coaches. The hub rotated to provide each approaching coach with an available dock. As the coaches drew close enough, the mining hub caught each one in a tractor beam and drew it into position, a mother hen gathering in her chicks at the end of the day.

Elsa felt the tug of the tractor as it caught her coach. The vehicle gently sidled up to a free dock set into the giant hub, and the automated system began unloading. She waited patiently while the cendrillon ore was sucked out of her coach and stored deep within the hub to be processed.

Her day's numbers scrolled across the controls as her newly harvested ore registered in the system. She couldn't help but smile in triumph; she had beaten her old record for one day's ore haul.

When unloading was complete, the airlock between mining hub and coach engaged with a hiss of equalizing pressure. Elsa unbuckled her harness, sliding it past her helmet. While heavy shielding protected the coach from lava and from solar flare radiation from Aschen's sun, cooling the cabin of each coach enough for human comfort would be a waste of money. Each cinder wore a spacesuit, creating his or her own tiny livable atmosphere inside the furnace of the coach.

Elsa punched the door controls and stepped into the open airlock. Supercooled air blew from vents around the airlock, and smoke rose from her suit as it cooled rapidly. Once her suit reached the appropriate temperature, the second set of airlock doors slid open.

She emerged into the employee center of the rotating mining hub, which was a welter of activity. Cinders hustled out of their suits and scampered about in their grey undersuits, all eager to snag an available shower stall in the post-shift rush. Supercooled ash from their suits drifted gently in the air, no matter how careful they tried to be. The thin soot that settled on their undersuits and skin was an unfortunate byproduct of their work; no matter how the miners scrubbed, a few smudges of soot always seemed to remain after showering. There was no help for it, and it had quickly prompted the cendrillon miners' nickname: Cinders always smelled slightly of brimstone, always had a touch of soot in their hair.

Elsa quickly shed her suit and put it in her locker until her next shift. Each suit was adjusted to the individual, but hers had been custom-made—being the shortest cinder in the locker room had one advantage. She climbed on the bench just outside of her locker to enable her to reach the shelf where her helmet belonged.

Behind her, the whine of hydraulics signaled the hub's rotation and the arrival of several more cinders. A moment later, Bruno came through one of the airlocks and pulled off his helmet.

"Heads up," the veteran cinder said to Elsa as he walked past her to his locker. "Nebraska wants to see you when you're finished here." He straightened Elsa's helmet on its shelf as he walked by.

Elsa groaned. "Why?"

Bruno shrugged. "Some paperwork thing; she didn't say."

Jaq, one of their newer crewmates, chimed in from his locker farther down the aisle. "Want me to fake an episode of cardiac arrest in front of her desk? Or I could activate the alarm system."

Elsa laughed. "I appreciate the offer, but no. I'd best just get it over with." She sighed. The mining office manager seemed to despise her, and it bothered Elsa more than she cared to admit.

Bruno gave her a shrewd glance. As if reading her mind, he said, "Don't take it personally. She hates everyone. And she obviously hates her job even more," he finished dryly.

"You watch, I'll win her over one of these days," Elsa vowed, rubbing at a patch of soot on her undersuit. "I really thought the candy would do it."

"You couldn't have known she couldn't process sugar. That wasn't your fault," Jaq said, gathering his belongings to enter the men's showers.

"Yeah, well, it didn't exactly put me in her good graces." Elsa gave up on the soot; she was just rubbing it more deeply into the fabric.

"I wouldn't worry. She doesn't have good graces to be put in." Bruno's usual hangdog expression didn't vary, but his eyes twinkled at her from behind their crows' feet.

Elsa smiled. "I do feel sorry for her, though. She must be lonely." She craned her neck to look at Bruno around the door of her locker. "You know, the other day I saw her carrying some sort of case, down near the personnel quarters. I waved at her, and she spooked and took off. Well. In as much as she can really take off," she amended. "You'd have thought I caught her smuggling contraband, from the look on her face."

Bruno frowned. "What kind of case was it?"

Elsa shrugged. "Some sort of musical instrument case, maybe? It was half as big as she was." She closed her locker with a bang. "I'm hitting the showers. I'll see you on the shuttle."

Bruno waved at her and hung his suit in his locker.

After scrubbing as much soot as she could from her hair, Elsa emerged from the women's changing rooms into the shuttle waiting area. At the end of each shift, shuttles ferried the cinders from the mining hub to the main space station, where the commerce center and personnel quarters were located.

The shuttles docked and disgorged their cargo of the next shift's workers. As soon as the coaches were unloaded and checked for any damage, they were sent straight back out with fresh cinders aboard. Elsa waited until the new workers had streamed past into the locker rooms, waving at a few members of the swing shift whom she knew personally, before she boarded the now-empty shuttle that would take her shift home.

Elsa chose a set of six seats, three on each side facing each other, and buckled herself into one of them. She was so small that the harness didn't really fit, no matter how she adjusted it, but the alternative was to be tossed around the temperamental shuttle. Bruno plunked down next to her. Jaq and Gus, another crewmate, took two of the seats opposite as the shuttle filled with cinders.

"Have you heard the news?" Gus asked as he struggled to buckle his harness over his rather ample stomach. *One size fits all* continued to be a lie perpetuated around the galaxy.

"What news?" Elsa asked.

"A frigate from the galactic fleet is stopping at Aschen," Jaq interjected before Gus could get a word in. Gus glared at him.

"What in the worlds for?" Bruno asked.

Gus put a hand over Jaq's mouth to stop him from answering. "Rumor has it they're passing through for a little shore leave before shipping out to patrol the outer edge of the quadrant," he replied. "I heard it from one of the stewards who orders the fuel and supplies for the ships docking at the station. The station received a requisition so large, it can only mean a frigate is arriving."

"Any idea which ship it is?" Elsa asked. *A proper frigate, docking at Tremaine Station? How did we get so lucky?*

Gus shook his head. "I'll keep my ears open, though."

As the shuttle launched itself from the mining hub, the artificial gravity shut off for a moment, not an unusual occurrence on the old transports. Jaq flailed an arm and just managed to catch his floppy hat as it drifted from his head.

Bruno groaned. "Again?"

The shuttle intercom crackled. "Sorry, ladies and gents, won't be but a moment."

There was a startled yelp from behind Elsa. She twisted in her seat to see that the occupant of the seat back-to-back with hers had been thrown into the air by the jolt of the launch and the sudden loss of gravity. The drifting cinder was tiny, slimmer than Elsa and not much taller. She had somehow flipped upside down, and her silvery cornsilk hair waved gently as she floated past Elsa's chair.

"Hello," the drifter said, and her voice had an unusual lilt Elsa had never heard before; she couldn't place the accent. "Slipped clean out of my harness. Now what?"

"Best watch out," Bruno warned. "The gravity could come back on at any—"

The intercom crackled simultaneously: "There, now, told you it wouldn't be long."

Elsa reached up as high as she could (which wasn't very), snatched at the drifting woman's hand, and just managed to catch her thin, cool fingers. She pulled hard, and the woman bent like a whip, swinging right-side up over Elsa and her friends. Elsa yanked the woman down into the seat next to her by her feet just as the gravity came back on, and the woman fell the last few inches into the chair.

"Many thanks," she gasped, clutching the armrests but grinning at Elsa. "I fell asleep," she admitted, hastily buckling the harness around her. She was so slender, Elsa could easily see how she had slipped free. "I should know better. The gravity cut out yesterday as I was first arriving at the station, but I just hung on to the harness to stay in my seat. I could have cracked my head like an embryo."

"Sorry, like a what?" Gus asked.

"Er, like an unborn . . ." she trailed off, gesturing vaguely with one hand. "You know, the kind that you eat." She looked from Jaq to a horrified Gus.

"Do you mean an egg?" Jaq asked. His voice had an odd tone, and Elsa glanced at him. He was staring at her new seatmate. With good reason, Elsa realized, as she caught a glimpse of the woman's eyes: She was a fay. That explained the hair, at any rate.

"Yes! Thank you," the fay replied.

Elsa coughed delicately. "Er, I'm glad you weren't hurt." She kicked Jaq, who finally closed his mouth. "You'll have to pardon us. We've never seen a fay before. I wasn't completely sure you were real," she confessed.

The fay laughed, a sound like a carillon. Her unearthly, quicksilver eyes gleamed merrily. "Oh yes," she said, "very real, as you can see. Though not many of us have left the homeworld yet. I'm a bit of a pioneer," she said, tossing her head and smiling. Her fine hair settled around her shoulders, thistledown soft.

"I know every cinder on this shift," Bruno said, "but I don't believe we've met. You say you're new?"

"Aye, brand. Today was my first day on shift."

Jaq rediscovered his tongue. "Welcome to Aschen, in that case! If you ever need anything, just you look us up and we'll come a-running." He grinned widely.

Gus elbowed Jaq in the ribs, ignored the dirty look Jaq shot his way, and said, "I'm Gus, and the lout here is Jaq. The one with the hound-dog face is Bruno."

The fay turned to fix Elsa with an unsettling, alien stare. Elsa forced herself not to look away. "And my tiny savior?" the fay asked.

Elsa laughed. "You're one to talk. I'm Elsa. And you?"

"I'm called Marraine," the fay answered. "Or at least that's close enough to what I'm called." She paused. "I don't forget a favor, Elsa." Again, that unblinking stare.

Elsa smiled. "No worries, glad to help. What brought you to Aschen? You're a long way from home."

"Oh, I have my reasons," Marraine replied. "A healthy desire for exploration primary among them. When starships from elsewhere first visited my homeworld, we asked them what made them come to our part of the galaxy in the first place. 'Because it was there,' they told us. I thought it an intriguing reply."

The shuttle jarred as it docked with Tremaine Station proper, and Marraine unbuckled her harness and rose before anyone could comment.

"Enchanted to meet all of you," she said. She looked at Elsa. "And thank you again for your help. Should you ever be in need, I'm at your service." She turned and was gone, slipping through the disembarking crowd.

Elsa blinked, and Bruno shook himself as if waking from a dream. Jaq hadn't moved since Marraine stood.

"I guess it's true," Gus said. "They really don't blink. She never did, the whole time."

"Her eyes were incredible," Jaq said, looking dazed.

"When the fay homeworld was first discovered, I heard there was some debate about whether the inhabitants were human or a separate species," Bruno mused. "I'm still not sure myself. She was beautiful and unsettling, certainly, but I don't know that I'd call her a different species."

Elsa stood up and hustled the boys out of the seats. "Who are you and what have you done with my crewmates? You've all been magically transformed into love-stricken teenagers. Now, let's get out of here before the shuttle leaves with us still aboard."

Still discussing their new acquaintance, the cinders emerged from the shuttle bay into Tremaine Station and were immediately caught up in the bustle of the crowds. Many people were hurrying home, some were shopping at the array of vendor booths, and some were dining at the assortment of available restaurants. The Tremaine Mining Company was one of the largest in the galaxy, and its holdings stretched across the stars. Aschen was lucky to have its own full-fledged space station nearby; most chthonian worlds boasted little in the way of civilization. Tremaine Station was home to the mining company offices and quarters for the cinders, but it was also rapidly becoming a port of call for galactic commerce. Cendrillon buyers came through almost daily, and a growing number of goods traders made it a regular stop on their routes as well.

Close your eyes and squint, thought Elsa, *and you could almost imagine this was a planetside city.* Not that she had visited many such cities since becoming a cinder; she had been bouncing from one mining station to another for the last several years, chasing the cendrillon.

"Want to catch a bite?" Gus asked the group at large.

"Suits me," Bruno replied, ever amiable. Jaq was still daydreaming and ignored the question, so Gus grabbed his arm and pointed him in the direction of the food vendors.

Elsa clapped a hand to her forehead. "I forgot about Nebraska."

"Ooooh. Better run," Bruno said.

"I'll catch up with you later. Message me with your restaurant choice so I can find you later?"

"Naturally," Gus replied, making a shooing gesture with his hands.

"Thanks!" Elsa tossed the reply over her shoulder, already on her way.

CHAPTER 2

IKE MOST STATIONS AND starbases, Tremaine Station established its own schedule based roughly on Earth-standard time. Although it was evening by station reckoning, the mining company offices still gave off a mild hum of activity. Shifts worked on Aschen almost round-the-clock, meaning that office staff always had work to do on their end.

Elsa braced herself as she approached the central desk for the mining company and the domain of Nebraska, who took her data-pushing duties very seriously. Excruciatingly seriously. Elsa pasted a smile on her face, took a deep breath, and rounded the corner to Nebraska's desk . . . which was empty.

She let out her breath and stood on her tiptoes, trying to see over the cubicle walls nearby—a fruitless exercise, given her stature. She walked over to the closest set of cubicles, which was shared by Priscilla and Camilla. The clones were, in Bruno's words, a few test tubes short of a lab, but their tendency to over-share was harmless compared with Nebraska's passive aggression.

"Hello, ladies," Elsa said, popping around the corner. "Have you two seen Nebraska? She wanted to talk to me, but she's not at her desk."

The clones looked up from their work in unison. The color of the day was apparently turquoise; the clones always dressed alike, and they usually wore outfits composed entirely of different shades of the same color. One of the clones—Elsa wasn't sure which—answered, "She should be back in a minute. She just stepped out to change her dressing."

Elsa's eyebrows rose. "Her what?"

"That cat of hers scratched her again," the same clone continued.

"Only creature alive who's meaner than she is," the other interjected morosely. "Must be the devil incarnate."

"The scratch got infected, oozing pus. Nasty business," the first clone said. "Did we ever tell you about the time we got poison oak?" she asked, changing topics with whiplash-inducing speed. "It was so bad, the pus seeped through the bandages."

Elsa sighed. At least now she knew which clone she was talking to. Both conversed mainly in non sequiturs, but Camilla possessed a ghoulish relish for all maladies, and Priscilla was obsessed with reincarnation and her past lives. Elsa briefly wondered just what the clones' original DNA donor had been like. "Yes, Camilla, I think you mentioned it."

"I have pictures of the rash somewhere on here," Camilla muttered, scrolling through files on her commlink.

"That's quite all right," Elsa said hastily. "Priscilla, do you know what Nebraska wanted to talk to me about?" *In other words, how badly am I in trouble,* she thought.

"Your last report had an error," the other clone answered. "We heard her banging data folders around. She made another cinder cry later, though, and that always makes her feel better. She's probably in a fairly good mood by now. Do you know she's been listening to the same ten pieces of music every day? If we hear one more of Bach's cello suites, we're going to throw ourselves out of the airlock."

"I'm sorry," Elsa began, but Priscilla cut her off.

"Not that it would be the first time, you understand."

Elsa blinked. "Sorry?"

"In one of our past lives, when we were part of a starship pirate's harem, kidnapped because of our captivating beauty to serve at a smuggler's whim. We lost our one true love, so we threw ourselves out of the airlock."

In the long moment it took her to muster any sort of reply to that, Elsa heard a faint squeak down the hall behind her. The clones paled. "You'd better go," Priscilla said. They hunched over their work.

Elsa sighed. The squeak grew louder. She pasted the remnants of that big smile back on her face and turned to face her nemesis.

Nebraska stood at the central desk, glaring at her with her one human eye. The other was no doubt glaring as well, but Elsa couldn't tell; Nebraska was a cyborg, and her left eye was artificial. Her right leg, also artificial, squeaked ominously when she walked the halls, giving the other employees just enough advance warning of her approach to feel a shiver of dread.

"Good evening," Elsa chirped, determined to begin civilly. "I hope your day went well?"

Nebraska said nothing but managed to do so disdainfully. She sniffed the air. Elsa surreptitiously took a whiff herself. She couldn't smell anything, but she was immune to the odor of soot by this time. Nebraska, however, had a nose like a bloodhound and wasn't shy about reporting Elsa to the supervisor for "reeking like a chimney." Nebraska swore the smell aggravated her asthma. Elsa didn't fully understand how a cyborg with artificial lungs could even have asthma, but she wisely kept this observation to herself.

If she could smell brimstone, Nebraska chose not to comment on it. She smiled. Her face didn't seem to know what to do with the unusual movement. Elsa resisted the urge to shudder.

"Could have been worse," Nebraska finally said.

"You wanted to see me?" Elsa asked.

Nebraska pointed dramatically to a stack of reports. The one on top had been highlighted in an alarming shade of orange. Elsa leaned over to read the note. "'Correct and return to me,'" she read aloud. "What did I do wrong?"

"I've marked your mistake."

Elsa scanned the first page. "Well, I see the typo on the third line." In her haste to submit the end-of-week report, she had tacked an extra H to the end of a word. "I don't see any important errors, though."

"Please do as I requested."

Elsa blinked. "You mean you printed out the report, marked the typo, and waited to file it, so that you could hand it to me, I could go into the digital file, fix the typo, and resubmit it to you . . . instead of just removing the letter yourself?"

Nebraska's artificial eye whirred disconcertingly. "Do you have a problem following instructions? Please do as I requested."

Elsa took a deep breath, held it for a second, and smiled. "I'll send the corrected report in tonight." As she lifted her much-maligned report from the stack, she glimpsed a fuel requisition order underneath. Nebraska was frighteningly old-fashioned and still occasionally insisted on hard copies of a document. The name on the requisition caught Elsa's attention, and her eyes widened.

"It'll be late by then, of course. You'll have to log the time and submit a notification of tardiness," Nebraska said with relish.

But Elsa was only half-listening, caught up in her discovery. "Sure, have a good evening, Nebraska." She left the office as quickly as she dared.

Choosing a food vendor always took longer than it should have. Bruno waited, a long-suffering expression on his face, as Jaq and Gus argued the merits of crepes versus burgers.

"You might as well eat nutrient cubes," Gus complained. "An hour after eating a crepe, and you're hungry again. They're practically air."

Jaq shook his head in disdain. "You call that food?" he asked, gesturing at the burger vendor's menu. "That's an edible coronary." The burger vendor shot him an irritated look.

At last even Bruno's legendary patience gave out. He came up between the two younger men, grabbed an elbow apiece, and steered them across the station's food plaza. "Pasta it is," he decreed.

The other two men acquiesced with a readiness that would have been surprising to those who didn't know them well, but Bruno was well aware that their bickering was an expression of their friendship. *There are limits, however, to how much friendly banter a hungry man can take*, he thought, looking over the menu options.

"Should we get something for Elsa?" Jaq asked.

"I know she likes the lasagna," Gus put in. "I'll order her a piece."

"She may be awhile," Bruno warned. "Depends on how long it takes Nebraska to vent her frustrations."

"I don't understand Nebraska," Jaq said as he selected his entrée and scanned his commlink over the payment terminal. "Hating everyone at that level of intensity has to be exhausting."

"She was always prickly," Bruno said quietly, "but she wasn't always so vicious."

"Really? What happened?" Gus asked, surprised.

"It was a few Earth-standard years ago," Bruno said as they left the vendor to find a table. "She was just starting a temporary assignment as an ore inspector, didn't intend to be there long—she always thought working for the mining industry was beneath her."

It wasn't an uncommon viewpoint. Cinders, though a necessary part of the galactic economy, weren't held in high esteem as individuals. With its high pay and dangerous reputation, the job did tend to attract the desperate. *I should know*, Bruno thought.

He continued as they all sat down at an empty table. "Nebraska was caught on a transport shuttle when a massive plasma storm hit the station. The shuttle was all but torn apart, and Nebraska almost didn't survive." Bruno paused, remembering the sight of Nebraska on a hoverbed as the rescue team took her to the infirmary. Suddenly his pasta marinara didn't look so appealing.

He cleared his throat. "Her recovery was . . . lengthy. Afterwards she was guaranteed a permanent position with the mining company as part of her compensation. She didn't want to stay, but the pay was decent, and there's still a bit of a stigma against cyborgs on some worlds, after the Galatea Rebellion. Everyone's going the synth-flesh route these days. I guess she figured this was as good as she was likely to get."

Gus picked at his dinner quietly, more subdued after hearing the story, but Jaq still looked skeptical. "I know she's miserable here," Jaq said, "and I feel badly for her, but that doesn't excuse the way she treats people. I heard Anastasia quit because of her, and you know how tough she is."

"Oh, believe me, I agree," Bruno said. "Her misery doesn't entitle her to pass it on to other people."

Before he could continue, klaxons sounded throughout the station, cutting off all conversation. Bruno stood up, heart pounding, as he looked at his commlink for a more detailed notification. Jaq dropped his fork in his spaghetti with a splat.

"What is it?" Gus asked, fumbling for his own commlink. "A storm?"

"No," Bruno replied, heart rate slowing. "Looks like it was a false alarm for us here." He sat back down. "The notification says the alarm was only meant to sound in the mining hub. There was some seismic activity on Aschen's surface, and they're recalling any cinders currently in the southern hemisphere. No injuries or damage."

"Oh." Jaq fished his fork out of the sauce, wiping it with his napkin. The klaxons continued to blare. "So why aren't they shutting the alarm off here?"

Bruno snorted. "The mining supervisor sent the alert. You know what he's like. Probably hasn't even figured out that he triggered the alarm here too."

Gus winced at the racket. "I bet the clones could shut it off. Those two can hack into anything."

Jaq had his commlink out. "I'm messaging them now," he muttered around a mouthful of spaghetti.

Looking far too pleased for someone coming from a meeting with the cyborg, Elsa approached their table just as the klaxons fell silent at last.

"It's a miracle!" Gus said. He pushed the lasagna in front of Elsa as she sat down.

"What, that I survived the trip to the main office, or that the alarms finally shut up?" she asked. "And thank you," she added, giving Gus a smile.

"Both," he replied.

"Here's another one for you. I have news you won't believe," she said, throwing her report down in the middle of the table triumphantly.

Jaq squinted at the report from where he sat in his chair, teetering on the back two legs. "Nebraska still hates your guts, and you can't spell? You're wrong. We do believe you."

Elsa ignored him, and Bruno bit back a laugh. "The rumors about the frigate are true. Hold on to your helmets—the *Sovereign* is docking here!"

Jaq's chair hit the deck with a thump.

"Blow me down and close the airlock!" Gus exclaimed. "Where did you hear that?"

"I saw a fuel requisition on Nebraska's desk. The requisition was for a single ship, and the quantity needed could only have been for a frigate. More importantly," she said, "the name on the requisition was Jacob Tsarevich." She took a dramatic bite of lasagna.

Bruno whistled long and low. "Captain Tsarevich. Never thought I'd even be in the same star system with him, let alone on the same space station." He couldn't deny feeling a thrill at the prospect.

"He must be getting up in years, isn't he?" Gus asked. "I've been hearing tales of his exploits since I was a boy."

Jaq nodded. "Me too. On my homeworld, they called him the *Roi des Astres*—the King of the Stars. Have you seen the recordings of the Battle of Castle Nebula?"

Better than that, Bruno thought, remembering the sight. *I was there.* But he only nodded. "He's unmatched as a strategist—though they say his son Karl may be almost as good. Perhaps even better."

Gus scoffed. "I can't believe that. The Prince better than the King?"

"Well, his mettle is yet to be tested in the way his father's was, I'll grant you that," Elsa replied.

"Does his son still sail with him?" Jaq asked.

"There were rumors that Karl might take over the *Sovereign* when his father finally retires," Bruno said. "He should—he grew up on that ship, and he's the senior lieutenant. No one knows her better."

Jaq gave him a sidewise glance.

Bruno shifted in his chair. "What? We all have our interests. Mine happens to be the fleet." He didn't add that his interest could be termed obsession; ever since his own discharge from the fleet years ago, he spent an inordinate amount of time keeping up with the latest news.

"Why would the *Sovereign* be coming here, of all places?" asked Gus.

"I've been thinking about that," Elsa said, scooting her chair closer. "Initially, talk was that a frigate might stop here on its way to patrol. That wouldn't really make sense, though. A whole frigate, just to patrol the Periphery of the quadrant? It's a waste, even more so if it's the *Sovereign* they're sending. I think the fleet must be reinitiating the deep galactic exploration program." She leaned back, watching the reactions her statement produced.

Jaq cried, "What!"

Gus waved a hand in dismissal. "There's been no official notice of that, and nothing at all has been done with the exploration program since before the war."

Bruno, however, nodded slowly. "It makes sense. True, no exploration has been done in almost fifty years, but the peace has been solid for a decade now. It's logical for the fleet to return its attention to former goals, now that the region is stable." He hoped that was the case, anyway: no one wanted to relive the war.

Elsa slapped the table, making her half-eaten plate of lasagna jump. "Exactly! And even though things seem stable for now, it would also make sense to keep talk of the expedition to a minimum, which explains why we've heard nothing till now. News of the departure of one of the fleet's best could cause old enemies to prick up their ears, wondering if this is their chance to make a move."

"Do you know when the *Sovereign* is arriving here?" Jaq asked.

Elsa shook her head. "I didn't see the arrival date on the form."

"We'll know soon enough," Gus answered. "Much as they want to keep this quiet, the preparation work for fitting out a frigate—and accommodating its crew on shore leave—will require that most of the station occupants know about it."

Bruno couldn't argue with that. It was impossible to keep secrets aboard the station. *Well*, he thought, *nearly so.*

He rose from the table. "I think I'm going to call it a night." He picked up Elsa's report from the middle of the table and handed it to her. "Oh, don't forget about this, or Nebraska will have your hide."

She took it from him. "I'll submit the corrected report online and log the late submission right now. Maybe that will make her happy."

Bruno raised an eyebrow at her.

"Fine," she conceded, "there's little hope of that. But after today's news, I don't feel too badly about the situation anymore." She smiled, looking like an excited little girl, and not for the first time Bruno wondered what she had been like as a child.

She glanced at Gus and Jaq, who were caught up in a debate over the *Sovereign*'s specs, and she moved around the table closer to Bruno, lowering her voice. "When I heard the klaxons, I thought they may have been sounding for another plasma storm," she said, her eyes searching his face.

Bruno looked away. "It did bring back memories," he said. Nebraska hadn't been the only casualty of the storm. Of the group at the table, only Elsa had been there that day, years ago, when he was still licking his wounds from a failed fleet career. One side of his mouth rose in a half-hearted smile. "Not that those memories ever really left."

"It wasn't your fault," Elsa said earnestly. "None of it was. I know you look out for all of us like a father would, but you weren't responsible—"

"Yes, I was," he snapped. Gus and Jaq looked over the table in surprise at his tone. Elsa sent them a reassuring smile, and they resumed their discussion.

"I was responsible," Bruno continued more quietly. "I suspected the shield wasn't going to hold. I should have disobeyed the station's orders. I didn't." His already-rough voice rasped even deeper in his throat. "And lives were lost as a result."

Elsa put a hand on his shoulder and gave him a little shake. "Regardless of what you may think, that burden doesn't lie with you," she said, holding his gaze with her own. "We do dangerous work; risk comes with the job description. You can't protect us all," she said with a small smile.

Perhaps not. But he could try.

CHAPTER 3

IN THE EVENT, GUS was right: By the end of shift the next day, news of the *Sovereign*'s arrival hummed throughout the station.

"A *week*, can you believe it?" Jaq said as they all filed into the shuttle after their shift. "There's no way everything will be ready in a week, even with every staff member scrambling."

"Oh, they'll make it happen," Gus said, buckling his harness. "My steward friend says they're receiving a boatload of temporary employees today, borrowed from the Charger 751 starbase for the event."

Elsa noticed Jaq craning his neck to see over the seats. "Looking for Marraine?" she teased.

He shot her a look. "Nothing wrong with being friendly," he said. He pulled out his commlink and pretended to be absorbed in it. Suddenly he sat up straight. "Check your messages! We were just invited to a station-wide party in honor of the *Sovereign*'s arrival."

They all pulled up the message on their commlinks. Bruno raised a bushy eyebrow as he read the details. "There's going to be dancing?"

Gus shrugged. "I've heard that the captain enjoys ballroom dancing."

Elsa stared. "How in the worlds do you know that?"

Gus held up his hands, looking the picture of innocence. "I have a very trustworthy face; people tell me things."

As the week passed, the end-of-shift commute became a free-for-all of speculation among the cinders as excitement built. The furor truly exploded, however, on the day the *Sovereign* docked at the station.

The observation deck of the station was packed with people, and vendors with windows in their shops were allowing people to cram inside so they could see the frigate come into port—for a fee. The cinder crews created their own workaround to the problem by paying the shuttle pilot to take the scenic route back to the station from the mining hub after their shift. The cinders craned their heads to see out of the shuttle windows.

"Anything?" Elsa asked, tapping her fingers on the armrest. She and Marraine were too short to see over the other cinders' heads.

Jaq shook his head, not taking his eyes from the windows. "Not yet."

Gus whooped. "There she is! Aft starboard."

A hush fell over the shuttle.

Elsa unbuckled her harness, stood up in her seat, and locked her feet around an armrest in case the gravity shorted out.

"Good thought," Marraine murmured, doing likewise so she could catch a glimpse.

And there was the frigate. Silvery white, she glided towards the station, space sails still set. Even as Elsa watched, they gracefully furled, tucking away like the wings of a bird. Her heart clenched unexpectedly at the sight, a reminder of her home; her father used to take her to watch the ships dock at her homeworld. She remembered how he proudly pointed out her mother's ship, and she recalled the thrill of knowing her mother would be home with them soon. *Except for that last time*, Elsa thought. She swallowed past the lump in her throat.

"She is beautiful," Marraine breathed.

The *Sovereign* passed on to its dock, the largest Tremaine Station could provide, and the cinders lost sight of the majestic frigate behind the bulk of the station.

Elsa sat down. If the others noticed that she was silent for the rest of the trip home, they mercifully didn't comment; but for a long moment, Marraine watched her with unblinking eyes.

Gus was correct again. On the day of the party, the cinders received a message that Captain Tsarevich himself would be leading the dance, and his son would also be in attendance. Excitement on the shuttle reached critical mass on the cinders' last commute home before the party.

"I could swear I just heard a grown man squeal," Bruno said in disgust. "Everyone is losing their heads over this."

Jaq was in an agony over whether or not to invite Marraine to go to the party with him.

"Just do it," Gus hissed. "You're almost out of time. The thing starts in a few hours."

"But what if customs are different on her planet? What if asking someone to a dance is a big deal? I don't want to accidentally marry her!" Jaq paused. "Well. I mean, it wouldn't be so bad . . ."

Bruno threw his hands in the air.

Elsa skimmed through her messages on her commlink, only half-listening to the drama unfolding around her. She groaned.

"What?" Bruno asked.

"Nebraska wants me to report to her office again tonight."

"What for? Doesn't she know everyone will be getting ready for the party?"

"She doesn't say, but I better head over there now before the office closes." Elsa squared her shoulders, determined not to let Nebraska spoil her evening.

When the shuttle docked at the station, Jaq lagged behind the others as they disembarked. He drummed his fingers on the shuttle doorframe, yanking them out of the way as the automatic door attempted to close. "You folks go on," he said. "I'm, ah . . . I'm going to see if I can catch Marraine."

Gus high-fived him. "Look who's all grown up and going on dates with aliens. I'm so proud."

Jaq scowled at him.

Elsa caught sight of Marraine's silvery head among the group of cinders disembarking from the next shuttle. She herded Gus and Bruno away. "Come on, let's leave him to his wooing."

"But I want to see this," Gus protested.

Jaq pointed to the main station door. "Out! Or so help me, we're eating crepes every night for a week."

"Stars above!" Gus exclaimed in mock horror, hustling to the exit. Elsa and Bruno followed at a more sedate pace.

Once outside, the trio parted ways. "Time for me and Gus to go make ourselves look pretty," Bruno deadpanned. "We'll see you at the party. Don't let Nebraska keep you too long."

"Believe me, I won't stick around a minute longer than I have to," Elsa assured him.

When she reached the hub, one of the clones was already waiting to speak to Nebraska, who was engaged in an intense conversation over the comm line. Elsa heard cello music just barely audible over the steely-toned comm discussion. The clone fidgeted nervously, looking lost without her identical companion.

Elsa smiled at her. "Glad to see you haven't taken a header out of the airlock, in spite of the excessive Bach. What are you in for?"

The clone looked miserable, but before she could answer, Nebraska slammed a hand down on the comm controls, ending the call. The clone nearly leaped out of her purple shoes.

"Sun, moon, and stars above, what an idiot," Nebraska swore at whatever poor soul she had been talking to. She turned on the clone, who took an inadvertent step back before the force of the cyborg's one-eyed glare. "What do you want?"

"Er, which server would you like us to store the latest galactic fleet files on?" The clone's voice wavered.

Nebraska's single eye stared back at the clone, unblinking. The clone grew increasingly uncomfortable as the pause lengthened. She tried a tentative smile.

"In the tertiary drive folder," Nebraska snapped.

"Oh, all right—"

"They've always gone in the tertiary drive folder." Still no blinking. The artificial eye whirred, adjusting the focus slightly.

"I was just check—"

"They go in the tertiary drive folder."

"Yes. Of course." The clone conceded defeat and scuttled back to the relative safety of her cubicle.

Elsa took a deep breath. "You wanted to see me?" she asked.

Nebraska wordlessly handed her the shift duty roster, which Elsa had already checked at the beginning of the week.

"Oh, I've already entered my shift schedule into my calendar, but thank you," she said, puzzled.

"There have been some changes," Nebraska said.

Elsa frowned. Her shifts rarely varied. "Oh?"

"You've been placed on the beta shift for tonight."

Elsa's eyes widened. "Tonight? We were told that all shifts were cancelled for the evening so the cinders could attend the gathering. The whole station has the night off."

Nebraska had the grace to look slightly ashamed. "Cendrillon hauls weren't quite what we predicted. It was determined that one coach had to be sent out, or the station wouldn't fulfill the cendrillon quota for the month." She wouldn't meet Elsa's eyes. "Someone has to work the shift, and you were chosen at random from amongst the top haulers."

"I'll just bet I was," Elsa replied, unable to keep the bitterness from her voice.

Nebraska drew herself up, artificial leg clicking. "Are you presuming to imply that you were chosen unfairly? I have the records here: The computer chose your account at random. If you would like to take this up with the mining supervisor, you are welcome to do so."

"I'll consider it," Elsa replied icily. As Nebraska well knew, it was too late now for her to get an appointment with the supervisor before the party.

In the tense pause that followed, the cello suite playing at Nebraska's desk was plainly audible. Elsa turned to leave, not trusting herself to remain civil, when something clicked in her memory.

"Nebraska," she said, swinging back around, "are you going to the party?"

Nebraska looked down at her desk. "No," she replied. "I've never gone to the station gatherings before, and no one wants me there."

Elsa hesitated a moment before continuing, feeling as though she were putting her naked hand inside a thruster intake valve. "You should go," she said softly. "They've brought an orchestra, you know. Borrowed it from the Charger 751 starbase just for the occasion."

Nebraska raised her head but remained silent.

"I know the station isn't where you want to be," Elsa said gently. "This could be your opportunity to find somewhere you *do* want to be."

Nebraska blinked her single eye.

Elsa gave her a small smile. "I should go," she said.

She walked back to the shuttles, wondering if they would even be running. She took her time. There was no rush now, with nothing to get ready for.

One shuttle was standing ready, doors open. Elsa walked inside and took a seat, buckling herself in. The shuttle felt so much bigger, empty of cinders. She resisted the urge to cry. It was only a party, after all.

CHAPTER 4

JAQ WATCHED MARRAINE STEP down from the shuttle threshold, her bright hair contrasting vibrantly with the dark metal of the hull. He drew a deep breath and approached her. But his breath was immediately snatched away the moment he drew near, for she turned and gave him a beautiful smile.

"Hello, Jaq. Did you have a good shift?" she asked.

"I did, thanks. I hope you did too." There, that sounded fairly suave, right? At least moderately polite.

She slid to one side to allow the last few cinders past her, silver hair swinging with the motion, and something about her movement struck Jaq as so otherworldly and out of place that he blurted, "Why are you here?"

She arched an eyebrow at him, which somehow made her look much more human. "I was trying to go home to my quarters."

"Sorry, yes, I meant—" he floundered, stopped himself, and tried again. "I meant why are you working for the mining company? The only people who take jobs as cinders are adrenaline junkies or folks who need money fast, and somehow you don't strike me as falling into either category."

She gave him a shy smile. "I suppose I must seem like an odd bird out of air."

Jaq attempted to translate the mashed idioms. "Er, a fish out of water?"

She cocked her head at him. "I don't think that's an accurate metaphor. A fish out of water would be dead."

He thought about this for a second, frowning. "Yeah, actually. Sorry, continue."

"Anyway, it's traditional on my world for young people to go away on their own and explore for a time after they have completed their education but before choosing a particular career. We call it a bridge age."

Jaq nodded. He had heard of similar traditions before.

"The fleet visited my world for the first time while I was growing up," she said. "Mine was the first generation to realize there was something beyond our planet. How could I decide what life I wanted, when there were so many choices on other worlds, about which I knew nothing? I decided to take my bridge age offworld." She dropped her eyes, shy again. "Mine has lasted rather longer than usual," she admitted, "but it turns out there are many things to see in the galaxy. Who knows what I'll find next?"

"Do you plan to move on soon, then?" Jaq asked.

She smiled at his crestfallen expression. "We shall see. I've not seen enough of mining life to satisfy my curiosity yet. We've not done any sort of mining on my world in centuries."

He frowned, curious. "What do your own people call your world? I don't know that I've ever heard a name."

"You wouldn't be able to pronounce it. Haven't you noticed, though, the inhabitants of every world call their home the same thing? World, earth, land—the meaning is the same, whatever the language might be.

Everyone believes his or her planet really is the *world*: the universe, the entirety, the only place that matters. We're only just beginning to depart from that self-centric way of thinking."

She was right, Jaq realized. "That's part of the reason why you left," he said. "You wanted to see the real world—all of it, not just the universe of your own planet."

She gave him a long look with those unblinking, silvery eyes.

That's . . . all manner of disconcerting, he thought. He kind of liked it.

"Very astute," she said finally, surprise in her voice.

He *didn't* like that. "It happens once in a while," he said, trying (and, he thought, probably failing) not to sound miffed. Being the youngest in his family, he was accustomed to people underestimating his abilities, but he didn't enjoy it.

"Oh, I meant no offense," she said hastily. "As I've travelled, I've run into a curious dichotomy," she said, frowning. "On the one side, many offworlders pursue exploration and knowledge, and on the other, many pursue profit. It's as though humans are attempting to better themselves but haven't yet managed to move past their greed. The latter has been particularly evident on Tremaine Station," she added, mouth twisting in disgust. "The preoccupation with profit, at the cost of human happiness or even human health, is disturbing." She eyed Jaq again. "So I'm sure you can understand my surprise at meeting a kindred spirit here." She studied him for a moment. "Why are *you* here? You don't seem to be an adrenaline junkheap, so did you come here for the fast money, as you called it?"

He resolutely did not smile at her error, an action made easier by his embarrassment. He looked away. "I did," he admitted, wishing it weren't the case after her indictment of the galaxy's greed. "I come from a large family, and credits were scarce while I was growing up. I took the job so I could send money back to my parents."

"Don't be ashamed of that," Marraine said, and the fervor in her voice made him look up again. "That's the best reason I've heard for joining a cinder crew, and I commend you for caring for your family. We value familial responsibility very highly on my world."

"I know you said I wouldn't be able to pronounce it, but would you mind telling me what you call your world?" he asked. "I'd like to hear how it sounds," he added shyly.

She laughed and said something incomprehensible.

He blinked. "Could you say that more slowly?"

Slower didn't help. He took a stab at it anyway. "Let me try. Hayzeltry?"

She laughed again, and he gave her a rueful smile. "I know, I'm garbling it, but that's the best I can do."

"It's not bad, really." She tried out his mangled version of the word. "Hayzeltry. I like how it sounds, even if it doesn't sound quite right to a fay's ear."

She glanced at the time on her commlink. "I'm sorry to go, but I should go get ready for the party. You ask so many questions! I believe you had one more, however." She tilted her head inquiringly.

"I did?" he said blankly. "Oh! I did." He cleared his throat, straightened his shoulders a fraction, and forced himself not to fidget. "Would you do me the honor of attending the party with me?"

"It would be my pleasure," she replied.

"I'll pick you up at your quarters?" He hadn't intended it to sound quite so much like a question.

Another big smile. He could get used to those. "I look forward to it," she said, touching his arm with cool fingers.

His commlink chimed just then, and he fully intended to ignore it.

"Hadn't you better get that?" she asked.

"Oh. Uh, yeah." If it was Gus, he thought in vexation, he swore he—but it wasn't Gus. His eyebrows shot up when he saw the name on the commlink. "Nebraska?"

The shuttle docked at the mining hub with a soft bounce—strange, the gravity worked just fine when there was no one to appreciate it—and Elsa walked into the deserted locker room. It was silent in the way only a normally busy room can be when it is empty. She climbed up on her bench to reach inside her locker and pull her helmet down off of the shelf. The click of her helmet locking into place on her suit echoed throughout the room.

Her coach launched itself from the mining hub into an eerie quiet. Elsa was used to the initial chatter of all of the cinders coordinating the beginning of their shift. *At least working alone means I can fly anywhere without worrying about interfering with another coach's trajectory,* she thought, trying to find a bright side.

Out of the corner of her eye, she saw something glint as she fell towards the planet's surface. She leaned forward to look through the view-screen back the way she had come. She could just see the edge of the *Sovereign*, glimmering like a jewel in its dock on the far side of the station. Elsa sighed and turned back to the task at hand. She skimmed over the planet's surface, adroitly avoiding a gout of flame that erupted nearby, and did not let her gaze drift upwards towards the station again. No point in torturing herself. She had a job to do.

Her focus meant she did not see what was approaching from the direction of the station. Her comm line buzzed, making her jump inside the quiet cabin.

"Mind if we come play in the pumpkin patch too?"

The voice was Bruno's, but she didn't understand. "What?"

"Looks like she's keeping the ore all to herself, kids," Bruno said, and she could hear the smile in his voice.

She finally saw them: three coaches making their way towards the planet's surface. "Jaq? Gus?" she said, incredulous.

"You were expecting terrifying space monkeys, maybe?" Jaq said. "Of course it's us."

"If we work fast, we can all go to this shindig," Gus said.

Elsa's grin spread across her face. "You guys are the best. But even with all four of us working, we'll still miss the beginning of the party. Are you sure you don't want to go back? I'd hate for you to miss the festivities on my account."

"I believe you mean all five of us," a cool, silvery voice replied. Another coach emerged from the shadow of the others.

"Marraine?" Elsa said in disbelief.

"The same. I told you I don't forget a favor, dear."

"But how did you all even know to come here? I just found out about the shift myself!"

"You won't believe it, but Nebraska told us," Bruno replied. "She said you had to work the shift and implied there would be no repercussions if a few extra coaches just so happened to launch."

If Elsa's vision became a bit blurred, it was only because her viewscreen was clouding up. Or so she told herself. She cleared her throat. "Thank you," she said simply. "You're all getting a big hug as soon as we get back."

Bruno harrumphed. "All right, enough chatter. Let's get this cendrillon loaded."

The crew filled their coaches in record time and flew swiftly back to the mining hub to dump their cargo. Elsa fidgeted in the airlock as her suit cooled, and she hit the door controls when the suit was still faintly steaming.

Jaq and Gus were already in the locker room. She grabbed them both and gave them resounding kisses on their cheeks before she was even out of her suit. Jaq squeaked. Bruno emerged from his airlock and turned it into a group hug, and as Marraine arrived, Gus grabbed her hand to pull her in, helmet and all.

Bruno realized the indignity of his position and coughed. "Don't we have an event to get to?" Laughing, the group broke up and began shedding their suits.

"Elsa, I have something you might be able to use," Marraine said, pulling off her gloves.

She slipped out of her suit and carefully lifted a wrapped item out of her locker. "This was made on my world. I haven't seen anything quite like it anywhere else in my travels." She handed it to Elsa.

Elsa unwrapped the layers of paper surrounding the item. She gasped. "Marraine, I can't accept this! It's far too generous."

Marraine smiled, her strange eyes shining. "It's unwise to reject a gift from the fays, child. Take it and enjoy it. You've earned it." She dropped a kiss on Elsa's forehead, feather-light.

Elsa hugged her tightly and then wrapped the package back up. Her smile seemed a permanent fixture by this point. "I accept, with gratitude. Just let me go clean up. It would be nothing short of criminal to get soot on this."

CHAPTER 5

AMILLA AND PRISCILLA HAD never seen so many people on Tremaine Station. The party was located in the vaulted central atrium of the station, and the crowds packed in so that they could catch a glimpse of the *Sovereign*'s crew, especially Captain and Lieutenant Tsarevich. The clones, wearing purple dresses with purple stockings and purple shoes, were leaning over the balcony of the second level, looking down at the people swirling below. The dancing was expected to begin any moment.

"There he is," Camilla said, elbowing the other clone. "This is our chance."

The captain and the lieutenant caused a stir the moment they strode in, imposing in their long dark coats. The rest of the *Sovereign*'s crew had foregone the customary uniforms in favor of more colorful civilian wear.

The clones took a service lift down, avoiding the worst of the crowd, and emerged behind the Tsarevich men as they walked into the atrium.

Priscilla grabbed Karl Tsarevich's arm, causing him to start. "It's so wonderful to see you here!" she exclaimed, as though they were old friends.

"We've been looking all over for you."

"Do I know you?" the lieutenant asked, a little bewildered.

Priscilla nodded solemnly. "From a past life. We were soul mates. It'll all come back to you."

"You perished, beheaded by barbarians," Camilla supplied helpfully. "I'm sure your luck will be better this time around."

From an upper level, Elsa looked down on the scene as the clones clutched their prize. Karl, poor soul, looked slightly panicked and a little amused, which was typical for someone newly introduced to the clones. As Elsa watched, Camilla led him to a table with hors d'oeuvres, and Priscilla handed him a plate filled with something unidentifiable before he could refuse. Elsa saw him take a bite of the finger food and pull a subtle face. He surreptitiously slipped the offending delicacy into a potted plant next to him when the clones were momentarily distracted by the sight of his father choosing a dance partner.

She snorted. "Charming."

Bruno appeared at her side, looking very dignified in his best clothes. "Marraine and the boys are already downstairs. Are you going to join this party, or are you just going to hover up here?"

Elsa took a deep breath, a little nervous in her unaccustomed finery. "Let's go."

Bruno offered her his arm, and they walked down the staircase together.

The Charger 751 orchestra was tucked next to the staircase, and the musicians happened to begin playing dance music just as Elsa and Bruno reached the bottom steps. Several heads swiveled to look in the direction of the sound—including Karl's.

There were several audible gasps from the people nearby when they caught sight of Elsa—or rather, when they caught sight of Marraine's gift.

The gown Elsa wore was unearthly in every sense of the word. One look and everyone could tell this was something from another world. The dress shimmered, silvers and blues glimmering like the light of an alien moon on the sea. It looked *wrong*, somehow, but breathtakingly, exquisitely so.

Karl, truth be told, would have taken advantage of any excuse to escape the clones—Camilla was regaling him with the tale of the gruesome demise of her cat, Kumquat, and Priscilla was staring at him with too much adoration for comfort—but he was intrigued by the woman standing at the foot of the stairs, looking terribly foreign and heart-wrenchingly lovely at the same time.

Bruno moved away from Elsa, giving a strange little bow, and she glanced at him in puzzlement at this unexpected courtly behavior. He looked past her shoulder. She turned, and there was Captain Tsarevich's son.

He was on the short side, she noted with some surprise. Still taller than she was, of course—everyone was—but noticeably under-height for a legendary space hero.

"Hello. Would you care to dance?" he asked.

Elsa dredged up dim, cobwebby recollections of an attempt at learning to dance back in her early school days and was not sanguine about her abilities. "I'm not very good," she admitted.

"Not a problem," he said with a tinge of desperation. "We'll wing it. I'm just not sure I can handle another gruesome feline death."

Elsa laughed and took his offered hand. He seemed very human for a hero about whom parents told bedtime stories to their children. "Mmm, Camilla does have bad luck with pets. Did you hear the story about the exploding tumor?"

Karl guided them out towards the center of the area being used as a dance floor. "Not yet, thank heaven. Please, don't spoil it for me."

Marraine danced past with Jaq, who looked amazed by his good fortune. Elsa waved at the couple.

Karl did a double take. "Is she a fay?" he asked in awe.

"She is," Elsa replied, focusing intently on her feet so she didn't tumble into the potted plant like the hors d'oeuvre. "Have you met any before?"

"Only once, years ago. We've not been to the quadrant containing the fays' homeworld in a long time. I was entranced—they were very beautiful, and very kind."

Elsa couldn't agree more after the events of the day. "Very kind indeed. Marraine gave me this dress for the evening, and I've never worn anything so fine. She said there were crystal shoes to go with it, but I think I would have inadvertently killed one or both of us by now if I'd attempted to wear them."

"Crystal shoes?" he inquired, quirking an eyebrow. "That sounds like a terrible idea."

"Marraine admitted they were awfully uncomfortable, which isn't too surprising," Elsa said. "Apparently they're traditional footwear on her planet for ceremonial occasions."

Karl winced remarkably like Elsa had when Marraine told her about the shoes.

"I know!" she said. "Fearful thought."

Karl paused, struck by an idea. "Wait. Traditional for both men and women?"

She froze for a moment before bursting out laughing. "You know, it didn't occur to me to ask. I'll have to visit someday and find out. There are so many places I haven't been."

"Where is home for you?"

It should have been a difficult question for a cinder who bounced from one mining world to the next, but she answered without thinking. "Here," she replied, surprising herself. "This is where my friends are." She added, "I was born on Anser."

Her partner cleared his throat. "That's a hard place to live. Were you, ah, there for . . ."

Elsa's smile faded. "The battle? I was, though I was very young and don't remember much. My mother was killed in the action. She was serving aboard the *Wilhelm* as a propulsion expert."

Karl broke rhythm for just a second. "I'm very sorry," he said soberly. "The loss of the *Wilhelm*'s crew was a terrible tragedy."

Elsa gave him a gentle smile. "Thank you. My father and I missed my mother very much, but we were proud of her."

"Is your father here on the station?"

Elsa couldn't imagine her father ever living in a place like this. "No, unfortunately he also passed away several years ago. He wasn't one to leave the homeworld, though. He was a glacial geologist; he loved Anser because of—not in spite of—the cold and snow."

Karl flushed. "I'm sorry, I seem to be doing nothing but opening old wounds this evening."

Touched by his concern, she hastened to reassure him. "Not at all, please don't feel badly. It's nice to talk about my parents. I haven't in some time." Elsa paused to concentrate on a particularly tricky—at least for her—turn. "Actually, your arrival reminded me of some of my favorite memories with them," she confessed.

"How so?"

"Our family loved to see the ships come in. My mother adored the *Wilhelm*, and my father would always take me to see her when she docked." Elsa met Karl's eyes, a little shy. "I watched the *Sovereign* come into port a few days ago. She's magnificent."

Karl's face lit up. "She is that! I love her dearly. I don't often see her from the outside, of course, but whenever I do . . . it's enough to make your breath catch in your chest."

He had an infectious smile, Elsa noticed. "Indeed it is. You know . . ." She paused speculatively and looked around the atrium. "The observation deck is probably fairly clear right now. Would you like to go see her?"

"Gladly," he said with such fervor that Elsa had to bite back a laugh. "Oh," he said, remembering his manners, "unless you'd prefer to dance? I don't want to deprive you of all the entertainment."

Elsa's lips twitched in mischief. "The risk to your toes increases exponentially the longer we dance; I'm having trouble talking and dancing as it is. We can always come back. The dancing will probably be going for hours if your father has anything to say about it."

The observation deck was at the top of the atrium, so they could still hear the strains of music when they walked off the lift. But their attention was entirely consumed by the ship in front of them, looking like a bird frozen in the moment of flight.

Elsa did indeed catch her breath. "Imagine, sailing among the stars in that," she murmured, unable to suppress a twinge of envy.

Karl walked up to the window. "She's a good home to us," he said, gazing outside. "Not that there aren't times when I get sick of life aboard ship," he conceded. "But those times are rare."

"I'm glad you realize how fortunate you are," Elsa said. How might her life be different now if she had shipped out with the fleet instead of becoming a cinder? She trailed her eyes across the frigate's hull, trying to imagine it.

"Believe me, I do. Especially now, in these times of peace." He put out his hand to touch the glass idly. "The *Sovereign* wasn't meant to wage war, though that's what she's spent so much of her life doing."

"It does seem wrong that something so beautiful should be used to take lives," Elsa agreed. "Whoever designed her clearly had more than killing in mind."

Karl turned to her, his eyes thoughtful. "What was it like, growing up on Anser? So much death was dealt out in the skies over that planet."

"Life returns to normal eventually. Or life becomes the new normal, I suppose." She shrugged, not because she didn't care, but because she cared too much. "Some things didn't really change." She told him of days and nights on the snowfields, star-gazing in the crystal-sharp air, hearing the snow geese in the night. "During the autumn, I often woke to the sound of the geese flying south. Their cries made me restless; I wanted to run after them to places I'd never been." She gestured to the *Sovereign*. "The sight of her makes me feel that same ache, almost physical—as though it's time to be off and see new sights."

He listened, rapt, and in turn she asked him for stories of his life, growing up aboard a frigate. He told her of the early days of families being permitted on board, what it was like with so few other children around, going from one colonized world to the next.

"One of my favorite planets to visit is New Gaul," he said. "It's not a place for thrilling adventures, but I enjoy its tranquility. And the food is superb," he added with a roguish grin.

Elsa chuckled. "My friend Jaq is from New Gaul," she said. "You two should share recipes."

"Really? We were there recently, actually—just a quick stop for repairs. The sails took some damage in an asteroid belt crossing when we had a bit of trouble with the main shielding emitters."

Elsa raised an eyebrow. " That shouldn't have occurred. Zero-point energy collectors like the *Sovereign*'s Casimir sails are designed to have separate shielding specifically to avoid that problem, and power can be routed through several auxiliary routes in case of damage to any one section."

Karl stared at her, mouth open.

Feeling terribly bold, she laughed and tapped his jaw shut with a finger. "My mother was a propulsion expert, remember? I learned about solar sails and drawing energy from the ground state of fields in the vacuum of space around the same time I learned to ride a hoverbike."

"Stars above, why aren't you serving in the fleet?" he asked, dumbfounded. "Propulsion experts are always in high demand."

"Not always," she said. "Not on Anser, not after the battle. The fleet dock was destroyed; no one was shipping out from the port. My father worked hard to rebuild the planet, but he took too much on himself; I didn't realize he had gone into personal debt, trying to help some of the families in our region." Her mouth twisted in sadness. "Not until he passed away and I was left to pay it off. I needed a high-paying job, and the fleet doesn't pay much to those starting out, as you know," she said, looking up at Karl. "I started on a different career path at a young age, and by the time I had earned enough that I might have been able to quit, I'd missed the ideal time window for fleet training for my age group."

She knew she sounded wistful, but she couldn't bring herself to regret her decision—not most days, anyway. Again she glanced sideways at Karl, who looked stricken. "Oh, it's not so bad!" she said, laughing at his expression and at herself for her maudlin ramblings while she should be enjoying her time with the golden boy of the fleet.

She tapped a finger against the glass. "If I'm honest with myself, I know I could still have gone and made a place for myself there." She turned to face the lieutenant. "But by then I'd found a family here. We live in a pragmatic galaxy, at least in my corner of it; when I found unconditional kindness here, I hung onto it. It's a rare thing, in my experience."

He looked long and hard at her, and she couldn't read his expression. "I think I envy you your perspective," he said finally. "If we all shared it, the worlds would be a very different place."

The music drifting up from below changed subtly, and he seemed to realize he was gazing at her too long. He smiled. "We should rejoin the party," he said. "If I'm not mistaken, that's a tango, and this will be worth watching."

Elsa tilted her head. "Why?"

"You'll see."

Bruno and Gus stood to one side of the dancers, watching with amusement. Dancing wasn't really Bruno's forte; but he found himself enjoying the sight, even if it did unearth memories.

Do I still have mine? he wondered, watching the captain's long coat swirl as he danced. He had worn that coat with such pride, long before his days of wearing a cinder suit.

Gus nudged him with an elbow, jostling him from his thoughts. "Do you think I could come up with an excuse to talk to the King?" he asked.

Bruno grunted, his attention suddenly focused on an unexpected party-goer on the other side of the room.

"Are you even listening to me?"

Bruno nodded, then shook his head. "Not really. Take a look over there," he gestured with his chin.

Gus turned. "Where?"

"By the orchestra, next to the stairs."

Gus raised an eyebrow. "Is that Nebraska? She never comes to station gatherings."

"Mmmhmm." Arms crossed, Bruno watched the cyborg with narrowed eyes.

Gus glanced at him. "What is it?"

"She's been talking with the music director from Charger 751 for some time."

Gus cocked his head. "You think she's up to something?" He watched her for a few seconds. "She doesn't look particularly vicious at the moment. Anyway, I thought she was turning over a new piece of circuitry, so to speak; she was almost nice earlier."

Bruno snorted. "People—even cyborgs—don't change overnight. She was almost *too* nice earlier."

"If you ever stop worrying, you won't know what to do with yourself." Gus glanced at his commlink as a tango piece began. "It's almost midnight. I'm going to dance a bit more before calling it a night."

Bruno lifted a hand in farewell.

When they emerged from the lift, Karl stepped straight back into the dance, drawing Elsa in. He looked over Elsa's shoulder, turning her until she could see that side of the room.

"My father loves a tango," he said.

Captain Tsarevich had snatched the hand of one of the station vendors, who happily allowed herself to be dragged onto the dance floor. The captain glided smoothly across the space, expression set in concentration. Elsa laughed out loud; she couldn't help it. Seeing the distinguished Captain tango suavely across the floor was so incongruous with his fearsome reputation. He dipped the station vendor, and she yelped.

Karl twirled Elsa, and her skirt fanned out like rippling water. When she moved back into his hold, she said, "I never thought I'd see the King of the Stars cut loose like that."

Karl cringed. "You have no idea how quickly that nickname grew old aboard ship. No one likes to work for the King."

"You've heard they call you the Prince, haven't you?"

He blinked, plainly horrified. "I haven't. That's even worse."

She laughed. "I wouldn't complain. Plenty of people envy you, the son of a famous captain, sailing the stars in the flagship of the galactic fleet, and now, of course, exploring new star systems . . ." She arched an eyebrow at him.

He glanced around and lowered his voice. "You've heard about that?"

So they had been right! She tried and failed to keep the smugness from her voice. "Not exactly. But we surmised it."

"*We?*" His voice rose an octave.

She gave him a wide-eyed, innocent look. "My friends and I. It didn't take much effort to put the facts together."

Karl groaned. "I told my father there was no keeping a secret like that."

"I'm not sure it should be kept secret," Elsa replied. "I think it would give people a lot of hope, knowing that the fleet has gone back to exploration like in the early days. Everyone is sick of the war. We're ready to set the past aside and be wide-eyed explorers again."

"We?" he asked again, more calmly. "Does this mean you'd like to gallivant across the galaxy in search of new worlds?"

Her eyebrows rose. "Are you inviting me?"

"Depends. If you're not working with propulsion, what is it that you do?"

Elsa hesitated. The fleet crewmembers didn't seem to look down their noses at cinders the way some of the station-dwellers did, but she was still reluctant to divulge her profession to the lieutenant. "I'm in . . . collections," she said.

He frowned, puzzled. "Debt?"

She shook her head. "Ore."

He opened his mouth to ask a question, but before he could do so, klaxons sounded, drowning out the music. Elsa snapped her head around, looking for her crew. She caught sight of Bruno pushing his way through the crowd, and Jaq and Marraine were cutting across the floor to intercept him.

"I have to go," she told Karl quickly, dropping his hand and backing away.

"What is it? What's happening?"

"Trouble. I have to hurry. I'm sorry!" She hitched her skirt up with one hand and took off at a run, dodging bewildered dancers.

Karl watched her leave, eyes narrowed in thought, before pulling his commlink out of his pocket to call his ship.

CHAPTER 6

ELSA CAUGHT UP WITH her crew at the shuttle dock, where a milling group of cinders was already waiting. "What's the trouble?" she asked Bruno. She heard the shuttle dock with a clunk.

"Major solar flare activity," he called over his shoulder as he moved towards the doors. The shuttle filled with cinders, still dressed in their best finery. Jaq rescued the train of Marraine's gown from being stepped on by another miner.

"So?" Gus continued the conversation as the cinders hastily buckled themselves into their harnesses. "Flares happen all the time."

"Not like this," Bruno answered, his jaw tight. "The ensuing plasma cloud is going to be huge."

The voice over the intercom spoke, sounding tense. "Sensors have discovered a massive coronal ejection in the wake of recent solar flares. It's much larger and is travelling at a much higher speed than any previously observed. We're recalling all satellites to Tremaine Station to avoid damage, but the station itself is in serious danger due to its proximity to a storm this size. Magma rain is also expected on the planet's surface, which is likely to halt mining for the next several days."

"Magma rain?" Marraine murmured. "That doesn't sound good."

"That part isn't unheard of," Elsa said distractedly. "Particularly hot spots on the planet actually cause the rock to vaporize. As it rises, it starts to condense into droplets. Eventually it falls back to Aschen's surface."

Marraine shook her head, a human gesture she was trying out. "Molten rock falling from the sky? No one back home would believe people willingly work under those conditions."

Jaq grinned. "To be fair, it's not always molten. Sometimes it cools enough on the way to solidify again into tiny rock particles."

"When that happens, we don't mine," Gus said.

Bruno remained silent; Elsa knew his thoughts were elsewhere.

"Oh, I'm glad you draw the line somewhere," Marraine said, throwing her hands in the air. "So what exactly are we supposed to do about the plasma cloud? We can't very well tug the station out of the way of the storm." She paused. "Can we?"

"No," Elsa said, finally pulling her gaze from Bruno, "we can't. But each coach is already equipped with shielding to handle plasma and radiation, due to the nature of our work."

"We link the shields together and form a larger shield to protect the station," Jaq said, his eyes bright with excitement. "I've never been part of it myself," he amended. "But I've been through the training."

"Elsa and I were part of the shield wall in '56," Bruno said. His face was unreadable. Jaq's smile slowly vanished.

"I'm sure everything will go smoothly," Elsa said into the heavy silence that followed.

"What happened in '56?" Marraine whispered to Jaq.

He shook his head. "I've been mining less than a year, so I wasn't here yet. I heard there was some kind of overload. The training seminars just said there was a design flaw in the coaches that has since been remedied."

The shuttle docked, and the cinders poured into their respective changing rooms, slipping out of their party clothes and into their undersuits as quickly as possible. They gathered in the locker room, the sight of the entire crew carrying their dress clothes incongruous in the industrial setting. Elsa hastily tucked Marraine's gown into the bottom of her locker, out of harm's way.

Bruno stood near the airlocks, arms folded, waiting for the others as they suited up. "Marraine, I know you're new at this. The station will automatically send instructions to your coach console, but if you have questions, you just ask."

She nodded tentatively, as though she wasn't quite used to the human gesture.

Bruno caught Gus's arm as he went by. "Keep an eye on those two," he said, nodding to Jaq and Marraine. "Make sure they both stay safe. Jaq knows less than he thinks he does." Gus nodded and clapped him on the shoulder.

Elsa climbed on the bench to snag her helmet and jumped back down. She pulled it over her head as she walked to the airlocks, pressurizing the seal. Bruno checked it anyway. She gave him a look.

"We're going to be fine. Stop being such a mother hen," she said, attempting to lighten the mood.

He pretended she was successful. "Someone's gotta do it." He kissed the top of her helmet. "Now scoot."

"Yessir."

Elsa stepped inside the airlock, and through the view panel she saw Bruno put his own helmet on.

Once inside the coach, she wasted no time launching. Somehow Bruno still beat her out of the gate, and his coach was waiting. The crew assembled in a loose configuration near the mining hub. Navigational data fed into their systems from the station, and the crew gradually moved into position between the station and the sun. Each coach was within sight of the others, but they were spaced as widely apart as could be and still link shields. As more coaches launched from the mining hub, they added themselves to the net, forming a growing wall in front of the station like a swarm of bees in front of their hive.

Nothing happened. It kept happening.

"So . . . now what?" Marraine's voice finally broke the tense silence that had settled over the comms.

"We wait," Bruno said. "If we link shields now, we'll only drain our energy unnecessarily."

Another long silence. The coaches hung in space. Elsa tapped her booted foot compulsively.

"So, anyone know any good games?" Jaq said.

Almost before the words were out of his mouth, Bruno shouted, "There!"

They couldn't see anything—but their sensors could. The control boards lit up with warning. The plasma cloud was coming.

"My sensors are acting up," Gus complained. "I'm getting ghost readings."

"No, you're not," Bruno said.

Something in his voice made Elsa look up, startled, even though she couldn't see him. "What?"

"They're not ghost readings. They're multiple clouds coalescing." He paused, and when he spoke again, his voice was heavy with dread. "This isn't going to work."

The order came through from the station: Link the shields.

Elsa closed her eyes. "Bruno," she said, "is there another option?"

She knew how much it was costing him to remain the calm, strong leader in the face of his memories. Spread too thinly, the shield wall of '56 had overloaded—and the deadly storm had savaged the cinders trying desperately to maintain the net, leaving several of them dead. Bruno had known the line couldn't encompass the whole station, but he had obeyed the station's order to maintain his crew's position. Most of the station had been saved—at a cost Bruno deemed too high.

When he spoke now, his voice was steady. "None that I know of, sweetheart. We'll have to give it our best shot."

Elsa took a breath and powered up her shields as the other coaches did the same. A bright net of energy spun out between the coaches, glittering and arcing in front of the station. It looked so fragile, Elsa thought. If only there was some other way to bolster it! She looked again at her controls. She hoped the readings she saw there were wrong. If they were accurate, the net would blister and crumble.

Unacceptable, she decided. She would not sit by and watch the same disaster happen again.

She connected her comm line to the station. "Priscilla, Camilla, are you there?"

The reply came in chorus. "Yes, how can we help you?"

"This is Elsa. Get me the *Sovereign* immediately," she ordered. "I need you to put me through to their bridge. And patch in Bruno too," she added.

"But you have to go through the proper channels, at least five sublevel communication protocols. You can't just talk to the *bridge*, Elsa!" one clone said, scandalized.

"Priscilla," Elsa said quickly, taking a guess and figuring she had a fifty-fifty chance of being right, "I heard about how you two hacked into the station comm system as a prank during the holiday party last year. I know you know how to bypass all of those codes. Now unless you want every circuit on the station to fry, and probably some of us in the process, *put me through to the bridge."*

A pause. One of the clones cleared her throat. "Right away."

Elsa exhaled.

"And this is Camilla, by the way," the clone said, sounding annoyed. "Okay. You and Bruno are both hooked up to the *Sovereign's* bridge now."

Suddenly nervous, Elsa grimaced, simultaneously praying that a senior officer would be on the bridge, someone other than the captain. Tango or not, he was still intimidating, and she didn't know how likely he would be to take orders from a cinder.

"Attention, *Sovereign*," she said, striking what she hoped was a note of respectful authority. "We request your assistance immediately at the shield wall."

She heard a strangled sound from Bruno as he realized what sort of conversation he was listening to. She pressed on, ignoring him. "Your sensors probably haven't detected it yet since you're docked on the far side of the station," she continued, glancing at her own controls, "but there is a combined plasma cloud heading towards the station. The coach shield wall will not be sufficient to protect Tremaine Station. We, ah, respectfully request that you—"

The voice that interrupted her did not belong to the King. "Bring us in to the shield wall," Karl ordered to someone else on the bridge. "You want us to shore up the shield wall, yes?" he asked Elsa.

"Yes," she said, exhaling again. Bless him, he caught on fast. "Yes, we do, Lieutenant."

"Where do you need us?"

"Bruno, where would they do the most good?"

She could all but hear Bruno scrambling for a suitable response. "Below the shield wall. You can focus your dorsal shielding to expand and overlap the net. Uh, sir."

Elsa glanced through her viewscreen. She could see the plasma cloud with her own eyes, and it was moving rapidly.

"I'm afraid you'll have to be sharp about it," she warned. "We're out of time. Priscilla, Camilla, still on the line?"

"Of course," they said.

"Pass the word through the shield wall. Make sure they know what we're about to try. Everyone will have to maintain their positions precisely." It wouldn't be easy, she knew; when the storm hit, the turbulence would be intense.

"Already done," they said.

"Is there anything else you suggest?" the lieutenant asked.

"Aside from prayer?" one of the clones whispered.

"No, Prince—er, no, sir," Bruno said, tangling his words. "Just get into position quickly. We can't hold it without you, and if the wall fails—"

"Understood," the lieutenant replied crisply.

Considering the unprecedented size of the storm, no one needed to be reminded. Aside from the probable annihilation of the cinders, the first line of defense, the station would suffer terrible damage; the outer sections and their inhabitants would likely be destroyed.

Elsa tried to control her breathing, tried not to think about the past, and willed the *Sovereign* to hurry. From here she couldn't see the frigate leave its dock, and she resisted the temptation to ask if anyone else could see it approaching. *The lieutenant knows the danger*, she told herself. *He'll get the ship into position as quickly as he can.*

Then she caught a glimpse of shining white hull rising into the lower corner of her viewscreen, and she began to believe this just might work. The *Sovereign*'s dorsal shield reached out to the shield wall like a tentative hand, linking tightly and binding them all together.

"Cutting it a little fine," Elsa muttered. She had just enough time to brace herself.

The plasma cloud slammed into the shield wall, and Elsa's coach rocked with the impact. Energy blazed across the shield wall. The viewscreens on the coaches darkened to prevent ocular damage, but even so, Elsa could barely see out against the glare as she fought to maintain her position.

The shield wall held against the onslaught, deflecting the energy away from the station. Elsa could only imagine what the light show looked like from aboard Tremaine Station, surrounded by coruscating fire. She shaded her eyes with a hand as she checked her controls.

"Everything is holding steady so far," she said.

"Looks good on our end too," the lieutenant said.

She had forgotten the line was still open. The crew members were quiet as they rode the storm for nearly an hour, saving their energy to wrestle the coaches as they bucked and twisted in the energy blast.

Suddenly Jaq yelped, shattering their intense concentration. His coach spun out of the net, gyrating wildly. The edges of the coach shields on either side grew together to close the gap . . . but Jaq was on the outside, caught in the cloud.

CHAPTER 7

J AQ BLINKED GROGGILY, HIS head aching from where he'd smacked it against the back of his helmet during his spin. Judging by the amount of shouting over the comm lines, he had blacked out for a few seconds.

"Jaq?" Elsa called, sounding as panic-stricken as he had ever heard her. "Jaq!"

He tried to focus on his controls, but without the buffer of the energy shield, his coach was being flung about by the plasma storm, making diagnosis of the problem difficult. "My shield emitter overloaded," he replied, voice shaky.

"Good to hear your voice," Gus said, sounding nearly as unsteady.

Jaq tried a few maneuvers. "My navigation is fried. Must have blown out all primary systems." He kept his reply brief so the others wouldn't hear the terror he was trying to mask. His stomach already roiled with nausea, one of the first symptoms of radiation sickness. He tried not to think about how much radiation was hitting him every second he was unprotected outside the shield wall.

Bruno cursed viciously. He was nearly at the opposite end of the wall, too far away to do anything personally.

"I'll get him," Gus said quickly, but before he could do so, Jaq saw another coach flit out of the formation.

"No, I've got him," Marraine's cool voice murmured in his ear through the comm line.

"Marraine, Jaq may have already received a lethal dose," Bruno said, holding the desperation in his voice tightly in check. "If your shield blows too—"

"You forget," Marraine said, her voice calm and alien, "I'm a fay. We have a higher resistance to these things."

A combination of panic and bile rising in his throat made it hard for Jaq to speak. "No!" he finally managed to croak. "Get behind the wall."

"Don't order me about, Jaq Perrault," Marraine said briskly.

He sat there, completely helpless, as his coach continued to jostle alarmingly. He willed her to hurry at the same time that he wished she would turn back. He wondered if she had lied about her radiation resistance just to make him feel better, and then he wished the thought hadn't occurred to him. If she died because of him—he, who was probably as good as dead anyway . . .

He blinked quickly, unable to rub his eyes because of his helmet, and did not permit himself to finish that thought.

Her coach reached him in moments—their positions had been close to one another in the net—and Marraine extended her shield around his coach, gently drawing him closer with her coach's energy field. She tugged him back to the wall, but it was slow going. The shields weren't designed for towing, especially under these conditions.

Jaq promised himself he would not throw up inside of his suit, but the vow was becoming increasingly difficult to keep as the radiation sickness symptoms intensified.

Over his comm line, he heard someone's gloved fingers tapping on the console in an agony of impatience. "*Sovereign*?" he heard Elsa ask.

"I'm here," the lieutenant answered.

"Can our people come to your sickbay? It's closer than the station's infirmary, and they're going to need immediate medical attention."

"Of course." Jaq heard him snap an order at someone else to prepare the sickbay for radiation patients.

At last Marraine and Jaq moved through the shield wall, which was still glittering with lightning tracery as the plasma storm continued to rage.

"Jaq?" Bruno said. "Can you hear us?"

Jaq muttered a reply, focusing more on his rebellious stomach than on his enunciation.

"Say again, Jaq?"

"He says you cluck like a mother hen, Bruno," Marraine said, laughing.

Jaq heard a smile in Bruno's voice. "You two get to the *Sovereign*, quick as you can. Fay or not, I want you to get checked out, Marraine."

"If she won't go, I'll carry her," Jaq proclaimed. He was barely able to hold his own head up, but that was beside the point.

Marraine laughed at him again, a sound like silvery bells, as she pulled him to the safety of the *Sovereign*.

Out of the corner of her eye, Elsa saw the two coaches disappear into the *Sovereign*'s shuttle bay. She released a breath she didn't know she had been holding. They would be well taken care of now, at least. There was nothing more the cinders could do for them.

Except hold the shield wall, of course.

There was a noticeable thin spot where Marraine and Jaq had been, and Bruno ordered the cinders to spread out to compensate.

"Any idea how long this will last?" Gus asked.

Priscilla (or Camilla) broke in. "Solar weather reports indicate the worst of the cloud will have passed in the next few hours."

Gus chuckled. "Is everyone and his brother still on this comm line?"

A readout on Elsa's display caught her attention. Her eyes widened in dismay. "Bruno?" she said tentatively. "We have a problem. Check the readouts on your emitters' power grid."

Bruno swore. "I see it. I bet all of the other coaches are in the same shape. The grid is already showing stress—no way it'll last another couple of hours."

"Bruno," Gus said, "if we lose just one more coach, the wall won't—"

"I know. Give me a minute."

There was silence over the comm lines as the cinders focused on maintaining their positions, now an even more tenuous balance without Jaq's and Marraine's coaches.

"Okay," Bruno said a few moments later, his voice definitive. "I've temporarily muted our comm lines to the clones and to the *Sovereign*. Fall back from the mining hub. We're going to let the storm take it. There are enough of us to protect the main station if we're not spread out so far, trying to encompass the hub as well. The mining supervisor just confirmed that no one is on the hub right now; the full contingent of cinders is out here."

Elsa's brows shot up. "The mining supervisor told you to sacrifice the mining hub?"

"Nope," Bruno said tersely. "But that's what we're going to do. I'm sending you new navigational data now to synchronize our withdrawal to a tighter perimeter around the station, and I'm sending it to the *Sovereign* as well. They won't know it's not station-authorized."

"You do realize you could get fired for overriding the station's orders, right?" Gus asked. "Not that I'm against this plan," he clarified, "but I just want to make sure we're all on the same screen."

Bruno was undisturbed. "I'm aware. I didn't disobey once when I should have done. I'm not making that mistake twice. People's lives are worth a lot more than a pile of molten slag from the armpit of a hell-planet. The cendrillon in the hub can vaporize, for all I care. Ready?"

Elsa grinned. "Ready."

In perfect synchronization, the cinders withdrew from in front of the mining hub, and the *Sovereign* slowly drifted backwards, keeping her dorsal shields in contact with the wall.

Elsa watched as the stress display on her power grid went from orange to yellow. "It's working," she said. "That should buy us some time."

The storm broke against the relatively unshielded mining hub, instantly searing all of the circuitry aboard. With its own minimal shielding stripped away, the hub was laid bare by the plasma as portions of the outer hull were peeled back by lashing tongues of energy. Elsa saw chunks of cendrillon, solid in the cold of space, explode silently out of the ore processors. *So much for our quota*, she thought, and found that she didn't care at all.

Two hours later, Lieutenant Tsarevich's voice came back on the line. "I just received a report from sickbay. Marraine is experiencing some nausea but didn't suffer any lasting damage. She's being treated and should be fine in a few hours."

"And Jaq?" Bruno interrupted.

"Jaq has suffered more extensive damage, but our doctor tells me he will make a full recovery in time. We have him in treatment, and he'll need to stay in a medical facility for at least a week." Karl paused. "The doctor reports that he is quite upset over the possibility of losing his hair and is running a fever, but is otherwise doing well."

Elsa laughed in relief as the comm lines exploded in cheers.

"Thank you for your help, *Sovereign*," Bruno said. To Elsa, he sounded as though he were holding back tears.

"It was our pleasure," the lieutenant said.

"Not to cut this short, ladies and gents," Gus said, "but it looks as though the fun isn't over yet."

Elsa looked at her sensors. A second cloud was hard on the heels of the first. The coaches all checked their positions and hunkered down to weather the blast.

The second cloud wasn't as dense as the first, but it was dispersed over a wide area. The shields all held, but the interminable fire outside was wearing everyone down. As the hours passed, the ache in Elsa's shoulders increased. They were all feeling the strain of holding the formation after wrestling with their vehicles for so long.

At last the storm passed, and whatever other debris Aschen's sun hurled was minor enough that the station's own shielding could handle it. Finally, blessedly, they all received the recall order from the station.

The *Sovereign* gently disentangled her shields and moved back into her station-side dock.

"Thank you again, Lieutenant," Elsa said softly, not sure he was still listening.

"You're welcome," Karl replied. "I hope all of you can get some rest."

Elsa fervently hoped so too. She withdrew her coach from the wall, wincing as she rolled her shoulders and finally took her hands from the controls. Her eyes stung from squinting against the brilliant light of the plasma for so many hours. She stared uncomprehendingly at the chronometer, too tired to figure out how long they had been battling the storm.

"Too long," Gus said when she voiced that question over the comms. "I don't want to see the inside of a coach again for a week, at least. How will we get home? We can't dock at the hub, obviously."

"Fly into the main station's shuttle bay," Bruno told them all, his voice blank with exhaustion. "If anyone dares give you trouble for entering without authorization, tell them to take it up with me. They can only fire me once."

The coaches swarmed inside the shuttle bay, parking anywhere they could find a space, and the cinders stumbled out, shaky but unharmed.

CHAPTER 8

WHATEVER FEELINGS OF TRIUMPH the cinders felt about surviving the storm and protecting the station had completely dimmed by the time they disembarked. Most of them were silent, bone-weary.

It was Gus, surprisingly, who pulled everyone into another hug before they all left, the other cinders streaming past them on their way to their quarters.

"I'm sorry," he told Bruno. "I said I'd look after them."

Bruno thumped him on the back. "Nothing you could have done. And it all ended well."

And yet Elsa seemed unable to shake the sense of gloom as the cinders went to their quarters. She fell across her bed, still in her undersuit and not caring in the least how much soot she got on her sheets. She was asleep in moments.

The cinders slept the entire day, exhausted beyond measure, but they dragged themselves out of bed to visit Jaq that evening. Marraine had stayed aboard the *Sovereign* with him.

Elsa and Gus boarded the shuttle to the ship. Bruno messaged to tell them he would catch a shuttle ride a bit later; the mining supervisor had requested a meeting with him. No one expected that to go well.

Elsa and Gus found themselves fidgeting on the ride over to the frigate. Elsa twisted her fingers in her lap. "Have you ever been aboard one?" she asked Gus.

He snorted. "A cinder, gallivanting aboard a ship of the line? Not likely." He craned his neck to look out the window. "Never even seen one this close up before."

Wing-like, the graceful, glittering lines of the *Sovereign* filled their view as they docked with a gentle nudge. Elsa and Gus exchanged glances and braced themselves before stepping through the airlock. Unaccountably, Elsa's heart was hammering in her chest.

A crewman was waiting for them. He saluted cautiously, unsure what to do with them since they had no official rank, before escorting them to the sickbay.

Elsa caught herself glancing down every hallway, looking for something. For what, she wouldn't admit, not even to herself.

The halls were brightly lit and spacious, more like a station than a ship. It didn't feel claustrophobic at all, though Elsa realized this may have been due to the fact that there were so few people. She commented on this to the crewman.

"Aye," he said, "we're flying scarce, I'll admit. It was a volunteer-only mission, and volunteers were a little thin on the ground once folks heard how long it would be before we put back into port. Still, we're managing."

Elsa was quiet, thinking, and Gus silently drank in the sights.

The sickbay brought them back to reality. Though it, too, was gracefully designed, it still smelled like an infirmary and no mistake: antiseptic and that indefinable hospital smell. But Jaq was there, looking very pale but like himself, and his grin when he saw them lit up the room. Marraine was seated at his bedside, looking less alien in the already-alien environment of the frigate.

"How are you feeling?" asked Elsa when the initial round of greetings was past.

"Not too bad," Jaq replied, "but they tell me I'll be stuck here—or in the station infirmary, more like—for some time. The *Sovereign* will be departing in a couple days, so I'll be dumped on the mercies of the Tremaine doctors."

"So soon?" Elsa murmured. "I didn't realize she would be sailing so quickly." Now why did that make her stomach plummet so?

"I'm sorry too," Jaq said. "I'd hoped to see more than just the sickbay while I'm here, though perhaps I still might. Lieutenant Tsarevich sent me a get-well message and said he hoped to give me a tour before I left."

"Have you, ah, seen him then?" asked Elsa, looking carefully at the bulkhead as she spoke.

Jaq shook his head. "He sent his apologies, but he's been busy overseeing the repairs."

"What repairs? Was the *Sovereign* damaged?" Gus asked.

"Only minor damage, he assured us," said Marraine. "Still, they want to make sure all is well before shipping out, and this is their last chance to get spare parts for some time." She turned to Elsa. "Just think of it! They're to be gone a whole year, travelling to places no one has been—or at least, no one for a very long time." She paused, flexing her long fingers absent-mindedly. "It is a tempting prospect, is it not?"

"Tempting indeed," Elsa said, doing a fair job of keeping the wistful-ness out of her voice. She watched Marraine work her fingers again. "Are you cold?" she asked the fay suddenly. She realized that the ship was noticeably cooler than the station; suddenly those long uniform coats favored by the fleet seemed less of a fashion statement and more of a necessity.

Marraine rubbed her arms. "A little. Our resistance to radiation may be higher than yours, but evidently our resistance to the cold is lower."

Jaq moved as though to whisk the blanket off his bed, but Elsa beat him to it, shrugging out of her jacket. "Here," she said, handing it to Marraine with a smile. "This is the equivalent of a warm day for someone Anser-born." Her smile fell suddenly as a thought struck her. "Oh, Marraine! Your dress was aboard the mining hub. I'm so sorry . . ." Elsa winced, imagining that beautiful gown torn apart by the plasma storm.

But Marraine wasn't concerned. She waved a jacket-covered arm. "It's just a dress, dear. We saved everything of importance." Her eyes flickered to Jaq, but he didn't notice.

"So where's Bruno?" the patient asked. "I thought the old codger would have come along."

"Oh, he will," Elsa said. "The supervisor called a meeting, but he said he would be here as soon as it was over."

"And so I am," said Bruno from the doorway. He walked in, stopping to ruffle Jaq's hair. "This still seems to be attached, for the moment," he said.

Jaq batted his hand away. "Not if you keep messing with it."

Elsa watched Bruno. "Well?" she asked. "That meeting was awfully short."

Bruno took a deep breath. "The hub is inoperable, not that that's a surprise to anyone," he said, sitting on the edge of Jaq's bed. "It'll take months to rebuild. The company wants to pursue mining here—Tremaine Station is too large an investment just to let Aschen go—but mining won't be back in operation for six months at least. They'll be sending the official announcement tonight, and they said they'd let us go over to the hub in our suits tomorrow to collect any belongings that may have survived."

"What will we do for six months with no work?" Jaq asked.

"Most of the cinders are being reassigned, at least temporarily, to other mining stations. No single location needs this many cinders—there are almost one hundred of us, all total—so they're dividing everyone up based on how much experience they have. They're sending a few veterans and a few newbies to each station, so you'll likely end up in different places." Bruno ran a hand over his face, looking older than his years. "That's assuming you all want to continue mining, of course. They're prepared to offer a severance package."

"Did they offer you a transfer too?" Elsa asked carefully.

Bruno snorted. "They offered me the door. They thanked me for my service, for what that's worth, but they can't afford a cinder who doesn't follow orders."

"That's unfair," Jaq said, hauling himself up to sit straighter in the bed. "You're the best leader they've ever had, and they know it. What else could you have done? They could've lost the whole station if not for you."

Bruno shook his head. "They admitted that, but they need a scapegoat for this whole affair. I'm expendable."

"I suppose there's no use in us hunting for jobs around the station," Gus reflected, "since fewer staff will be needed to run the commerce center as it is, without the cendrillon buyers coming through for several months. I guess we'll have to leave." His expression was that of a lost child.

"There's always ice mining on Europa," Bruno said doubtfully. "Maybe they would take the five of us on as a complete crew."

"Are their mines still open?" Jaq asked. "I heard a rumor they were thinking about closing."

Bruno shrugged. "We can check."

Marraine shook her head, getting the gesture just right this time. "I don't understand you people," she said, her voice brisk. "We just saved the station. We're all alive and safe, and we're together for the time being. We should be celebrating, not sitting around looking like someone kicked our frog."

"Dog," Jaq said absently.

"Close enough." Marraine reached down and pulled a bottle from her bag tucked away behind Jaq's bed. "I slipped back to the station earlier for some wisp wine I brought from my homeworld. I was saving it for a special occasion, and today is it." She poured servings for all of them in the disposable cups from the infirmary's water dispenser. "No more gloom," she commanded.

Soon after, the sickbay was ringing with laughter, and word got around the *Sovereign* that those cinders certainly knew how to have a good time.

CHAPTER 9

A FEW HOURS LATER, Karl slipped into a much quieter sickbay. Marraine was still sitting near Jaq's bed. Jaq himself was asleep, curled on his side, hair disheveled.

"I'm sorry I couldn't come sooner," Karl said softly so as not to wake the patient. "I heard there was a group of cinders visiting. I wanted to thank them for their service, but I couldn't break away from my duties until just now."

Marraine smiled. "They were sorry not to have seen you, I think. It did Jaq good to visit with them, though now the doctor says he'll probably sleep for hours." She looked at the sleeping cinder fondly. "It's just as well. If he were awake he'd only be worrying."

Karl raised an eyebrow. "Worrying? What about? Is his condition more serious than we initially thought?"

Marraine shook her head, silver hair swishing. She liked the action. "There will be no mining on Aschen for months. We're all to be reassigned to other mining worlds, but our crew won't be able to stay together."

Karl frowned. "I'm very sorry to hear that. Where will you go?"

She sighed. "You'll think it silly of me, maybe, to grow attached so quickly, but I've felt at home here with this crew, and I'm very sorry to leave them so soon. But, truth be told, I'm not sure mining is right for me anyway. I'd like to continue to explore. Maybe I'll try my hand at a different job—perhaps at Charger 751." She reached out to brush Jaq's hair from his face. "But we shall see. We're all rather adrift for the present. Bruno's mined for years; it might be too late to teach that particular wolf new tricks. But it wouldn't surprise me if Elsa decided to try something other than mining. Maybe I can convince her and Jaq to come along with me."

Karl hid a smile at Marraine's idiom. "Bruno and Elsa," he repeated the names. "Were they on the comm line during the storm?"

"Yes," Marraine said proudly. "Bruno watches over us like a father, and no one thinks on her feet faster than Elsa."

"They were extremely capable, and when it was all over, I regretted not asking their names. So much was happening so quickly, and there was no opportunity to thank them."

"Oh, you've already met them," Marraine said. "You danced with Elsa at the party."

Karl blinked in surprise. "Of course, she said you had given her the dress! I was an idiot for not asking her name, but I thought there would be time—and then the alarm sounded, and there wasn't any time at all. I've been racking my brains to come up with a way to find her ever since. Once I thought about it, I realized she had to be a cinder. Even if she hadn't torn across the atrium at the sound of the alarm, I noticed a smudge of soot on her jaw while we were dancing."

He realized he was rambling, and he fell silent, thinking for a moment. Marraine watched him with her bright, unblinking eyes.

He made his decision. "Marraine," he said slowly, "you mentioned wanting to explore. Do you think the rest of your crew might feel the same way?"

Marraine's eyes sparkled.

The next day the entire cinder crew, minus Jaq, rode the shuttles to the mining hub to gather their belongings. The shuttle pilots had to dodge debris fragments to reach the dock, but the employee area, located in the center of the hub, had been spared the worst of the storm damage. Artificial gravity still worked, but life support had not yet been restored, so the cinders wore their suits as they made their way to the locker room.

Elsa patted her locker door affectionately. It was dented from where something had obviously careened into it during the upheaval yesterday, but she was able to force it open.

"Marraine!" she cried in delight, picking up the dress from the bottom of the locker. "Your dress is still intact." She tried to hand it over, but the fay shook her head.

"Please keep it," Marraine said, smiling. "It was a gift."

Elsa thanked her, once again touched by the fay's generosity. She climbed on the bench to reach her top locker shelf, fumbling blindly to make sure she hadn't left anything up there. "Maybe wherever I end up will have stepstools," she said.

"Darling, forget a stepstool—you need stilts," Gus said.

Elsa threw a towel from her locker at him. She smiled, but she felt like crying. She was going to miss this so terribly.

Finally everyone had everything gathered. Marraine cleaned out Jaq's locker for him, piling his belongings on a bench, and the rest of them helped her carry his things to the shuttle. They piled all of their gear at their feet and in extra seats, taking off their bulky helmets as soon as the door sealed.

Bruno's face didn't look nearly as long as usual, a sure sign that he was depressed. Gus was sniffling into his sleeve and pretending he wasn't. No one really felt up to talking, but no one wanted to part ways either. As they disembarked to go their quarters, they made plans to meet later.

Elsa and Gus helped Marraine carry Jaq's gear as they all wrestled with their own suits. The three of them dropped Jaq's belongings off at his quarters.

Elsa shifted her gear and Marraine's dress to her other arm so she could set Jaq's things down. "Oh," she exclaimed. "This is Jaq's helmet. I wonder where mine is. Do either of you have it?"

Marraine and Gus checked their piles. "Nope," Gus said. "Maybe you left it on the shuttle?"

Annoyed with herself, Elsa looked through everything again. "I must have. I'll run and check right now. See you both later."

They waved as they headed to their respective quarters.

By the time Elsa reached the dock, the shuttle had already departed again. She sighed and pressed the wall comm. "When will the shuttle be back?" she asked the operator.

"Should be within the next hour."

"I believe I left some personal belongings on board. If you find a helmet, could you please return it to Elsa Vogel? I'm in D1950."

"Will do, ma'am."

"Thank you."

The moment Elsa returned to her quarters, Marraine called her via commlink. "Check your messages. You'll be glad you kept the dress," she said, something unidentifiable in her tone, and hung up.

Elsa brought up her list of messages, and an invitation immediately caught her eye. She read it and laughed aloud.

"Back to the *Sovereign* so soon?" she murmured, unable to wipe the smile from her face. She accepted the invitation.

Karl left the *Sovereign* and boarded the shuttle to Tremaine Station for his meeting with the station master. His father had quickly agreed to Karl's suggestion to host a reception aboard the *Sovereign* for the cinder crew and the station staff in recognition of their service.

He had still to convince his father to accept his second, more ambitious plan.

Karl buckled himself into the harness, and a moment later was glad he had done so. The gravity shorted out. An apologetic voice came over the intercom. "Very sorry, Prince, the gravity's a bit temperamental. Should be back up in a moment—or rather, back down." The shuttle pilot chuckled at his own bad joke.

Karl bit back a sigh. That nickname had caught on far, far too quickly. Just as well he was going to the far-flung limits of the galaxy; it seemed he would have to in order to avoid the moniker.

Something caught his eye, floating in the corner of his vision. He twisted as much as the harness would permit. A helmet drifted down the aisle of the shuttle, and he reached out to snag it as it came within his grasp. It was very small, he noted—almost too small to belong to an adult. He wiped the soot-smudged faceplate with his sleeve, turned the helmet over in his hands, and caught his breath. Someone had written the letters E.V. on the lining inside the back of the helmet. A slow grin spread across his face.

CHAPTER 10

THE NEXT DAY, THE shuttles were packed full of laughing cinders dressed again in unaccustomed finery as they made the trip over to the *Sovereign*. The reception was held in the ship's meeting hall, and the poor orchestra members, still on loan from Charger 751, were pressed into service once more. Let it never be said that Captain Tsarevich ever threw a party without dancing.

It was the captain's son, however, wearing the long dark coat of the fleet, who greeted every cinder as he or she entered, with a wide smile and a firm handshake for everyone. And if he scanned the crowd a few too many times for a particular diminutive cinder, no one commented. A few did comment on the fact that, for some reason, the lieutenant had what looked like a cinder's helmet tucked under his arm.

Bruno wheeled Jaq into the reception area, a medic hovering anxiously behind them. "Really, sir," the medic said, "I'm not sure this is a good idea! My patient—"

"Your patient wouldn't miss this for the worlds," Jaq said. "Wheel me over to the lieutenant," he told Bruno imperiously.

"Watch yourself, young lord," Bruno grumbled. "Radiation sickness or not, I'll still trounce you."

Karl grinned to see them approach. "Jaq, how are you?"

"Feeling quite well, though he doesn't believe me," Jaq said, jerking a thumb at his hovering medical attendant.

"Oh, one evening surely can't do too much damage," Karl said to the attendant.

"We'll make sure he doesn't wear himself out," Marraine said, walking up and giving Jaq a smile like a gift. Jaq flushed. Marraine took the wheelchair handles from Bruno and winked at him.

Bruno gaped. "You can blink?" he whispered.

"That's a tale for another time," Marraine said mysteriously, and wheeled Jaq away towards the dance floor.

Karl laughed before turning to Bruno to offer his hand. "You must be Bruno. I wanted to thank you personally for what you did the other day. You made the right decision, whatever the mining officials may have told you. A level-headed man like you is to be prized, and I was particularly impressed with how your crew worked together."

Bruno shook his hand, a little awed. "Thank you, sir!"

"Please don't; everyone's been 'sir'-ing me all evening. Call me Karl." He scanned the crowd for what must have been the eighth time. "Er, Bruno," he began hesitantly, "are all of the cinders here?"

Bruno glanced around the room. "Just about. Except Elsa, of course. I believe you've met her."

Karl nodded mutely.

"She'll be along in a jiffy. She was glancing over the shuttles, looking for a lost helmet of hers." Bruno narrowed his eyes at Karl. "Rather like the one you're holding, as a matter of fact."

Karl blushed, but before he could answer, the clones approached and entered the conversation. Today's color was yellow, evidently. From across the room, Bruno saw Jaq pretend to be blinded by their bright clothing.

"Why *do* you have that helmet?" one of the clones asked Karl.

He polished its surface with his sleeve absently. "I think it belongs to a cinder I met at the party," he replied. "I wasn't able to get her name before the trouble began, and I mean to return it tonight." He added, "I doubt it would fit anyone else on the station, it's so small."

"Why, that helmet belongs to one of us," the clone said. "We've both misplaced ours, haven't we?"

The other clone nodded vigorously. "Don't you remember? You met both of us at the dance. We had no idea you were so impressed." She smiled in an attempt at flirtatiousness.

"Let us try on the helmet," said the first clone, pulling the helmet from his grasp. "If it fits, you know it was us."

"I don't think—" Karl began helplessly, but the clone was already tugging the helmet on her head. Bruno struggled bravely not to laugh.

"There, see?" Pricilla said breathlessly, her voice muffled by the helmet. "It fits perfectly."

"But you can't even see out of it," Karl said gently. The helmet was clearly too small, and since she couldn't pull it down all the way, the faceplate was mainly over Priscilla's forehead instead of her eyes.

"Let me try," said the other clone. She wiggled the helmet off of her double's head.

Karl frowned. "But you're clones. You're the same size—" Over the clones' shoulders, he saw Bruno shake his head in warning. "Er, never mind," he said. "Go ahead."

Predictably, the helmet didn't fit Camilla any better. "But we spoke to you at the dance," she said in despair, wrestling it back off of her head.

"Yes, I recall," Karl said, not unkindly. "You made me most welcome, and I am grateful to you."

Bruno rescued him. "If I could talk to you for a moment, sir?"

"Of course. Ladies, if you'll excuse me?"

The clones were crestfallen, but they were out of arguments. "If you can't find who you're looking for," Priscilla said wistfully, "you know where to find us."

Karl took each one's hand, bowed low, and kissed their hands in turn. "Thank you, Priscilla and Camilla."

He and Bruno walked to a quiet area of the room, leaving the clones nearly beside themselves. "That was kind of you," Bruno said. "They're both lonely, and they've not had easy lives. They'll be talking about that kiss for weeks."

Karl smiled. "You're quite the softy yourself."

Bruno shrugged, but his eyes twinkled. "Don't go giving me away, sir. I have a reputation as a surly curmudgeon to uphold."

"Your secret's safe with me, but only if you quit calling me 'sir.'"

The older man laughed. "Fine, Karl. Now, if you don't mind, we don't get food like this every day—I'm going to avail myself of your buffet table."

Karl made a shooing motion with his hand. As Bruno moved away, Karl left the room and hurried to the shuttle bay.

When he arrived, he only saw the guard on duty. "Excuse me," Karl asked her. "Have you seen the cinder Elsa?"

"I'm here," said a voice behind him. He spun around.

Elsa was wearing the fay dress again, and it glittered under the *Sovereign*'s lights. "I apologize for being late to your reception," she said with a smile. "But to be fair, I believe you owe me an apology too." She gestured to the helmet under his arm. "The Prince, a common thief? Think of how people will talk."

He held the helmet out to her, grinning. "Forgive me," he said. "I'm sorry you've been hunting for it. I found it on the shuttle and wanted to return it in person."

She took it from his hand, baffled. "Why?"

He let out his breath carefully. "Truth be told, I wanted an excuse to talk to you again. I have some news." He looked suddenly shy. "I hope you'll think it's good news. My father is announcing it to the rest of the station crew right now, I expect."

She tilted her head inquiringly.

"Marraine told me about the cinders' situation, how you'll all be separating to work elsewhere, at least until Aschen is back in business." He paused. "Elsa, I grew up on a ship, seeing how a tight-knit crew interacts, and what can be accomplished when crew members care for one another. I saw that with your cinder crew, the way you all worked together so seamlessly. To pull apart a bond like that is almost a crime."

Elsa watched him closely. "I agree with you. But what else can be done?"

"As you discovered, the *Sovereign* is going on an exploratory mission. We'll be away from port for a year, and as a result, all of our crew are volunteers—those who were willing to leave family, forego the chance of promotion earned in battle, and travel far from the civilized regions of the galaxy. We're not running a skeleton crew, exactly, but it's not much better. We could use crewmembers who are already dedicated to one another, accustomed to dealing with space machinery, used to risk without much reward in return." He hesitated again, unsure how to phrase this.

Elsa was holding her breath, her heart racing. "You can't be saying what it sounds like you're saying."

Karl finished in a rush. "I know, not all of the crew will want to come, and I know it's terribly unorthodox, bringing aboard crew who aren't fleet-trained. The jobs available are hard: only crewmen positions. But my father agreed to offer them to the cinder crew, if you're willing to throw your lot in with ours."

Elsa made a noise between a laugh and an exhale. "Your father agreed? So this was your idea?"

Karl smiled. "It was. I will admit to some . . . selfishness in motive. You spoke so passionately about exploration. This seemed a way to provide you the chance to embrace that passion. There may even be a chance for you to gain propulsion training while you're aboard . . . if that's something you want."

Elsa said nothing, turning the helmet over in her hands. She didn't trust her voice.

Karl dropped his eyes. "I know it's not without sacrifice," he said. "Perhaps you want to stay with your chosen profession—it would make sense. And you hardly know me. Not that that need affect your decision!" he added hastily. "This is an offer of employment, not . . ." He waved his hand in a vague gesture, trailed off, and finally looked at her again.

Elsa was silently laughing at him, having regained her composure after watching him lose his. "I'm honored to accept your offer," she said.

Karl's face cleared. "You'll come with me then? I mean, with us, aboard the *Sovereign*?"

"Most happily," she said with a grin. "Who knows what we may discover on the edge of the galaxy? You may find that you need a cinder one day, out there."

A cheer drifted down the hallway. The King had clearly made his announcement.

"I think I'm well on my way to needing one already," Karl said quietly, his voice lost in the uproar. He offered Elsa his arm. "Shall we join them?" he asked more loudly.

The clones all but ran into them as soon as they entered the hall.

"Elsa, you'll never guess! We're to be promoted!" they chorused.

"You're not leaving Tremaine Station, are you?" Elsa asked.

Priscilla (Camilla?) shook her head. "Nope. We've had enough of exploring during our former lives. We're going to be taking over Nebraska's position!"

Elsa knew the clones were efficient, despite their quirks, but she was still surprised that the mining officials possessed the wherewithal to see it. "And what about Nebraska?"

Hearing a squeak behind her, she flinched. Old habits died hard.

"I'll be going to Charger 751," Nebraska said as Elsa turned around. "I've never enjoyed working on a mining station," she continued. "Perhaps you, ah, noticed."

Elsa said nothing, in as noncommittal a way as possible.

"I was speaking with the orchestra members. Maybe you don't know," Nebraska said almost bashfully, "I love music. They're going to have an open position soon."

"For a cellist, right?" Elsa asked. "I knew you were learning to play."

The clones' faces were mirror images of shock. "We didn't know that," one of them said. "So when you played those same pieces over and over, driving us crazy . . ."

"It was because you were trying to learn them?" the other finished.

Nebraska turned her head slowly, artificial eye whirring, and fixed the clones with a glare that could have blistered the paint off the bulkhead.

They quailed. "We're . . . we're going to go," they said in unison, and fled.

Elsa struggled mightily not to laugh. She cleared her throat. "I'm so glad to hear that, Nebraska. It sounds as though you'll be very happy."

Nebraska's mouth twisted in what may have been a smile. "I don't know if I'd go that far. But it will be an improvement." She seemed about to leave but turned back to Elsa. "And I do congratulate you on your new opportunity," she said, only a little bit grudgingly. She left before Elsa could say anything more.

"Will wonders never cease," Bruno said as he approached with Jaq and Marraine in tow. "It's been a shocking evening." He shook Karl's hand wordlessly in thanks.

"Did you hear, Elsa?" Jaq interrupted, practically bouncing in his chair as he rolled up.

Marraine put a slender hand on his shoulder to settle him. "Jaq Perrault, be still."

"I did!" Elsa answered. "Will all of you accept the captain's offer?"

Gus snorted. "Are you daft? I wouldn't miss it for the worlds."

Marraine smiled. "Jaq and I also accept. I hunger to see more of the world. And I don't think I could stop him from following me," she said, glancing down at Jaq, "radiation sickness or no." Her tone was stern, but her eyes shone.

Elsa turned to Bruno at last. "And you, my friend?"

Bruno heaved a sigh. "I had thought myself too old for a career change, but I find all of this youthful enthusiasm infectious, if exhausting." He flashed Karl a nervous look. "If the fleet will have me back . . ."

Gus waved a dismissive hand. "The regulations you supposedly broke that earned you a discharge aren't even active anymore. I'm sure they'll take you on, especially since you'll only be a crewman." He glanced around at his friends, who were staring open-mouthed at Bruno.

Bruno was staring open-mouthed at him. "You *knew*?" he asked, flabbergasted.

"What?" Gus said, shrugging his shoulders. "I hear things."

"You were in the fleet?" Elsa gasped. "Why didn't you ever say so?"

Bruno tore his shocked gaze away from Gus with difficulty. "I was discharged, as Gus said, for breaking regulations. In those days, families weren't permitted aboard fleet ships—we were still fighting the war, and ships of the line were considered front lines. No civilians allowed." He paused.

"Bruno. Are you *blushing*?" Elsa asked, stunned.

"I smuggled my wife aboard," he confessed. "And we got caught."

"You old dog!" Jaq exclaimed.

Marraine shushed him. "What happened to your wife after you were discharged?" Her face was serious again.

Bruno met her gaze, his face somber again. "She was killed in the war. Just before the Battle of Castle Nebula," he added, turning to Karl. "I know the death toll on her planet would have been much higher had your father not arrived when he did." He looked at the lieutenant with something like pleading on his lined face. "Still want me aboard, after hearing all this?"

Karl said nothing, but he pulled the man into a one-armed hug.

Bruno smiled, such a rare occurrence that Elsa found herself mirroring it without conscious thought when he turned to face her. "Then yes," he told her. "I'll come with you."

Elsa kissed him on the cheek, blinking hard. "Thank you," she whispered in his ear.

The music struck up, and dancing couples began to fill the center of the hall.

Karl turned to Elsa. "May I have this dance?"

She smiled and gave him her hand.

ABOUT THE AUTHOR

STEPHANIE RICKER is a writer, editor, and tree-climber. She adores the cold and the snow but lives in North Carolina anyway, where she enjoys archery, hiking, canoeing, and exploring with friends.

Stephanie's fiction has been published in *Bull-Spec*, a magazine of speculative fiction, and in four consecutive editions of *The Lyricist*, Campbell University's annual literary magazine. She was the editor of the 2009 edition of *The Lyricist*, which won first place in the American Scholastic Press Association Contest. Stephanie's non-fiction has been published in an assortment of medical magazines and newsletters, and her senior thesis on Tolkien was published in the 2009 issue of *Explorations: The Journal of Undergraduate Research and Creative Activity for the State of North Carolina*.

You can find out more about Stephanie and her writing on her blog: www.QuoththeGirl.wordpress.com

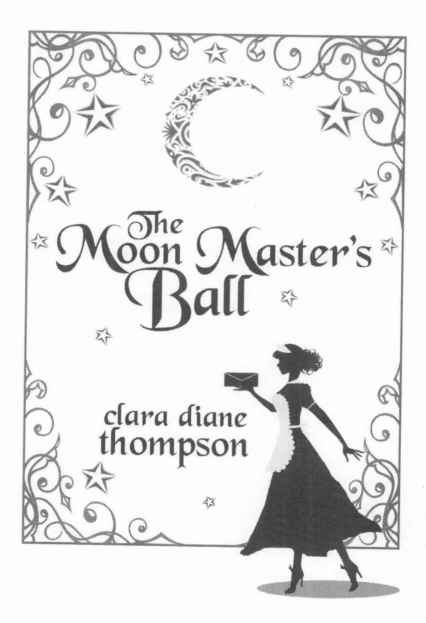

The Moon Master's Ball

clara diane thompson

To my wonderful family for all the many ideas.

1

EAVES SWIRLED on the moonlit streets of Winslow village as Tilly Higgins sped past closed shops, her arms wrapped tightly about herself to keep out the cold autumn wind. The thought of hot cider made her quicken her pace, and she ran up to a crooked little inn, opened the door, and rushed inside.

Apple Tree Inn, the nightly gathering place of all Winslow residents, and in many ways the core of the town's happiness, always had a warm fire crackling on the hearth and was known for its good cider and company. Low ceilings and the smell of cooked apples made the inn feel like home to anyone who would wish to enter, and clusters of candles glowed softly on each table, lighting up all corners of the room.

"Tilly! We were beginning to think you wouldn't come tonight." Bruce, the rotund butcher, spoke around his pipe from his warm seat by the fireplace. His comment was followed by murmurs of agreement throughout the inn.

"Sorry," Tilly answered as she unwound the scarf from her neck and unbuttoned her coat, revealing an ankle-length maid's dress. "I had quite a bit of work to finish up." She walked to the rough wooden counter near the back of the room where Caroline, the owner of Apple Tree, was serving up her famous cider.

"You seem upset, Tilly." Caroline, who was like a mother to almost every young person in the town, addressed Tilly without even looking at her while pouring fragrant cider into an aged mug.

Tilly didn't respond. Instead, she sat in a rickety chair and waited for Caroline to hand her the drink. "Thanks." She sipped it and closed her eyes.

"Do you want to talk about it?" Caroline leaned over the counter, brushing a graying strand of hair away from her eyes.

Tilly set down the mug and fingered a small chip on its rim. "You know about the new family that just moved into Baker Woodlow's old house across the street?"

"Aye. But none of us have seen hide nor hair of them since they arrived two days ago!" Caroline squinted. "Whatever can this new family have done to make our girl so unhappy?" The inn suddenly became quiet as the other villagers heard mention of the newcomers and listened to what Tilly had to say.

"The mother, Mrs. Carlisle, sent her application in to Lord Hollingberry. She and her daughter will be working at Winslow Manor, and Mrs. Carlisle got the position of head housekeeper."

Outraged whispers rippled through the room, rising above the growling of logs shifting in the fireplace. Caroline was silent for a moment then patted Tilly's hand, offering her a comforting look. "I know how hard you've been working for Lord Hollingberry. You've devoted the past two years of your life to your duties at Winslow Manor! It don't seem right that he gave this new woman the position and not you. But cheer up, sweet girl. Perhaps they'll be a nice family to work with. You never know."

Satisfied, the other inn residents resumed their own conversations. But Caroline's kind remarks didn't make Tilly feel any better. She had already sunk into the bowels of self-pity—in her mind she played out a scene of voicing her angry thoughts to Lord Hollingberry. But deep down in her heart she knew she was wrong. She was too young to be a house-keeper; girls of seventeen served as maids. Besides, several of the other girls working at Winslow Manor were far more experienced than she.

But Tilly still felt a bit slighted by her employer. Lord Hollingberry had taken her under his wing two years ago, when her father died, and allowed her to stay in a small room by the kitchen in Winslow Manor. Due to his kindness, Tilly worked long and hard. She was grateful for all he had done for her; and yet, since she had labored so faithfully, she couldn't help expecting some kind of promotion . . . however unrealistic that may be.

Mrs. Carlisle was now in charge of Winslow Manor—a disgruntling fact, but one Tilly had to accept. This was how normal maids were treated, and Tilly wanted nothing more than to lead a normal life.

Just as she took another sip of cider, someone grabbed her shoulders from behind, and the hot drink sloshed into her lap. Startled, she jumped out of her chair and snatched a rag from the counter.

"Whoops! I didn't think you'd make a mess on yourself."

Dabbing at her now cider-spotted maid's uniform, Tilly glared at the young man responsible for jolting her. "Rodger. I might have known. What are you doing, sneaking about and scaring defenseless girls?" She threw the soiled cloth at her friend and smirked, forgetting her self-pity for a moment.

Rodger grinned and tossed the rag back at her, then leaned against the counter while Caroline poured cider for another villager. "Oh, you know. A boy has to tease a girl every once in a while or else he ceases to exist."

"Is that so?" She smiled at Rodger. He was the sort of person everyone liked. If he walked into a room, he undoubtedly knew everyone in it. Rodger was a little on the short side, and a mop of unruly brown hair dangled in his sparkling hazel eyes. But it was his friendly personality that made him completely charming.

"I heard what you said. Everyone did. And we're all on your side." He became serious and looked at her the way a little boy would look at a wounded puppy.

"There aren't sides." Tilly shook her head but was secretly happy that her friends supported her. "Thank you, though."

Rodger winked at her. "Anytime." Then, with a glint in his eye, he abruptly changed subjects. "So, will you be going this year?"

She set her mug down and bit her lip. "Going where?"

"You know where I mean. It's time you had a bit of fun, and you've never been before! I'll be your escort, if that makes you feel any better."

"Rodger, I *have* been before, and I saw something that frightened me very much. I've never forgotten it . . . not to mention I don't care for magic."

"You're a big girl now! Why don't you give it another try?"

"I'll think about it." Tilly knew this was the only answer that would satisfy him, at least temporarily. She watched him walk over to the coat rack and slip on his short tweed jacket.

"You want me to walk you home?" he asked, wrapping a blue scarf around his neck.

"No. I'll be fine." She smiled at him as he ambled to the door.

"Goodnight, fair maiden!" Rodger bowed dramatically, and someone in the inn clapped. With another flourish he stepped outside.

Tilly decided she was ready to depart as well. The next day she would meet Mrs. Carlisle and her daughter, and she wanted to be well rested for the encounter.

"Goodnight!" she called to everyone in Apple Tree Inn, then buttoned up her coat and headed towards Winslow Manor. The wind felt even colder now that she had been inside the warm inn, and she covered her mouth and nose with her scarf. As she walked home, the heels of her laced-up boots clicking hollowly on the cobbled street, she looked around at the little town she had grown up in.

The village of Winslow was the quaintest place imaginable, and rustling leaves and scents of fall made it more whimsical than ever. Little groups of cottages with pumpkins on their steps were scattered throughout the village, and at the end of the main street, towering above them all with authority, stood Winslow Manor. No gate or wall separated Lord Hollingberry's great house from its neighbors, and the village folk were proud of its stately position; it provided a sense of security and welcoming warmth.

Tilly sighed again when she thought of meeting Mrs. Carlisle and her daughter. For the past few years of her life she had worked alongside other maids who didn't get in each other's way. It was hard work, to be sure, but she and the other maids had developed their own method of cleaning and organizing which the two Carlisle women were sure to uproot. Change was necessary, she reasoned with herself, and the Manor was Lord Hollingberry's and no one else's. If he wanted his bed to be made one way or another then he would tell Mrs. Carlisle.

But for all her reasoning, Tilly wasn't convinced that she and this Mrs. Carlisle would be compatible.

The street's emptiness caused chills to crawl up her spine, and she suddenly wished she had accepted Rodger's invitation to accompany her home. A gap between the cottages and Winslow Manor gave her a perfect view of Bromley Meadow—to most people, a place of magic and delight.

To Tilly, a place of fear.

She knew it wasn't wise to stop and look at the meadow on such an eerie night, but there was something enticing about the silver halo the moon cast over the rolling hills. She peered to her left and gazed at its haunting beauty.

The meadow itself had never seemed terribly extraordinary to Tilly, but extraordinary things did occur amongst its soft grass and swaying dandelions. Rodger was hoping she would go to Bromley Meadow this year, but she didn't think she had the courage.

An image of blood-red eyes and sharp yellow teeth flashed in her mind.

Tilly rushed around behind the manor and flew to the back door, desperate to get away from the moon's glow highlighting the meadow.

Calming herself, she stepped over the threshold and into the kitchen to find Mrs. Gregson, the cook, sipping tea quietly at a small table, a plate of freshly baked cookies before her. All of the other servants went home each night, but since Tilly was an orphan and Mrs. Gregson was widowed, Lord Hollingberry insisted that Winslow Manor be their home.

"Hello, Mrs. Gregson. Busy day?" Tilly knew that warm cookies and tea meant Mrs. Gregson wasn't feeling in the most favorable of moods.

The cook lifted her red face and looked at Tilly, gesturing to the seat across from hers. "Sit down, Tilly. I've got somethin' on my mind that needs to be said."

Tilly raised her eyebrows and sat as the cook had bidden her, nabbing a cookie and munching on it while waiting for the older woman to speak.

"I don't like this Carlisle business," Mrs. Gregson began. "You and I have worked together for two years, and everything has turned out splendidly! I don't get in your way, you don't get in mine. We both get to do things how we want to. But now Lord Hollingberry—I'm not sayin' anything bad 'bout him!—has given this woman the keys to the house and is allowing her to tell us and everyone else what to do. Mrs. Carlisle is a stranger to Winslow. She don't know the way things work here." The cook poked an emphatic finger Tilly's way then sipped her tea again.

"I agree with you, of course." Tilly tucked a strand of her black hair behind her ear. "Lord Hollingberry knows what he's doing, though, and has his reasons. But don't think I'm not just as upset as you are, because I am." She finished off her cookie and rubbed her hands together, dropping crumbs in her lap.

"Go on to bed, Tilly." The cook heaved a sigh. "Thank you for listening. I'll see you in the morning."

Tilly told her friend goodnight and slipped from the kitchen. Once safely in her room across the hall, she took out a matchbox and lit a candle by her window, then sat down on her bed and looked around the small space she called home.

An oak wardrobe stood in front of her, and to her right a floor-length mirror leaned against the wall. A vase on a little table sprouted the marigolds and ferns she had picked that morning, and a clump of dried lavender was suspended above her window. It wasn't a large space, but Tilly loved it. Her room was a safe haven.

She stood again, looked at herself in the mirror, and realized how tired she appeared. Her dark maid's dress brought out the shadows under her eyes, and she had grown thin in the past few months. Tilly suddenly realized that what she really needed was a holiday from cleaning.

She thought about what Rodger had said. He was right; she did need to enjoy herself and have a bit of fun. Tilly slipped on her nightdress and blew out the candle.

Some minutes later, after she had turned to one side then decided she was more comfortable on the other, a scuttling noise caused her eyes to open wide. Ears alert, Tilly glanced towards the window. A shadow darted just beyond her vision.

She fumbled desperately for the matchbox. Keeping well away from the window, she held the lighted candle towards the glass and squinted, her trembling hand causing wax to spill over.

The wavering light revealed no menacing creature.

Once her heart had calmed, Tilly exhaled slowly, blew out the candle, crawled back in bed, and forced her eyes closed. She told herself there had been nothing outside, nothing peering in at her from the darkness.

Nothing at all.

2

THE SUN'S early rays slowly woke Tilly. She opened her eyes, feeling rested and happy, only to have that feeling crushed by the sudden remembrance of the invading Mrs. Carlisle and her daughter. She sat up and rubbed her eyes, allowing herself a few moments of tranquility before the day's mad rush began.

"Tilly!"

Mrs. Gregson's voice bellowed at the door, accompanied by a frantic rattling. "Tilly! You've slept too late! The Carlisle women are comin' up the front steps right now, and everyone else is already lined up to meet 'em!"

"Coming Mrs. Gregson! Thank you!"

Now Tilly understood why she felt so rested. How stupid of her, sleeping in on a day like this! She leapt up from her bed, mentally thanking Mrs. Gregson over and over again. A minute later she was dressed, her hair up under her maid's cap. Dark, unpinned tendrils fell in her eyes. She scrambled to the back door and rushed around to the front of the Manor, lining up beside Ellen, her fellow maid.

"You're late," Ellen whispered the obvious from the corner of her mouth.

Tilly didn't respond but watched as Mrs. Carlisle climbed to the top of the steps, her daughter following close behind. The woman curtsied to Lord Hollingberry, and the daughter followed suit.

"Well, well. We're quite happy to have you here, quite happy. I know the girls will be glad to have you as their authority. Glad, yes, they'll be glad." Lord Hollingberry was in the habit of repeating himself several times over, and he looked as though he could be blown off the steps of Winslow Manor if a strong enough gust of wind hit him.

The lord was a dear old man who loved his servants and treated them as though they were his own family. Tilly often thought he must have been tall and handsome in his youth, even if he was hunched over and wrinkled now, much like a candle exposed to too much heat. He had big eyes that resembled a pug's, and, like a pug's, they watered when he got excited, so he was often dabbing at them with his handkerchief.

Tilly hoped neither he nor Mrs. Carlisle had noticed her absence, although Lord Hollingberry always observed more than people thought.

"Come inside, and I'll introduce you to the girls." As he ushered Mrs. Carlisle and her daughter through the door, Lord Hollingberry called over his shoulder to the maids. "Come along, girls. Come along."

As she and the other maids lined up side by side on the foyer's gleaming hardwood floor, Tilly was able to get her first good look at the two Carlisle women. Mrs. Carlisle was only a bit taller than Lord Hollingberry. She had a plump face, a long, crooked nose, and dark eyes. Tilly thought Mrs. Carlisle should have seemed like a sweet old lady, but the plumpness made her look disgusting rather than grandmotherly. Instead of firm round cheeks and chin, hers were soft and sagging, giving her a lazy appearance. In fact, her skin almost looked leathery.

However, after one glance at the daughter Tilly realized, with an unreasonable pang of jealousy, that the girl was nothing like her mother: She was very beautiful.

"Now, since you're all here, I'll introduce . . . Oh, dear me! Where is Mrs. Gregson?" Lord Hollingberry left the small group and teetered down a hallway towards the kitchen stairs, muttering, "Excuse me. Excuse me."

The maids stood mute in front of Mrs. Carlisle and her daughter, feeling a bit awkward. The old grandfather clock's silver chime seemed thunderously loud as it echoed throughout the house.

But it couldn't deafen their ears to another sound ringing up through the floor.

"I'm not goin' out there with *that* woman!"

Everyone in the foyer could hear Mrs. Gregson's voice bellow from the kitchen beneath their feet, followed by the soft voice of Lord Hollingberry.

"Mrs. Gregson! Please, dear lady. You'll quite like her, I'm sure of it. Come upstairs for me. Please."

After more muttering from Mrs. Gregson, which they couldn't quite make out, Tilly heard the approaching footsteps of Lord Hollingberry and his cook.

"You'll have to pardon Mrs. Gregson. She wasn't feeling quite up to meeting anyone today, but I convinced her to come." The kind old man patted Mrs. Gregson's shoulder before she walked over and stood grumpily beside Tilly.

"Mrs. Carlisle, I would like to introduce you to Daphne, Florence, Laura, Ellen, Tilly, and Mrs. Gregson, our cook. Girls, meet Mrs. Carlisle, the new housekeeper, and her daughter, Drosselyn. That is . . . correct, isn't it?" Lord Hollingberry put a finger to his chin as he turned questioningly to Mrs. Carlisle's daughter.

"Yes sir, that's right." Drosselyn answered sweetly and smiled at the maids before her. "I do hope we'll all get to be good friends."

Mrs. Gregson snorted and clenched the spatula in her hand as though she might challenge the newcomers to a duel at any moment.

"Well, well." Lord Hollingberry looked fondly at his maids and then turned to Mrs. Carlisle. "I suppose I'll leave you all to start your new routine." He chuckled slowly the way old men do, and turned, creaking sluggishly upstairs to his study.

"Well!" Mrs. Carlisle clapped her hands briskly and smiled. "I certainly am excited to get to know you all. But first, let me inform you that this house is to be run on a strict schedule. I shall tolerate no tardiness whatsoever." She looked pointedly at Tilly and Mrs. Gregson. "I shall not allow any of you to be lazy, and you will have no male callers here at the manor." Mrs. Carlisle was certainly adept at making up rules. She turned to the rest of the girls. "Now get to work!"

She clapped her hands again as though this would spur them on to do her bidding. Slowly the girls went about their usual tasks. Tilly caught Mrs. Gregson's eye, and the two shared an exasperated look before Tilly headed upstairs.

"Mrs. Gregson?" Mrs. Carlisle stopped the cook as she was making her way to her kitchen. "My daughter and I require tea, if you please. We'll take it in the parlor." With that, she turned and ushered her daughter into the room, closing the door softly behind them.

Mrs. Gregson looked up at Tilly, who had watched this exchange over the banister; then she gave a grunt and stomped off to make a pot of tea. With a shrug, Tilly hurried on up to join the other maids.

She found them huddled in the upstairs hallway, muttering. ". . . and did you see her daughter? Standin' there, lookin' at us like she was so much better!" At Tilly's approach they looked guilty for a moment but relaxed upon seeing their fellow maid.

"Tilly! What do you think about them?" Ellen asked, and all four girls turned to hear Tilly's opinion.

"They'll take some getting used to." Tilly swiped absent-mindedly with her feather duster at a painting of Lord Hollingberry's late wife.

Daphne, an attractive brunette, snorted. "That's not an answer. I can tell you don't like them either. And where is her daughter now? I was under the impression she would be a maid alongside us." She picked up her bucket, dunked her rag, and swirled it angrily in the water before wiping off a stained-glass window at the end of the hall.

Tilly frowned and answered her friend without looking at her. "They're having tea in the parlor. Those women are marching around here like they've lived in Winslow all their lives!" She couldn't suppress her feelings even though she knew it was wrong to be talking in such away to the rest of the girls. But if Lord Hollingberry had wanted a housekeeper other than herself, he should have chosen Daphne! She was twenty-one, smart, and had been working at Winslow Manor longer than anyone else save Mrs. Gregson.

"I'm sorry." Tilly brushed her duster violently over Lady Hollingberry's face, nearly knocking the painting off the wall. "This just doesn't seem right."

A door suddenly opened, revealing Lord Hollingberry's hunched frame, and the girls froze like rabbits caught in a trap. All of them had forgotten they were working just outside his study.

"My! Does it take so many maids to clean one hallway?" He laughed quietly and rubbed his sagging chin with his fingertips. "I know you are all upset about Mrs. Carlisle. I do believe I would be upset if I were you, too!" He clasped his hands behind his back. "But I have my reasons for bringing her here. Let her do what she wants. But for now, why don't you all spread out a bit, hmm?"

The girls muttered, "Yes sir," and Tilly began to leave with them. But Lord Hollingberry put out a staying hand. "Not you, Tilly. Come into my study. Come in, come in."

Tilly looked quickly at the painting she had nearly knocked down and wondered if Lord Hollingberry somehow knew she'd been rough with it. Meekly she stepped into his study, waiting for some kind of rebuke.

"Ah, yes!" he said suddenly. "You're a bright girl, Tilly. Very bright. That's something I've always admired about you." And he returned to the hall, lifted the portrait off the wall, and carried it past her into his study. Had she somehow damaged it?

But he said only, "If you would please close the door, my dear . . ."

She hurried to obey. He didn't seem upset. Perhaps he *wasn't* planning on scolding her.

When she turned back to the room, Lord Hollingberry stood gazing down at the painting of his wife. He suddenly seemed not quite so crooked and bent, not so wrinkled as before. He glanced at Tilly. "Aminia would have enjoyed your company, of this I am sure." Then, to Tilly's surprise, he slipped the portrait into a cupboard, shut it away, and turned back, brushing off his hands.

"I don't like Mrs. Carlisle. In fact, I quite despise the woman. But there are greater things taking place here, Tilly." His expression was grave.

"I . . ." Tilly was at a loss for words.

The old man continued as though oblivious to her discomfort. "There are greater things taking place." He said this to himself, as though remembering something he had long ago thought forgotten.

"Would you like me to go, sir?" Tilly inched towards the door, not understanding exactly why he wanted to speak to her.

"Do you recall, Tilly, the time you asked if my wife and I ever had a child?"

She stopped moving and thought carefully. She seemed to recall an instance when she had asked Lord Hollingberry this. "Y—yes sir."

"And what did I tell you?"

She bit her lip. "You told me that you and your wife lost your child."

He sighed and looked at her with a faraway expression. "That wasn't entirely true. We never had a baby of our own. I was . . . a godfather of sorts. But what is true is that we lost him. Are you going this year?"

The question startled Tilly. "Going?" She played nervously with her feather duster and avoided his eyes.

"Yes, are you going?"

She didn't need to ask him where. He could only mean one thing. "I had a . . . bad experience when I was a child. You know I never . . . go." Tilly felt pressure welling up inside her.

In her mind's eye she saw the wispy shadow, yellow teeth dripping with saliva, and glowing red eyes. All at once Tilly wanted to scream, to run away from Winslow Manor and Mrs. Carlisle and Bromley Meadow. But Lord Hollingberry's earnest eyes kept her feet planted on the soft rug in his study, and she realized he was grasping her small hand in his large knobby one.

"Things are about to change. As I said, there is something greater at work here. I need you to be here. You are special, Tilly; I know it. And I'm going to need you to go this year. For me. And . . . for someone else. Can you do this for me? For Winslow?"

Tilly wanted to say no, to shake her head and tell him he wasn't acting like himself. But she felt her head nodding up and down in spite of what her heart was telling her to do, and she heard her voice whisper, "I'll try."

"Thank you. Thank you, my dear."

And then Lord Hollingberry was once more hunched over and frail, pulling his fob watch from his vest with shaking hands that had been strong a moment ago.

"Goodness me! Look at the time. You have work to do, and I've kept you too long. Too long." He opened the door and ushered her out of the room. "Goodbye! Work hard, dear." The old man started to close the door behind her but then quickly opened it again. "And don't tell any of the other girls this." He tapped the side of his nose as if they were both children sharing a secret. "We want things to work out properly, you know."

His eyes began to water, and he dabbed at them with his kerchief while closing the door, leaving a terribly bewildered Tilly standing in the corridor, holding her feather duster limply at her side.

Lord Hollingberry stood a moment before shuffling over to his desk. He groaned as he sat down in his plush, paisley chair, but then thought about Tilly and smiled. Sweet girl, that. Poor dear had no idea what she would have to do in the upcoming days. Was she ready?

The old man frowned at the question in his mind.

No matter if she was or wasn't, he told himself. It had to happen *now*.

Muttering quietly in agreement with himself, Lord Hollingberry leaned forward and lifted a sheet of thick ivory paper from his desk. Dabbing the nib of his pen in the inkwell, he began to write in smooth, long strokes. After folding the paper up, he stamped the Hollingberry seal on it. His wrinkled hands flipped the letter over and addressed it to:

The Moon Master.

3

TILLY REMAINED quiet the rest of the day, mulling the strange conversation she had shared with Lord Hollingberry over in her mind and preparing what she would say to him when he asked her to go.

"No, Lord Hollingberry, I'm afraid I can't go . . ." She sighed heavily while sweeping out the mud tracked into the foyer by the new arrivals. "Oh, that's no good." Frowning, she leaned on her broom, trying to think of another way to phrase the sentence. "Lord Hollingberry—"

"Tilly!" Ellen rushed into the foyer. "Tilly, there's only one room left for us to clean! And we figured you were the best one to tidy up the parlor." She grabbed the broom from Tilly. "I'll finish this."

Tilly chuckled at her friend. "*None* of you wanted to brave the dangerous Mrs. Carlisle and her daughter?" She shook her head. "I can't believe they're still in there. They've been sitting in that room all day!" Tilly looked out the windows framing the front door and saw that the sun was setting. "Fine. I'll finish up. You all owe me."

"Yes, we do!" Ellen replied happily as Tilly headed off to the parlor.

Approaching the parlor door, Tilly slowed then stopped, uncertain. Should she knock? Common courtesy dictated that she should, so only after thumping her knuckles against the thick wooden door and hearing a soft "Enter" did she walk into the room.

The parlor's walls were painted a soft blue that looked like the sky was just preparing to display its stars. A long window in the center of the room offered a perfect view of Bromley Meadow. Two settees graced the room, and three chairs, the cushions of which had been stitched delicately by Genevieve, the village's most renowned seamstress.

The room's prettiness was darkened, however, by the two silhouettes lounging in those lovely settees and chairs.

"Yes?" Mrs. Carlisle turned her head slightly when Tilly entered; then she smiled. "Ah, Tilly the Tardy! Come to clean the parlor, have you?" She chortled.

Tilly gritted her teeth. "Yes ma'am. It won't take long. I've only got to dust." She entered the room and began to do just that, hoping some dirt fluffed into Mrs. Carlisle's lungs and made her miserable.

"You missed a spot."

It was Drosselyn who spoke this time. Tilly didn't acknowledge that she had said anything.

"I said you've missed a spot. Right there."

Tilly turned to see Drosselyn pointing languidly from her seat, her luxuriant hair framing her face like the dark petals of a flower.

Tilly brushed over that spot vigorously.

"You seem to be a smart girl, Tilly," Mrs. Carlisle stated.

"Thank you, ma'am." Tilly continued to dust, eager to leave the room and go to Apple Tree Inn with the rest of the girls.

"There has been much talk of something exciting happening soon. If you could enlighten us to what this special occasion is, we would be most eager to hear."

Tilly clenched her hands and moved to the other side of the room, turning her back to Mrs. Carlisle. "I can't say that I could, ma'am." She didn't want to talk about it. Not to them.

"How disappointing! It seems as though everyone here knows what's going to happen except us. Isn't that right, daughter of mine?"

"Yes, Mother." Drosselyn responded in monotone as though she spoke the words every minute of every day.

"I'm sure you could tell us *something*," Mrs. Carlisle continued, fixing her small, staring eyes upon Tilly.

"Yes ma'am. I could." Tilly turned around to face the two reclining ladies. "But it's not a pretty story and not something I wish to tell. All I can say is that you'll know what this 'special occasion' is when you see it. Look for it in Bromley Meadow."

Mrs. Carlisle's face didn't change. She did, however, click her teeth together in a thoughtful manner. The sound repulsed Tilly.

"Thank you," Mrs. Carlisle said, her head twitching oddly.

Tilly finished dusting the last table and left the room in a whirl, her face flushed with anger. She marched down the back stairs to her room, grabbed her coat and scarf, and rushed out of the house as quickly as possible.

Those women! Disgusting, detestable, prying, rude, snobbish—

"I was wondering when you'd show up."

For the second night in a row Rodger startled Tilly half to death. She spun about, letting out a gasp. Rodger leaned against the back wall of the manor as though he was about to fall asleep.

"Scared you good, didn't I? And I wasn't even meaning to!" He laughed and walked towards Tilly, his presence like a breath of fresh air.

"Ellen said you were staying to finish up, and I thought I'd escort you to the inn, since I'm such a dashing, protective man."

"Thank you, Rodger." Tilly's voice caught when she said his name, and his quirky smile suddenly vanished.

"Was today really that bad?" All joviality left his face, leaving nothing but concern in its place.

She nodded numbly and sniffled when he put his arm around her.

"You need to be 'round people who love you tonight. Come on. Let's get to the inn. What happened?"

Tilly let out an exhausted sigh. "It's . . . Everyone wants to know if I'm *going*. And I don't want to. It scares me, Rodger! I know that everyone else here loves it, but I saw something different than the rest of you!"

"You don't have to go, Tilly. It's all right. You can stay home all week when they come, bundled up in your blankets and drinking hot tea with honey." He smiled one of his most infectious smiles and patted her shoulder.

Tilly nodded. "You're right. I'm sorry. It's been quite a long day."

"That's all right. Perhaps we'll toast some bread with cheese over Caroline's fire tonight. And we can have some fresh cranberry sauce with it as well! Eggs sound good to me, but I know you're more for the bread and cheese . . ." He continued talking as they headed to the inn, lifting her spirits with every word.

But in spite of Rodger's assurances, she huddled beneath his arm, feeling the need of some protection against the sightless stare of Bromley Meadow looming behind them.

HE NEXT day Tilly scrubbed the kitchen floor while listening to Mrs. Gregson rant about Mrs. Carlisle and her daughters. "They didn't leave 'til past dark! If they ever *did* leave. I never saw 'em go."

"Wait." Tilly sat back on her heels and looked up at Mrs. Gregson. "They're not even here yet. It's half past seven."

Tilly the Tardy indeed!

"I'll be right back, Mrs. Gregson." Tilly dropped her scrub brush and nearly overturned her soap-filled bucket in her haste to scramble up. Ignoring Mrs. Gregson's questioning shout, she dashed upstairs and into the parlor and began cleaning furiously before the new housekeeper could set up camp in the room. "Daphne! Ellen! Could you come help—"

Then she glanced out the parlor's large window and staggered backwards, bumping into a table and sending a vase full of flowers crashing to the floor. Tilly gripped the table with both hands and squeezed her eyes shut. *Calm down. It's not as though you've never seen it.*

But, in truth, she could never get used to the sight. Every autumn for ever-so-many years, she had seen this phenomenon occur. One minute there was nothing but dandelions atop Bromley Meadow, and the next minute . . .

It had arrived.

Tilly could hear the excited shouts of other villagers as they saw it too, but she wasn't listening. The memories of that terrifying moment of many years ago flashed through her mind, and she felt bile rising in her throat.

"Tilly! It's here! Lord Hollingberry has given us the *whole* week off!"

The other maids rushed about the house, never stopping to notice Tilly's terrified state. Already she saw families hurrying out to Bromley Meadow to have a grand time. Shops closed and children were let out of school . . .

. . . For there, reaching up to the sky, was a massive tent painted in the most magnificent colors. Emerald-green stripes, deep-burgundy stripes, gold stripes, and even peacock-blue stripes adorned the tall tent; and scattered around it were little, aged wagons of pastel colors and booths with vendors awaiting their first customers.

A slight fog still clung rebelliously to the meadow's rolling hills and, as the sun shone down, the grass twinkled with dew. It was a beautiful sight to the people of Winslow and, while they rushed to get ready for the day, the thought of it danced about in their minds. For a week there would be nothing but fun in the village.

Bromley's Circus had arrived.

While down on her hands and knees cleaning up the broken vase and flowers, Tilly pondered Rodger's suggestion of the night before. Once her work was finished, she decided, she would bundle up in her room and not come out for the whole week. And she would ask Mrs. Gregson for tea. Perhaps she would read the book Daphne had lent her.

Her thoughts stopped abruptly when she heard a noise coming from underneath the wooden floorboards. It sounded like scratching and . . . something else. Whispering. Scratches and whispers.

Tilly pressed her ear to the floor, and the whispering got louder, though she couldn't pick out any specific words. The noise sounded familiar, as if she had heard it once a long time ago. But it ended abruptly when Lord Hollingberry stepped suddenly into the room.

"Tilly? Why are you still here?" The old man looked around the parlor and smiled. "My dear wife loved this room." The smile faded a little as he looked at Tilly again. "Come along now; leave the cleaning for another time. Do you remember the conversation we had yesterday?"

Tilly gulped and scrambled to her feet, trying to think of a way to escape Lord Hollingberry's question. "I—I do, sir."

As she stepped into the foyer, he closed the door behind her and spoke very quietly, as if afraid someone might overhear. "My dear, I know something happened to make you afraid of the Circus. It *is* a strange place, after all. But I need you to suppress that fear and do something for me."

Tilly was already shaking her head frantically, her face pale. "I'm sorry, sir, but I can't. I just can't."

Once more, Lord Hollingberry's voice and manner became strangely young. "What if I told you that a man's fate rests in your hands?"

"Sir, please, you aren't making any sense—"

"When have I ever lied to you? I've taken you in, given you a home, and treated you with as much kindness and consideration as you could wish. Now grant me this one favor," he said just above a whisper. "I'm only asking you to go to the Circus, find Indigo Bromley, and tell him you must see the Moon Master to deliver this letter from me. It's as simple as that."

Lord Hollingberry stretched out his hand to Tilly, offering her an ivory letter with a midnight-blue wax seal.

Tilly shook her head. "I'm sorry, I—"

"Tilly. What is happening right here, right now, is bigger than your fear. Be brave. I will make sure you are protected from any harm."

It was a simple task. Take the letter, go to Indigo Bromley, and give the letter to the Moon Master. Simple.

And yet she was terrified.

But Lord Hollingberry had been so good to her. She should stop complaining and complete this small task! With this thought firmly planted in her brain, Tilly held out her hand and allowed Lord Hollingberry to place that crisp letter in her palm.

"Thank you, Tilly. Thank you so very much." Lord Hollingberry turned to leave, but she stopped him with a question.

"Why can't you take it, sir?"

The lord slowly looked at her over his shoulder, a deep pool of sadness rippling in his eyes. "I was banished from Bromley's Circus a long time ago."

With that, he left.

Tilly walked slowly down to her room, every step more resistant than the last. She inspected the letter and wondered what sort of message was scribbled within it. Then she looked in her mirror, folding back the collar of her maid's uniform. A long white scar ran from her neck down to her collar bone.

She let out a sob and sat on her bed. Why had she agreed to go back?

5

"*WHERE* IS my blasted necktie?"

Indigo Bromley always made doubly certain his personal wagon was set up behind the main tent in order to best avoid the Winslow residents rushing to buy Circus wares. But at present he couldn't think about his Circus. A weightier matter consumed all thought: He was missing his peacock necktie with its emerald pin, and a magician cannot be a magician if he is not properly dressed.

"Scatter! Scatter, come here this instant!" Bromley looked in his mirror and made sure every hair of his black beard was where it should be. Delicately he twirled the tips of his mustache. Then he placed his dangling ruby-and-diamond earring in his right ear. "Scatter! Where is that little—"

"I'm afraid you cannot disturb Indigo Bromley." The guard outside his door spoke in a low grumble.

"Oh, but I *must* see him!" A girl's voice replied. "It's a matter of the utmost importance!"

"Sorry, miss. Have you seen the magic pumpkin carvings? You might enjoy that."

"Please, Lord Hollingberry sent me!"

Indigo Bromley stopped searching for his necktie and peeked around his curtain at the girl outside. She was young. Pretty, too, and she looked absolutely petrified.

Hoping to make a dramatic entrance even without his necktie, Indigo Bromley flung open the curtains of his wagon and flared out his long, green-and-black, sparkling coattails.

"Let her in, Dudlow," he said in a deep, unidentifiable accent. With a shrug, Dudlow let the girl step into the wagon. Bromley closed the curtains again and turned to her, twirling his mustache absentmindedly. "And what is the beautiful lady's name?" He bowed and grasped her fingertips, planting a kiss on them.

She snatched her hand away. "Higgins," she said in a trembling voice. "Tilly Higgins. Lord Hollingberry sent me. I have a letter, you see." Her hand shaking, she pulled out a letter with the Hollingberry seal on it.

"Hmm." Indigo Bromley extended a ring-clad hand to take it, but Tilly jerked the letter out of his reach.

"M—my instructions were to show it to the Moon Master. No one else."

Bromley raised an already-arched eyebrow. "I see. I don't think you'll like him very much. You're already quite frightened about something, and he'll only scare you further."

Tucking the letter away, Tilly took a deep breath. "But I still must deliver the letter to him."

"Very well." Indigo Bromley turned away from her. "Scatter!" He bellowed out, making Tilly jump. "Jittery, aren't you?" The magician smirked.

"Yes sir." Tilly lowered her gaze and hoped Bromley would hurry and take her where she needed to go. She heard a rustling noise beneath the wagon. Looking down, she saw a hole in the floor. The rustling noise got louder until a little white head poked up from the hole. Tilly jumped backwards and knocked into Indigo Bromley's full-length mirror, nearly sending it crashing to the ground.

"Good heavens, girl, watch what you're doing!" Bromley barked, and then addressed the white mouse climbing up from the hole in his floor. "Scatter. It's about time you got here."

The mouse chattered then looked at Tilly almost apologetically.

"Take the girl to the Moon Master. And find my necktie!"

With a chirp, Scatter gestured with its tiny pink paw for Tilly to follow. She didn't move.

"What's the matter, girl?" Bromley looked exasperated.

"I'm not . . . not fond of . . . rodents." She wrung her hands and glanced at the mouse again.

"Neither am I. Now go with Scatter to the Moon Master. Or you can give *me* the letter."

Tilly didn't respond. Steeling herself, she followed Scatter from the wagon and past the guard to the main tent.

This tent was as gigantic as she remembered, towering high above the village below the meadow. Its curtains were open wide as if they wanted to embrace each visitor, but Tilly didn't feel up to a hug. It was too crowded inside, and she only wanted to get away from the noise and the pushy vendors. The mouse bounded inside then turned to look at her with his glistening black eyes. When she didn't move, he sat on his haunches and began to clean his whiskers.

"Hello, Tilly! Beautiful day, isn't it?" the village folk asked as they passed her and strolled into the Circus. Tilly nodded and smiled at each one, knowing she must look silly standing there outside the tent, quivering with nerves.

Closing her eyes, she tried to forget about the small but terribly powerful creature that had attacked her. It had been nighttime that first time she came, so perhaps the creature was nocturnal. Or maybe, after all these years, it was dead.

Yes, it was surely dead, she told herself and plunged into the tent. She clutched the letter tightly inside her dress pocket and followed Scatter deeper into the lights and shadows of the Circus.

The noise of vendors calling to village folk and the villagers calling back was deafening. Her ears felt suffocated by the noises, and she ran to keep up with the mouse, which wound between peoples' legs and scurried under booths.

"Scatter! You're going too—Oh, excuse me!" Tilly apologized when she bumped into a man and sent his hat flying to the grass.

"Quite all right," the man grumbled as he placed the hat back on his head, then watched in astonishment as she turned from him to follow a small white mouse through the thick crowd.

Scatter led her, weaving across the length of the Circus tent until they reached its farthest and darkest corner. Tilly glanced around, wondering where the Moon Master could possibly be. At least it was quiet in this area. There was no interesting act or delicious food to attract anyone. In fact, there was nothing in the corner at all.

But then, as her eyes adjusted to the darkness, Tilly noticed a pair of green curtains that reminded her of a dense forest covering the entrance of a small black wagon. The mouse climbed up to it and scurried underneath the curtains, leaving Tilly to assume she should follow. She spread the silk apart cautiously and peeked inside.

"Hello?" She slid between the curtains and entered the black wagon, her eyes opening wide as she looked around. Candles lit up the small space, illuminating the piles of velvet ribbons distributed about the room. Each ribbon was more unique than the last, and Tilly walked closer to inspect them. Gems she had never seen before inlaid every strip, making them finer than the most expensive ribbons one could find at a dress shop. There were stones as black as night sewn into a ribbon the color of an aged rose. Tilly reached out her hand to touch it.

"I believe you've entered the wrong wagon."

She jerked her hand back like a child caught stealing a cookie and looked around for the speaker. A man who must have been standing in a back corner of the wagon now slowly approached her. "Are you lost?" he asked with a voice that reminded her of chocolate and caramel mixed together.

"I . . ." Tilly stared up at the strange, tall form before her and wondered how he could stand so perfectly straight in such a small space. He was painfully thin, and his dark clothes hung on his gaunt frame, making him appear willowy and fragile. Yet something about the way he held himself made Tilly certain he was anything *but* fragile. His pale face was young, though he was older than Tilly. Chestnut hair hung in his wintry grey eyes, just brushing his shoulders when he tilted his head to study Tilly.

"Are you quite well?"

Tilly gathered herself and blinked several times. "Y—yes. I'm fine. Are you the Moon Master?"

His eyes narrowed. "Who's asking?" There was a hint of hostility in his voice.

"My name is Tilly Higgins. Lord Hollingberry sent me. I have a letter." She held out the letter to him, making certain he could see the Hollingberry seal.

"Lord Hollingberry?" He took the letter gently from her grasp and opened it a bit awkwardly with one hand. His eyes scanned the paper several times before he folded and held it back out to her.

"Don't you want to keep it?" Tilly looked from him to the letter.

"I have no need to." He watched as she took the letter from him and placed it back in her pocket.

"I'll just . . . I'll just be going now." Feeling awkward, Tilly took a step backwards and startled when something dashed past her feet. Scatter climbed up to the Moon Master's shoulder and perched there like a proper parrot. Placing his paws on either side of his Master's ear, the mouse leaned in and whispered. The Moon Master smirked and patted Scatter's head with one finger.

"Well, we won't tell him you've made it into a nest, will we?"

Tilly turned to leave, giving the lovely ribbons one last glance.

"Wait."

She turned around when the Moon Master spoke to her.

"Take a ribbon, please, Tilly Higgins." He gestured generously.

Even though her task was accomplished—even though she wanted nothing more than to escape the Circus—Tilly paused and looked at the beauty before her. Giving the Moon Master a cautious glance, she fingered a yellow ribbon with green gems.

"May I?" From a near pile he selected a pair of ribbons the color of a frosted violet with gems that shone like stars. "These are my favorite." He held the two ribbons out to her.

"Thank you. They're lovely." Tilly took them and rubbed the silkiness between her fingers. She could not help noticing that he only ever used one hand.

"Have we met before, Miss Higgins?"

The Moon Master's question shocked Tilly, and she looked sharply up at him. "No. We haven't," she said a bit more emphatically than she meant to. "I never come to the Circus. I only came now because Lord Hollingberry requested it of me."

"I see. Forgive me if I offended you." He dipped his head graciously and then nodded to the curtains. "Make your escape. I know you're dying to leave."

Without further ado, Tilly left the Moon Master and the mouse on his shoulder, suddenly feeling claustrophobic.

When the curtains were closed again, the Moon Master sat down in his rickety chair, placing his head in one palm. "I scared her away, Scatter. I spoke too soon."

The mouse patted his cheek.

"Follow her. Make certain she is safe."

With a loyal chirp, the mouse darted off his master's shoulder and followed the young girl, who was running towards the safety of Winslow village.

ONCE WELL away from Bromley's Circus, Tilly stopped to catch her breath, sitting down in the meadow's grass. The sun was setting behind the Circus tent. She couldn't believe she had gone back. The day seemed too surreal to comprehend. But, at Lord Hollingberry's request, she *had* returned to the Circus, and she *had* seen the Moon Master. The task was done.

Why had he seemed to recognize her? And what was Lord Hollingberry's connection to the strange Moon Master? Tilly felt her dress pocket, remembering the letter tucked inside, waiting to be read. Little caring whether or not she was doing the right thing, she pulled it out and fingered the broken seal.

"Tilly! What are you doing here?"

She shoved the letter back into hiding and looked up at Rodger approaching with his two little sisters. Rising, she brushed herself off, trying very hard not to look guilty. "Hello, Rodger. I'm just on my way back to Winslow Manor." She offered the two girls clinging to his hands a shaky smile then started to walk past them.

"Wait a moment." Rodger let go of his sisters and stopped her. "Just last night you were upset about the Circus, and now here you are, sitting in Bromley Meadow. What made you change your mind?"

It was a reasonable question, but Tilly certainly didn't feel like answering, nor did she think it was right to. After all, she didn't have all the answers; Lord Hollingberry did.

"I was running an errand. Please, Rodger. I don't want to talk about it."

Rodger pursed his lips and watched her walk away, noticing that she took a shuddery breath. Glancing towards the Circus, he saw Ellen waving at him. He waved back, then leaned down to his sisters and said, "Girls, see Ellen over there? Go to her, and she'll take you around the Circus. I'll be right back." Then he ran to catch up with Tilly.

"Mind if I walk you home?" He appeared beside her and sauntered along, hands in pockets.

Tilly turned to him, somewhat aggravated. "Not today, Rodger. Go be with your sisters." She walked faster, but Rodger sped up and dodged in front of her, walking backwards.

"Well, I *feel* like walking you home. Is that all right?"

Tilly sighed, truly not wanting his company at the moment. "If you wish."

Rodger grinned triumphantly. They made quick progress back to Winslow Manor since Tilly set such a fast pace. Neither one said a word until they reached their destination.

When they stood at the back entrance, Tilly turned to Rodger. "Well, I'm here, safe and sound. Go back to your sisters, Rodger." She opened the door, but Rodger drew it shut again. She sighed. "What now?"

"I want to make sure you're all right." He gazed upon her with all the concern in the world, which only made Tilly angry.

"Do you?" She crossed her arms and glared at him. "Fine. I'm not all right. In fact, I've had a completely horrible day, and I *don't* want to talk about it. I've been used, and I've been scared, and I just want to be *left alone.*"

Rodger took a step closer, a strange expression on his face. Then he reached out and gently took her hand. Tilly pulled half-heartedly away, only making his grip tighten. "In case you didn't notice, Tilly, I *care* about you, and I want to be sure you're safe."

"Stop it, Rodger! You're being ridiculous." She pulled away again.

"Very well." He let go of her and grinned, albeit ruefully. "I'll leave you alone. Just promise me you'll take care of yourself."

Tilly nodded. Then she rushed inside, closed the door, and leaned her back against it, breathing hard. When she cautiously peeked out the window, Rodger still stood there gazing at the spot where she had been. Then he turned back towards the meadow without the usual jaunty spring in his step.

Without wasting another minute, Tilly sped up two flights of stairs to Lord Hollingberry's study, only just stopped herself from barging in, and raised her fist to knock on the door. She hesitated, however, when she heard voices from within the room.

"She's back. It's time." That was Lord Hollingberry's voice.

"Are you absolutely certain? We only have one shot at this, or that poor boy will be—" A woman was speaking, but the lord cut her off.

"You don't need to tell me the consequences if we fail. This isn't going to be easy, but we must take a chance." He emphasized the last phrase by pounding his hand on his desk.

Feeling a bit wicked for eavesdropping, Tilly knocked on the door to alert them of her presence. There was a long pause, and then she heard

Lord Hollingberry's voice say, "Come in."

She opened the door and inhaled sharply when she saw Caroline, the innkeeper, sitting in the chair in front of Lord Hollingberry's desk. "Caroline?" Her voice quavered when she spoke.

"'Ello, dear." Caroline rose and faced Tilly, placing her bonnet on her head. "I was just leaving." She walked towards the gaping young girl then turned to face Lord Hollingberry, who had risen politely. "Proceed as you so desire." With these words she left, patting Tilly on the cheek as she brushed past.

"Come in, Tilly. Come in." Lord Hollingberry waved her inside, and she shut the door behind her. "My, you seem a bit flustered!" He chuckled, but stopped quickly when Tilly didn't join in. "Did you do as I asked?"

Tilly nodded. "I did. The Moon Master appears to have seen me before. Also, a mouse rode on his shoulder and whispered in his ear."

"Ah well, things haven't changed much." Lord Hollingberry walked around his desk to her. "I'm sorry, dear girl. I know that must have frightened you a great deal."

She clenched her hands but didn't speak.

"I wish you would trust me. You must know I would not have put you in that situation if it weren't absolutely necessary. Remember, there is something greater taking place."

Tilly sighed and rubbed her forehead with one hand. "Why won't you *tell* me what that 'something greater' is?"

Lord Hollingberry gazed upon his maid, his tired old eyes full of compassion. "I cannot. The time is not yet right." He brushed a strand of hair out of her eyes and smiled at her. "Why don't you go clean yourself up, hmm? Get some sleep. You've earned a good rest."

Tilly felt her anger evaporate, leaving only tired confusion in its place. She nodded, turning to the door.

"And Tilly?"

She looked around.

"*He* isn't your enemy. Try to understand that."

Tilly tried to speak but found she had no words. With a little shake of her head, she left the study and hastened down to her bedroom, collapsing on her bed. Something crackled in her dress as she did so, and she pulled out the letter she had almost forgotten about. Too tired to feel guilty about reading a private message, Tilly slid her finger under the broken seal and saw only two words scrawled across the page.

Her heartbeat quickened, and she felt as though she would faint at any moment. She read the words again, making certain they were real. Sure enough, those letters were not some odd illusion caused by her exhausted brain.

The only words on the crisp piece of paper spelled out a name:

Tilly Higgins.

SCATTER SQUEEZED himself under the back door to follow Tilly inside the manor. He quickly scampered to a dark corner from which he watched her charge upstairs, but he didn't follow. His master had told him to make sure she was safe, so he would have to search the house and make certain.

Starting in the basement, the little mouse began inspecting each floor of the house quickly and silently, his delicate nose and whiskers twitching back and forth, picking up all manner of scents. Crumbs caught on his whiskers in the dining room, and he sniffed spilt tea on the drawing-room carpet, but none of these scents were hostile.

The mouse scurried to the upper floors, thankful that Lord Hollingberry did not keep a cat, and checked the rooms there. Nothing.

Scatter was about to leave when he thought perhaps he could bring back some cheese for his Master. Oh, that would make him so happy! And then he would pat Scatter's little head and tell him, "Thank you!"

Yes. Scatter would bring back cheese. He scuttled down to the foyer, his pointy nose telling him which direction to go, but suddenly stopped, whiskers twitching. There was a room he had not noticed before.

The parlor.

How had he missed it? The white mouse made his way into the room . . . and immediately wanted to dart back out again, for the room reeked of magic. Magic always stank.

But there was another foul smell concealed in the room. He sensed it beneath the floorboards. Scatter's large ears fanned out when he heard a sound, and he crept cautiously closer. Despite the stench, he kept his nose pressed firmly to the floor, determined to know what was causing the smell.

Then the loyal creature's tiny heart began to pump harder, faster, filling with fear. He realized what was hidden under the floorboards.

And what was concealed beneath the floorboards knew he was there, too.

Scatter barely had a moment to bound backwards and dart for the door before a hairy paw with claws twice the size of his small body smashed up through the floorboards, sending splinters flying through the room. The black paw slammed down again on the wood, claws scraping horribly until they fell into the hole again.

Scatter knew he had to escape before the creature leaped out from its hiding place. Desperately he headed for the nearest door and barely managed to squeeze under, then skittered down the front steps and bounded towards Bromley Meadow. He nearly flew across the cobbled drive, his tiny paws pounding furiously. He had to get to his master! He had to tell him that the girl was *not* safe!

The meadow lay just ahead when there was a crashing sound behind him—the creature had broken through the door! Dodging between tall blades of grass, Scatter gasped for breath. Soon he heard deep grunting and a vicious snarl. His enemy was gaining on him more quickly than he had anticipated!

The Circus still seemed to be miles away. Scatter's legs and lungs burned from running so far and so quickly. At last the mouse reached the tall tent, slipped inside, and ran around the edge of it, unnoticed by the crowds of people.

He was almost to his master; his master would protect him! Only a few more feet to go, then he would be safe!

Scatter leapt towards the booth with the dark green curtains, but something caught the fur on his back, suspending him in mid-air. Hearing a guttural growl that sounded almost like some kind of twisted chuckle, he closed his eyes.

Pain erupted throughout Scatter's tiny body.

8

TILLY WOKE up wearing the same dirty dress she'd worn the day before, still clutching the letter with one hand. She blinked groggily, feeling a bit disoriented, and got up. Leaving the crumpled letter on her bed, she staggered over to her washbasin, slipped out of her dress, and splashed water on her face.

What did it matter if Lord Hollingberry had given her the whole week off? There was nothing for her to do but go to the Circus, and she wasn't about to do that. So she pulled out her maid's uniform, preparing to work all day.

But first she headed to the kitchen for a bite to eat and some company. Mrs. Gregson was the only other person in Winslow who remained unmoved by the Circus's charisma. In fact, she called it "a place of cheap tricks and bamboozlers." Tilly and the cook rarely discussed Bromley's Circus; they were each happy to know that the other agreed on the subject and left the topic alone.

"Morning, Mrs. Gregson!"

The old woman snorted. "Morning, indeed. It's past ten! You, my girl, are turning into a sleepyhead." She chuckled to herself and took out an egg, cracking it over a copper bowl.

Tilly scrounged up a piece of leftover apple pie from the night before. "You certainly seem happy this morning." Settling at the table, she took a bite.

"It's just nice to have the house all to ourselves. You and me and Lord Hollingberry. *That's* the way it should be all the time."

Tilly smiled and chewed on pie, wishing she could feel as carefree as Mrs. Gregson. Finished, she rinsed her plate in the basin. "If you need me, I'll be cleaning the dining room."

The hours passed slowly and easily. Tilly spent them working and stayed out of Lord Hollingberry's way, determined not to think about the Circus again. However, no matter what she did, Bromley's Circus and the strange Moon Master kept flashing before her mind's eye.

Why had he asked if they had met? She would certainly remember someone like him. Yet his voice had seemed somehow . . . familiar.

There were also the ribbons, the Moon Master's gift. They were beautiful, far too beautiful for her! Nevertheless, she kept them.

And then there was Rodger.

Was he actually interested in her, or was he merely fond of her as a friend? Tilly had never thought of a relationship between the two of them; Rodger had been her friend and support ever since they were children. She had never noticed him acting strange around her until yesterday, after she left the Circus. Hopefully she was only imagining his interest.

She closed the drapes in the front drawing room and took a deep breath. Another day was almost over. Soon the week would be past and the Circus, gone! She wasn't feeling sociable enough to head to Caroline's inn that evening. Rodger would probably be there, and she wanted to stay away from him for the next few days. With any luck, whatever feelings he had suddenly developed for her would soon evaporate.

"Tilly?" Lord Hollingberry called from somewhere nearby.

Tilly squeezed her eyes shut. She had thought herself safe from any odd conversations that day, but apparently she'd been wrong.

"Tilly, are you quite well?" He sounded anxious.

Reluctantly Tilly stepped into the foyer, only to see Lord Hollingberry staring fixedly into the parlor . . . which she had forgotten to clean. How strange! Until that moment, Tilly had been sure she'd cleaned every room in the house.

"I'm here, sir."

He turned to her quickly. "Thank God you're all right!" he said, breathing a sigh of relief. "You didn't notice the . . . the parlor?"

Tilly shook her head and hurried to join him. "I'm sorry, I didn't even think about it. I'll clean it right—" Her sentence ended abruptly when she looked into the parlor for the first time that day.

There was a hole in the middle of the wooden floor. Claw marks led from this hole to the doorway where they stood, then across the foyer to the Manor's front door, which bore another hole, as if something had plowed straight through the wood.

How had she not seen this?

"Tilly," said Lord Hollingberry, "I need you to deliver another message for me to the Moon Master."

If Lord Hollingberry had asked her the same question earlier that day, Tilly would have refused without a moment's hesitation; but now there was a hole in the floor of the parlor. Whatever had caused it was bound to be more sinister than the Moon Master.

So, once again, Tilly felt the weight of a letter in her pocket. She also felt, pressing against her heart, the weight of something much bigger and more important than her fear of the Circus.

Lord Hollingberry was surely telling the truth when he insisted there was something much greater taking place in the village of Winslow.

A LOW FOG was rolling in. Tilly tucked her coat tightly around herself as she trekked towards colorful Bromley's Circus. The afternoon had been cool and wet, and heavy clouds cast a gray shadow over Winslow, yet people scurried excitedly past her towards the Circus. The sounds of children laughing and people gasping in astonishment made the twinkling merry-go-rounds and inviting vendors even more appealing. Lanterns adorning a nearby carousel were eerie yellow orbs glowing through the fog, yet somehow they cast the Circus in an entrancing light. Tilly almost wished she didn't hate the place so much.

But beneath all the glitter and false magic lay something deep and sad which she couldn't quite understand. She felt sorry for everyone in the Circus, even the foppish Indigo Bromley. Perhaps she was wrong to feel such hatred towards this otherworldly place. Everyone else in Winslow adored it. She reminded herself that she, too, would have loved it if not for the horrible night when her neck was scarred.

"It's Tilly, isn't it?"

Tilly had been so caught up in her thoughts that she hadn't noticed she was skirting the edge of the main tent, unmindful of where she was going. She turned around to see who had addressed her.

"Y—yes. It is." To her great dismay she recognized Mrs. Carlisle's daughter. "I'm sorry; I can't seem to recall your name."

The young woman laughed, waving her hand dismissively. "Don't worry about it. My name is Drosselyn. I recall that you were late the day we arrived. Mother was quite upset with you."

Tilly nodded, recalling that horrible morning. Was it only two days ago? So much had happened since then!

Drosselyn smiled and nodded at Tilly's coat. "That's quite lovely. I adore those silver buttons." Then she snapped her fingers as though an idea had struck her. "Do you know there's a *dress* shop here, and all the dresses were made by the faeries of the Winslow Wood themselves?" Her eyes were wide as she waited for Tilly to respond.

"I didn't know. But there aren't *really* faeries in the Wood." Tilly felt a smile tugging at the corners of her mouth. Perhaps Drosselyn wasn't quite as bad as her mother.

"No, I suppose there aren't. But it's awfully fun to think there are." Drosselyn grinned and tugged on a shiny brown curl. "Why don't we look at the dresses together?" She seemed truly eager, even hopeful.

"Oh." Tilly looked behind herself at the huge tent towering above. "Perhaps some other time."

"It's just that Mother is at home," Drosselyn persisted, looking a bit like a child who had just dropped her candy in the muddy grass. "I couldn't convince her to leave." She frowned.

"Well, I'm afraid I have something that I must get done. And I'm not terribly fond of this Circus." Tilly looked cautiously around, as though the creature that haunted her dreams might spring upon her at any moment.

"Oh?" Drosselyn took a step closer. "Why aren't you?" She tilted her head, still playing with her hair.

"Just . . ." Tilly thought desperately for an excuse. "Childish reasons."

"Perhaps you're afraid?"

Tilly blinked. "Excuse me?"

Drosselyn's smile was sweet as honey. "I would be afraid if I were you." Her sweet bearing vanished for a moment, revealing a steely look of determination and . . . jealousy? Tilly couldn't quite tell.

But the moment passed. "Well!" Drosselyn smiled brightly, the strange expression gone from her eyes. "I'll leave you to accomplish that *something* you were about to do before I apprehended you. Goodbye."

Tilly watched Drosselyn until she disappeared into the crowd, heading off towards a shimmering emerald-and-gold tent, over the entryway of which hung the banner "Tippets and Pumpkins." Taking a step backwards, Tilly shook her head. It would appear that odd conversations were becoming part of her daily routine.

As she stepped into the main tent once again, she couldn't help but marvel at the huge poles reaching up to support the heavy canvas, and at the various stunning acts taking place all around her. Trying to ignore a woman walking across a thin rope high above her, Tilly maneuvered around diverse onlookers and headed towards the Moon Master's wagon at the back of the tent. It seemed stranger than ever without the mouse guiding her, and she suddenly missed the small companion who had so unsettled her only the day before.

She found herself standing in front of the dark green curtains, and for a moment she wished there was a door instead so she could knock. "Um . . . hello?" she called out, feeling awkward. "It's Tilly Higgins again. I have another message from Lord Hollingberry."

There was a long silence before she heard the Moon Master's melancholy voice. "You may come in."

Tilly spread apart the curtains and stepped through. It was darker inside the wagon than it had been the day before. "H—hello?" Once again, she couldn't find the Moon Master. Could he blend in with the shadows? Tilly jumped when he suddenly appeared as if emerging from the back of the wagon.

"Yes?" He stared at her blankly, and she saw that his eyes were red and puffy. He looked almost as though he had been weeping.

"Lord Hollingberry has another, um, letter for you." Tilly pulled it from her pocket and handed it to him, trying not to stare at his disheveled clothes.

He took the letter without even glancing her way, again opened it with only one hand, and read it quickly before folding it back up and stuffing it inside his shirt. "Thank you." He turned his back as though to leave, but stopped abruptly. "When you leave, would you mind telling Indigo Bromley that it's time?" His normally rich voice was strangely dull, much like the hollow hoot of an owl.

"It's time? That's all?" Tilly asked.

He nodded. "Yes. Goodbye, Miss Higgins." He began to walk off into the shadows of the wagon, and Tilly wondered if it was really as small as it appeared.

"Wait!"

He stopped, not turning around to face her.

"I . . ." Now that she had stopped him, she didn't know what to say. For some reason she couldn't explain, Tilly felt that letting him dissolve back into the darkness would be wrong. "Are you all right?" She didn't know why she cared. Her mission was almost accomplished; she should talk to Indigo Bromley and then go home. But the Moon Master's shoulders, which had seemed so strong the day before, now seemed weak, crushed.

He turned his head until Tilly could see his angular profile. "Do you recall the mouse on my shoulder yesterday?"

She nodded. "Yes. Scatter was his name."

The Moon Master's hand clenched into a fist. "He . . . he was killed last night. And what's worse even than his death"—he turned slowly to face her, passion suddenly strong in his voice—"is that they killed him for no *reason*."

Tilly blinked. "Who? Who would do such a thing?"

Lifting one hand to his face, the Moon Master rubbed his eyes. "Forget I said anything at all, Miss Higgins." He waved her away and began to move back into the shadows. "Forgive me for darkening your day."

Then he was gone again, and Tilly almost felt inclined to follow him. Who had killed Scatter? And why?

The Moon Master didn't appear to be completely of a sound mind. Perhaps the mouse had simply run afoul of a hungry cat, and he had convinced himself that a creature more sinister had killed his pet

Something told her this wasn't the truth.

Tilly frowned as she stepped out of the wagon. Somehow she had become more a messenger than a maid in the past few days. Now another message for Indigo Bromley. Yesterday she had found the magician in his personal wagon outside the main tent, so she maneuvered her way towards the exit. Her life seemed crazier than the bizarre acts playing out around her. Would she ever lead a normal existence?

"Well, well. Hello again, Miss Higgins."

Tilly nearly jumped out of her skin before she recognized the familiar voice of Indigo Bromley. He chuckled. "Still as jittery as ever, I see."

Tilly exhaled slowly. "I was looking for you."

"It would seem you *weren't* looking, since you walked past without even noticing me." Bromley's deeply accented voice rumbled from his throat. "What is it that you require, little maid?"

"The Moon Master told me to tell you that . . . it's time. That was all he said."

All charm evaporated from Indigo Bromley's bearing. His face looked ashen. "You're . . . you're *sure* that's what he said?"

She nodded. "Yes. What does it mean?"

He looked away from her and cleared his throat.

Tilly suddenly wished she could take back the question. "Well . . ." she said, backing away from him. "I'll be leaving then."

Indigo didn't respond as she slipped away. He stood frozen, looking like a flamboyant and colorful statue. His extreme reaction upset Tilly. Everyone around her knew something big and terrible that she didn't know, and they were all playing with her as if she were a doll in a child's game. Determined not to be left in the dark any longer, Tilly marched towards Winslow village and the small inn that was lazily puffing smoke from its chimney.

She wouldn't go back to Winslow Manor just yet. Whatever this web of secrets that had formed around the village and the Circus was, Lord Hollingberry and Caroline were at the center of it, Tilly was sure. It was time to take out her feather duster and brush away the cobweb of secrets woven throughout her life.

It was time to speak to Caroline.

Mrs. Gregson was enjoying her day alone in the kitchen. Little was on her mind as she stirred together the ingredients to a lemon poppy-seed cake, Lord Hollingberry's favorite. No one else was home but the lord himself, and although the cook was terribly fond of Tilly, she was glad to be alone. She bustled about her domain, thinking there was nothing better in life than a clean kitchen. The back door creaked and she heard someone enter. It was probably Tilly, home from wherever she had got off to.

"Tilly?" the cook called as she squeezed some lemon into the batter. "Would you mind handin' me the—" Mrs. Gregson stopped. It wasn't Tilly who had entered after all.

Anger swelled up from her chest and shone brightly in her eyes as she saw Mrs. Carlisle in *her* kitchen.

"Hello, Mrs. Gregson. What are your skilled hands baking today?" Mrs. Carlisle asked as she roamed the large space, gazing at different pots displayed on the walls.

Mrs. Gregson huffed. "Get out."

"I suppose the reason your food is so utterly delicious is that you use magic to make it. Am I correct?" Mrs. Carlisle continued, ignoring Mrs. Gregson.

The cook grabbed a sturdy nearby pot and brandished it menacingly towards Mrs. Carlisle. "You're mad!" she stated.

The invading housekeeper chattered her teeth thoughtfully before muttering foreign words under her breath.

Mrs. Gregson started to move towards the woman she so despised. "What's that gibberish you're mumblin'? I said, get out!"

Before she quite knew what was happening, Mrs. Gregson's raised arm froze and the pot slipped from her grasp to clatter on the floor. Her eyes felt heavy, and though she fought to keep them open, her eyelids slid shut. She fell, joining her pot on the hard kitchen floor.

Mrs. Carlisle clicked her teeth again, shaking her head as she focused her small black eyes down at Mrs. Gregson. "I expected more from *you*."

Then she slipped quietly from Winslow Manor, scurrying quickly back to her home.

10

ILLY HASTENED down the street with her back towards Winslow Manor, trying to ignore its imposing shadow that leaned over the other houses to glare disapprovingly at her. She knew Lord Hollingberry wouldn't commend her for going to see Caroline behind his back; but since he wouldn't answer her questions himself, Tilly felt that she must ask her old friend instead. Perhaps nothing unusual was going on in Winslow. Perhaps she was simply being used as a courier between a delirious old lord and a crazed young man.

But why had Caroline been talking to Lord Hollingberry the day before, when Tilly had just returned from the Circus? Tilly had never known them to have any sort of relationship before.

She mulled these thoughts over as she mounted the steps of Apple Tree Inn, noting absent-mindedly that weeds were reigning supreme in the flower garden. Pushing open the inn door, she felt the chill of an absent fire in the hearth. In fact, there was no hearth at all in the small room. No chairs or tables were set up, and no candles glowed placidly in the corners.

Indeed, this didn't appear to be Caroline's inn at all.

"You were right, Mother. It *did* work."

Tilly whirled around to face the person who had just spoken behind her. Drosselyn closed the whining door and looked at her mother, who was stepping out of the shadows.

"Of course it worked. My magic always does, silly girl." The old woman chuckled and rubbed her hands together, looking at Tilly with glistening, beady eyes that resembled a rodent's. "But I have to say that *was* surprisingly simple."

"M—Mrs. Carlisle. Drosselyn." Tilly nodded to each of the women. "Hello. I seem to have entered the wrong place. Silly me." She smiled, hoping they would do the same. But their returning smiles made her stomach clench with sudden dread.

"Oh, no," said Mrs. Carlisle, taking a step nearer. "You came to the right place. Didn't she, dear?"

Drosselyn tossed her hair over one shoulder and sighed, apparently bored with the whole ordeal. "She did."

"I don't think you understand—" Tilly began, but Mrs. Carlisle cut her off.

"Don't play innocent, darling." The woman walked towards her. "We have you now, and we also took care of your little fairy godmother, so don't expect any rescue attempts. Mallory?" Mrs. Carlisle turned to the shadows and addressed someone. "Escort Tilly the Tardy to the basement, will you?"

A dusty old floorboard creaked, and Tilly peered into the shadows. A pair of glimmering red eyes stared back at her from the darkness. As the creature moved into the dim light, a large, strong body with black, matted hair and yellow teeth that looked sharp enough to gnaw through anything followed. The scar on Tilly's neck suddenly began to itch as she backed desperately away.

There, directly in front of her, stood the monster from her worst nightmares.

The rat had found Tilly again at last.

Fair maidens in fairy tales were constantly fainting when horrible beasts caught them in their foul clutches. Back when Tilly's father had read the old tales to her, she remembered looking up at him, scrunching her nose and saying, "*I would never be like that, Daddy.*"

If only her father could see her now! She had fainted dead away like a proper fair maiden after glimpsing the dreadful creature that attacked her so many years ago.

Tilly groaned as she slowly woke up, her eyes opening to slits. She wished she were still asleep, because no monster and no mad Carlisle woman could invade blessed unconsciousness. Hoping it had all been a dream, she forced her eyes open wide and scanned her surroundings.

An old staircase led down to the dirty floor of what Tilly assumed to be the basement. It was dark; the only light came from a flickering lantern beside her feet. She shifted her weight and tried to move her hands, but swiftly realized they were bound firmly in place with a rough rope.

Lord Hollingberry had tried to convince Tilly that something greater was taking place in Winslow, but she hadn't believed him. Now she was the prisoner of a woman who seemed to have magic on her side. Though Tilly had never completely believed in magic, she was quickly developing faith in it.

Moth-eaten rags in the corner of the basement suddenly rippled, sending dust floating to the ground and startling Tilly out of her thoughts. She remembered Mrs. Carlisle telling the rat to escort her down to the basement. Was it still down here with her?

Not wanting to see but unable to tear her eyes away, Tilly watched the pile of old clothes with growing anxiety. They shifted again before a mouse—a perfectly normal, small mouse—came scuttling out from underneath.

She breathed a sigh of relief, struggled to sit up with her back against the wall, and searched the area for a way of escape. From what she could see by the dim light, there was nothing in the basement of any use to her. Unable to believe that she was actually tied up in a housekeeper's basement, she closed her eyes and blamed the Circus for all her misfortunes. That horrible place had been haunting her ever since she was a child, and Tilly hated it with every ounce of passion in her heart. It was unjust that she should be here, tied up, and at a complete loss as to why.

A scratching in a dark corner to her left startled her. Tilly pretended not to notice. She focused on wriggling her hands out of her bonds, determined not to be distracted. If she could just loosen the knots—

"*Ooorian.*"

Tilly froze.

"*Oooriaaann.*"

The voice whispered again, sounding more persistent. The scratching noise sounded again, and Tilly's head whirled towards it. Familiar glinting red eyes beamed out from the darkness underneath the staircase. Tilly squirmed, trying to escape her bonds faster.

The rat crept out from the shadows, staring at the girl, who writhed desperately.

"Get away." Tilly shifted awkwardly. When it didn't stop moving, she tried again. "Please, *stop!*"

To her dismay, the rat approached more quickly. "*Stop it!* Just leave me alone!" She began to sob, the long scar on her neck throbbing with horrible remembrance. Still the rat continued until it was next to her bound hands. Then, to Tilly's increasing terror, it began to climb up her arm, latching its long claws into the sleeve of her dress and proceeding up to her shoulder.

"Get off me! Get *off me!*" She shook her shoulder, but the rat only coiled its thick, scaly tail around her arm, balancing itself there. With maddening slowness, the rat placed one paw on her cheek and the other on her head, its sharp claws somehow not scratching her.

The rat leaned in, its black snout close to her ear. Tilly shook uncontrollably, waiting for the creature to kill her, to swipe its deadly claws across her throat and be done with her.

But that blow never came. Instead, the rat took a shuddery breath and whispered in her ear.

"Help me!"

VEN AS the rat repeated its whispered plea, there was suddenly a loud bang from above, as though someone had opened the door to the house and let it swing to hit the wall. Two voices began talking tensely, but Tilly couldn't tell what they were saying. The rat, still perched on her shoulder, appeared to listen as well; but when the door at the top of the basement stairs opened, it leapt down and dove into the darkness, its tail following behind like a pale snake.

Two dark figures creaked down the stairs and approached Tilly. "Are you all right?" one of them asked.

Tilly's tears stopped flowing when she realized who was speaking to her. "L—Lord Hollingberry?" She sniffled.

"That's right, love, that's right." As the lantern's light touched his face he smiled, warming Tilly to the bone with his kindness. How could she have ever been upset with the dear old man?

"'Ello, Tilly." The person hovering behind the lord spoke, and Tilly remembered there was someone else in the room.

"Caroline?" She might have known the innkeeper would be with him. Tilly leaned forward as Lord Hollingberry untied her.

"Yes, dear." Caroline offered her a motherly smile.

"What . . . ?" Her eyes got blurry again from tears, and Lord Hollingberry patted her back.

"It's all right," he soothed her. "I know this is all a bit surprising. We really *were* going to choose a better time to tell you, but circumstances being what they are . . ." Lord Hollingberry's voice faded away as he helped Tilly stand up, groaning as he did so. "There, that's better. Goodness me, I'm not as young as I once was!" He began to hobble off towards the stairs.

"Wait." Tilly looked into the shadows beneath the staircase where the rat had escaped. "There was a rat."

Caroline shot Lord Hollingberry a look. "So you were right. They *do* have one."

He shushed her as he scooped up the lantern from the floor and held it towards the corner still shrouded in darkness, where the rat had disappeared. Caroline wrapped a protective arm around Tilly's shoulder when in the gloom of the flickering lantern they saw the rat huddled with one paw over its eyes. It suddenly looked so much smaller than before, so much less terrifying. It was chanting over and over again something Tilly couldn't quite understand.

"*Ooooriann . . . Ooooriann . . . Ooooriann . . .*"

Lord Hollingberry looked back at Caroline. "I think we have a convert."

Caroline nodded. "Do you suppose it's the one that was in your parlor?" she asked.

"No," Lord Hollingberry said firmly. "Whatever was in the parlor was far fouler than this fellow and cloaked in magic."

"What is it exactly?" Tilly asked, nervously moving closer to Caroline.

Lord Hollingberry didn't look at her as he responded. "It's a Dorian Rat."

"But what *is* a Dorian Rat?"

Caroline looked at the rat and then at Tilly. "They were given the name Dorian Rat because it sounds as though they are always whispering the name 'Dorian.' They serve anyone brave enough to capture them, and they can shape-shift. Never seen one do it, though."

Tilly looked back at the rat and suddenly felt pity for it. Perhaps it wasn't the same one that had given her the scar so many years ago. "Can you help it?"

"Of course, dear! And we will. But we need to take care of you right now." Caroline herded Tilly to the stairs and started up. "Bring the Dorian Rat," she called over her shoulder to Lord Hollingberry. "After you take care of him, meet us back at my place."

"All right. I'll see you in a bit, Tilly. I'll see you in a bit."

As Lord Hollingberry hobbled off towards the Dorian Rat, Tilly almost cautioned him against getting too close. But then she reminded herself that Lord Hollingberry was so much more than he seemed. If he could set her free from the Carlisle women, then he could take care of a rat. Tilly and Caroline made their way upstairs and into the main room of the Carlisle women's house.

"Where are they?" Tilly asked, avoiding a dusty gray rocking chair. The place looked long deserted.

"Mrs. Carlisle and Drosselyn?" Caroline asked. "They've gone. Don't know where, but I'm sure we'll run into each other again before the night is over." She opened the front door and ushered Tilly outside.

They trudged across the street toward Apple Tree Inn. "What I don't understand," said Tilly, "is how I mistook that old shack for your inn." She followed the innkeeper up the steps.

"A simple masking spell, dear. Anyone might've fallen for it." The old woman bobbed inside her inn, pulling Tilly along with her. "Come now. I have something to show you." She giggled like a schoolgirl and led the way behind the counter to a small hallway. Tilly, who had never passed that counter before, hesitantly followed, wondering what her friend could possibly want to show her.

At the end of the hallway, Caroline bent over and pulled up on two iron rings, revealing the basement below. "Come along!" she called to Tilly as she began to thump gaily down the stairs.

"I think I've had enough of basements for one day," Tilly groaned, but nevertheless followed the woman.

She should have known Caroline's basement would look nothing like Mrs. Carlisle's. As Tilly stepped off the last step, her boots touched floorboards of polished cherry wood. A basket of ripe, red apples sat over in a dark corner beside a glowing fire on the hearth. Several of the apples had rolled onto the floor and warmed themselves in front of the fire, their scent filling the room. A crystal chandelier suspended from the center of the ceiling looked entirely out of place, but its pendants knocking together caused a lovely chime to ring throughout the basement. It was altogether a warm, comfortable arrangement.

But lovelier by far than the apples or the fire or even the chiming chandelier was the gown displayed on a dressmaker's form in the center of the room.

With her hand over her mouth, Tilly walked towards it, unable to resist its beauty. Folds of luxurious creamy silk peeked out from beneath a frosty lavender overlay, and the bodice was soft velvet of the same color. As she circled the dress, Tilly saw shining silver buttons marching up the back of the dress like little round soldiers.

"Like it?" Caroline asked, her voice brimming with excitement.

"It's beautiful!" Tilly fingered the velvet and looked back at Caroline. "Whose is it?"

The innkeeper smiled. "It's yours, dear."

Tilly stepped away from the dress as though it were the plague. "What?" She looked sharply at her old friend.

Caroline ambled over to a settee Tilly hadn't noticed before and sat down. "I believe now is the time for some explanations." She patted the cushion next to her and waited for the girl to sit. "There is going to be a ball tonight, and you must attend." She spoke in a low voice as though they were planning something devious. "The Moon Master's Ball, to be exact."

Tilly choked. "The Moon Master from Bromley's Circus?" Her eyes opened wide.

"The very same, love." Caroline nodded.

Tilly shook her head. "What is this about?"

"It's about my wife."

Tilly and Caroline both turned to see Lord Hollingberry at the base of the stairs, the Dorian Rat perched on his shoulder.

Tilly's lips parted in another question, but Lord Hollingberry held up his hand, stopping her. "My wife," he said, his eyes misty in the firelight, "was fairy godmother to a boy named Jasper."

"But there's no such—" Tilly began.

Caroline interrupted her. "Don't say that!" she huffed, looking like a plump cat that had missed dinner time. "Magic is very real, and the sooner you start believing in it, the wiser you'll be."

"Years ago I accepted a boy—an orphan like you—named Jasper to be my ward." The old man spoke to the floor. "I met his godmother and fell in love. But our happy life together didn't last as long as we had hoped. Jasper was cursed, and my dear wife gave her life in one final attempt to save him."

Lord Hollingberry slowly approached, dabbing at his eyes. "Since Aminia died, unable to save her godson, by the laws of magic I am not allowed to visit him."

Realization dawned brightly upon Tilly. "The Moon Master is Jasper?"

"Yes, my dear. You probably wouldn't remember him; you were only a child when he was cursed. But every curse has a way to be broken. Jasper has one night when he can have the chance to be free by finding someone to save him. And after all these years of waiting, he has chosen tonight to be that night." He reached out a hand and clutched Tilly's shoulder. "If he isn't freed, he will belong to Mrs. Carlisle . . . and that poor boy doesn't deserve such a fate."

Pressure bubbled up inside Tilly's chest. What did they expect *her* to do? Hadn't she done enough already? She shrugged off Lord Hollingberry's grasp, got up quickly, and walked towards the fire, avoiding his penetrating gaze. "What do you want of me? I must go to the ball? And do what, exactly?" she asked bitterly.

The Dorian Rat leaped off Lord Hollingberry's shoulder, landing heavily on the ground. It scuttled close to Tilly's feet, causing her to back away. Reaching out a paw, it tugged at her skirt as though asking her to listen to what it had to say.

"Get away!" Tilly pulled her dress away from its claws. "I've had enough of you!"

Flattening its ears against its head, the rat ran into the shadows and hid itself there.

"What?" Tilly rubbed her nose with the sleeve of her dress, glaring at Lord Hollingberry and Caroline, who were staring at her. "I'm sick of secrets and darkness. I want to have a normal life!" Tears of frustration welled up in her eyes. "I just . . ."

Tilly dropped her forehead into the palm of her hand and sneaked a sideways look at the beautiful dress. She thought of the Moon Master's wintry eyes, eyes which had seen so much more sorrow than she had. She thought of the way he held himself, so powerful and yet so beaten down. She thought of poor Aminia, and of the woman's devoted husband who was trying so hard to save the young man he couldn't even speak to. And she thought of Caroline . . .

What exactly was Caroline's part in this?

With a little gasp, Tilly spun about to face the innkeeper. Even though she had guessed the answer already, she asked, "Who are you?"

Caroline's brow crinkled. "Didn't I say?" She squinted her eyes and thought. "S'pose I didn't. Well, dear," she smiled brightly, "I'm your fairy godmother."

The Moon Master sat shrouded in the cold darkness of his cursed wagon. If the night had been normal, he would have candles lit.

If the night had been normal, he would have been listening to Scatter's latest news about the Circus: whether there had been any accidents, if Indigo Bromley was in a foul mood, or if the clown's dreadful act had improved at all. The Moon Master glanced at the little corner to his right where a peacock necktie, somewhat shredded, had been arranged into a cozy nest. An emerald pin lay discarded beside it, Scatter having found no use for it.

The little mouse would never sleep there again.

Dark thoughts flitted across the Moon Master's mind, for the recent visits of Tilly Higgins had stirred troubling memories. He idly rubbed one of his ribbons between his fingers. His jaw clenched as he thought over his life of ten years ago. He and Aminia and Lord Hollingberry had all been so happy.

Then, on his fifteenth birthday, Mrs. Carlisle had gone hunting for him.

He squeezed his eyes shut as though he could somehow shut out further recollections. But he couldn't. Visions of Aminia leading Mrs. Carlisle away from Winslow and sacrificing herself for her beloved godson played out in his mind. Her death had been in vain, however. Mrs. Carlisle had cursed him regardless of Aminia's death. His long fingers clenched the ribbon angrily.

At least Mrs. Carlisle knew nothing of Lord Hollingberry's relationship to him.

And the girl . . .

Perhaps there was hope after all. His brow furrowed when he thought of the danger she was in. Surely Lord Hollingberry would keep her safe.

But no matter how much he reassured himself, he couldn't suppress the feeling of dread growing in his chest. He stood, slowly, and drew a shaky breath.

The Moon Master must prepare for the ball.

12

ONCE AGAIN Tilly found herself unable to refuse Lord Hollingberry's wishes. As he had said, there *was* something greater taking place, and it was up to Tilly to free the Moon Master from Mrs. Carlisle.

How she was supposed to accomplish this was beyond her reckoning. Jasper had been held captive for many years under a curse that allowed him to leave his wagon for only one night to find a girl brave enough to save him.

Otherwise, he would be Mrs. Carlisle's forever.

Tilly hated vagueness, and Caroline and Lord Hollingberry were nothing *but* vague. Now, alone in the cozy basement, she paced the floor, pulled at the collar of her dress, and fretted. Lord Hollingberry had left for Winslow Manor after saying he had unfinished business to address, and Caroline was bustling about upstairs.

The fire popped unexpectedly, causing Tilly to jerk and peer cautiously at the shadows where she had last seen the Dorian Rat. It hadn't reappeared since she told it to leave, and Tilly felt a little sorry for speaking harshly to it.

Someone began creaking down the stairs, halting her guilty feelings about the rat. To her relief, it was Caroline. "Hollingberry is outside, waiting for your grand appearance." Grinning, Caroline walked over to the ballgown and held out her hand to her goddaughter. "For you," she said.

Tilly looked at the two ribbons in Caroline's hand and accepted them gently. "How did you know about them?"

"I didn't," she replied. "Hollingberry did. He knew Jasper would give them to the girl he believed could save him. Thank goodness Mrs. Carlisle didn't get a hold of them!"

Tilly rubbed the ribbons between her fingers, admiring the shining stones. "They're more than just ribbons, aren't they?" she asked, her voice soft.

"Yes," Caroline grunted as she fumbled with the buttons on the gown. "They were Aminia's last gift to him. Get out of that dreadful thing you have on." She gestured to her goddaughter's dress.

With a clap of Caroline's plump hands, a tub overflowing with bubbles appeared before the fireplace. Tilly suddenly realized how grimy she felt. A minute later she was basking in a magical bath of the most perfect temperature. Her back and arms had ached since her imprisonment in Mrs. Carlisle's basement, but now all pain slipped away as her fairy godmother rubbed a light, sweet-smelling ointment into her hair then rinsed it out. Tilly's scalp tingled delightfully.

"Caroline," Tilly began drowsily, the smell of apples lulling her to sleep. "How did things go so terribly wrong with Aminia and Jasper?"

Conjuring a white lace robe from mid-air, Caroline handed it to Tilly and returned to the gown, admiring her own handiwork. "Amina was teaching Jasper the ways of magic in a land far beyond Winslow." She recounted the tale with a frown. "During their travels, they met another fairy godmother, Mrs. Carlisle, and her goddaughter."

Tilly listened intently, not wishing to interrupt her godmother's story.

"Jasper never was a handsome sort of fellow, but he always has possessed a certain charm that makes him appealing." She glanced towards Tilly. "Drosselyn found him *very* much to her liking, the spoiled little milksop. Jasper, in turn, liked her very little."

Caroline paused to pull a stray thread off the dress. "You can imagine how this angered Mrs. Carlisle. Her magic was so powerful that Jasper and Aminia fled, taking refuge here in this obscure little village and . . . Mrs. Carlisle pursued. You know the rest. He's been cursed these past ten years. When Mrs. Carlisle and her goddaughter returned to Winslow, we knew the time had come."

Tilly suddenly realized that she didn't feel anymore as though Caroline and Lord Hollingberry were forcing her into helping them. She truly wanted to help them, not because of Lord Hollingberry's kindness, but because it was simply the right thing to do. Jasper had suffered and so had she. They were the same in many ways, she thought.

But there was one question still lingering in the back of Tilly's mind. "Why did Lord Hollingberry invite Mrs. Carlisle into Winslow Manor?"

Caroline grinned triumphantly. "Ah! We tricked Mrs. Carlisle quite well, Hollingberry and I. She never knew that Aminia was married. And she never suspected any connection between Lord Hollingberry and Jasper. We've been able to keep a close eye on that Carlisle woman since she came back!" The fairy godmother sniffed, quite delighted with her own cleverness. "Come now," she said. "We've got to get you ready for the ball."

Minutes later, Tilly was wearing a gown more beautiful than she could ever have imagined. She couldn't help but twirl, watching the silken folds of cream and lavender fan out like the petals of a rimed tulip.

"Slow down, girl!" Caroline sounded annoyed, but the smile on her lips said otherwise. Tilly's godmother pinned up her hair in soft curls, adding sprigs of dried lilac throughout. When the girl, who in recent years had worn only a maid's uniform, looked at herself in the mirror, her heart thrilled with delight.

"You look stunning, my love," said Caroline. For the first time, Tilly saw tears shining in her fairy godmother's eyes. "But we're not done yet!" Caroline wiped the tears away quickly and told Tilly to sit on the settee. "Where are those ribbons?" she looked around the room.

Tilly held them out to her, and the old woman snatched them away. "We'd best get you to that ball quickly! Midnight will come before too long." She draped the shining ribbons across her goddaughter's feet.

"What happens at midnight?" Tilly asked, once again confused.

"Hush, I'm thinking." Caroline tapped her chin with one finger. "Oh, how does that old rhyme go? Ah, yes." Rubbing her hands together, she cleared her throat and closed her eyes.

"Light, show yourself pure and strong,
Save a man from evil's throng.
Take a form, small and white,
Give this girl the strength to fight."

When Caroline had uttered the last word, something happened to Tilly's feet. She felt a coldness slide across each foot up to her ankle, but it wasn't an unpleasant feeling. It reminded Tilly of slipping her feet into a cool set of sheets before bedtime. She looked down to see what exactly was happening and saw a pair of shining crystal slippers adorning her feet. The violet ribbons laced through tiny holes in the slippers and tied into delicate bows at her ankles. They made Tilly feel even more beautiful, and she touched the crystal gently.

"They're gorgeous," she whispered.

"So are you. Come along! Your carriage awaits."

Tilly followed her godmother back upstairs, stumbling a bit from the heavy folds of her dress, and out to the front of the inn. Lord Hollingberry was standing in front of a majestic horse-drawn carriage, his breath visible in the starlight.

"Tilly!" He stared at her. "You look stunning."

She was about to respond when she looked a little more closely at the carriage, and her mouth dropped open. "A *pumpkin?*"

Lord Hollingberry looked from her to the carriage that was indeed shaped like a pumpkin. "I realized my carriage was terribly old and dirty, so I had to improvise. There was a nice little pumpkin sitting out in the garden, and I think, overall, it looks quite nice. Yes, quite nice." He nodded to himself and then stepped forward to help Tilly climb into it.

"Did Aminia teach you that trick?" asked Caroline. "You seem to have forgotten a coachman. *You* certainly can't drive it." She crossed her arms, and one of the horses attached to the carriage snorted in agreement.

"Naturally I picked up a few things from my dear departed wife. And I did not forget a coachman. What do you think took me so long over at Winslow Manor? I had to create a spell from scratch! Plus, I had to rescue Mrs. Gregson from a nasty sleeping enchantment I imagine our friend Mrs. Carlisle gave her."

"Mrs. Gregson? Is she all right?" Tilly asked, panicked.

"She's rampaging about the Manor at the moment, but yes, she is quite all right. I suspect she had the misfortune to be mistaken for your fairy godmother! And now, Tilly"—Lord Hollingberry motioned for her to lean out the carriage window and look where he pointed—"meet your coachman."

Leaves rustled beside the inn, and Tilly watched as a man, a very tall man, stepped out from the shadows, tugging awkwardly on his coat. His wispy black hair was braided down his neck, and his narrow face looked as though it had seen far too much sorrow.

Caroline gasped. "Is that the Dorian Rat?" she asked, mouth agape.

"Mallory is his name," Lord Hollingberry said soothingly. "And he is on our side. He wanted to help Tilly."

"Is he quite safe?" Tilly asked, not taking her eyes off Mallory.

Lord Hollingberry nodded. "Absolutely."

"Well, then," Tilly said, drawing a shuddery breath. "Take me to the Ball, Mallory."

13

T HE PEOPLE of Winslow had scarcely left Bromley's Circus since it arrived, and they milled about Bromley Meadow, bubbling with excitement. Men, women, and children alike wore attire they had purchased at the Circus. The pumpkin carriage rumbled easily up the meadow and stopped once it arrived at the colorful Circus tent. The tent's curtains were closed, and a platform had been set up outside, with a huge silk banner hanging above it reading "The Moon Master's Ball."

The steady murmur of the village folk's voices rang through the cool night air, lending the atmosphere a festive vibe. Tilly shivered as Mallory opened the door to the carriage, offering her his hand. She ignored it, determined not to forget he had once been a rat, and walked into the thick crowd.

"I hoped I would see you tonight," a soft voice said behind her.

Tilly turned, knowing full well to whom the voice belonged.

"You look beautiful," Rodger said, his eyes scanning slowly across her dress.

She tucked a loose strand of hair nervously behind her ear, annoyed when it popped back out. "Thank you. You look . . . very nice as well." She stumbled over her words, trying not to show her uneasiness at being around him.

He laughed his most contagious laugh and shook his head. Then his face became suddenly serious, and he took a step closer, speaking in a low voice. "What are you playing at, Tilly? You've turned so mysterious of late. We used to be friends." He touched the back of her hand hesitantly.

Tilly stepped backwards, giving him a stern look. "I believe our friendship changed the day you wanted it to be something more." Biting her lip, she looked at the lush grass beneath her feet. "I'm sorry—"

"Don't be." He shook his head. "You've changed, Tilly. You've become . . . distant." Rodger stuffed his hands into his pockets. "I thought you felt something for me."

She opened her mouth to say that she *did* feel for him—as a brother and friend. But he held up his hand.

"I wish you all the happiness in the world."

He left her then, his dark green jacket disappearing into the crowd, leaving Tilly with many unsaid words sitting on her tongue. She swallowed them and turned, nearly bumping in to her coachman.

"Mallory!" she exclaimed, and he looked at her with an expression she couldn't identify. "Get back to the carriage. You aren't needed here." Tilly moved to step around him, but he stopped her.

"I . . ." His voice was deep and strong, and he appeared to be shocked when it left his mouth. "I must protect you."

"If I need protection from anything, it's from your kind." Tears stung her eyes as she thought of her lost friendship with Rodger. "Now please, return to the coach."

"It was not my kind that killed the white mouse," Mallory said quietly.

But Tilly didn't hear. The voice of Indigo Bromley swept over the meadow, sufficiently stopping any chatter and making heads whip around towards the platform.

"Ladies and gentlemen! Welcome to the Moon Master's Ball! Tonight I will introduce to you a man of mystery and magic." Bromley paced about the wooden stage, his colorful coattails swishing behind him. "He has chosen to reveal himself to you all this evening, and *only* for this evening will you be permitted to know him." Bromley stopped and winked at a group of plump old ladies who had forced themselves to the front of the crowd. "I give you the glorious, the stupendous Moon Master!"

He disappeared in a puff of smoke, leaving a lone figure standing where he had been. The crowd went silent in anticipation as the smoke cleared, giving Tilly a complete view of the Moon Master's tall form.

As he stepped into the light, she saw that he was no longer the broken man confined in an endless wagon. He was strong, standing tall above the people of Winslow with grace and authority. He wore a coat of dusky blue and silver that shimmered in the moonlight and emphasized his cool eyes. Those eyes flitted across the crowd, lighting a moment longer on Tilly than on anyone else.

Then he spoke:

"Welcome, dear people of Winslow. You have supported this Circus throughout many years, and for this, I thank you." Placing his hand over his chest, he dipped his head in acknowledgement. "As you well know, I am the Moon Master, and I invite you to celebrate life, freedom, and courage here tonight in this colorful place."

The Moon Master smiled, causing women to swoon all across the meadow. Then with painful slowness, he raised his arm, looked up at the sky, and snapped his fingers. The light of the moon was snuffed out as though it were nothing more than one of the weak candles flickering in

Apple Tree Inn.

The crowd gasped in astonishment. An inky blackness settled around the people of Winslow, and Tilly could hear the panic rushing into their voices as they asked what was happening.

But before the panic truly took hold, a light shone in front of them. It was only a small golden sliver at first, but it grew by the second. The curtains of Bromley's Circus were opening, and the people of Winslow rushed towards the light, thrilled anew with their beloved Circus.

Tilly followed behind, not desiring to be crushed by the wild towns-folk crowding around her. For a brief moment she wondered where Mallory was. Probably already in the Circus, she thought, skulking around in some dark corner.

Pushing all thoughts of the rat-man aside, she lifted the skirts of her ballgown, displaying her crystal slippers, and entered the tent. Endless rows of tables had been set up under the big top. There were no odd acts taking place, and members of the Circus troupe looked relatively normal as they offered dainty entrees to the villagers.

A man offered Tilly what looked like a baked mushroom wrapped in lemongrass, but she declined, her stomach suddenly in knots. What was she to do here? It was certainly a strange night at the Circus; though really, when had the Circus been anything but strange?

"I hoped I would see you tonight." A silky voice spoke the same words Rodger had said earlier, yet with a completely different meaning. Tilly turned at the sound of his voice, thinking that while Rodger had sounded apprehensive and worried, the Moon Master sounded earnest and thankful.

"Hello, Jasper." Tilly fiddled with her hands, feeling the absence of one of Lord Hollingberry's letters to play with.

His eyes lit up. "It's been so long since I've heard my name. I had almost forgotten it." The Moon Master offered her what was barely recognizable as a smile. "I am glad you were first to say it."

Tilly squirmed under his unwavering gaze. "Oh. Well. I'm glad I know it now. I felt strange calling you the Moon Master." She laughed half-heartedly at herself and crossed her arms to ensure that they wouldn't hang ungracefully.

"You now know my sad story then." He placed his hand lightly on her back to direct her towards a table serving a sparkling red drink.

Tilly nodded. "Yes. I'm sorry about A—Aminia," she stuttered, wondering if she should have brought up the fairy godmother.

"That is the saddest part of my story," he stated. "Losing someone close to you is more haunting than a life of cursed solitude." Jasper picked up a glass and filled it with the drink, handing it to Tilly.

She took it. "What is this?" she asked, inspecting the different berries floating inside.

"Dewdrop punch," he said. "The berries are gathered early in the morning in Winslow Wood and are made into this drink. The sparkles you see are the dewdrops themselves." His eyes smiled at the incredulous look she gave him.

Tilly took a cautious sip and then another. It tasted like the early morning air one breathes in on cool days when the fog is still drifting about the earth. Tilly had never thought such a taste could exist, but as she sipped the drink again, it transported her to an image of ripe berries frosted over with dew.

The sound of a clock chiming ten echoed across the tent, causing Tilly nearly to spill her drink. She set the cup down on a table and noticed that Jasper's posture had gone stiff with tension.

"Miss Higgins?" The Moon Master's silky voice made Tilly's eyes snap up to his face. "Would you care to dance?"

It was then, as Jasper led Tilly towards the dance floor, she noticed that the Circus no longer looked like a Circus at all. The tent was gloriously draped in luxurious cloths of ruby, gold, emerald green, and peacock blue. It looked like the dance hall of a grand palace. An orchestra started playing a simple waltz, and Jasper led Tilly through the steps. He held her with only one arm, his left arm hanging limp at his side. She tripped several times, Jasper's constant grace making her feel inadequate.

"Why," Tilly asked to cover a misstep, "did Mrs. Carlisle imprison you?"

His arm tightened about her waist. "She imprisons everyone who does not give her what she wishes."

She looked around at the people serving the villagers. "You mean everyone else in the Circus is captured as well?"

"Sadly, yes." He nodded and spoke no more on the topic.

Tilly looked at his lifeless arm. "What happened . . ." She paused, unsure if she should finish. "What happened to your arm?"

Jasper sighed but continued to lead her flawlessly through the dance. "Many years ago, in the black of night, a little girl strayed away from her parents. When she happened by my wagon, I watched her, enjoying her innocence of the horrors of life." His voice was entrancing as he told his story. "I sensed that she was special. That one day, she might even be able to help me." He looked pointedly at her. "But my enemy sensed this as well."

Tilly's breath began to come in shallow puffs. "Stop, please." She didn't want to know where this story was going.

"She was attacked by a strange, large rat, and I reached out my arm in an attempt to help her," he continued, heedless of her attempts to silence him. "Since Isla Carlisle cursed me to never be able to leave the wagon, my arm was crushed instantly, and the girl"—Jasper looked sadly at the scar on Tilly's neck—"was left with a scar that changed her life. Remember, Tilly."

He drew her close and whispered in her ear. "Your enemy is my enemy."

She pulled away from him and stumbled from the dance floor. All her life she had thought she was the only person who knew of that scar and the horrible story that went with it. Jasper moved to follow her, but a glistening mass of pink silk got in his way.

Drosselyn stood before him, gazing up at the tall man from beneath her dark eyelashes. With the look of a cat who knew it would get its way in a moment, she held out her hand. Tilly, watching from a distance, saw color rise to Jasper's cheeks. Was he blushing? Or did he flush with anger?

Tilly held back, observing as he began to dance with Drosselyn, wondering what part she played in Mrs. Carlisle's evil, trying to recall details of Caroline's story. Soon the clock chimed eleven, reminding her that Caroline had mentioned something happening at twelve. But her brain felt strangely fuzzy. Finding her appetite, Tilly sampled the delicacies being served, hoping food would fill the emptiness she felt when watching Jasper with Drosselyn.

"Enjoying yourself, darling?"

Hearing Mrs. Carlisle's voice behind her, Tilly spun around, barely able to swallow the mushroom she'd been chewing. "You're not welcome here," she stated flatly.

Mrs. Carlisle chortled. "I'd imagine I'm *not*." She gazed upon Jasper and Drosselyn. "Look at them. Such a lovely couple, and so completely in love." The old woman turned her gloating gaze back to Tilly. "He will be hers before the night is over."

She took a glass of dewdrop punch and sipped it. Then she set down her drink and looked at Tilly with her awful, rodent-like eyes. "You should leave now if you ever want to lead a normal life. You can stay with your godmother, Mrs. Gregson, if ever she wakes up." When Tilly didn't move, she snapped, "*Now*, before that chance expires."

A whirlwind of thoughts rushed through Tilly's head. Lord Hollingberry counted on her to save his godson, and she owed it to herself to help a man who had suffered at the hands of evil. Just as she had suffered all those years ago. And Scatter . . . the patient little mouse whose death had been useless.

Just as useless as Jasper's life would be if she didn't save him.

"I'll never leave," she said.

Mrs. Carlisle shrugged. "Your choice."

The silvery chime of the clock rang again, alerting Tilly that it was midnight. Jasper left the dance floor and ran towards her. He barely had enough time to reach her and whisper, "Be brave!" before the lights extinguished all across the enormous tent.

Pandemonium broke out as people ran into each other, screaming and frantic without the moonlight or light from the tent. It was pitch black, but Tilly stayed where she was, too frightened to move and wondering where Jasper was.

Then she saw a light. Not a familiar golden or silvery light like the sun or the moon, but a red light. Two red orbs floating in the air close together. She knew instantly that it was the light of a rat's eyes, and she backed away, terror ramming in her throat.

"*Silly girl!*" a raspy voice uttered. "*Thinking you could defeat me!*"

Tilly collapsed to the ground, crawling away backwards in a final attempt to escape the rat.

"*Did you really think he could ever be yours?*" the rat asked. "*He is Drosselyn's and only hers, you filthy little swine. I should have destroyed you that night long ago!*"

Tilly screamed when she saw the eyes rise up into the air, imagining the rat pouncing on her as she crouched defenseless in the darkness.

But it never descended upon her, for a second pair of red eyes joined the first rat's; the two beasts collided in mid-air, grunting and squealing as they fell to the ground. Tilly scrounged desperately around in the blackness, hoping to find a fork or knife with which to defend herself, but she found nothing.

Then and there, although her heart pounded desperately, Tilly realized that this was her time to free herself and Jasper from the hateful, wicked godmother who had kept them both in bondage for so many years. She stood, resolutely bracing herself.

Taking a step towards the scuffling, shrieking noise of battle, she saw a faint light peep out from beneath her skirt. Another step, and the light grew. Tilly's glass slippers were glowing! Moving closer and trying not to think of what she was about to do, she raised her foot, aiming the pointed heel of the crystal slipper towards the larger of the two creatures squirming on the ground. With all her might, she plunged the crystal heel down into the heart of her opponent.

A dreadful squeal sliced through the tent and echoed throughout the silence of Winslow village.

14

SLOWLY, AS if afraid to come back too soon, the candles in the tent flickered to life, lighting up a huge, hairy rat much larger and uglier than a Dorian Rat. A crystal slipper was embedded in its chest.

With a death rattle, the rat changed form, melting from a horrible creature into an even more disgusting woman. And then the body of Mrs. Carlisle faded away until it was nothing but dust on the grass. Tilly's lone slipper, which had slid from her foot after she stabbed the rat, now sat pure and untainted by the grotesque godmother's blood.

Tilly stumbled backwards, tripped, and sat down hard. Hot tears flowed down her cheeks, and she didn't bother to wipe them away. All in one night she had faced and killed her greatest fear, and the sense that her world would be safe again flooded her heart with relief.

As her senses slowly returned, Tilly heard heavy panting. Turning, she saw Mallory crouched nearby with long, bloody scratches running down his arms and chest. Not bothering to stand, Tilly crawled over to where he sat and hugged him, apologizing and thanking him over and over for protecting her in the darkness.

All around them, terrified townsfolk ran to escape the Circus, not wanting to be trapped in midnight shadows again. They flowed past like a brook weaving its way around a pebble, and Tilly watched them go. Among them she saw the familiar forms of Ellen and Daphne hurrying away, and, between the girls, someone she knew all too well. Rodger had a protective arm around each of her friends. At the entrance he let go of the girls and ushered them out of the Circus, then turned around to see if anyone else needed assistance. His eyes met Tilly's, and he rushed towards her, fighting his way through the fleeing crowds.

"Are you all right?" he asked once near, shoving a fallen table away and kneeling down to Tilly's level.

Finding it hard to look him in the eyes, she nodded reassuringly. "I'm fine." Only then did she realize that Mallory was no longer beside her. How had he vanished so completely?

Rodger tugged on her hand, encouraging her to stand up. She rose awkwardly, the lack of a second slipper disrupting her balance.

"Let's leave this place." He wrapped an arm around her waist and began to tow her towards the exit.

"No, Rodger, I'm fine." Tilly slipped out of his grasp and looked sadly at her old friend. "You go on. Take care of Ellen and Daphne."

"Tilly," he spoke her name softly. "Always you've been afraid of the Circus. Now I can't seem to get you away from it."

Tilly smiled sadly at the irony of the situation.

"You've been up to something these past days. Tell me what it is," he persisted.

She shook her head. "It's too much to explain right now. Go on, Rodger. Leave. I'll catch up with you later."

"What?" He took a step towards her. "No. I'll never leave you."

She thought her heart must be cracking slowly in two. "I . . . Rodger, I meant what I said earlier. There's nothing . . ." She closed her eyes and chose her words carefully. "There's nothing between us but friendship."

Rodger looked down at his boots. "You really believe that?"

She nodded slowly. "I do."

He looked up at her, the familiar twinkle barely visible in his eyes. "Well, then." He offered her a rueful smile. "Whatever you say." He turned to leave, intending to catch up with Ellen and Daphne and escort them home.

"Rodger!" Tilly called after him and he turned, eyebrows raised. "I'll see you at Caroline's tomorrow night." She smiled, hoping he would do the same.

"'Course you will!" he responded. "You've got a lot of explaining to do." With a roguish wink, he followed the crowd out of the Circus, a bit of dash returned to his bearing.

"No! Please, I didn't mean to! I didn't mean any of it!"

Dreadful wails fell upon Tilly's ears, and she turned to see who was screaming so desperately. Drosselyn clawed frantically at Jasper's arm. He wrenched himself out of her grasp, and she collapsed on the grassy ground.

"I'm sorry! I'm so sorry!" She buried her face in her delicate hands.

Jasper looked down at her and sighed. "I forgive you."

Drosselyn's sobs quieted, and she looked up at him hopefully. "You . . . you mean—"

He cut her off, saying, "I mean *nothing* but that. I forgive you, Drosselyn. That is all." When her piercing wails began again, Jasper walked away, pinching the bridge of his nose and looking downward. His eyes lit up, however, when he saw Tilly limping towards him.

"Tilly," he said, reaching out to take her hands as he met her halfway.

"How can I ever thank you for what you've done tonight?"

"I was bound by Mrs. Carlisle as much as you." She couldn't help smiling at his tousled clothes and hair. Caroline hadn't lied when she said there was a certain charm about Jasper.

"That girl really did love me, I think," Jasper said suddenly, glancing back at the heartbroken Drosselyn. "A strange, twisted love. But strong enough that she wished her fairy godmother would enslave me until I agreed to be hers." He shuddered.

Tilly gently squeezed his hands . . . and suddenly realized that she held *both* his hands. "Your arm!" she cried in delight.

"Yes, it returned to normal as soon as you broke the curse." His eyes, filled with gratitude, no longer seemed wintry.

The rest of Carlisle's Circus slaves, also freed from her magic, rushed from the tent with noisy excitement. Even Indigo Bromley was running away with glee.

"Come on. Let's get out of here." As Jasper urged Tilly towards the exit, she took two steps and remembered something.

"My slipper!"

Jasper followed her gaze to her lonely glass slipper in the grass and stooped to pick it up. Then he went down on one knee at Tilly's feet and looked up at her with a smile. She obligingly lifted her skirts, and he placed the slipper back on her foot then tied the ribbon securely at her ankle.

Tilly felt too shy to say anything but gladly took his offered arm. Together they walked toward the tent's entrance.

Glimpsing a shadow from the corner of her eye, Tilly turned back to find Mallory following close behind them. "Please join us, Mallory," she invited him with a genuine smile.

When Jasper, too, thanked him for courageously defending Tilly, the rat-man seemed nearly overwhelmed by the attention. But he did keep close behind. At the tent's entrance they all stopped.

The night was pure and fresh, holding no terror of vengeful fairy godmothers in rat form. It was the perfect autumnal night, Tilly thought. But when the tall man beside her snapped his fingers, the moon returned to the sky, making it more perfect still.

"How do you do that?" she asked, looking up at him with bright eyes.

He grinned. "Magic."

Tilly chuckled. "I doubt the people of Winslow will want more of the Circus after tonight!"

They laughed together, and even Mallory joined in. But when the three of them stepped out of the tent, Bromley's Circus was no more. It disappeared just as it did every year, although this time Tilly doubted it would ever come back.

"I daresay I'm in the mood for some of Caroline's apple cider," Jasper declared, his voice content. "It's been far too long."

Tilly smiled. "So am I. Although I have no idea how she makes it so delicious."

Jasper shot Tilly a look. "You mean you really don't know?"

"What?" she asked, peering up at him in the moonlight. "Do you?"

He leaned down and whispered in her ear. "She uses magic to make the cider. *That's* why her inn is so famous."

Again Tilly laughed, absolutely brimming with happiness. As the trio walked home, Jasper held her hand. And for the first time in many years, she felt truly safe. Lord Hollingberry and Caroline would be waiting for her when they got back, and they would recount the night over a warm cup of cider. She had found a loyal friend in a Dorian Rat and perhaps something more in the mysterious Moon Master. It wasn't the normal life she had dreamed of since childhood.

But it was a good life. A life she wanted to live.

ABOUT THE AUTHOR

CLARA DIANE THOMPSON lives in the swamps of Louisiana with her loving family, dashing dog, and a very confused frog that resides in the birdhouse outside her window. Aside from writing she enjoys playing guitar, singing, Broadway plays (particularly *The Phantom of the Opera*), ballet, tea with friends, and long BBC movies. An enchanted circus may or may not appear occasionally in her back yard.

You can find out more about Clara and her writing on her blog: www.ClaraDianeThompson.blogspot.com

Eager for more stories by
Five Glass Slippers authors?

Self Preservation has never looked more tempting . . .

If you enjoyed *A Cinder's Tale*, get ready . . .

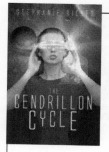

Looking for more fantastic fairy tale retellings?

TAKE PART IN THE NEXT CONTEST

An all-new collection of stories releases Summer 2015

www.RooglewoodPress.com/Fairy-Tale-Collections

Other Exciting Books from
ROOGLEWOOD PRESS:

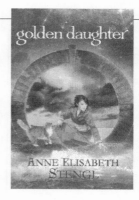

A dainty but deadly bodyguard, Sairu is committed to protecting her mistress, the mysterious Dream Walker. But how can she guard against enemies she can neither see nor touch? For the Dragon moves in the realm of nightmares . . .

Golden Daughter
Coming November 2014
by: Anne Elisabeth Stengl
www.GoldenDaughterNovel.blogspot.com

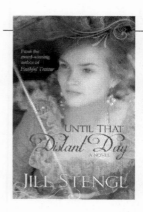

In the early days of the French Revolution, Colette dreamed of equality for all. But those days are passed, and the bloodshed creeps ever closer to home. Can Colette find the strength to protect her loved ones . . . even from each other?

Until That Distant Day
by: Jill Stengl
www.UntilThatDistantDayNovel.blogspot.com

ROOGLEWOOD PRESS

Find Us on Facebook
www.RooglewoodPress.com

Made in the USA
Lexington, KY
26 June 2014